S M O K E

Deirdre Macken is a journalist, columnist and member of a volunteer bushfire brigade. She has worked for the *Australian*, the *Age* and the *Sydney Morning Herald*. She lives in Sydney with her husband and three children. This is her first book.

SMOKE

DEIRDRE MACKEN

MANDARIN

I'd like to thank my sister, Mary Horarik Macken, for her wise and gentle advice.

Published 1996 by Mandarin
a part of Reed Books Australia
22 Salmon Street, Port Melbourne, Victoria 3207
a division of Reed International Books Australia Pty Limited

Typeset in Garamond by J&M Typesetting
Printed and bound in Australia by Australian Print Group

National Library of Australia
cataloguing-in-publication data:

Macken, Deirdre.
    Smoke.
    ISBN 1 86330 579 3.
    I. Title.
A823.3

For Roger, Nicole, Kate and Toby

Sydney Gazette, November 11, 1804

The whole of Tuesday night, the face of the country was covered with detached fires, which presented a spectacle at once awful and romantic. Had the wind shifted to an opposite quarter, while the excessive rage of the conflagration lasted, it would be difficult to compute the possible damage which might have ensued.

Chapter one

It was a hot and smoky night. Emily breathed in deeply. She dragged the bush smoke back into her lungs. They jangled with anticipation. Emily had been an ex-smoker for three years. Her lungs were yet to get the message. They liked nothing better than slipstream. Even slipstream from a bushfire. Emily breathed deeply again. She wanted to end this impasse. Either take up yoga again or start smoking again. She turned on the TV instead.

'... enveloping the volunteer firefighters. The flames are leaping four storeys into the air. There seems little hope for the homes but it appears all the residents have been taken to safe refuges. One firefighter has just told us to retreat, so on this scorching first Wednesday of the new year, this is Scott Gormley of channel 11 news.'

'Go, Scott, go,' yelled Emily at the small TV screen, which was dancing yellow and orange as the news camera panned back over a burning landscape. Emily bounded off her lounge onto the floor to mimic Scott Gormley, her body taut, crouching low in defence; her face turned from the torture of the heat. A good mimic of the reporter's dramatic pose, just before the burly firefighter had grabbed him by the elbow and muttered something like, 'Off you go, now.'

'Anyway,' said Emily, still talking to the TV as she settled back into the lounge, 'Barry on channel 6 got much closer to the fire than you, Scott.' Emily chuckled while she recalled the bedside interview with Barry Wells that had been broadcast a few nights ago. He was sitting upright in a hospital bed with his toes bandaged and elevated. Even as a patient, Wells had the posture of the television journalist – upright and attentive. As Wells relived his horrifying moment for the eleventh interview of the day, the only jarring note of his face-to-camera account was the stiffness of his pyjama top collar. Emily still wondered whether he had ironed his pyjama top especially for the interview. Had Wardrobe from the station popped down to the hospital? But everyone was used to seeing Barry in his starched army fatigues, so perhaps no one else noticed the incongruity of his collar.

It was Barry's sartorial vanity that was partly to blame for his injury. A few years ago, Barry had appeared at the television station in army fatigues because he was covering a story on military manoeuvres. They laughed at him at the station. Said he looked like a lost Army Reserve cadet. But the viewers liked the look. Besides, the authority of the outfit allowed Barry into areas other journalists couldn't penetrate – police blockades, emergency services road blocks, and into the photo albums of bereaved old women. Soon Barry was being featured in news promos in his camouflage gear. 'It's one way to make sure the news editor gives you the gutsy stories,' Barry told his colleagues. He now had four neatly pressed sets of army fatigues and two pairs of steel-capped boots.

It was the boots that gave him the problem. Steel absorbs heat. By the time Barry was feeling the heat in the steelcaps on that thirty-eight-degree day in a fire-ravaged southern national park, he had been standing on hot ground for five minutes. When he moved closer to a flaming stump, his steelcaps came alive with heat. Barry's boots were shin-high lace-ups. On a sober evening he took a good forty seconds to get them off. Out on the burning ground of the national park, flailing at his laces like a berserk chicken plucker, it took almost a minute. By then his skin had softened, turned an angry red and was blistering.

The station still had the footage of Barry's agonising hop across the hot bush floor but hadn't broadcast it yet. 'A bit tasteless,' Barry told other journos. They nodded in agreement. They knew that even if viewers never got to see Barry's waltz, they would see pirated copies of the tape. And they wouldn't have to wait for the end-of-year spoof tape.

Emily felt much better now. Yelling at the news was almost as satisfying as an hour-long session of that new sort of massage, reiking. She wondered whether she should start reviewing television professionally. She'd written enough of it. Well, enough scripts. Only one had caught the imagination of the SBS head of documentaries at a time when he still had funds to divest. 'What ethnic appeal has it got?' he'd asked her over the phone. So courteous yet so curt. Emily had mentally reeled through her script about an inner-city terrace filled with university students whose creativity was confined to bed. And she remembered the Islander who made an appearance in the second scene. A bedroom appearance.

'Solomon Islanders,' she'd said to the SBS producer, 'and their difficulty adjusting to Australian urban life.' She hadn't lied. She just diverted the plot when he asked to see a treatment.

Wandering over to her kitchen, which was little more than a busy-looking corner of the small flat, Emily contemplated writing a television review column. No, she thought, not just TV – radio reviews too. She felt as qualified as anyone else if only because from the moment she woke up and switched on the radio to her constant flicking through the channels late at night, she lived media. She mentally rewrote, recast, edited and criticised the media all the time. It was her constant companion. Her guide to life. Her church. And her family.

Mooching around her kitchen benches, pulling drawers open and staring unseeing into the pantry, Emily was still shouting comments back to the television. They were the sort of comments one throws across the lounge room to a spouse – familiar, chiding, abbreviated. If one was standing with her in the kitchen one would feel inclined to look towards the living area to see who she might be addressing.

She stopped suddenly. Agitated, she looked around the living/ dining/kitchen area of her flat. She had no idea what she was doing in the kitchen. She searched the flat for a memory. It was devoid of prompts – not for her memory or her personality. Furnished from drive-in decorating stores, and filled with accoutrements of the right colour – duck-egg blue and sand – nothing jarred and nothing demanded attention. Everything in the flat was right for its purpose and position but the overall impression was one of impermanence. The flat said nothing about where Emily came from and less about her aspirations. The impression the flat left on her friends was so slight that it was difficult for them to remember any detail of it once they had left. Emily received many ill-fitting decorative presents from friends.

Pasta, thought Emily, breaking her reverie. The single woman's dinner date. She filled the saucepan with water. TV dinner of the nineties. Looking over the rooftops of inner-city apartments towards the setting sun, she breathed deeply again. On cue, her lungs jangled awake. The sun was sinking into a mucky brown carpet of smoke. It was mired in the dirty horizon, she thought. She breathed deeply again and thought of her father gazing over the bushy hilltops from his verandah. She realised why she felt agitated.

'Bugger Dad, why did he have to build his house in a national park tinder box!' Emily muttered as she grabbed her cordless phone to push hash 4. Fourth most common person in her life. Fourth biggest responsibility. As the tones drummed, she tried to target the source of her anger. Was it Scott Gormley and his nightly bungy jumps into 'the worst fires in Australia's history!'? Or her father for living alone, for being too damned independent, contrary, macho, irresponsible? Or herself, for not having a life?

'Hi, Dad,' she said. Her voice softened at the sound of her father's. 'Are you all right down there, Dad?'

'Yes, yes,' he replied, rising from silent mode into urban conversation lilt. 'My flu went last week.'

'I meant the fire,' said Emily. Her anger was stirred by his annoying cheeriness.

'I'm having a cup of tea while I watch the sunset and I'm speaking to my favourite girl, so I must still be alive,' Carmody said. 'I would inform you if the house burnt down, Emms.'

'I would hope you'd inform me of what was happening well before that, Dad. I hate the idea that you're all alone down there with these fires rampaging around your area.'

'You make them sound like a bunch of serial killers.'

'Well, they are killers. Two people have died already. Dad, I don't know what sort of news you've been listening to down there but this is not a firemen's picnic. I suppose you've heard that Sydney is surrounded. That these are the worst fire conditions ever. That the Lord Mayor is getting condolence letters from the President of the United States ...' Emily paused to get the sarcasm out of her voice. Couldn't. 'That brown sky outside your window, Dad, is not the slipstream from the public bar of the Crest hotel.'

'You've been watching too much TV, Emily,' said John Carmody. He was more relieved than angry to hear his daughter's chidings. He was always happy to hear from her. Even when she thought she was angry with him. There was a strangled tone of caring beneath her sarcasm. As she spoke, he imagined her face. She'd be running her hands through the well-worn track in her hair. Lucky she had a lot of it. He tried to decide whether her brow would be knotted with tension, adding sharpness to a face that always seemed so alive. He'd always thought Emily would be pretty if she could just remain relaxed. She had warm, light brown eyes and even features. But she was so reactive to the world that expressions were always sprinting across her face – knotting, compressing and twisting her features. Sometimes Emily practised an expression of ennui, the pose of a pale-faced, pouting model. But the air of worldly sophistication would only last until the next expression barged onto her face. Carmody guessed his daughter would not be wearing her haute couture expression tonight.

Emily was still chatting. John Carmody let her words wash over him like a warm surf. He had felt lonely today. And was surprised that he had felt that way but, he thought, as Emily massaged him with words, it had been a dramatic day.

He had risen at five a.m. with an old nightmare trailing off into his wakening mind. He'd barely made the transition back to reality when he snapped awake with the realisation that his nostrils were tingling with the smell of burning bush. A sensual, summery smell. The smell that pervaded his youth – barbecues, burn-offs and campfires. And occasionally bushfires.

His second big breath of the morning confirmed it. There were bushfires outside. Quite a distance away. Lots of them. Burning slowly, going nowhere. There was no wind. But the fires were closer today than they were yesterday. As his eyes registered the density of the ash and dust in the air, the hairs on top of his head tingled. The animal response to fear woke him fully. And shocked him. He was always surprised when his body responded to something before his mind had recognised it. Like now. When his body was registering a portfolio of environmental stimulae and, without intellectual input from him, presenting him with an invoice of fear.

He rolled out of bed. Best way to get out, he thought. With creaky knees and stiff back, he either rolled out of bed or stayed there debating whether to get up at all. He had developed the roll into something resembling a rugby roll. More to save face than impress his bedsprings. Won't be putting in for the Olympics, though, he thought, and ambled up to the mirrored wardrobe.

He caught sight of himself in the mirror and, briefly, he saw someone else. Someone older, bulkier and sadder-looking than himself. It was, he realised, a reflection of himself before he had time to compose himself for a reflection of himself.

He straightened himself to his full height – a hundred and seventy centimetres and shrinking fast. He tucked his tummy in a little – eighty kilos and losing the fight. And he searched the mirror for himself. He was nearing his sixties but his face looked as if it had seen more time under the sun than that. The wrinkles cut tracks across his forehead, like a poorly built railway line. More wrinkles cupped his mouth and fanned out from his eyes. When he was talking to friends, his crow's feet and a slight curl at the end of his mouth gave the impression of a man who was about to crack a joke, or someone who was hearing a good one. But when he was alone and his face relaxed, it dropped into sadness. It used to worry him that people meeting him when he was concentrating on something would invariably say, 'Cheer up, buddy,' or 'It can't be as bad as that.' It didn't happen too much any more. Most of the people he met knew him well. Or at least they knew his facial expressions.

He pushed the image of himself aside as he opened the door of his wardrobe. He fossicked past the all-weather jackets in his wardrobe, past the fishing gear, and grabbed a green, grungy pair of overalls from the end coathanger. His firefighting outfit. It hadn't seen action for a while. These days he wore it more for clean-outs than burn-offs. He smelt the fabric to see if he could still detect traces of bush smoke. It smelt of old sweat and a musty wardrobe. He hadn't thought about putting his firefighting gear on, or he couldn't remember thinking about it. But he pulled it on anyway.

He stiffly walked out to his verandah, as he did every morning. Shaking hands with the world, he thought. Sometimes, he could tell what his day would be like if he listened attentively. He sniffed, rubbed the rails and he listened. He cocked his ears for the sounds of the bay below, for the bird calls and the sound of wind passing through casuarinas. Sometimes he listened to silence. The silence was worst because it usually meant nature was preparing for a drama, tucking its head into burrows, nestling into tightly packed foliage, standing still with nose tipped and eyes darting.

It was silent this morning. The birds hadn't appeared. Food scraps that had been flung over the verandah last night had been ignored by lizards, ants, wallabies. The hot air was coming in

from the north, languidly elbowing through the lax branches of
casuarinas and the crinkly leaves of gums. It hugged him, filled
his nostrils with a thick, warm warning and wafted insouciantly
into his house.

As his eyes scanned the horizons he was mentally counting the
particles of ash per square metre. It was thick – the horizon ended
at the hillsides half a kilometre away. His eyes itched already. He
looked along at the neighbouring houses that could be seen
above the tree tops. They too looked hazy – as if they had been
drawn with a blunt pencil. He looked to the east. A little clearer.

The houses of Flint Bay were strung out along the hillside, like
loose teeth in a bandit's mouth. It was the sort of housing config-
uration that evolves when there is no road to impose discipline on
the streetscape. Houses had been built to catch views, or to nestle
behind a stand of trees, or to take advantage of a relatively flat
patch of earth. Most of the houses had been sited on a whim. The
Leonard house ended up where it was because that was where
the builder's supplier had dumped the building materials.

The houses were all within shouting distance of their neighbours – a few were cheek by jowl. The only link between the
houses of Flint Bay was a track that wound along the waterfront.
The track performed many roles. It got people from the wharf and
their moorings along to their homes, it loosely defined private
property from national park and it was a meeting place for residents. At some stage, everyone in Flint Bay met everyone else on
the track. Certainly, it didn't take long to meet Mrs Parker. She
pottered around her front garden to trap passersby into conversation. That part of the track was called Parker's station. Residents
walked briskly past Parker's station.

Most of the houses were built between the Second World War
and the seventies and, except for a few follies from the eighties,
most were humble in their aspirations. A deck, a few large windows, lots of bunks and furniture handed down from the long,
empty summers of the forties and fifties.

Flint Bay didn't feature prominently in property listings of real estate agents. Some street directories didn't even put it on the map. It was one of those areas that was passed down from generation to generation. Carmody had been in the Bay for ten years. He had been president of the association once, he was de facto supervisor of maintenance programs due to his engineering background and he was de facto deputy of the fire prevention team. He was one of the most liked figures in the community. But most of the residents of the Bay still thought of him as a newcomer.

Things to do, he thought to himself as he turned away from the view of the bay and walked back into the house to the kitchen. He turned on the radio and began fossicking through cupboards for plastic containers. One by one he filled them with water. Later he would flavour them with glucose. Just like the women did for his father and uncles up in the mountains when they would fight fires for days, replenished by sweet water, sandwiches and eye washes. He wouldn't put the glucose in now. Didn't want to panic.

'... is the summer we've been dreading,' boomed the voice of the fire chief on the eight a.m. bulletin, 'no decent rain for seven months, the undergrowth is thick, dry. Already this Wednesday morning we have eleven major fires burning to the north-west and south of Sydney and dozens of smaller outbreaks. At the moment they are not threatening residential areas but if the wind picks up from the north, we're in trouble.'

As Carmody listened, he let the tank water flow over the spout of the plastic container down his age-pocked hands. The cool wash of water was soothing, like the soft touch of a woman. And bloody stupid! He spun the tap closed and chided himself for wasting water. God knows, his life may depend on having those final drops of water in his water tank. At that moment, the wind picked up a little. Rustled from its sleep. Taunted from its lassitude.

'Kettle on?' cried a voice from the back door. It was Bo, who lived in a house along the ridge. Bo banged his boots against the back door steps and shuffled into the house. A bit like a dog that shuffles and side-steps onto new territory, excited but nervous.

'I'm onto my second pot, Bo,' he lied. 'Come on in.' He was surprised to hear from his neighbour, who spent most of his time in his one-room fibro hut with his dog, his collection of branch sculptures and a yellowing pile of *Reader's Digest* from the fifties and sixties. Bo's subscription had lapsed in 1968. The year his brother died. No one had told him how to renew the subscription. So he reread old issues in the twenty minutes of kerosine light he allowed himself every night.

Old Bo looked wilder every time John saw him. It was like the stories he read of children living with animals. Slowly they come to resemble them. Bo was coming to resemble his dog. His shuffling gait; eyebrows pulled down over eyes, hooding them. His skin was darkening. Hair was closing in around his face. John Carmody's grandchild, Joel, had screamed the first time he'd seen Bo down the track. Lucky for him, Bo was down-wind at the time. Bo not only resembled his dog, he smelt like his dog too. It wasn't an unpleasant smell – it was the smell of damp carpet and carnivorous breath – but it was a disturbing smell because it wasn't a smell that you associated with human beings.

'I thought you'd help shift my box. Down the hill,' said Bo. Getting straight to the point. 'Time to move things out of the cabin. Mum's things and all. What with all this smoke,' Bo talking more to the sky outside the kitchen window than to Carmody.

He often had trouble understanding Bo. The bushman was so unused to talking to people that his syntax had contracted into tight half-sentences. Carmody had never thought of Bo as backward, but he was so tight with words and he found exchanging words so painful that the resulting conversations were inevitably constipated. One walked away from an encounter with Bo with not much to mull on. Nor did one ever get a greater understanding of Bo, of where he had come from or, most pertinently, where he was mentally living at the moment.

John Carmody wiped his hands clean and muttered, 'So you've got a pile of photos to shift down to the water?'

Bo looked stricken. 'No, I left those. Just got a few notes ... and a couple of branches ... and a few ...'

'No matter, let's get to it,' Carmody said, walking out of the kitchen. He noticed Bo was slow to move. He thought for a minute that maybe Bo was waiting for that cuppa. Or going deaf. But then he realised Bo was listening to the radio. Attentively.

John listened too. 'We've been down the ridge road,' a voice on the radio crackled loudly, 'and the fires have already swept through the rear of the Hills district. It's a front of about two kilometres and firefighters have been forced to retreat to the back-yards of threatened homes. With winds currently only a few knots, firefighters are confident they will be able to handle the front of the fire as it moves behind the houses, but they are not even trying to stem the front as it moves further into the park.'

The fires couldn't be news to Bo. And it wasn't like Bo to panic at the news that a fire front was ten kilometres to the west of the bay. Carmody looked at the bushman from the corner of his eyes. Bo seemed more intent on the face and dials of the radio than on the news report. Obviously, it was the radio that was intriguing him. Maybe, thought John, he hasn't listened to a radio in a long time. Quite possibly – the radio had disappeared when his brother's kids came and cleaned out most of Bruce's possessions.

Bo and John were quiet during the walk up to Bo's hut. Bo's dog, Sheila, clipped happily along beside them. Carmody watched the bush as a surgeon observes his next morning's patient. Noting weaknesses, escape routes, fallback positions, dry spots, areas where bush rubbish had collected, weakened trees. He tried to gauge how the hillside would cope with a spot fire. In these con-ditions, he concluded, it would only take a single burning ember to turn the hill into a bonfire.

After half a kilometre of hard slog up the hill and along its steep banks, they reached Bo's cabin. It was built on a large flat

rock and overlooked the backyards of neighbours. As he entered
Bo's place, John suspended his senses. He held his breath and
didn't encourage his eyes to adjust to the dusty darkness. He
hadn't been inside this hut since … Carmody could hardly
remember the last time. Months, six months, maybe more.
Carmody recalled the first time he had visited Bo. It was shortly
after he had arrived in the Bay. He made the mistake of visiting
Bo on spec. Just to introduce himself. Bo had nearly bolted in
fright. But when Bo recovered, he grew to like John Carmody.

Through the veil of bush smoke and a reluctant eye focus, he
could still decipher the layout of Bo's cabin. There was a single
bed to his left. The lumpiness of the mattress defied the clinical
precision of the bedmaking. Only nurses and old soldiers make
their beds like envelopes, noted Carmody. A kettle, packets of tea,
assorted biscuits, sugar and flour shared a small 'kitchen' bench
next to the door. On the other side of the cabin was a small table,
stacked with *Reader's Digests* and a chair. Just one chair.
Testimony to Bo's entertaining program. John had always wondered about Bo's toilet. But had never asked.

In the middle of the hut was an old tin trunk that Bo was
groping in the half-light. Together they lugged it down the hill to
the waterfront, where Bo had already scouted a spot just above
high-tide mark.

'This weighs a ton, Bo. What have you got in this treasure
chest? The bones of your dead relatives or something?' asked
Carmody. He scrambled over the rock to position the trunk.

Bo appeared to have already forgotten he had company. He
paused briefly at the top of the boulder, 'A few of Mother's old
things. Stuff,' he said, moving off again.

'But it weighs a ton,' Carmody persisted. He didn't normally
pester Bo for a conversation but Carmody was curious about what
sort of things Bo valued. The wildman had never showed any
interest in material possessions. Certainly his hut and his lifestyle

suggested that Bo didn't value much that was man-made. And yet the weight of this trunk belied that.

'There's nothing of treasure in there,' said Bo, more resolute. Carmody let the matter drop.

The rest of the morning, John had paced the verandah, alternately wondering what treasures Bo had stashed away on the shoreline and whether he too should take his keepsakes down to the waterfront. He had already packed most of the old photos, records, newspaper clippings and the few trinkets that once belonged to his wife, but he hadn't moved them to safe ground.

He knew he should move them just as a precaution. He'd buried them behind the rocks on the water's edge twice before. In the fires of '72 and '63. To bury them seemed an over-reaction. Not to bury them seemed a denial of the hot winds that were now rippling over the water, stroking the casuarinas and sucking the moisture from his skin and hair. He spent the afternoon in indecision.

But he didn't tell this to his daughter, who had paused at the other end of the phone line.

'Dad, are you listening to me? Don't you care where I go on weekends away? One day I'll go off on a special weekend and I'll be grabbed by the Moonies and taken off to Seoul for a mass wedding ceremony.'

'As long as you avoid the mass murderers,' said Carmody.

'Tell me about your day, anyway. Have you had any advice on what happens if the fires come into the Bay? I hope you're not planning on greeting them with your garden hose!'

Carmody chuckled as he remembered the fire hose that was already laid out over the front lawn, having been tested twice in the last three days.

'Don't be dramatic, Emms. I've just been sorting through some old records and rearranging things,' John Carmody said to his daughter, adding, for her benefit or possibly his, 'I'll call you if I need some help.'

Chapter two

Jack withdrew from Sarah with a groan. Deflating in more ways than one. Nimbly he executed a body roll that would clear him of the wet spot. He hated the wet spot. Wished she'd do something about it.

'What would you have me do, Jack?' said Sarah when he had once raised his discomfort about the matter. 'Tie a hand towel around my arse for the duration? Or should we remain locked together like two dogs and crab-walk into the shower?' At the time, the idea of a crab-walk appealed to him. But he didn't pursue the line with Sarah.

As Jack completed his roll out of bed, he noticed that his stomach no longer crinkled when he bent over. It rolled. A pasty, slightly dimpled roll.

'Gotta get some more exercise,' he said to Sarah, slapping her bottom as he passed her on the way to the ensuite.

'Thanks a lot!' Sarah said brusquely.

'No, no, not you! I was referring to myself. Why would you think I was referring to you?' said Jack, adding in a mutter, 'You're so bloody defensive about everything these days.'

'Maybe I'm a mite peeved because you don't bother coming home until after midnight, then you poke me awake with an erection and make love to me with all the tenderness and emotion of a mechanic doing his sixth grease and oil change of the day.'

Sarah tore the sheet away from herself and flipped her legs onto the floor. Her body, after thirty-two years, one child, several years' cross-training and a brief period of bulimia (a practice she reluctantly gave up when her teeth began discolouring) was sylph-like. With just a modest top-up of silicon. Clothes tended to drape her body, lying lightly on her curves. She had a mesmerising effect on most men – even Jack after nine years of marriage.

As Sarah overtook Jack to claim the bathroom first, Jack was trying to recall what had started this morning's fight. It didn't take much to start a fight with Sarah these days. They seemed to be triggered by anything. Certainly he couldn't remember provoking them, or feeling aggrieved with her before they started. But every time Sarah looked his way she seemed pissed off about something. In fact, Jack thought, grabbing his towel to take to the other bathroom, Sarah was beginning to look like a pretty girl who turned into a disappointed woman. Sour.

By the time he had banged on the bathroom door and heard Joel yell back that he was 'sitting', he was getting worried. He hated it when Sarah's moods were unreadable. He felt like a cloven-hoofed beast that had bolted through a garden, terrorising the fairy at the bottom of the glen.

Flowers, he thought, get her flowers. Not today, that would be too obvious. On Friday, just to show he's thinking of her, just to show that he thinks of her at times other than his tumescent wakenings, just to show –

The phone buzzed him from the kitchen wall. Jack wandered over to it, hoping that it wasn't a friend of Sarah's. He didn't want to exchange pleasantries and he was already planning on exiting the house without having to talk to his wife again.

'What are we going to do about Dad?'

Jack hated the way his sister never introduced herself on the phone. She presumed that Jack would recognise her voice as easily as if she had just walked into the room. It implied an intimacy he no longer felt for her. If, indeed, he ever had felt it.

'And who might this be, on this bright and beautiful day!' replied Jack. He stared out the window at a sky he noticed was not bright at all. It was a dull, white sky – a fact he hadn't noticed through the shutters of his bedroom and the cool of his air-conditioning. As Jack pushed the kitchen window open, the morning gob-smacked him. It was a hot, raspy day.

'Which planet are you living on, Jack? What day is it? Do you have any idea that it is Thursday, to be precise January 6?' She read his pause well. 'It is the day that hell arrived on earth. My barometer is already reading thirty degrees. The health department has alerted asthmatics to stay indoors, the emergency crews have … Jack have you listened to the news at all?'

'Oh and what will the radio news services tell me that could be of any interest, other than the purient?' asked Jack, getting tetchier as his bowels began pressuring for their morning release.

'It might tell you whether Father is going to die today,' said Emily, on the verge of tears. She realised that while she had spent half the night worrying about her father, imagining the inferno that was crackling its way through the undergrowth to his house, her brother had not even thought about his father.

The pause at the end of the line confirmed it.

Jack felt his pulse lighten when he thought of the news report about the bushfires he'd heard on the way home last night. And another he had heard the night before. And he had never thought of his father. Not once. But he wasn't going to panic now. Not for the satisfaction of his sister.

'What do you want to do about him? He's a grown man. He knows how to turn on a hose. If he needs a lot of water, there are volunteer firefighters with big trucks of water and if things get rough he can walk out of there and lodge an insurance claim,' said Jack. He hated himself just a little as he acted the smartarse.

'Well, I'll tell him that, Jack. I'll say, "Don't worry, Dad, Jack is going to send you an insurance claim form. He's got everything organised."' Emily was shouting now, the tension of the restless night releasing itself down the phone line. 'And in the meantime,' she continued, 'you can let Dad burn in the bush just the way Mum did.'

'Get a hold of yourself, Emily. That last comment was way beyond bounds. What the hell do you mean by that comment? Mum didn't die in a bushfire. You make it sound as if her death was someone's fault.' Jack switched the phone to his other ear. He tended to do this when he wanted to change the subject of conversation. As if a physical switching of the phone would prompt a mental switch. He was breathing heavily. He exhaled heavily to burn up some of his indignation.

'Okay, okay, I didn't mean it.' Emily's voice wavered down the line, conciliation in her tone.

Jack wasn't ready to forgive. He was tempted to hang up. But that would be the sort of thing Emily would do. She'd love to spark a drama over this. He let the silence stretch and then said, 'I'll check on him. Okay? I'll give him a call and ask if he wants help.'

'I called him last night,' said Emily quietly. 'He seemed okay then but he may have been putting on the bravado for my sake. So if you could call him this morning and ... oh I don't know, just see how he is, I suppose.'

'Goodbye, Emily.'

He was still smarting half an hour later as he drove his Jaguar through the morning peak-hour traffic. His sister was always spinning dramas around him. Most of his childhood memories revolved around her demands for him to be a part of her fantasy. He'd be squatting happily over a colony of slaters or ants, devising ways to divert them from their paths or building alternative tunnels for them, when the shadow of his sister would loom over him.

'Come and be the prince in my play,' Emily would demand of him, dumping some stupid costume onto him. There was no denying Emily. Or at least it had never occurred to him that he could say no to her. Not during his first twelve years of life with her. Invariably he'd spend Saturday afternoons climbing up the sweet pea lattice to rescue Princess Emily, or smashing rocks in a loincloth while Emily wielded a willow whip.

But they had never talked about the biggest moment of drama in their lives. The death of their mother had been passed over so quickly it still hung between them. Like smoke, he thought, looking through the windscreen at the hazy sky. He stopped at a red light and gazed at the smoky landscape of North Shore suburbia. It was like a gauze curtain across his vision. Yes, he thought, the memory of their mother's death hung like smoke in a room – an ethereal presence, rarely acknowledged. But it still played on their senses. Skewered their outlook.

As his car moved off from the red light and crested a hill, Jack could fully appreciate the gritty panorama of suburbia. It was strange, he thought. Cloudy days normally have a dull, comfortable light, a wet taste. Today the sky was filled with a hard, shiny light. Briefly he was tempted to wind down his window and check the outside temperature but he decided to turn on the eight a.m. news bulletin instead.

'… fires simply devoured these homes. Nothing anyone could have done would have made any difference. By late yesterday afternoon there were only two houses left standing in the whole of Beattie Street. This morning as the residents of Beattie Street sift through rubble – ' Jack let the news report wash over him. The excited hyperbole of the journalist, set against the background of fires swooshing and cracking, was strangely soothing. It was almost as though he felt safe while the fates were otherwise occupied. Simply because something dramatic was happening elsewhere in the world, there was a good chance it wouldn't be happening to him today. He remembered hearing a report on radio once where a critic had referred to it as 'the guilty compassion of the armchair witness'. Maybe, thought Jack, he was just growing cynical. He tuned into the news bulletin again.

'… it's not efficient to send out crews to every one of those outbreaks. We simply don't have the resources to do that. We probably couldn't make much inroad into those fires in any case and we must hold our power until the fronts reach populated areas.' A calm, almost laconic voice filled the cabin of the Jaguar.

'But as minister,' retorted the interviewer, 'isn't it your responsibility to protect the national parks, the wildlife in them and, in particular, some of the species that are already threatened, such as the snub-nosed possum?'

'I thought it was the snot-nosed possum,' replied the minister, droll. Jack burst out laughing. He loved hearing people take the mickey out of journalists.

'It doesn't seem, Minister, that you're taking this issue seriously. There are many Green groups who feel that your policies and practices of fire management completely disregard wildlife concerns.'

Jack could hear the deep breath being taken by the minister and could guess what was coming. The inevitable backdown, the placating tone, the promises that would enable everyone to go back to work knowing that even if no one was doing anything, everyone had voiced the right intentions.

He switched the radio off and drove into the parking station. Reviewing the interview he had just heard, it dawned on him that if, indeed, firefighters were not bothering to fight fronts in crown land or national parks, then the situation must be serious. He'd never heard of firefighters electing to let fires burn unchecked.

Grabbing his briefcase and his mobile phone as he walked towards the lift doors of his building, he pressed hash 9 for his father's number.

'Dad, how are you?' he said, hearing his father's gravelly voice.

'Jack, good to hear from you. How's my mate little Joel?'

'Fine, Dad, but how are you?' persisted Jack. He watched the lights of the lift buttons descend to the ground floor.

'Fine, Son, that flu is cleared up all right, a bit of fluid hanging around the bottom of the lungs but that'll go.'

'Sorry, Dad, I didn't know you'd been sick. You should watch that fluid, it could easily progress onto pneumonia, you know.

But I'm really ringing about the fires. I just heard the Thursday morning wrap-up on the radio and they all sound pretty excited about the whole thing. Emily's in a tizz about the threat, in fact by mid-morning she'll probably be on your verandah with a mob of men in yellow overalls, a garden sprinkler and Evian spray!' Jack noticed that the lift was about to arrive. He couldn't terminate the conversation with his father already. Nor did he want to natter in the lift. He detoured to the fire stairs.

'Well, we've all been pretty busy, getting things in preparation. A few residents haven't got much in the way of garden hoses, much less fire hoses. And, of course, the water tanks are already low. The Greys' tank only has ten or eleven rungs of water left.' Jack Carmody obligingly recounted the duties he had attended in the Bay during the last couple of days.

By the time his father had filled him in on the Greys' water tanks and the O'Conners' firetrap under the house, and the moisture content of the vegetation down at the Bay, Jack had walked up two flights of steps, unlocked his office, picked up his mail and begun flipping letters on his desk. He'd just retrieved a Law Society letter from the pile when Jane poked her head into his office and mouthed 'hi'.

Jack looked up from the letter, momentarily forgetting his father on the end of the line and said 'good morning' to Jane in such a warm, pregnant tone that his father was silenced.

'Is Sarah there?' asked John Carmody.

'No, no,' said Jack too gaily, 'it's just one of the other solicitors, Jane Tully. But listen, Dad, if you need me to come down there and hold the fort with you for a while, just give me a call. I'm sure I'd be able to escape the office for a little while and if not, I might be able to arrange some help down there for you.'

'No, Son, don't be silly. These fires are just giving us all a good practice.' John Carmody was so certain that he had just lied to his son, he blushed. He waited for his son to state the obvious; to reprimand him for his false bravado.

Jack was grinning across his office at Jane's reaction to hearing his offer to his father. She pursed her lips in mock admiration. As Jane fossicked around in the library for a reference book, Jack straightened in his chair and tilted his head in what he hoped was a patrician pose. He almost succeeded. Jack had a promising face – if you started at the top. His dark thatch of hair was the envy of every bloke who was getting nervous about his hairline. It slung generously across his forehead. His eyebrows carried on the thick, dark tradition. His eyes, too, were dark, although too small to be kind. Disappointment set in further down his face. His lips were thin, his chin stopped short and a slight jowl to his cheek suggested flaccidness.

'Okay, Dad, I've a conference to go to tonight but let us know if I can do anything. No other news to tell?'

Carmody failed to detect the ennui in his son's question. 'Did you know Roger Burton is stepping down as association president and he wants me to take on the job again?'

'Oh yeah,' said Jack disinterestedly, 'that sounds interesting. Does it involve much work?'

'It does, really. It means organising all the community working bees, making sure someone does a bit of fundraising. Sometimes you have to write letters to various governments and departments – chase up problems in the surrounding bush with the national parks ...'

'Well why do you want to do it? Didn't you do that job once before?' interjected Jack.

'Yes, I just said so. Frankly Roger doesn't think too many other residents are ... well capable is not the word ...'

'Say it, Dad, they're too dumb.'

'I wasn't going to say that at all. I meant most of the people down here aren't very extroverted or assertive.' John Carmody was feeling disappointment sinking into his bones as he talked with his son. The feeling was familiar. Conversations with Jack were always at cross-purposes.

'Do you get paid for it?' demanded Jack.

'No, don't be silly.'

'What about a government grant?'

'No, why would they give the people of Flint Bay a government grant?'

'Listen, Dad, I'll talk about details at another time but all you have to do is change the name of the organisation, make it the Flint Bay Historical Society or the Flint Bay Sporting Association and apply for a grant. Don't ask for much or they'll ask too many questions. Ask for four or five thousand, say you need to erect a plaque or repair an orienteering track and you'll have a cheque within weeks.'

'But why would they give money to a group they have never heard of?'

'You've got articles of association, don't you? And signed-up members? That's legal recognition. The only thing you've got going against you is you're middle-class Anglos who live in a safe seat. But the government has to give little bits of money all over the state so no one will look too closely at the big bits of money they pump into the marginal electorates. It's now known as whiteboard diplomacy – they get a big whiteboard of the whole state and pin lots of dots around it to signify grants allocated …'

'You're kidding me, Jack.'

'Dad, listen I've really got to go. But leave it with me. I'll track down some forms, get the low-down on when applications have to be in … just let me do that for you.'

'Okay, Jack.'

Jack cursed as he hung up. Jane had just left the room. He wondered what reference she was after, or whether she had come in for a reference at all. Certainly she had used his library a hell of a lot since she arrived in the firm a few months ago. It may have been close to her office but there were other libraries. Jack leant back in his swing chair, stretched his arms to the ceiling and cracked his knuckles.

'You'll keep, Janey,' he said to himself, 'till tomorrow night at the conference. Have a few drinks, let down the hair, meet a few contacts, rub shoulders with each other, rub … yes, Janey, I'll see you Friday night.'

Chapter three

Emily perched on the edge of a spaghetti-weave chair and flipped the manuscript to the first page. Her audience had a distracted air but was quiet. So she began.

'The waitress was taking their lunch order when she felt his hand slide up her dress. The touch was so light she wasn't sure what was happening. When she realised what was happening, she held her breath to stop herself yelling or gasping. Slowly, inconspicuously, she edged away from him. His hand clenched around her thigh to stop her.

'The waitress didn't say anything. She stood there staring at the woman who was ordering meatballs while her partner sat beside her with his hand up the waitress's dress, stroking her inner thighs.

'Meatballs,' the waitress repeated to the woman. The words croaked out. The woman looked up from the menu, ran her eyes over the waitress's grease-streaked uniform and said nothing.

'And-will-that-be-all?' the waitress added, operating on remote control as the man's hands grabbed her buttocks. The woman looked at the space in front of her as if reading an imaginary menu. The waitress tried to match the blank expression – dumb blonde to dumb blonde.

'The cafe hummed in the background. Vaguely familiar celebrities were edging past too-small tables. Suddenly the man reached up to grab the waist of her pantihose! For a minute the waitress felt like yelling "Stop!" or "Rape!" Something – anything! But how could she yell "Rape" while standing in the middle of a crowded cafe? She mouthed her protests silently.'

'Oh, Emily, just get us a coffee, or we'll yell rape,' said Bernadette, pushing her friend out of the chair. Kate smiled as Emily lifted herself off the chair that she had only just sat on.

'Don't you like the script?' said Emily.

'Is it a script? Or is it just another one-page treatment that will end up at the back of your desk with all the others?' said Bernadette. She gave Emily her disappointed schoolmistress look.

'Ouch.' Emily folded the script back into her bumbag.

'Okay, okay, I'm sorry. It's just that we hear so much about your new ideas for feature films or TV soaps and you never finish them,' said Bernadette.

'Well this one is a goer.' She swept her hand around the cafe. 'The inner-city cafe is the nexus of urban life. If you set a TV serial in a hip cafe, you can explore every issue of urban angst – workforce issues, relationship issues, the single woman's lifestyle. You've got the opportunity to introduce crime, with a hold-up or drive-by shooting. You've got an opportunity for lots of – '

'Sex?' interjected Kate.

'You said it, I didn't,' said Emily.

'Honestly, Emily,' said Bernadette, leaning back in the spindly cafe chair, 'the rest of us don't reel off R-rated films in our minds every time we hit a boring spot in life. I sometimes wonder how often you live in the real world.' She looked curiously at her friend's profile. 'Life is not a film script.' She paused for dramatic effect. 'You can't slow-mo reality while you run the reel of your own imagination.'

While Bernadette folded away the menu, Emily opened her order book, mostly for the benefit of her boss, whom she noticed was staring at her from behind the espresso machine. Perhaps her friends were right. Even as she looked at her boss she was panning in on the steam above the machine, mentally poking a microphone towards the ceiling of the cafe to pick up the hubbub of mid-morning conversations, creating the next scene of CAFE BABYLON.

She knew she was putting her imaginary camera to her eye a lot these days – often without premeditation. She'd be talking with someone and suddenly she'd be filming them, adjusting the volume of their voices, panning in on their lips, sometimes even setting a sound track to the scene. But she'd reconciled her outlook as that of an artist. She doubted anyone got angry with Monet because he saw a bluer sky than anyone else; she didn't think Mozart was chided for humming lullabies while he attended to his daily ablutions.

Emily was now miffed. 'Are you going to hop slowly through Centennial Park tomorrow morning?' she asked Bernadette.

'If you are referring to my Friday Tai Chi sessions, Emily, then the answer is yes. And if your middle-class paradigm cannot allow you to experience anything other than a hopping feeling with Tai Chi then I'd prefer you didn't come with me.'

'Didn't you spend a whole weekend doing Tai Chi at the Holistic Centre's weekend just last month?' Kate said, turning in her chair to confront Emily.

'It was a vibrational healing weekend,' retorted Emily, 'and, no we didn't do Tai Chi. We did reiki and shell healing.'

'Shell healing?' Kate dropped her menu on the table.

'Shell essences,' Emily said. She didn't want to pursue this conversation too much further. She'd had a dreadful time at the Holistic Centre. She was castigated for her attitude twice by the man in charge of the program. The Enabler, he was called. Emily had *wanted* to believe! She liked shells! She had collected them when she was young. Just because she couldn't hear the music of their soul didn't mean she was antagonistic towards them, as the Enabler had claimed.

Her friends were looking at her. Waiting for her to explain shell essences.

'You've heard of essential oils, haven't you?' Emily said by way of explanation.

'Yeah, but shells don't smell,' said Bernadette.

'Oh,' flustered now, 'they have a presence, they're supposed to have a music. They represent the sea, time, the wind. We can absorb their essence into our bodies.'

'You mean, like those sharks' teeth that men wore around their necks in the eighties?' said Kate.

'I suppose so,' said Emily. She hadn't seen the association between sharks' teeth and shell essences before. But it made sense. She remembered a date in 1982 with a bloke who wore a particularly large shark's tooth. The tooth had impressed her. He didn't. He was obviously counting on the shark-tooth talisman to compensate for his inability to carry a conversation.

'Did you ever meet a good-looking guy with a shark's tooth?' Emily's question met with silence. She too was mute as she searched the archives of her dating history for a bloke's face that was more interesting than the shark's tooth around his neck. Silence. 'I think the shells work more like crystals,' concluded Emily.

'I thought you had a bad experience with crystals,' said Bernadette smugly.

Emily wasn't going to grace that remark with a reply.

'Some people hop slowly through crowded parks, others suck crystals. Each to their own,' said Emily.

'I don't know why you keep flirting with New Age if you've got such a negative attitude to it. Deep down you think it all sucks, don't you?' said Bernadette.

'I'm open. I'm open to anything,' said Emily, brushing off her apron. 'It's just that none of them have given convincing returns yet.'

'Spoken like a true reductionist. Everything is reduced to its return. To its yield. Who gives better dividends – Buddha or Christ; crystals or yoga?' Bernadette was flapping the menu in front of her face as she said this.

'Just give me a break and order something,' said Emily. 'The way the boss is staring at me, I'll be sacked by the time I get back to the servery.'

'Two cappuccinos and a water,' said Bernadette. 'So we won't see you tomorrow?'

'No. I'm going to Dad's place at Flint Bay to help him fight the bushfires.' Emily quickly shut her order book and began waltzing off. She was good at timing exits. This exit was timed so her friends could digest the news of her mission of mercy without being able to question her about it.

'What do you know about fighting fires?' said Bernadette to Emily's back, more as a parting comment than a question. Without turning around to face her friends, Emily lifted her hands in a sassy gesture. She couldn't answer the question anyway. She wasn't sure she was serious about joining her father for the fire. It seemed like a good line at the time.

It was the way she made a lot of decisions. They'd just announce themselves halfway through a conversation or she'd find herself doing something she couldn't remember deciding to do. Still it surprised her that decisions about her life got made somewhere at the back of her mind where she didn't have easy access. Intuition, she called it, if ever asked to account for her impulsiveness.

But she was worried too. Her conversation with her father last night had nagged her all morning. She felt he was underplaying his fear. And, she had to admit, she was getting curious about these fires.

'You were at that table so long, I figured your friends must be ordering like a busload of American tourists,' Joseph, her boss, chided as Emily returned to the servery.

Joseph had a tray of coffees ready to take out to a table. As Emily busied herself, she could see Joseph's jaws were set hard with concentration. Emily had seen him look like this when he was fighting with his wife.

'I was reciting the menu to them,' said Emily. 'If you would bother to write down a list of all the cakes and specials, I wouldn't have to spend so long crouching over tables parroting through the menu for patrons.'

Emily knew she'd gone too far when she saw Joseph bristle. She hurriedly collected cutlery and serviettes to reset a table and was turning on her heel when Joseph said, 'Emily, I've just done the roster for the next week. Mum's in Friday and Saturday so don't bother coming in tomorrow or the next day, okay? I'll ring you next week, if we have any shifts available.'

She nodded. The gesture acknowledged the retrenchment slip that Joseph had just verbally delivered her. Emily moved out of the servery to scrub down a table – head down so her friends wouldn't see her tearful flush.

The embarrassment hurt most. Emily had never been sacked before. She'd moved through dozens of casual jobs but it was almost always she who quit. On the couple of occasions when she'd detected a growing disenchantment from the boss, she'd thrown in her apron before the inevitable.

The anger gnawed at her as she scrubbed a recently vacated table. Scrubbed the grease off, then the paintwork and, if she kept at it, there wouldn't be any timber laminate left. She was pissed off at this cafe anyway. She was pissed off with patrons who demanded much and tipped poorly. She didn't think the fifty-cent tips they left deserved the familiarity they demanded. She'd been here almost six months – long enough for the regulars to recognise her. Long enough, they thought, for her to memorise their ritual orders. Fifty-cent tips won't buy you my memory, she wanted to yell at the regulars.

Joseph presumed Emily enjoyed the familiarity. When someone asked Emily for 'the usual', Joseph would wink at her or nod his head in acclamation. Emily would grimace and remind herself that the proprietor just wanted her to become another woman under his control – mother in the kitchen, wife at the front door and friendly little waitress at his side.

She didn't want anyone to think of her as part of their family. She didn't want anyone to think of her as a waitress. She didn't want anyone to think she was nice. Emily hated people who made assumptions about her. She was the only one who knew exactly what she was. Or would be. She, Emily Carmody, was a script writer. Of feature films. One day she would also be a director. Of feature films. But Hollywood had not discovered her yet. Nor had the Australian Film Finance Corporation. In the meantime, she had to work tables. Like every other artist of merit.

As she walked back to the servery, Emily forced herself to think haughty. To lift the chin, like an offended artist – misunderstood but still dignified. Her lips contracted over her mouth. Passing Joseph, who was examining the espresso machine like he'd never seen one before, Emily couldn't resist a parting jibe.

'So, Joe,' she said, using the name his mother used on him when he did something stupid, 'you'll call me next week, eh?'

'Sure, Emily,' Joseph murmured, still not meeting her eyes.

Emily's retort ended there but the phrase stuck with her. It repeated itself as she wrapped up her apron, picked up her bag and stormed out into daylight.

'I'll call you next week,' Emily repeated to herself. 'I'll call you next week.' It was strange how employers had began using the phrase that cowardly men had been using on women for so many years. With similiar sincerity. 'I'll call you next week,' said all the blokes who passed out of Emily's flat on a Sunday morning. 'I'll call you next week,' they said as they jiggled themselves into their pants.

'Isn't that what Michael Douglas said to Glenn Close in *Fatal Attraction?*' Emily would reply as she rolled over, languidly she hoped, to face the bloke. Most of the men – hell, there had only been a couple in the last year – paused when they heard her reply. She loved that brief pause, that flicker of fear, that jump in the heart rate that suggested that these guys weren't entirely confident that she was joking.

So they'd laugh. Loudly. And she'd laugh then, loudly, even though she didn't think she looked attractive when she laughed. Especially in the morning. She didn't lose that startled, crumpled face until at least forty-five minutes after waking. So when she laughed first thing in the morning, she resembled Judy Davis in a bad temper. It made the men more nervous.

For all her bravado, Emily usually did want the blokes to call again. Sometimes, if she had a particularly fun night and the bloke had seemed a little special, she let herself believe that he would ring again. But long after she'd cleared away the wine glasses and washed the sheets and rushed home for the next few days to scan the answering machine, long after she'd checked with the telephone company that her phone was working, she wished that she wasn't such an optimist.

Today, ambling down the streets of inner Sydney, she wondered how Glenn Close might handle a brush-off from a boss. Maybe she would come into the cafe every day and sip cappuccinos in a corner table, staring at the boss, seductively fingering her table knife …

'Joseph,' Glenn Close would pant during late-night calls, 'I'm waiting for your call. I'm waiting now. Outside your house. Near the bunny hutch. Have you checked your bunnies recently, Joseph?'

'Cut,' Emily said to herself, forcing herself to look up from the pavements to engage in reality. The sky had a textured appearance, as if she were looking at the world through chiffon curtains. She rubbed her eyes to clear her vision. Without success. She breathed deeply. With some satisfaction. If the smoke is this thick in the middle of the city, she thought, what would it be like on the edge? Suddenly Emily felt the need to be informed. She hadn't heard a radio report since early that morning. Anything could have happened since then.

By the time she'd unlocked the two locks to her front door and turned off the alarm, Emily was feeling nervous. Not so much because she had just lost her main source of income, nor because she had just missed the midday news wrap-up, but because now there was no reason not to join her father.

Chapter four

Emily tramped up the hill, watching ants and lizards scatter in the shadow of her footfall. The bush floor scrunched beneath her sandals. Emily knew this patch of ground well, partly because it marked the beginning of her Easter visits, partly because this was where her brother had kicked her in the back of the knee and made her leg collapse. But the main reason she felt intimate with this ground was because the hill was so bloody steep that the earth reared up to block any other vistas.

Today she was taking longer to complete the journey between the wharf and her father's house. At thirty-two years of age, Emily had just passed the peak of her fitness – a fitness that relied heavily on the air-conditioning and padded floor of a gym. She had done her routine Friday morning class just a few hours earlier but nothing in that class was as strenuous as the walk up this hill.

As she opened the back door of her father's house, Emily was greeted with a musty smell. It was the mark of a house inhabited only by a man. She always wondered why male households had that distinctive smell. She suspected it was the sheets in need of a change. But it could be the lack of a female scent; the perfumes, deodorants, shampoos, conditioners, scented moisturisers and toiletries that women bring to a house. Maybe women's hormones neutralise male hormones. Once, she had asked an expert about the smell of an all-male household. The aromatherapy masseur suggested that single males leave a scent to attract females, the same way dogs scent their territory. A whole household of males, the masseur said, creates a riot of smells, with each male smell trying to overcome the others. Eventually, when a female stumbles onto their territory, the masseur said, she will follow the trail of the strongest scent.

'That's right,' murmured Emily, 'and when a household of men all turn their underpants inside out on the same morning, the smell is actionable.' Emily had never met a natural therapy practitioner with a sense of humour. This one was no different.

The smell was comforting. It meant Dad. But when she walked into the living room and saw boxes full of papers, photograph albums, bits of cheap tourist trinkets from Asia and framed portraits, she felt another presence.

Someone's riffled through all Dad's treasures, she thought. A thief is ripping all this off! Emily was crouching for a blow, her eyes scanning through the room. If the stuff is still here, so is the robber! Emily let her backpack slip quietly to the floor. She padded across the room. Without realising it, she had put her imaginary camera to her eye and was zooming the lens around the bric-a-brac. Here was an old gold cross – zoom – her mother's favorite silver – zoom – a teaspoon from Raffles Hotel in Singapore. Her camera swooped around the room in an erratic path. Its frantic efforts to focus reflected the desperation of the search.

With her senses distorted by the behaviour of her camera and her body operating in slow motion, Emily's hearing was acute. Wind rubbed through the leaves of paperbark trees and clinked the tackle of yachts in the bay. A blowfly brained itself against the kitchen window. A rustle came from the bedroom. The thief. Emily did a quick flashback to the scene where the thief would have entered her father's house. He would be big, dirty and mean. His face looking as if it had eyeballed countless back alleys. He wouldn't have tiptoed in because he didn't care about being caught. He would have burst into the house with a make-my-day expression on his face.

Emily padded along the hallway to her father's bedroom, wondering why she was sneaking up on a man who could rearrange her body with a few lazy punches. She was breathing so lightly she felt she was going to faint. The rustling sound got louder as she closed in on her father's bedroom. She had no option now. She had to stride up the hallway, fling open the door of the bedroom and confront …

'Dad!' she screamed.

John Carmody had been reading a letter that his wife had written a few weeks before she died. He was not so much reading the words – he knew the words by heart – he was looking at Maeve's handwriting. Examining the letters that had been formed with excruciating care. The effort to contain her quivering fingers had resulted in handwriting that still seemed to vibrate with tense courage. The shape of the letters, he thought, was like a subtext. Their costive message was a different one from the words his wife had put together.

When Emily burst in, he'd been immobilised by the screech of his daughter. By the time the shock had left his system and allowed him to breathe again, he'd guessed at what had been happening in his daughter's mind during the last few minutes.

'Ah, Emily, I'm glad to see you too,' said Carmody. He suppressed a chuckle well enough to maintain the blank-faced persona his daughter found so infuriating.

'What the hell are you doing?' said Emily, trying to disguise her foolishness with anger. 'What are you doing lounging around with all these old letters while the contents of the house have been turned upside down.' She pointed to the bed covered with old letters and documents, the old travel cases on the floor, the framed photographs that were propped up beside the bedside table. 'Are you moving house or something?'

'I'd say "or something" is closer to the mark, Emily. I'm getting a few precious things together, just in case I have to take them down to the water to protect them from the fires.' Carmody continued to refold the letters. 'I was surprised when you rang to say you wanted to come down for a visit.'

'Well, you've been here for days preparing for a fire. I thought – '

'Weeks,' said Carmody.

'What do you mean?'

'I've been on watch here for almost two weeks. I know the big fires have only reached the city in the last couple of days, but most of the residents have been getting prepared for the worst since the heatwave began.'

'Bit pessimistic of you, isn't it?'

'Just careful,' said Carmody, squeezing letters into their old envelopes. Emily stared at the letters. She bit her lip when she saw her mother's handwriting – the handwriting that had once scrawled across school lunch orders; writing that once underlined the mundanities of her life; handwriting that so often said 'be home soon'.

Her father's brisk handling of the letters didn't disguise his care. Watching him refold them, Emily thought of a priest at mass, reverently refolding his linen napkin after sipping at the chalice. Emily had never seen her father in a sentimental mood. He wasn't the sort to linger in the past, pawing keepsakes like talismans. She certainly hadn't thought her father still dwelt on her mother's death.

'She's been gone eight years, Dad,' she said as an invitation to her father's thoughts.

'I know. I know.' Quietly. Apologetically. 'I got distracted by them while I was collecting everything that should be saved.'

Emily looked at the pile of letters written on hospital letterheads. 'I didn't know she'd written so much,' she said. Waiting for a response. She looked down on her father's sandy-grey head as she stood beside his bed, adding, 'I don't know if I could read her letters. Is there a lot of pain in them?'

'She was in pain towards the end but she didn't want to take anything for it. She kept flushing her drugs. I suppose I should have insisted but ... I couldn't even get her to stay in hospital to have the operation which could have –' He paused. 'I didn't have much more success convincing her to take her medicine.'

'She was very determined,' Emily said as an invitation, hoping her father would open up more. He didn't. 'But I suppose the fact that she died in a fire saved her from awful pain she may have encountered closer to –' Emily struggled to find a kind word for it. 'Well, you know – closer to her time.'

'Come on, let's get all this stuff down to the water's edge,' said Carmody. Emily watched him fold the carton's lid over its contents, place it on the bed and stand up to survey the room. She, too, looked around for something to do and finally stacked some framed portraits of long-dead relatives in a spare box. Nothing was said for a while. The presence of Maeve Carmody hung in the air.

'Maybe I should read some of her letters,' Emily said. 'I don't really want to. But it would be good therapy.'

'Therapy?' said Carmody. He looked at the box on the bed, thinking of carting it out. But he changed his mind and picked up another box from the floor.

'They say it's good to get intimate with the death of a loved one. You know, hold the stillborn baby, talk to it, give it a name. You're supposed to throw yourself into the grieving process and I didn't – well we didn't get much of a chance to … Dad, we didn't even have a wake for Mum. It was like we couldn't wait to bustle her off into the afterlife – ' Emily's voice trailed off as she caught her father's dark expression.

'Your mother's letters aren't therapy,' replied Carmody. 'What do you want to do with them? Workshop them?' Carmody hugged a box to his chest. The lines on his forehead rutted heavily. He wanted to be gone, to be out of that room. He looked around the room, searching for other items that he might carry out. He couldn't see anything. But he wasn't really looking. He knew his daughter was right.

'If it will help, you can read the letters later. After the fires have decided what they are going to do down here.' He paused, still looking around the room rather than at his daughter, who was restacking old books into neater piles. 'You may as well keep the letters,' he added, unable to resist a jibe. 'The therapy might take a while.'

'I didn't mean to usurp your interest. I'm just trying to come to terms with it. I still have nightmares. And we've never really talked about it. So – '

'Okay, Emily, I said you can have the letters. Now let's get all this stuff down to the waterfront while we still have time.'

As they carted their booty from the bedroom to the back door, Emily tried to find less hurtful ground for conversation. The smoke reminded her.

'Is it that bad?' said Emily. 'I mean, look out there. It's a beautiful beach day, calm, warm and there's not a flame in sight. In fact, the air seems a lot clearer now than it has for days. Maybe the worst is over.'

Carmody felt his neck bristle. Something Emily had said rang alarm bells. He turned to look out the window of the lounge room as he was passing. He examined what he could see of Flint Bay. There were no fires, no falling ash and the morning sea breeze had helped clear the smoke. The most telling sign of imminent danger was the lack of activity. There were only a few boats left on their moorings. The bay was bereft of water traffic. The track that wound along the waterfront was empty and there were still no birds to be heard. Something else nagged at him.

The wind. Emily had said it was a calm day. Carmody focused on a gum tree to judge how rapidly its leaves were moving. Not much. The north-easter that had been blowing strongly all day, clearing the area of smoke, was dying. North-easters don't normally wane until after sunset. If they die at two p.m., they are shifting direction. This wind was shifting.

'If this wind is turning into a nor'westerly then there's a lot we have to do,' said Carmody. 'We've got a meeting in the community hall at three o'clock and I want everything that I've packed to be down by the water by then.'

'What is the meeting for?' asked Emily. Standing behind her father in the hall, she rested her heavy box on her thigh.

'To discuss emergency procedures, roles, who's going to get what equipment. I think we should distribute the knapsacks and McLeod tools when we're at the meeting. We should decide who's in charge of catering. That might be something you can give a hand with, eh Emily, packing a few sandwiches, making thermoses.'

'Have you heard the latest news on the radio? I missed the midday wrap-up because I was on my way down here. God, anything could have happened.' Emily made a move into the kitchen to check for the radio.

'No, I haven't heard the news since this morning but the radio news isn't going to tell us where we can find enough hoses and tools to fight the fire.'

'Dad, if things get dicey here, we're not going to hang around with a spade in one hand and a packed lunch in the other. We'll have to be evacuated.'

'Most people won't leave their homes, Emily, even if a mighty fire front is bearing down on them. Especially if a front is heading their way!' said Carmody. 'Besides, it won't come to that. We're all just preparing for the worst possible scenario.' He shuffled out towards the back door.

'The worst possible scenario,' yelled Emily to her father's disappearing back, 'is a night at a Sydney motel at the expense of the government's emergency services budget!'

Emily and John Carmody were the last to arrive at the hall, and when they walked into the dimly lit space, Emily almost burst out laughing. It was the sight of Mrs Parker that tickled Emily. The rotund, middle-aged woman who normally ambled along the neighbourhood track dressed in paisley polyester dresses was kitted out in her dead husband's army uniform. A prettified version of an army uniform. She'd taken off the medals and braid and tied the slouch hat snugly around her chin with a cerise-coloured ribbon.

Walking to vacant chairs at the back of the hall, Emily felt Mrs Parker's gaze. She wiped her face with her hand, trying to hide her smirk. As she slunk into a chair beside her father, Emily noticed most of the residents were in various stages of battle dress. Some were equipped for a prolonged guerrilla battle in Vietnam, like Mrs Parker; others wore heavy boots and rugged pants but they'd hung onto their T-shirts; a few wore overalls pulled down at the waist, as if they were only half-convinced of the danger. Only a few were dressed like Emily – shorts, T-shirt and sandals – and most of them were children. Emily had planned to duck down to the beach for a swim after the meeting. She'd rethink that swim now. Something told her it wasn't good form to go for a quick dip while the neighbours were preparing for Dante's inferno.

The chairman of the meeting, Roger Burton, was ensconced on a small stage at the front of the hall. He wasn't too impressed with the late arrivals. He acknowledged them with a brisk tilt of his head and continued his address to the residents.

Emily allowed Mr Burton's drone to wash over her while she cast her eyes over the assembly. The jumble of old army pants, woollen jackets, tough boots, bowie-knives on hip belts, flasks in fishing jackets, slouch hats and bandannas reminded her of a sale she had once attended in an army disposals store. It was the smell of old wool and long-forgotten boots that prompted the memory as much as the sight of the battle-ready residents. Emily felt she had just stepped into a World War II movie – more *Dad's Army* than *Bridge on the River Kwai*.

'All this mob needs are helmets and rifles, and we could do a remake of *Dad's Army*,' she whispered to her father.

'Helmets are out the back. You can pick one up after the meeting,' replied Carmody.

Emily giggled uneasily. 'Get real,' she whispered.

Her father looked at her briefly. His face gave nothing away. Helmets? He has got to be kidding, she thought. This is how the extras on movie sets must feel. They walk into a scene they know nothing about, are handed a script they have never sighted before and are expected to play a part.

Mr Burton's overalls were criss-crossed with luminous strips of plastic. As bright as a traffic stopper. Although they were obviously not brand new, they had never been worn for any length of time. He was the only resident who had formally trained as a volunteer firefighter and although the area no longer had a brigade he was still deferred to in matters of fire. Emily had only seen him in his firefighting outfit once before, when he was standing at the head of a line of locals who were bashing the bush along the side of the path. 'Fire break,' he'd said in response to the bemused expression Emily had made on her way to the rock pool.

Fire break, thought Emily. Who are these people kidding? A monster fire is not going to come to a screeching stop when it reaches a one-metre break in vegetation. 'Whoooaaa', says the towering inferno as it hits the fire break, 'this is it. Gotta head back where we came from. There's a fire break here. Come on, guys, let's high-tail it outta here.'

'Under no circumstances,' droned Mr Burton, 'is anyone allowed to light their own backburn. Controlled backburns have trapped almost as many firefighters as wildfires have. It's only when we are positive that no one is left up the hill that we will set a backburn. And even then the lighting of a backburn will have to be timed precisely. So no backburns without reference to me.'

Emily squinted her eyes to look through her imaginary viewfinder. She panned her camera over the scene. Mr Burton was puffed up with I-told-you-so importance. The audience was attentive, and serious. Emily positioned her camera at the single bulb hanging from the middle of the ceiling. A blowfly buzzed around the lens, magnified into a horrifying size compared with the small figures in the audience below. The camera was misting with the hot breath of the audience. The microphone picked up the distant drum of cicadas. Emily watched the meeting through the lens of a fly – bulbous, distorting.

'We have roughly four sets of everything. Four fire hoses and eight knapsacks or backpack water carriers to those unacquainted with firefighting. We have eight or nine McLeod tools, a small pile of fire blankets and four pumps. We will be dividing the area into four groups with roughly eight households in each group,' continued Mr Burton to the assembly. 'Our main problem will be spot fires. There have been reports that spot fires are occurring three kilometres in front of the main fires. So no one should feel comfortable about the fact that the major fire threat is ten kilometres to the west of us at the moment.

'If the wildfires reach the Bay – and that is a big *if* at the moment – we might be able to respond with a backburn. The backburn line is virtually clear of vegetation and I'd like to say a big thank you to all those residents who have been slashing away at the line for the last few days. I know it seems improbable that we'll need the line, but we've got it if we need it.

'Now if a few of you ladies could get together some tucker. Nothing elaborate, just hand food – sandwiches, dry biscuits, drink bottles, thermoses, cough lollies or something to suck on and a supply of basic first aid - eye washes, bandages big and small, compresses, icepacks and whatever else you think might be handy. Remember, we won't just be dealing with possible burns. We have to be ready for heat stress, heat exhaustion, for injuries from falling trees or branches, for snake bites – '

Emily's camera had finished panning across the heads of dad's army and was roving rapidly to capture images of worried faces;

of pursed lips smeared with coral-tint lipstick; of a grasshopper immobilised on the windowsill; of Mr Burton's generalissimo performance; of her father's distant expression.

'The children will be leaving on the next ferry,' continued Mr Burton. 'We don't want to panic, but Mrs Schofields has offered to take the children to her place on the peninsula overnight. The next ferry will be the last one of the day, so make sure all six children are on it.' Mr Burton nodded to the children's parents as he said this.

Emily was dragged back to reality when she heard the words 'last ferry'. She looked around the hall. Confused. What the hell was Mr Burton planning? Children being taken away. The last ferry. Snake bites. It was moving too fast for her.

'Listen,' Emily said suddenly. Mr Burton stopped talking. The hall was quiet. Emily had surprised herself when she'd yelled out. She felt like slinking lower into her chair. She often found herself saying rash things when she had her camera to her eye. As if she were acting out the script in her mind rather than reality. A true hero of the screen – in her case truly tiny screen. It was too late to change tack now. She unwound her legs from her chair and stood up. 'Surely by the time snakes start running out of the bush to escape the fire, we'll be long gone,' she said. 'We'll have been evacuated, along with the fourteen thousand other Sydney people who now call the local community hall home.'

The hall was quiet. Most of the audience was trying to put a name and a face to the interjector without turning around in their seats to stare. Not all succeeded in stemming their curiosity. After leaving a few more seconds of silence as a reproach to Emily's rudeness, Mr Burton addressed her.

'Emily, anyone can leave Flint Bay whenever they like but most of us want to do what we can to protect our homes. I realise that half the houses in the area are weekenders and only half of those householders are here at this meeting, but we do have resources and we do have some experienced firefighters among us ...'

'Oh yeah, some of you guys may have fought campfires thirty years ago,' interjected Emily, 'but we're not talking about fires that have escaped out the back of a barbecue pit.' Emily paused, looking around the room. She was standing but she felt like disappearing into the ether. Her voice belied her inner timidness. Her hands streaked through her hair. They ended up on her hips. She let them slip down by her sides. She didn't want to appear bolshie. She didn't want to appear anything. But she was halfway there already. There was no turning back.

'Haven't you been listening to the media reports? These are the worst fires in memory. We're going to lose ten thousand homes. No one is *fighting* these fires. Even the bushfire brigades are just trying to redirect them. They're not standing in front of them with a knapsack.' Emily's voice lost its stridency. Her last comments drifted off, almost as if she were disowning them as they emerged from her mouth.

'I think what Emily is trying to say,' said Carmody, standing up, 'is that we have to be prepared to evacuate if necessary. There has been a message relayed from the water police that older residents, those with disabilities et cetera, should clear out now if they have another home to go to. But,' he added turning to his daughter, 'we owe it to ourselves and to each other to do what we can.'

'You don't have to be old or infirm to be hurt in these fires,' Emily said, turning to her father.

'No, but you have to be fit and strong to fight them,' a resident retorted from the front of the hall.

'And brave,' said another voice. More quietly. More pointedly.

The hall was silent in assent. Then another resident, Bruce Leonard, rose to address the meeting. Emily did not know Bruce well – he had a weekender at the far end of the bay. He didn't come up often and when he did he brought a horde of people to entertain.

'Can we, at least, get a fire boat stationed in the bay so if the fires come over the hill the boat can pump water onto the hillside?

I saw one of those boats on a documentary once and they can pump a lot of water. If just one of those boats could give the whole hillside a thorough soaking, the fires wouldn't have a chance,' he proffered.

'Bruce, it's the fires we have to soak, not the hill,' said Mr Burton. 'If there are no further questions then I suggest we disband and agree to meet again at eight p.m. tonight.'

A few minutes later, the meeting disbanded. Residents picked up their share of the firefighting equipment as they left the hall. Walking along the bush track with helmets tucked under their arms and a knapsack between them, John Carmody and Emily were mostly silent. Emily took her father's silence as a reproach. Carmody felt more disappointed than angry. How could someone as feisty as Emily be such a – a – ? Carmody struggled for a description. He settled on a term he had heard in the media but had never felt sure of its meaning. Until today. His daughter was a wimp. A victim. Carmody tried to reconcile the daughter who was walking beside him with the one who had grown up with him. The Emily he knew was a pugnacious child. And that Emily did not fit easily with the one walking beside him.

When Carmody recalled his daughter's youth, he saw a series of dramas, mainly because Emily always seemed to be caught in a drama. He recalled the fracas created when twelve-year-old Emily had refused to stand in the classroom corner after her teacher had caught her talking. The refusal began as a flip remark – more to impress school friends than flag a showdown. But Emily never knew when to back down. After she'd refused to eyeball the corner, saying 'That's not what I'm here at school to do,' Emily was sent up to the principal. There she had explained: 'I have come to school to learn and I can't learn anything if I am facing the wall, so I shouldn't be sent to the corner of the classroom.' The principal, just deprived of corporal punishment, had yet to learn modern methods of discipline. After a half-hour debate and a call to Emily's mother and, later, to John Carmody at work, a compromise was reached. Emily would stand in the corner for ten minutes but would face the class so she could still learn whatever lesson was being taught. By the accounts of her astounded classmates, Emily stood at the back of the classroom like a queen, puffed up with her first victory against institutional society.

There were many other dramas in Emily's youth. Most of them of Emily's making. In fact, thought Carmody, most of them were written, directed and acted by Emily. Not so, any more. Today, Emily was a critic. Carping from the sidelines.

'I see you've still got that fiery temper,' said Mrs Parker, who had trotted up behind John and Emily without either of them noticing. She sounded wheezy. To have caught up with them, Mrs Parker would have been jogging since she left the hall.

Emily turned to acknowledge Mrs Parker's presence. She tried to smile at Mrs Parker but it turned into a grimace. Is that what will become of me? she thought. A short, stout figure of a woman who bustles through life? A woman of crêpey neck and cat's-bum mouth? A woman whose mousy hair grows more disappointing with every year – a little thinner, a little greyer? The only interesting feature of Mrs Parker's face was her eyes. They danced in her face; they were quick to widen with excitement and even quicker to flirt with the old seadogs of the Bay.

Turning back to the track, Emily was tempted to give Mrs Parker another taste of her temper but she decided that would only encourage a dialogue she wasn't inclined to sustain.

'I see you're still taking good care of your complexion,' replied Emily, not bothering to look in Mrs Parker's direction. 'That slouch hat looks divine with the satin ribbon.'

'Well, dear, you'd better think about getting yourself some more sensible clothes. If a fire comes through here, you don't want to be caught with that flimsy clothing and sandals. I have an old pair of woollen jodhpurs that might fit you and I'm sure your father could find an appropriate top.'

'Mrs Parker, when the fire from hell comes through this area, I do not intend to be here to greet it.'

Mrs Parker had moved up beside Emily on the bush path, despite the fact the path only accommodated one person comfortably. John Carmody was happy to listen to the two women battle it out. His daughter, he knew, thought of Mrs Parker as a silly old woman, with nothing better to do than live vicariously. Emily didn't know that Mrs Parker had nursed a child for six months through a terminal illness – never complaining, never debating the issue, never breaking. She had also watched her husband die of stomach cancer. Mrs Parker had been an office manager before marriage in the fifties put a stop to it. She was still good at managing people and events. There just weren't enough people or events to keep her busy down here at Flint Bay. Emily, thought Carmody, was more like Mrs Parker than she would ever care to admit.

'Yes, yes, Emily, we've all heard how you feel about this. But this is no nugatory matter. We all have to be prepared to do our bit,' said Mrs Parker still puffing to keep up to the striding pace of the Carmodys – a pace that seemed to be quickening all the time. 'Now, John has told me that you've been working in a restaurant, so you'll be a great help getting the sandwiches, pikelets and supplies together up at my place tonight.'

Emily glanced in her father's direction. She could just imagine Mrs Parker pumping him for gossip about his daughter's vacillating career – university one year, film-making the next, working cafes one year, travelling to Tibet the next.

'Working in rest-torr-aunts,' said Emily, mimicking Mrs Parker's toffy pronunciation of the word, 'does not train you to become a tea-hand at a community event.'

'Perhaps not. But I'm sure you'll cope anyway.' Mrs Parker was not going to be deflected. 'We have to get some quick, easy-to-eat, high-carbohydrate foods together that the blokes can eat easily. The sort of food that can be carted out into the bush and eaten on a fire break, if necessary.'

Emily remained silent so her father could say something. She needed back-up. A diplomatic hand. Her father let the silence stretch.

'Mrs Parker,' she said, 'if the wall of flames comes to town, I'm not going to be handing out packed lunches to the brave fire-fighters. I intend to be evacuated. But if I *am* still in the Bay, I'll be in there fighting with a bloody garden hose. I'm not about to surrender all my feminist principles.'

'All right, dear, if you want to fight the fires, that's your choice. There are other women who can help me with the catering,' said Mrs Parker, 'just make sure you get appropriate firefighting clothes before the fires hit. Being prepared for all outcomes is no nugatory matter.'

Mrs Parker had to shout the last of her words because Carmody and Emily had veered off the track to head up to their house. Mrs Parker couldn't see John Carmody smirking. Emily did.

'Oh, that's very funny. Why didn't you help me out there?' Emily said.

'You were doing fine.'

'Sure, that's why I've been bulldozed into staying to fight the fires.'

'Your choice, Emily.'

'Why do you tolerate the old bag?'

'She's harmless, Emily,' said Carmody, glancing down the track to see Mrs Parker still waiting on the track for a farewell wave from him. He gave his customary wave and Mrs Parker strode off towards her place. 'In fact, she's a very kind person and very useful to have down here. She acts as the community secretary, keeping everyone up to date with lists of each other's phone numbers; keeping track of the communal equipment ...'

'Yeah, keeping track of everyone else's business,' retorted Emily. 'I can't believe there are still women whose role in life is keeping track of what everyone else in the world is doing. And what the hell does "nugatory" mean?'

'Mrs Parker likes to exercise her mind by looking up a new word in the dictionary every day. "Nugatory" must be her new word for today.' Saying this, Carmody's attention had already moved off the subject of Mrs Parker. He had paused halfway up to the house to catch his breath. And took the opportunity to look around. Emily paused too. There was silence. As their ears adjusted, Emily felt a pressure on her eardrums, the pressure of nothingness. She looked around and saw a bushland that was almost devoid of signs of settlement. The moorings in the bay were abandoned. Cicadas were silent. So too were birds. No motor sounds, no human sounds. There was no wind.

After a minute or two of stillness, Emily murmured, 'Eerie, isn't it?'

Carmody nodded. He too was absorbing the scene. Literally. Completely. From the soles of his feet, he was aware of the powdery dryness of the bush debris. There wasn't a gram of moisture left in the floor litter. There wasn't much moisture left in the live vegetation either. Carmody rubbed his hand along the branch of a small bush. There wouldn't be much more than ten per cent moisture in these plants. Just above survival level. His ears were humming with the expectant silence of the bush. His nose was monitoring the dust particles, the languid aromatic smell of a national park on fire. But most of all, Carmody was focusing on the messages that registered on his skin. Momentarily he closed his eyes to concentrate better on the tactile feeling of the bush. The air was as warm as a hug and as dry as a cough.

'Do you know what's happened?' said Carmody, opening his eyes. 'The wind has shifted to the north-west.'

Emily looked from her father's grey face to the panorama of the bay. 'I can't feel any wind but it does look a little smokier,' she said.

'You see the smoke before you feel the wind. First sign that the wind has shifted. Smoke. Coming in from the front. Heading our way,' said Carmody.

Emily loped up the hill after her father. She scoured the bushland. She felt that her father had seen something that she had missed. Was the wind direction that important? Or had he seen something else? As they hustled through the back door she caught sight of Bo further up the hill.

'Why wasn't Bo at the meeting?' she asked, closing the back door firmly.

'He was. He was watching from outside,' replied Carmody.

'Weird,' replied Emily. She headed for the radio and switched it on. The sounds of an Irish ballad tinkered through the kitchen.

'Forget the bloody radio will you, Emily,' said Carmody. 'We've got downpipes to plug and gutters to fill.'

'Where does Bo live?' asked Emily.

'Up in the shed, about halfway up the hill, along a little from us,' said Carmody. He was already sorting through plastic containers in the cupboard below the sink.

'Is he allowed to live there?' Emily grabbed a carrot from the fridge. The sight of Bo had made her nervous. She thought he belonged in an institution. Or possibly in one of those communal houses. Just for his own benefit, she told herself. People with special disabilities should be cared for. Someone who is so out-of-this-world, like Bo, should be closely watched. For his own good.

Carmody had detected the not-in-my-backyard inference in Emily's question. And he wasn't happy about it. 'Bo is allowed to live in his shed because he owns his shed. And he owns the land around his shed. He no longer owns the family house that is adjacent to his land but he owns the shed.' Carmody's voice was staccato with suppressed anger. 'The shed is the only thing Bo asks of the world. Will you begrudge him that, Emily?'

'I was only asking,' said Emily. She thought she should drop the subject but her curiosity was stirred. 'What does he do for a living?'

'He doesn't need money. He makes twenty or thirty dollars from the branch sculptures he sells to an art gallery but he doesn't really need that,' said Carmody, busying himself at the sink.

Emily felt chastised by her father's curt tone. He was obviously angry with her. Had been since the meeting. She wondered what she had said or done that had upset him. She didn't think about asking him what he was angry about. She knew that would be futile.

As if reading her pause, Carmody muttered, 'Sorry I'm a bit snappy but there's a lot to do ...' and his voice trailed off under the burden of the thoughts.

'It's just that he's so, so, apelike.' Emily mouthed the word 'apelike' with a disdain that screwed up her face.

'Who?' said Carmody, pausing. 'Oh, are you still on about Bo? He's not apelike. He's natural. For God's sake, he's a hermit. A common, garden-variety hermit.' Carmody softened. 'Don't hold that against him. Half of Australia was populated by hermits and outlaws last century.'

'Give me an outlaw any day,' said Emily, chomping on the carrot.

'There isn't much difference between the hermit and the outlaw,' said Carmody. He was filling more plastic containers with water. He stared out the kitchen window into the bush across the bay. 'In Australia's early days, outlaws often turned into hermits and hermits sometimes became outlaws. Australia's history is full of stories of outlaws who escaped to live in the bush or in fringe settlements. They'd get a plot of land, build a hut, grow vegetables and keep their heads down whenever authority came riding by. They lived all around this area, here and over in those hills,' Carmody said pointing to the hillside across the bay.

'Many of them were happy to be recluses. And for that matter, many of them never surrended their unlawful ways – they stole chickens and pigs or traded in a bit of contraband. But some of them became upright members of the community. Solid, quiet men who – '

'You make them sound like monks.'

Carmody paused. He recalled the line in a book he had once read on monks – 'a silence of heart and thought'. That was their aspiration, silence of heart and thought. To achieve that goal, monks had tramped off into the desert or mountains or bush. Often alone, always in silence and usually for life. It had been happening for centuries. So many lifetimes spent searching for that special silence.

Carmody turned to face Emily, wanting to explain that book to her. He saw her picking up the cordless phone and wandering out of the kitchen towards the spare bedroom. He changed his mind.

'Mostly they were quiet men who lived by themselves,' he said to finish off his previous thoughts.

'Thank God Ned Kelly never discovered the hermit within. We need some gutsy heroes in our knee-patch history,' Emily yelled on her way out. Adding, 'Mind if I make a call?'

'No, go ahead. All I'm saying is that Bo is simply part of a long tradition. Flint Bay is renowned for some of its notorious figures. There's a good reason this cove used to be known as Smugglers Cove. Even today the odd drug shipment comes through those heads in yachts.'

'Don't give me a history lesson again, Dad.' Emily paused at the doorway. She was about to walk away again when her father's comment about drug shipments lodged. 'How do you know drugs are still smuggled in here?'

'All you have to do is watch what's happening around you; stay in touch with your neighbourhood. It doesn't take a genius to figure something is fishy if an expensive yacht slips through the heads late at night with none of its lights turned on,' said Carmody.

'Next time a drug shipment comes in, give me a call!' Emily yelled from down the hallway. 'By the way, do you know Jack's phone number off the top of your head?'

'No,' said Carmody. And when he thought about it, he felt just a little guilty.

Chapter five

'G'day, mate. Jack Carmody here. How are you?'

Although flip in manner, Jack Carmody did not feel comfortable making this call. He didn't know Tom Cole well. They had gone to the same school, albeit a few years apart, and he had renewed acquaintances last year when Cole was appointed private secretary to the attorney-general. But Tom Cole didn't owe Jack any favours, especially now that Cole's minister, Fred Hanes, had been switched to the Emergency Services portfolio. Today, with fires ringing Australia's biggest city, Cole and his minister were exceedingly busy. It was not the day for a long-forgotten acquaintance to make a do-me-a-quick-favour call.

'I'm feeling top-notch, Jack, but bloody busy at the moment as you'd understand,' replied Tom Cole, neatly summarising Jack Carmody's position re favours.

Jack cursed his sister for putting him in this position. He recalled the call she made to him just half an hour before, at five p.m. on a Friday afternoon. Only Emily could expect action at five p.m. on a Friday afternoon. Only Emily could be insistent while making a call from under a duvet in their father's spare bedroom.

'Jack, these people down here are loopy,' Emily had said. She'd sounded like Marlon Brando as she spoke through gritted teeth and the layers of the duvet. 'They're getting tools prepared to fight the fire. They are making sandwiches to sustain them through a firefighting episode, for God's sake.' Pausing for a muffled breath. 'They think they are going to be in charge when a fire comes through here. They have no idea of what headquarters are saying. Some of them, Jack – ' she paused for dramatic effect, ' –

have turned off their radios so they won't hear any orders that are given by headquarters.'

'Emily,' he replied, trying not to calculate how much earning time his sister's call was costing, 'the chance of a fire coming into that area is remote and, if it does, evacuation is easy. The authorities will pile everyone onto a boat and take them out of there.'

'What if residents refuse to go?' said Emily.

'They can't refuse. The government now has legislation giving police and emergency workers the power to forcibly evict people from their homes in an emergency. Remember those Windsor floods of a few years ago when an old bloke refused to evacuate? The bloke who sat on his roof, giving the finger to media helicopters? The bloke who risked the lives of a dozen emergency workers because of his intransigence?' Jack exaggerated. 'Well, the government got so pissed off at the nightly footage of the old man waving his filthy finger at authority, they changed the law. So Dad and all the rest will have to go when police say so.'

'Can you find out what they're going do?' said Emily. 'Can you ask your friends in the government what their action plan is? I don't want to be stuck with a bunch of loonies waving a McLeod tool at a fifty-metre-high fire front.'

'What the hell are you doing down there if you don't want to help?' said Jack, calculating this call had cost thirty dollars so far.

'I came down to Flint Bay to make sure Dad was all right. No one else seems to care about him any more.'

'Don't lay that guilt trip on me, Emily. You went down there because you thought you could sit on the verandah, sipping gin and tonic as you watch the fires rearrange the national park. And now that the fires are getting a bit too close for comfort, you're sorry you even thought of going down there. I can read you, Emily.'

'You can't read me at all, Jack. All you can do is project yourself onto others, which is why all your relationships are so superficial.'

'You've got a gall, Emily, ringing me on a busy Friday afternoon and wasting sixty dollars of my time abusing me. If you've finished – '

'Okay, okay. I'm sorry. I'm just scared. I want to know what's going on. Everything seems so unreal down here. I thought it rained this afternoon,' said Emily, her voice breaking with emotion, 'I felt these faint drops of water. It was the weirdest rain. More like wet dog's breath than raindrops. But, shit, it was r-a-i-n, rain. I got so excited I ran inside to tell Dad. He came out and stood outside. He was unconvinced but couldn't understand what was going on. So I turned on the radio to listen for news of a southerly change. I was convinced a southerly had moved through Sydney and was just over our hill ...'

'Yeah, I heard too,' said Jack wearily. 'The fires are starting their own little weather systems, creating pockets of light rainfall in some spots. I'm not divorced from this whole thing you know, Emily. The city is shrouded with smoke, the traffic is impossible ...'

'Don't talk traffic to me when I'm staring into a bushland that is about to go *pop*! Just find out what your government mates are planning to do when the fires reach this mob of hillbillies.'

His conversation with Emily still galled him. But after he had settled down, he too was curious to know what the authorities had planned for places like Flint Bay.

Jack stared into the push-buttons of his phone and took a breath that he hoped would inspire a hail-fellow-well-met mood into his exchange with this busy bureaucrat.

'Tom, I just thought you could fill me in on the state of play with these fires. My old man is on the edge of the national park. You know, dug in like an old trooper. I thought I should know what the government policy might be if things should turn bad,' said Jack.

'Get him out of there,' said Tom.

'Well, yeah, sure. I suppose that's what will happen eventually anyway but, ah, what are you saying, you think I should insist that he leave the area already?'

'I can't tell you what headquarters will be deciding on any particular emergency front. All I can tell you is that we're not going to endanger the lives of firefighters or police by trying to save a few brick veneers. In these conditions we let the houses burn. We don't risk lives. We don't want to be sued by either firefighters or bereaved relatives for failing to use the powers of evacuation we now have enshrined in legislation.'

Tom paused to give Jack a chance to respond. Jack breathed deeply but didn't fill the pause. He didn't know what to say. He didn't know what he – or his stupid sister – expected of this bureaucrat. Answers probably. A hard-and-fast answer. It had been a while since he had talked with his political contacts.

'Listen, Jack, I've got to get going,' said the bureaucrat, filling the pause himself. 'Just tell your old man to save his arse and forget his fibro weekender or whatever he's got down there. Insurance will build him another home, it won't grow him another layer of skin.'

An hour later as Jack manoeuvred his Jaguar into peak-hour traffic, the image of the old man of the Windsor floods giving the finger to authorities stayed with him. He felt like that sometimes. Especially on days like today, which had begun with a stony silence from the wife and ended with a brush-off. Today he felt like giving the finger to the day.

Jack mused on yesterday's fight with Sarah while he mindlessly negotiated the Friday night traffic. Trying to discover the real reason for his fights with his wife was like swimming through mud. The cause was grey, amorphous, unattainable. And mucky. Was it really his comment on fitness that upset her? Was she unhappy with him even before he woke? Was she generally unhappy with him or with life? How far back into their relationship should he look for signs of disharmony or, more likely, lack of interest? When Jack thought of his past with Sarah, he looked through a photo album of memories. All the moments seemed frozen. In more ways than one. He clicked mentally back through frozen photos of the happy couple. They looked happy in the album, they seemed happy at functions. Functionally happy was more like it. Certainly they were never wildly happy together. Never recklessly happy.

No, they were like the photos themselves. A neat fit in the frame of life. If they had ever been happy with each other, it was because they had found in each other someone who fitted their image of a life partner – an attractive, well-educated person with good prospects and the confidence to negotiate their way around a formal table setting. He had always hoped the relationship would go beyond that. He'd presumed that marriage marked the start of love; that if he found someone who liked most things that he liked, then love would grow; that out of liking would come love.

But things were always getting in the way. They'd had so little time to work on their relationship. With his career and her study. And then a child. Three changes of address in five years. They'd barely had time to speak to each other, much less find out more about each other. Sometimes, when he worried that they seemed more like social partners than husband and wife, he wished Sarah would do something about it. Maybe organise things so they could spend some time together or arrange for some marriage counselling or get a few books on relationships. Still, he supposed most marriages were like that.

Jack suddenly remembered his decision to buy Sarah flowers. Nothing too elaborate, he thought, something small and dainty. A spur-of-the-moment posy. A highway bunch of flowers. He pictured the posy in the middle of their dining table tonight, surrounded by his wife looking fresh, coiffured and bored, plates of mignon, and himself trying to find a conversational link with his family that extended beyond the sauce bottle. He felt easier when he remembered that he would have to dash off to a conference straight after dinner.

The traffic funnelling onto the bridge closed in around the Jaguar. Jack suddenly had a cartoon image of himself being pulled along the highway on a conveyor belt to be delivered to his home where he would be tethered to a post and given dinner in a bowl by someone who expected him to be grateful. Tonight that was all he was going to be doing at home – grabbing a plateful of food and taking off again for the legal conference. Normally he wouldn't bother going home. But he felt guilty. Not just about the offence Sarah had taken over his comment on fitness and not just because he had been working late often. Jack shifted in the leather seat of the Jaguar. And thought of Jane. Guiltily. He knew there was no reason at all to feel guilty about the new partner in the firm. He'd done nothing with her, beyond that accidental brush at one Friday night's drinks. He wasn't even sure that Jane had registered the touch, the too-lingering-to-be-accidental brush. She'd kept chatting to Ronald as if hands brushed past her arse every day. But he knew her aloofness was the start of their con-spiracy of silence. It was in their eye contact – open, alluring, challenging, amused. It was apparent in the tone of their voices – warm, reassuring. Their undeclared intimacy was most apparent in their morning greetings, which were bright, alert, always wel-coming, but most of all, expectant.

Jack adjusted his trousers in the car seat and realised how much he was looking forward to seeing Jane tonight. He hoped they could escape to one of the bars in the hotel for a quiet drink. And let things develop. He hadn't booked a room in the hotel – a booking would have seemed like a commitment. And possibly premature. Jack had no idea whether single women jumped into bed with men after a few drinks these days. The women's maga-zines gave the impression that girls not only fucked on their first dates but also demanded 'sexual integrity and honesty'. Whatever that was. Didn't sound the same as fucking to him. Whenever Jack let himself wander down this route of fantasising, his eczema began to itch. Jack hadn't made a hotel booking but he had casually inquired about vacancies that night. Always briefed, was Jack.

As the traffic began freeing his Jaguar from its twenty-kilometre-per-hour grip, Jack reached for the radio dial.

'Tony Thomas has been at the fire fronts all day and is now just outside the area of most concern – Hornsby. Tony, are you there?' excited the radio voice.

'Yes, Marlene, this certainly is one of the worst hot spots at the moment. The change in wind late this afternoon has breathed new energy into these fires. Most of the day, things were, well almost under control because the north-easterly wind was tending to blow the fire back over burnt areas. Late this afternoon, however, the wind swung around to the north-west and immediately the front took off again.'

'What's in its path, Tony?'

'Mostly national park. One of the oldest and most popular of Australia's national parks with its amazing wildlife, wallabies, many, many birds, some say there are a few wombats in this area and, of course, the endangered snub-nosed possum. There are a few small housing settlements closer to the coast.'

'Tony, what's it like being at the fire front all day? You've been out there since just after dawn, it's now just after six p.m., you've been breathing that smoke, you've literally been feeling the heat, what's it like?'

'Marlene, it's unbelievable. I know most of the city is suffering from the effects of smoke, but when you are standing in front of these fires, the smoke tears at your lungs and the heat is almost unbearable. It's impossible to know where the fires are coming from or where they are heading. These fires just appear from nowhere and they are unbeatable. This, as the minister has already said, is the fire that can't be fought. Firefighters here are just trying to get the residents out, make houses as fire-proof as possible and cope with spot fires around homes. But when the main front comes through, we're out of here.'

'Yes, Tony, that seems the wisest course. Even for journalists covering the fire. There have already been injuries among the media.'

'That's right, Marlene. Scott Gormley is recovering in hospital. In fact, he has been inundated with well-wishers. But it just shows you, Marlene, that if someone as experienced as Scott can get caught in these fires, then no one is safe.'

'Tony, thanks for your time.'

Jack banged the off button as he swung the car through the gates of his Killara home. 'Bloody excitable journalists,' he muttered to himself. Jack was unperturbed by the news of the Hornsby fire. Briefly, he tried to imagine how much distance lay between Hornsby and Flint Bay – two kilometres? Five? Could be thirty kilometres as far as he knew. He tried to visualise the area, to see what bays, mountains, streams or suburbs might lie between Hornsby and Flint Bay. He couldn't imagine anything.

'For all I know, there might be another bloody city between the two areas.'

Chapter six

'The waiting is the worst,' John Carmody said to his daughter as he carefully made his way onto the verandah with two cups of tea. Emily was standing with her eyes closed, facing the hillside opposite, which was reflecting the glory of the sunset. As he got closer, Carmody could see that her hands were carefully wrapped around her nose. Carmody briefly wondered whether it was de rigueur to pick your nose publically these days.

'I've tried everything,' said Emily, turning around to take the tea cup. 'I've done visualisation, the mantra, self-hypnosis. Nothing works. Even alternate nose-breathing doesn't work. My throat is constricting. I can barely swallow ...'

'Why don't you lie under one of those diamonds of yours?'

'Dad, they're crystals, not diamonds. And I don't use them any more.'

Emily sniffed with disdain and turned away from her father. She didn't want to think about crystals any more. Not since she swallowed her favourite – shaped like an elongated pyramid. She hadn't swallowed it deliberately. One night while watching television she had absentmindedly picked up the crystal and begun sucking on it. Or, more precisely, drawing back on it. The doctor had told her not to worry too much about it – 'Aren't you supposed to sit under those things?' he'd asked when she explained what had happened. The doctor had suggested she check her stools for the next two days to make sure the crystal cleared her system. She never found crystals appealing after that.

'So you don't believe in that New Age stuff any more?' said Carmody.

'It's not "stuff". New Age is an exploration of new ways of seeing and doing things.' Emily paused. She'd heard this line before. From her friends. It hadn't sounded convincing then. 'It's a way of looking for what else might be out there. It's no different to the hocus-pocus of the Catholic masses you used to take us to as kids.' Emily looked at her father. And resumed her pacing.

'I suppose not. But in church you're supposed to think of others. All this New Age stuff seems designed to make you think only of yourself. All this focus on your mantra. All this alternative nose breathing. It must be hard to find what's out there in the universe if you're so focused on yourself.'

Emily thought about this for a while. It sounded right but she didn't like it. 'Well, it's even harder to focus on the real meaning of life, if everyone is always buzzing around, never emptying their minds, always out to make a buck or get a lay. At least I'm taking the first step towards enlightenment. If you can't focus on the immaterial world, whether that is through yoga, or with crystals or ambient music, then you haven't got a hope.'

'But Emily, you can't stand still long enough to drain a cup of tea,' said Carmody. He pointed to his daughter's legs, which were still pacing the verandah. He saw Emily's lips turn into her mouth. He'd made her angry again. 'Come on, Emms,' he said, 'let's just relax. There's nothing to worry about at the moment. We've done everything we can do. There's nothing left to do but watch the sunset and wait to see what the night brings. The gutters are blocked ...'

'With oranges!'

'You use anything you've got in these circumstances, Emily. They don't sell gutter-blockers at the local hardware shop.'

'Well they should. What are we supposed to say if the water leaks around the oranges and the house burns down. Do we tell the insurance company, "Sorry, our oranges must have leaked"!'

'The gutters are filled with water,' continued Carmody, choosing to ignore his daughter's hypothesis, 'both generators –

the electric and the petrol – have been checked and are set up next to the tanks, the pump is okay, the fire hose is laid out. Water bottles done. The junk's been moved out from under the verandah and the precious things are down at the water's edge,' said Carmody, reeling through the jobs that he and Emily had accomplished that afternoon.

Emily had thrown herself into the work, although he suspected that her zest for work was a form of denial. She kept referring to the fire preparations as 'playing fireman Bob'.

It never ceased to disappoint Carmody that his daughter was unable to cope with stillness. It was almost inconceivable to him that anyone could feel distressed by quietness. But here was his daughter, pacing the verandah, utterly unable to cope with just being here. Her body was wound tight, her fine features were pinched. Just watching her, he could see that it was physically painful for her to wait, to surrender to the aberrant clock of nature. If she hadn't been stuck here, Emily would have waved off hours ago. Bob O'Conner referred to Carmody's daughter as 'the tornado' because she arrived and left in such a hurry. Two hours was her average visit. Enough time for a cup of tea, a fire-blasted sausage, a stroll down the track, a quick chat, a manic tidying up. Then she'd leap – literally -onto the ferry. Tonight she couldn't leave. She was leashed.

'The smoke makes me think of Mum and what it would have been like for her,' said Emily. She'd finally stopped pacing.

Carmody responded to this unexpected twist by taking a slow slurp of his tea. He leaned over the verandah rail to stare at the ground. The sky was darkening prematurely tonight. He could hardly see the ground now. But he thought if he kept staring at the bush floor, the images of his dying wife would not reappear.

He breathed deeply, wearily. Smoke raked up his nose. After three days of breathing it, he barely noticed the smoke now. But the smoke brought memories for him too. Memories he had been avoiding. Flashes of the smoke that rose from the studio at the rear of his house – the smoke that took the life of his wife – months before she was due to die.

'This smoke is not even that dense and I feel claustrophobic. Imagine what it was like for her,' continued Emily, prodding her father into a response.

John Carmody didn't want to explore the death of his wife, so many years after it had happened. Not now, not tonight, not like this. They should have talked about it when it happened – after the funeral, on the first anniversary, sometime. But they hadn't talked of it and Carmody was content to leave Maeve's death as a series of private griefs.

'I can imagine the smoke burning her lungs now. I never could before. Once I stood over a barbecue to see what Mum would have felt. But it seemed stupid. Now I can feel a little of what she felt,' said Emily.

Carmody was getting angry with his daughter. Living vicariously again. Sucking on a drama. A prurient interest in matters that tore deeply into the hearts of others.

'What's your interest all of a sudden, Emily? You planning to make a movie of your mother's death or something?'

He knew he'd misjudged his daughter when Emily turned to him with a face contorted by emotion. Whirling past him towards the door of the verandah, she stopped long enough to spit out, 'I just thought this was something we should talk about. I've been waiting years to talk to you about it. I have been waiting years for the chill to leave your heart. And you still block me out. You've still got the door locked.' Emily had almost stormed off the verandah when something else occurred to her. She stopped. And turned around to face him. She looked into his sad face. She could barely see him through the film of tears. 'It's as if you died in that fire too!'

Tipping his tea over the rail of the verandah, Carmody listened to his daughter's footsteps striding across the lounge room, along the hall and, presumably, out the back door. He let silence settle

on the house again. And allowed his mind to drain. He felt buf-
feted. A close call with the tornado. He pushed himself off the
rail, straightened up and was about to follow her through the
house to make peace, when he heard her yell.

'Dad! I can see a glow on the horizon. Something is happening.
Come and have a look.'

Carmody strode into the house and through to the back door.
He dared not breath too deeply. Emily was frozen to the back
step, staring at the horizon. 'That's not the sunset, is it?' Emily said
as she felt her father arrive behind her.

'Don't get panicky. It's just the glow from the Hornsby fire, but – '
Carmody was already pushing in front of Emily to get a better view
of the south-west. Raising his body into a rigidity that he hoped
would inspire a flush of energy, Carmody tried to gauge exactly
where the distant fire was in relation to them. Probably five kilometres away, four hillsides. In the tightly woven facade of the bush
landscape, it was always hard to see the gullies, hills and slopes. But
Carmody had walked that area enough to know its hidden folds.

He took a breath to begin to explain this to Emily, but she
turned to him and declared, quietly but with tense vocal chords,
'It's heading this way, isn't it?'

'Come on, we have to find a decent outfit for you to wear.'
Carmody took Emily's elbow, unwilling to answer her question.
Unwilling, too, to ponder the glow on the horizon for too long.
'We've got another meeting in the hall at eight p.m. so we'll find
out if there's any news on this front there. At the very least we
should organise a roster for keeping watch during the night, make
sure we've got everything ready.'

Carmody pushed Emily into action mode, if only to forestall a
dramatic performance. As he fashioned a reasonably pragmatic
firefighting outfit for her from army disposal gear at the back of
his wardrobe, Emily muttered about catastrophes and evacuation,
frightening herself with dreadful scenarios, imagining demons that
weren't there. Or hadn't arrived yet. Carmody let her drone on

while he mentally took himself for a walk between his house and the wildfire to try to find out what lay between himself and the fire. As he let his mind roam the hilltops to his west, he tried to envisage whether it was more or less likely that a fire on the north-east of Hornsby would end up at Flint Bay.

The terrain of Flint Bay was steep, sandy and graced with only one small but reliable creek. There were big caves tucked high into the hillside – about halfway between the houses of the Bay and the area where he imagined the fire was sited. One of the caves still bore the handprints of ancient tribes and a few paintings of hunting figures. Carmody knew a lot about the former Aboriginal inhabitants of the bay through their paintings, through his reading of white history and through local legends. But he was most intimate with the ancestral neighbours when he sifted through their garbage dumps. The bay was littered with middens – sunny, sheltered spots where Aboriginal people had cooked their fish and sucked at fresh sea shells before throwing them on a pile. When the white settlers first came to Australia, they found middens that were up to eight metres deep. None in Flint Bay was that deep, but all had enough volume of shells and bones to weather centuries. Carmody liked to imagine the Aboriginal people reclining on their sunny rocks with fresh seafood platters, sucking on shells and languidly tossing them onto the pile. He wondered what they talked about around their middens — where the good catches were; whether the sharks had moved down the river into the bay yet. Perhaps they took bets on who could land a shell at the top of the pile. And keep it there.

Carmody's mental journey was interrupted when Emily insisted on finding another pair of army fatigues. The first had a hole that Emily just knew would prove a fatal weak spot in the forthcoming fires. Or so Emily had told him. 'I can feel it in my bones,' she'd said. 'This hole in the knee could be disastrous for me.'

While she fossicked around cupboards, Carmody mentally took himself back into the bush and tried to imagine how his

Aboriginal neighbours would have coped in a fire. Most of the hab-
itable caves were halfway up the hill. A dicey position for fire. But
if Aboriginal groups had torched the bush as often as the early settlers suggested, none of the fires would have been particularly big.
Mostly forest floor fires. Low fuel fires that were much easier to
escape or hide from. Besides, he thought, most of the fires would
have been started around their own campsites. Fire was always
with them. They carried burning embers in gourds like smokers
carry lighters. It was, the Aboriginal people reasoned, much easier
to restart a fire from smouldering branches than it was to light a
fresh fire with friction sticks. Carmody had once tried to mimic the
Aboriginal way of lighting a fire – two thin, strong sticks were
placed above a pile of dry leaves and the sticks were spun through
their hands to create friction. It had taken him several tries and
twelve minutes to get even a wisp of smoke. After that attempt,
he'd decided that if he had been Aboriginal, he would have carried
smouldering embers around in a gourd too. Waterfront groups even
carried fires with them in their dug-outs. Colonists were amazed to
see smoke coming from dug-outs that were so low in the water that
a family appeared to be sitting around a campfire in the middle of
the water. Most whites presumed Aboriginal people carried fire
onboard to cook fish. They did cook fish in their dug-outs but the
most likely reason for carrying fire across the water was so they
didn't have to wear out their hands lighting fires manually.

Emily was dressed, striding out of the bedroom and still talking
while Carmody was trying to envisage Aboriginal people fleeing
from fire. He couldn't. It didn't gel. Fire was their tool. It was their
most powerful tool. They used fire to flush out animals and trap
them. Fire didn't destroy their crops, it brought their food running
towards them. Or at least, cornered for an easy catch. Fire didn't
destroy their homes. Caves were protection from the flames and
their shelters weren't built to last anyway. Fire touched lightly on
Aboriginal lives.

Carmody again thought of the landscape that lay between him

and the fire. He saw the caves with the handprints of children. He saw the middens with their bacchanalian images. And he saw the foundations of white people's houses, dating back to the last century. No doubt some of those houses had been abandoned after a bad fishing year, or when authorities caught up with the residents, or when the husband left. Others had been destroyed by fire. But no matter how these houses came to ruin, all of them would eventually be touched by the flame.

'So why does everyone seems so bloody surprised to see a fire again?'

'What?' Emily cried as she headed out the back door.

Carmody didn't realise he had spoken. 'Nothing, nothing, I'm just consulting the muses.'

'What's your muse called?' Emily said when he had caught up with her outside the house.

Carmody looked at her for enlightenment.

'It doesn't matter,' said Emily. She didn't think her father would appreciate that Bernadette's muse was called Janet – a name Bernadette would call upon whenever she grew angry or exasperated. Emily had told Bernadette that muses shouldn't have names. Certainly not names like Janet. If muses must be named, Emily had said, they should have Greek names. Bernadette had retorted that she didn't know any Latin.

By the time they had reached the community hall, most of the other residents had gathered. The Carmodys were greeted inside the hall by Mrs Parker, full of bonhomie and smelling of bacon. Alex Solomon waved hello while nursing an empty beer can guiltily at his side. Most of the other dozen residents stood around the hall in little knots.

Strangely the smoke that had been getting denser through the afternoon seemed to have dissipated. Whether it was the clearing of the air, her proximity to the water or the atmosphere of action, Emily felt steadier as she nestled into the knot of people.

'Firstly, there's no reason to worry at the moment,' boomed Mr Burton. 'The fire is still well to the west of us but as the north-westerly is blowing, albeit at a slower pace than this afternoon, we should be prepared for the worst.

'As I said this afternoon, the great danger is from spot fires. Spot fires are being reported two, three kilometres in front of the main fire fronts. These fires are fingering out like a pianist's hands. But we should be able to handle spot fires if we catch them early enough. A fresh spot fire can be knocked down with fire hoses, knapsacks or even fire blankets if you have nothing else. In the absence of all those, the old McLeod can be used to move the fuel away from the spot fires,' continued Mr Burton with only the briefest glance toward Emily.

'I'm in regular contact with headquarters but it might be useful if everyone keeps an ear to news reports, although don't rely on them for the last word. A quick look at the window will often tell you more about what's happening – '

'What about I bring my portable TV down here to the hall?' interjected Solomon.

'If you like. We're not scheduled to have another meeting here but by all means bring a TV down in case we need to evacuate later. But before you settle in for the night make sure you have a good supply of water in your tanks, it would be wise to hose down your houses, the areas underneath the house and even the vegetation around the house.' Mr Burton paused, briefly scanned the faces around him for signs of questions and, maintaining eye contact, added, 'I hope you all have full water bottles and baths full of wet towels.'

Emily stopped rearranging the dirt on the floor with her shoes and thought of Mr Burton's last words. People only wore wet towels around their heads when they were escaping from a blazing house; running through fire. Wet towels were the last resort. And she realised that Mr Burton's reference to towels was more than a precaution. It was a declaration that he, and he presumed everyone else, was staying to the end. Dug in.

While Emily was digesting Mr Burton's words, Mrs Parker chimed, 'And food. I hope we all have a neat stash of portable food but if you're a bit understocked pop into my place, I've got piles of freshly packed goodies.'

Mrs Parker's interruption was taken as a sign that the meeting was finished. All too often Mrs Parker found that her contributions to discussions signalled a rapid dispersal of people. She took this as a sign of her authoritative way of summing up proceedings.

Just as the residents began filing out, Mrs Parker, stationed just outside the door to farewell everyone, spotted someone walking along the waterfront track with a hefty shoulder bag banging against his thigh.

'Oh my, a lost bushwalker,' said Mrs Parker, hurrying along the track to claim this new piece of interest.

'Good evening, Tony Thomas of 2YX news,' said the figure. He shook Mrs Parker's hand but continued to walk towards the people gathered outside the hall.

'Oh, it's a newspaperman,' said Mrs Parker. The residents turned to witness the arrival from the bush. A few swore they saw Mrs Parker give a small curtsy.

'Evening all, Tony Thomas of 2YX – that's radio, not press. So glad I've caught up with you all, I was beginning to think this place had already been evacuated.'

Emily peered at the newcomer from behind the backs of neighbours. He was, as Mrs Parker said, an interesting find. Tall – well, tallish – he carried himself with an easy purpose. As he emerged from the shadows into the torchlit group, he looked as if he knew exactly where he was going, as if he knew exactly where everyone else should be going, as if he was prepared to take them all along with him.

'How did you get here?' asked Mr Burton.

'Water taxi,' replied Tony.

'Police have been keeping all non-residents out of this area since this afternoon. Boats aren't supposed to be coming anywhere near the western foreshores unless it's for emergency services,' continued Burton.

'Sure, but I'm media,' said Thomas. Before anyone could dispute this, Tony Thomas was tracking onto another topic. 'If you wouldn't mind, could I have a few words with some of you for the next bulletin?'

Emily was intrigued – fascinated that this man could walk out of nowhere and claim the group as his own. As the reporter moved closer to the light streaming out of the hall, Emily could appreciate his features: blond – a quiet sort of blond – with looks that were pleasing without being memorable. Although he had a presence that was hard to deny, his appearance was easily forgotten ... except for one feature, which he was now bestowing on the small group. Tony Thomas's smile was wide, generous and apparently spontaneous. It hinted at intimacies yet to be established and it warmed those whom Thomas elected to include in his circle of charm.

Emily returned his smile. A few others acknowledged his request with shrugged shoulders. Everyone was mute. That was all Thomas needed to proceed. 'Well, if I could start with you,' he said, turning to Emily with a microphone he'd silently pulled out of his shoulder bag, 'are you evacuating right now?'

'Ummm, no, not now,' replied Emily, 'uummm I think we have to wait for the orders.'

'And I'll bet you can't wait for those orders,' asked the reporter, knowingly.

'Dead right. It's hell down here. Those fires must be only one or two kilometres away. I'm out of here as soon as the police arrive – '

'What about you, sir?' Thomas swiftly turned his microphone to Alex Solomon. 'Are you prepared for this front that seems to be heading straight for this area?'

'Yeah, I think so. As best prepared as we can be. Although if you've got any information on how this fire is travelling, we'd appreciate an update.'

'No doubt I'll have more information later,' continued Thomas in a seamless dialogue that was reducing those huddled around him into awkwardness. 'Given the toll these fires have taken in the last three days, you people must be very frightened at the moment.' Thomas took three quick strides over to his next inter- viewee, who was well back from the group, almost invisible in the shadows.

When Thomas's eyes met Bo's, he reeled back. Briefly he wasn't sure whether the creature was animal or human. Even when he decided that it was human, he knew he wouldn't get a reliable English response. The hooded eyes of Bo glared back at Thomas unselfconsciously. Thomas thought he heard the man growl menacingly under his breath.

Missing barely a beat, Thomas kept spinning onto the next nearest person. He found his microphone resting under the rib- boned chin of the woman who had first bailed him up on the pathway.

'Oh yes,' said Mrs Parker, taking the microphone from Thomas, 'this is more frightening than anything I've ever seen. Even people who have been in the other great fires say this is different. No one should take these fires lightly. But we are prepared. We've got our gear ready, we've got the hoses laid out, I've got cheese and bacon – '

Thomas grabbed the microphone firmly but politely back from Mrs Parker and, again without missing a second, continued a monologue into his microphone. 'As these fires rage unchecked through our outer suburban areas, another community – a small bayside community – is preparing to evacuate. Fear is becoming as common as Hills Hoists in our backyards, and here in Flint Bay you can smell fear on the breeze. This is Tony Thomas reporting.'

Tony Thomas immediately began packing his equipment away.

He wasn't happy with the outcome. It was at moments like these that he kicked himself for not being born in America. Americans always had an opinion. Even the poor, black Americans were able to stand in front of a microphone and say something interesting. In Australia, you were lucky to glean a useful comment if you spent the whole day standing in Pitt Street with tapes running. And the further you went from the centre of the city, the more tongue-tied they became. Once you got to the outback, the locals were unintelligible even on the rare occasions they chose to say something. Two centuries of locking their jaws to prevent the incursions of flies had rendered them speechless.

In the silence that followed Thomas flicking off the tape and repacking his microphone, Emily offered, 'If you need a phone to get that report back to the station, you're welcome to use one at our house.'

'Thanks, love,' said Thomas. 'I've got a mobile but we always prefer to use the wires. If we could head that way now, I'll make the nine p.m. news bulletin.'

Walking back up the track, her father and Tony Thomas in file behind her, Emily hoped that Thomas wasn't wearing steel-capped boots. She thought about asking him, but was afraid he might say yes. Or worse, pull an old army uniform from his bag. Tony Thomas was too good looking to be a bozo reporter. Surely.

When they arrived in the house, Emily whirled around the kitchen getting food and drink together while Thomas relayed his report to the station from the telephone in the lounge room. Her father had disappeared out the back. She desperately hoped the refrigerator would hold a beer brand a bit more sophisticated than ale. Preferably something European. It didn't. Emily grabbed a bottle of white wine instead and hoped Thomas had the public bar palate for which his colleagues were famous. She loved listening to the sound of his voice coming from the next room. He had a deep, corrugated voice that rumbled over her spine. It was a voice that was both soothing and sexy, perhaps because it hit a chord deep within the ear, where memories of lullabies and tribal chants lived.

By the time Thomas wandered back into the kitchen, Emily had laid out cheese, biscuits, olives and the bottle of wine. 'Hey,' she said, 'welcome to media headquarters for Flint Bay.'

'You're a journalist too?' Thomas plonked himself down at the table, instantly at home.

'Nooo,' said Emily already regretting the 'blonde' tone to her voice, 'I make movies. Documentaries mostly. That's why I'm down here, actually. I'm doing research for a doco on the bush, getting a feel for the-bush-in-crisis.' Emily paused, wondering what had brought on this rash of lies. Nervousness, she told herself. Then wondered how she was going to sustain the lies. 'Of course, I don't have a crew with me at the moment,' still flying by the seat of her pants, 'I'm just soaking-up-the-atmosphere.'

Thomas poured a glass of wine with an expression of trepidation. Emily thought, just my luck to strike a wine wanker. Thomas did not seem over-impressed with Emily's film project, either.

'Done many docos, then?' he said.

'*Solomanders at Sea*!' replied Emily.

Thomas raised an eyebrow. He was sparing with words when he'd packed the microphone away.

'It was a film about how Solomon Islanders feel lost when they come to urban centres, like Sydney. How they find themselves all at sea. Get it?' said Emily, pouring herself a glass of wine. And then continuing to fill the silence as Thomas sipped his wine suspiciously. 'It was an SBS funded project.'

'Oh, right,' said Thomas. Silence again. Emily looked out the window at the blackness. At least she couldn't see the smoke at night. She could just smell it. She breathed deeply, trying to imagine herself sitting with this bloke in a smoky bar, sipping on wine, exchanging body language full of promises.

Without warning, without thinking, Emily reached over for Thomas's packet of cigarettes, snapped one out of its soft packet and turned it into her mouth. Flicking a lighter to the tip of the cigarette, Emily watched while the end of the cigarette was warmed by the lighter. Then she breathed back.

As the tip crackled into life, Emily felt her lungs fill with smoke. Filled and then filled again. Her lungs expanded and expanded again. And then she felt it. The cigarette smoke with its dose of tar, nicotine and toxins danced around the inner linings of her lungs. And her lungs sang.

All those parts of her lungs that she had been denying for years came to life and sang. And danced. And vibrated. And wept with relief. Ah, the homecoming. The familiar fog of comfort.

Emily braced herself. She stared into the burning tip of her old friend and steadied herself for another embrace. Slowly, closing her eyes just slightly, she tipped her head back and did the draw-back again. A deep, long, loving drawback. And it happened again. The smoke caressed her throat, moved over the old terri-tory of her breathing fibres and into the deepest part of her lungs. It found its home. It caressed her soul.

Tony Thomas was staring at Emily now. He was astounded at this woman, not just because she'd swiped a cigarette from him with the desperation of an African girl at a UNICEF truck, not just because she'd gone off into a reverie that excluded him, but because of the change in her face.

As she'd sucked on the cigarette, her features had softened. The sharp, angular features were filling out. They filled out not with smoke but with contentment. With relief too. Pitiful relief. He reminded himself never to give up smoking.

Emily was keen for a third drawback but she'd just realised that Thomas was staring at her. She wondered whether she had said anything. Maybe she had sighed, or gasped with pleasure. She hoped she had not just delivered a *When Harry Met Sally* perfor-mance of cafeteria ecstasy. Thomas's face gave little away. His fea-tures seemed to have contracted. Warning of danger. Or excitement. Or possibly both.

'I'm so glad you're here,' said Emily. She was surprised she'd said it. So too was Thomas, judging by his expression. But his quizzical pout also suggested that he was pleased to hear this.

Emily registered Thomas's pleased reaction. She had already decided she fancied him. Even though he was arrogant. Perhaps *because* he was arrogant. But she hadn't meant the comment as an invitation to explore a relationship. Not yet, at least.

'Well, what I mean is that all the people down here are … well they're not loopy, they're just … they don't know what's going on. They think they can do something about these great walls of fire. They need some direction. The Water Police were here earlier in the day, but they've gone somewhere else so we're all alone.'

When John Carmody walked into the kitchen at that moment, Emily wondered whether he had been listening to their conversation. Carmody had, in fact, picked up the gist of her last words but made no acknowledgement. He was too intent on addressing the young man who was sitting at his kitchen table like he'd been reared there.

'You may have chosen the wrong spot to report the fires,' said Carmody, busying himself at the kitchen sink. 'That fire we saw glowing in the west seems to have receded.'

'What's happened to it?' asked Emily.

'Not sure. It may just have made its way down into the valley so we can't see it any more or it might have died down. In any case, I don't think you'll be getting a story too soon. The north-westerly is quiet at the moment, the weather bureau says there's a good chance of a southerly coming through tonight.'

'Oh fantastic. A cool, wet southerly,' said Emily silkily.

Carmody was unable to feel the same relief. Although he was keen to give the reporter the impression that the fire was history, he wasn't able to convince himself. In the half hour he'd spent on the back step trying to get acquainted with conditions, he'd grown more uneasy. The glow waned until it was little more than a suggestion of warmth on the south-west horizon. But he didn't believe a fire like the one that was tormenting the outer suburbs of Hornsby could die so quickly. He'd walked that terrain and had felt the twenty-five tonnes per hectare of fuel beneath the soles of his boots. It was lightly layered fuel – leaves, bark, small twigs, dead grasses and dried shrubs. Fuel with oxygen between its layers; fuel that had piled up under the thick flaky skin of paper-barks; debris that mounded under old turpentine gums to create a forest floor of bonfires.

But it wasn't just the amount of fuel on the ground that was frightening, it was the dryness of the bush floor. Months of scarce rainfall had reduced the debris to a lightweight, brown consistency that crinkled when he walked upon it. Some of it broke down into powder. Crispy bush, some wag called it. And after almost a week of heatwave temperatures, the moisture in the vegetation was down to ten to fifteen per cent. That hot, dry dog of a north-westerly had licked every scrap of moisture from the landscape.

Carmody sniffed the breeze again. The north-wester was abating but the air was still dry. Nothing wet or dewy about this night. Standing on his tip-toes on the back step, Carmody tried to see beyond the distant hills. Nothing. It had, he decided walking back into the kitchen, either died down with the abating winds, changed direction or stalled. Or it was hiding.

'I wouldn't be too confident about the southerly, Emily,' said Carmody, squinting into the fluorescent lighting of the kitchen.

'But the bureau said that a southerly would end it all. That's what we've been waiting for, Dad. Haven't you listened to any radio reports in the last few days?'

'There are different sorts of southerlies, Emily. There are wet southerlies, there are southerlies that peter out before they reach our ridgeline. And there are dry southerlies.'

'You seem to know a bit about bushfires,' said Thomas. 'Are you a volunteer firefighter?'

'No, I just watch the bush. I also fought a few fires in my youth and, like most people down here in the Bay, I've been involved in the odd winter backburn, although we haven't been able to do one of those for a long time. You don't have to be an expert to appreciate the power of these fires. Any drongo can look at the bush floor and see what happens when authorities stop people from doing controlled burns.'

'Oh, we're onto the bash-the-greenies bandwagon, are we?' said Thomas, shifting sulkily in his chair.

'No, the only greenies I'd like to bash are the political greenies. The ones who decide the bush is a sacred site that no man – especially no white man – is allowed to enter, that no one should endeavour to control.'

'The Kodak greenies – take a photo 'cause that's all you're getting out of the bush,' interrupted Emily.

'Those greenies don't love the bush, they don't really love the snot-nosed possum. They just hate people,' continued Carmody.

'It's the snub-nosed possum, not the snot-nosed possum,' said Thomas, quieter now. He wanted to back away from a confrontation. He was aware that he should not fall out irreconcilably with these people. He needed a house with a phone, and hopefully a fridge, for the next few hours, possibly the night.

'Well snub-nosed possums survived thousands of years of burn-offs by the Aboriginals – a routine occurrence then. The snub-nosed possum of Victoria survived the 1939 fires that threw a black blanket of ash over the state. It survived the 1974 fires and Ash Wednesday in '83. If it doesn't survive these fires it is because "green policies" have allowed a bonfire to build up on the floors of the forests.'

Carmody concentrated on clearing dirty dishes from the sink and sucked on his bottom lip. He hadn't intended laying a diatribe on the young reporter. He hated wasting his thoughts on people who treated debate as a political tool. He abhorred arenas where he who speaks slickest wins. Most of all he hated wasting his words on people he didn't think deserved them.

'So you think the worst is over down here,' said Thomas conciliatorily.

'I don't know,' replied Carmody, 'it could just be hiding.'

'You talk about the fire as if it's alive. A real personality-plus fire front.'

'Sometimes they behave as if they're alive,' said Carmody.

'Alive and thinking creatures? Things that can hide?'

'Why not?'

'Because fire is an element, or so my science teacher told me when I was eleven years old,' said Thomas.

'Please, Dad, stop this nonsense or Tony is going to think we're all loopy.'

Carmody started walking away from them, his left leg stiffening with late-night arthritis. 'Being loopy is not the worst thing that one can be these days, Emily.'

Chapter seven

Jack strode into the mirrored and marbled foyer of the hotel and followed the seminar signs across the foyer to the closed doors of the ballroom. Even from outside the room, Jack could hear the drone of a speaker inside. He sniffed the mixture of aftershave, perfume, wooded wines and spicy chicken half-wings and immediately felt at home. In fact, he thought, straightening his tie as he prepared to enter the ballroom, he felt more comfortable here in a city hotel than he had earlier that evening with his wife, his son and the gardening program on TV.

'Hate to leave you with the compost,' he'd said to Sarah as her Friday night gardening show blared on the TV set, 'but I really should show my face at this conference tonight.'

'Conference?' she asked without looking up from the television.

'"Ethics and the Law: Question Mark". It's being opened by the old attorney-general. I've missed half of it but I should be able to catch the keynote address and catch up with a few contacts afterwards.' Jack's voice trailed off as he finished the explanation.

Sarah seemed entranced by a segment on the gardening program about aphids. Jack got the impression she hadn't heard him. She switched off a lot these days. Especially when he talked about work.

'Why the "Question Mark"?' Sarah said as Jack retreated from the room.

'Uh?' called Jack, already nearing the front door.

'The question mark in the conference title, "Ethics and the Law: Question Mark"?'

'If you have to ask, you don't need to attend,' he replied.

Sarah waved him off without even a glance in his direction. The posy hadn't lifted the chill on their conversation. A romantic weekend might work, he thought. With champagne. And garden visits. And lots of sex. Maybe.

Jack kept fiddling with his tie as he listened at the ballroom doors. Then he heard a bustle of activity behind him and, as he turned, felt someone shouldering him out of the way. He was almost bowled over by the press of media bodies following Fred Hanes, Minister for Emergency Services, who was striding towards the ballroom like a hot young Hollywood celebrity. The camera lights and jostling news crews gave the minister a presence that his portly, flushed body would not otherwise deserve.

'Minister, what are you doing about the residents of Beattie Street who have lost their houses to the bushfires?' a reporter yelled above the racket.

'They are comfortably ensconced in a hotel with a hot dinner as we speak,' Fred Hanes replied, stopping just outside the ballroom to allow the pack to finish their questions.

'And what about Mary Peck who lost her house, belongings, her life savings and her canary in the fire? What have you done for her?'

'Mary Peck is also in a hotel tonight. Last I heard, she had had her dinner, was receiving counselling and the department was organising longer term accommodation for her with new furniture.' The minister paused as if trying to remember something. Then added, 'Hasn't *Face the Facts* just taken her out to an aviary and bought a new bird for her? A pretty yellow one, as I recall from tonight's program.'

Most of the reporters chuckled at this comment. Mary Peck's new canary had been promoted heavily all day. Everyone knew that Mary had a new bird. Even the minister. Especially the minister. The mood of the pack did not remain jovial.

'How long will these people be provided with shelter by the government and will it be a reasonable standard of shelter?' shouted a reporter from the rear.

'They are all in top-notch accommodation and – '

'I'll bet it's not the Regent Hotel,' piped another journalist.

'Why do you ask? Are you pimping for the Regent?' The minister smirked at his own joke and then gave reporters a solemn look. 'The government is doing everything it can for the victims of the fire. If they have any grievances I would expect to hear directly from them, not via you blokes.'

'And women – ' said a female voice.

'And sheilas,' retorted the minister.

'Minister, what are you doing attending this law conference tonight?' The question came from the minister's left elbow. This time Fred Hanes looked to see who was asking.

'Why, Mike, I accepted this invitation last month when I was still attorney-general,' he said, dropping his voice as the doors of the ballroom were pushed open and he entered. 'I didn't feel I could disappoint them, especially as the new attorney-general is on a study trip in Venice as we speak.'

'I'll bet you wish you were still in that portfolio,' whispered Mike Cottee. The other members of the media had trailed off, taking their lights, cameras and bustle. With just one reporter left at his side, the minister swung seamlessly from public mode to private chat.

'At a time when the state is facing the biggest disaster in fifty years, this portfolio will either make me in the eyes of the Premier, the voters and the history books, or it'll bury me.' The minister was talking under his breath so as not to disturb the audience. Or perhaps because the words were more of a private wish than the stuff of broadcasts.

'You sound reasonably confident of the challenge.' Mike Cottee intoned.

'You play your part and I'll play mine.' He began looking around the room. Obviously he hadn't spotted the person he wanted. The minister hated being left alone. He continued filling the pause. 'What about you, Mike? I thought you were the social affairs reporter for the station.'

'I was. Too many child abuse stories, feel-good cripple stories and I got sick of travelling to the forgotten fringes of the city for every story.'

'So now you're tackling the real power issues.'

'No, now I'm tackling the real crime issues.'

The minister laughed softly at this. Cottee didn't. At that moment, the chairman of the conference scuttled towards them, nodding greetings to the minister and gesturing for him to come to the stage.

Jack Carmody stood at the rear of the ballroom and watched the minister being escorted to the podium. He had been waiting on the fringes of the media hustle for a chance to shake the minister's hand. But the opportunity didn't arise so he remained on the edge, half listening to the minister's exchange with the media. Jack hated people who were overly pushy with celebrities. Nevertheless, he reminded himself to seek out the minister at the drinks session after the speech. Never hurt to have political contacts, even if they were of the wrong hue. Jack found his name tag on a deserted registration table and checked his watch. Just on eight p.m. He figured the minister's speech would wrap up the conference by eight-thirty. And then there'd be time for drinks. And hobnobbing. And new contacts.

The minister's speech was mercifully short. Within twenty minutes, Jack found himself standing in a crowded room clutching a drink and searching for familiar faces.

'Your timing is perfect. You have missed the boring introductions, the keynote speech, but you're just in time for cocktails.'

Jack turned, smiling already as he recognised the voice. Jane Tully was smirking at him. She had removed the severe dark jacket she had been wearing earlier that day in the office to reveal a sleeveless silk top. The combination with her shortish dark skirt was very Hepburn.

Jack was inordinately pleased to see her, not least because she had obviously been watching for his arrival.

'Let's be fair. I did catch the minister's speech,' replied Jack. 'Besides, the only reason any of these people come to these functions is to swap gossip, meet someone else who counts and drink half-decent wine.'

'I'd dispute the latter,' said a voice coming in on Jack's left side.

'Tom! Haven't seen you for yonks and then we butt heads twice in the one day.' Jack turned swiftly to shake the hand of the political contact he thought he'd lost.

'Has your old man found his way out of the fire yet?' said Tom Cole, staring intently at Jane and then adding for her benefit, 'Jack's old man is caught in some fibro hut at the edge of the national park. We've been trying to figure out ways to lure him out of there, haven't we, Jack?' Tom didn't wait for a response from Jack. He didn't want one. He was engaging with Jane. 'I'll bet you didn't know Jack comes from old bush stock?'

Jane was about to reply to Cole's query when Jack, unaware that the conversation was skirting him, replied, 'Don't believe a word this man says, Jane. I am not a bushy. I was raised in Lindfield and then the Hills district. Dad tried to outsprint the urban sprawl. Every time suburbia encroached on his street and solicitors began moving into the area, he'd move further out. Eventually he settled on a God-forsaken spot with the national park in his backyard and a nest of black snakes in the front yard. But he's happy.' Jack Carmody finished with a well-timed sip of wine. And a generous one at that.

'So the only thing that encroaches on his backyard now is a dirty great fire?' said Jane, paying more attention to her political opposite than Jack, to whom her question was addressed.

'Better than having lawyers move in next door, eh?' said the political adviser. To Jane.

Jack could feel himself being edged out of this conversation. He turned to claim Tom's attention with his body language. 'I presume you'll be sending a police helicopter down there if anything bigger than a Weber barbecue flares up.'

'Let me just give you one word of advice, Jack.' He finally turned to look at Jack. 'Everyone's being taken out of the danger areas. We're not letting the family budgie stay on in houses if there is any threat whatsoever.'

'Is it that bad?' asked Jane.

'You're Jane Tully, right?' said Tom, proffering a hand. 'Formerly with Corrs and Hanson? We met a couple of years ago.'

Jane looked pryingly at Tom. She remembered nothing about him, but liked what she saw: an interesting political animal with good contacts, big ambitions and, if the business gossip columns were correct, a taste for women.

'Yes, I think I remember,' she lied, 'but tell me, the government is obviously worried about these fires.'

Tom took a deep breath and glanced around him as if to check for eavesdropping. 'The briefing that has been given to the government indicates that this is potentially a huge disaster. Bigger than Ash Wednesday. Bigger than '39.'

'But they're just bushfires,' said Jane. 'They could take out a few bush cabins but they're not going to reach populated areas.'

'Jane, if you were to take a walk around the perimeter of Sydney, if you were to walk along the areas where the suburban house meets the Australian bush, you'd pass ten thousand houses. Every one of those houses could go up in smoke and, with the conditions that have been allowed to build up, many of those *will* go up in smoke.'

'What conditions?' said Jack.

'You know the score. No burn-offs for several years, not much rainfall, hot air, high winds,' said Tom.

'We know who's to blame for the lack of burn-offs,' said Jack, swigging at his drink and, spying the quizzical looks on Tom's and Jane's faces, adding, 'Well the government's anti-pollution laws have made it bloody difficult for anyone to do controlled burn-offs for the last few years.'

'The government has not been alone in that respect,' challenged Tom. 'Every time there have been attempts at burn-offs, our members get inundated with complaints from voters whingeing about the smoke, and the asthma. Even the suggestion of a burn-off has been enough to spark howls from the Greens in parliament. And then we have to cope with the national parks and their sensitivities to areas where endangered wildlife might be put at risk.'

'Don't complain to me, Tom,' said Jack, 'no one said government was supposed to be easy.' He turned to swap his empty glass with a full one on the waiter's tray behind him. He took a second glass and pressed it into Jane's hand. He raised an eyebrow in Tom's direction. Tom declined the offer. Jack continued, 'It's the government's role to balance all these interest groups and come up with the right solution. So far, the only solution your mob can muster is the political solution. And the political solution is not always the wisest solution for the bush. Or for the suburban fringe dwellers. Or, in the end, for any of us.'

'Still, it doesn't seem fair to blame it all on the government,' piped in Jane.

'You're right, Jane,' said Tom, happy to shift attention, 'and we don't intend to be blamed for something we shouldn't be held accountable for. We certainly won't be blamed for deaths. That's why we've decided to let the houses burn. They're covered by insurance or will be compensated by special emergency grants. But we don't want any bodies.'

'Is that the reason the minister was scaring the pants off everyone today, saying that we could lose thousands of homes to the fires?' asked Jane.

'Precisely. We have to make people realise how serious this situation is – '

'Oh yes,' interrupted Jack, 'and it's a neat political ploy too. In two weeks' time, when hundreds of houses have burnt to the ground and the media is hounding the government for its mishandling of the disaster, the government can turn around and say "we *should* have lost thousands of houses but we managed the disaster so well we kept the tally to just a few hundred." To turn disaster into triumph in politics you just have to put the right spin on events *and* get the pups in the media to buy into it.'

Jane and Tom stared at Jack gesticulating with his empty glass. Both were wondering whether he was drunk already. Tom turned to Jane, showing an exclusionary shoulder to Jack. In a quiet tone of voice, designed to contrast with Jack's outburst, he continued, 'It's important for the government to be seen to be pro-active. There is not much the government can do at this stage, except minimise the physical toll ...'

Jack was looking around the room as Tom Cole gave him what amounted to a dressing-down. At the edge of audience, Jack could see the minister leaving the ballroom surrounded by a hub of well-wishers.

'Your boss is leaving, shouldn't you follow?' he said hopefully.

'No,' said Tom Cole, 'he's heading back to headquarters. I know where to find him.' He was already disappearing into the crowd as he said this. With Jane Tully on his elbow.

Jack found himself in a group of junior solicitors and academics. For the next half hour he was forced to share inanities with people who didn't matter and probably never would matter. Occasionally he spied Tom and Jane in the distance, but they looked so engrossed he doubted he could butt into their conversation successfully.

As the trays of drinks began appearing less frequently and the crowds began thinning, Jack wondered whether he had drunk too much. He felt like he was on the cusp of bonhomie and blather. He thought he was still well within the confines of the former. The reactions of others suggested he'd crossed over. A while ago.

When he had been shouldered off even by the junior solicitors, Jack made an effort to stride to the exit doors while unpinning his name tag. He had abandoned hope of seeing Jane again that night. Certainly he knew he wouldn't need a booking for a hotel room. Except perhaps for himself, if he couldn't negotiate this ballroom floor with more aplomb.

Suddenly Tom appeared from behind him, also unpinning his name tag. 'Mate,' said Tom, 'I'd start laying down the law to your old man if I were you. I just heard from a journo that the fire front is moving into the western foreshores.'

The news sobered Jack a little. Or at least brought the first twinges of a hangover. 'Fuck me,' Jack said to himself as he busied himself with a name tag that just kept twisting around on itself, carving a deep hole into the lapel of his coat, 'just what I need tonight.' Then, finally meeting Tom's eyes, he said, 'Well, if that's the case, don't forget to send that police helicopter down to the Bay.'

Chapter eight

Beryl Parker dabbed her nose again with a lace-edged handkerchief. She sniffed the aroma of lavender that had been infused into its fabric. Closing her eyes, she invited images of dewy mornings and a verdant English countryside. The reassuring images were slow in coming today. The heavy smoke of the last few days had now permeated her household fabrics. Like a cheap motel room where the smell of heavy smokers and unemptied ashtrays is absorbed into every fibre of the room, bush smoke had now claimed Beryl's house. She knew she would spend weeks – months – coaxing the smell out of her cushions, curtains, rugs, linen closet, clothes ... The tally of her duties sent Beryl stalking around her cottage searching for cushions to beat.

She was still on the prowl when Roger Burton brushed past the seaside daisies that lined Mrs Parker's pathway, plonked his knapsack on her verandah and peered in through the flyscreen of the front door. He could see Mrs Parker standing very still in the middle of the lounge room with a cushion limp in her hand. He waited on the threshold for a while, trying to determine why she was frozen to the spot, when Beryl suddenly thrashed her cushion through the air. And missed the fly.

'If it upsets you that much, Beryl, we can fill the knapsack with flyspray and blow it out of the sky,' said Roger from the front step. 'Oh, Mr Burton, how nice of you to pop by. There's always one, isn't there?' said Mrs Parker, gliding down the hallway to open the door for him. 'I mean one fly – I wasn't referring to your being here. I'm so happy someone has taken up the invitation. Do you think the others will pop in for a cuppa? It's,' she glanced at the watch that hung loosely around her wrist, 'past nine o'clock now. Getting late.'

Mrs Parker looked behind Mr Burton as he stepped into the house. Mr Burton couldn't be sure whether she was looking for more people coming up the pathway or checking for flies that might sneak in behind his back. He suspected the latter.

Mrs Parker's floor gleamed. It always did, but Roger Burton thought the floor boards had a special glow about them tonight. Like the smile on the faces of family members on Christmas night. Too bright for comfort. As he walked into the small dining room of the fifties timber bungalow, Roger Burton understood something of Mrs Parker's day.

Laid generously but not extravagantly across the cedar table were platters of date scones, triangle sandwiches, a savoury loaf of bread, jams, butters, chutneys, tea cups turned onto saucers and a fly net draped over the lot. Roger Burton turned to her with his arms outstretched, breathing deeply the aroma of fresh baking, of bacon and lavender, and exclaimed, 'We're expecting a fire, Beryl, not the bowling club social committee!'

Mrs Parker smiled. She took this as a compliment and busied herself reheating the kettle (she had been boiling the kettle on and off all afternoon). She prepared a small plate of food from the buffet. Roger Burton headed for the big armchair in the adjoining lounge room and prepared himself for a half hour natter.

'I can't stay too long, Beryl. I'm due to begin my shift in the watch tower at ten,' he said.

'Oh, we've built a watch tower, have we?' said Mrs Parker, hovering around his armchair with the plate of food and napkins.

'No, I meant that metaphorically. Really, Beryl, for someone who has lived in the bush for as long as you have, you ought to be a bit more familiar with fire protection routines.' Roger Burton accepted the plate from her.

'Oh, I've been to all the fire maintenance days but you forget that I am normally pretty busy in the kitchen with the other ladies preparing things for you blokes to eat when you've finished bashing the bush.'

'Bashing the bush! Beryl, "bashing the bush" is an essential program of maintaining fire breaks. It's not a macho thing we do to prove to ourselves that we're real men,' said Mr Burton, hoeing into a scone. He began speaking again with the scone still in his mouth. 'If we'd been able to do some real burn-offs over the last few years we wouldn't be facing this disaster.'

Mrs Parker searched her mind for something worthwhile to add to the conversation. She remembered the word she'd looked up that morning. 'Yes,' she said, 'it's all very xeric out there at the moment, isn't it?'

Mr Burton swallowed his scone. He let her comment pass. 'Have you found Kurt's old fire hose yet?' he asked.

'No, I didn't pay any attention to where Kurt stored his fire stuff,' said Mrs Parker, gently wringing her hands as she perched on the edge of a stiff chair.

Roger Burton clanked his tea cup down into the saucer. He had become handyman for the widows of the Bay since his wife had divorced him seven years ago so she could go back to uni and study psychology. Why she needed to divorce him so she could go to uni, he didn't understand. Then or now.

He missed his friend Kurt most. Kurt Parker, married to Beryl, had been a garrulous neighbour, free with his back-slaps, with his beer and with his gardening equipment. Roger was always happy to encounter Kurt on the track or at the wharf. It made his day when Kurt gave him a shoulder hug and took him into his whirlwind of chatter, jokes and laughter. He felt lifted out of himself for a while.

Roger was surprised when Kurt died of cancer. Suddenly, almost hastily. One day a diagnosis was announced and, within weeks, a funeral was held. Kurt had died before Roger had even visited him. He hadn't even been able to decide how to talk about the cancer with Kurt before it was too late. For heaven's sake, he hadn't even settled on an appropriate way of scheduling a meeting with Kurt when the bloke had died. But he'd been visiting his widow regularly ever since.

He clanked his tea cup again. Mrs Parker's ears pricked up. She couldn't abide chipped tea cups.

'I suppose I do tend to assume that everyone down here has had some experience of fires,' he said.

'Frankly, I don't think I could extinguish a barbecue. I certainly can't light one.'

'I was in Gippsland in 1939,' said Burton, pausing. Those who knew something of the history of Australian fires normally greeted this statement with a few tisks, or shook their heads with silent concern. Those who didn't know the history usually replied like Mrs Parker, 'Oh yes.'

'The worst this century,' he continued, rousing himself from the armchair to pace the floor. 'They say the '83 fires killed more but the fires of '39 … there was nothing like them, before or since.

'Conditions were so bad leading up to the summer of '39 that the fire season started in August. Crown fires in August, imagine that. The whole of the state was parched even before summer arrived. It's funny, I've always associated fire with war. I think it's because Hitler's advance into Europe was being made at the same time as the '39 fires were spreading across the country.

'The conditions were ripe for the outbreaks. Two dry years, a very dry winter. Outbreaks began in earnest in October and they spotted all summer. There were fires in Gippsland, the high country, the border with South Australia. Every morning we'd wake up and look outside to see how close the fires were that day. Some days they were close, real close, and we'd go through all our fire drills again. Mum would bring the chooks inside the house because the chook house was right on the edge of the bush. It would take us kids hours to catch them and get them back into their cages again. One night, we missed a chook, went to bed without even knowing that the rooster was stuck behind my parents' wardrobe. It struggled free at five a.m. and hopped onto the lowboy to throw its scrawny neck back and greet the day. Almost gave Dad a heart attack.'

Mrs Parker was smiling fondly and sitting back in her chair. So Roger continued the story.

'When we got up in the morning, we'd turn on the ABC and listen to the rundown of areas affected. It was usually a long list of names of areas and town. Then came the warnings for other areas. Sometimes there was a report of the number of people who had died in fires or died of heat exhaustion the day before. Hitler's march through Europe was usually number two on the local news bulletins. I don't know which was more of a worry for us – Europe falling to Hitler, or our homes being wiped out by fire. Certainly, Hitler seemed a long way away from our lives.

'By January Victoria was baking. Funnily enough a lot of farms were quite safe because the drought had killed off all the grasses. But in the bush there were literally hundreds of fires. There was no rain on the horizon. All the cool changes kept getting pushed away down into the Tasman. It just kept getting hotter and hotter.

'If you believed in witchcraft, then you'd say the '39 fires were always going to climax on Friday 13 January. I tell you, Beryl, I don't believe in witchcraft or superstitions but after that day I've never felt entirely easy on Friday the thirteenth.

'It was forty-six degrees Celcius that day. It was so dry that if you opened your mouth for a while all the saliva dried up. You could almost feel the air sucking the moisture from your eyeballs. They were swirling, angry, confused winds. Seventy-one people died that day.'

Roger Burton paused. He realised he probably shouldn't be frightening Mrs Parker with tales of infernos. He looked at her from the corner of his eyes. She was motionless – except for her hands, which were massaging each other, as if to rub warmth into each other. He stopped pacing the floor and wandered over to the window overlooking the front path. 'Expecting anyone else tonight?'

'Oh I hope so,' said Mrs Parker. 'I asked everyone in our fire-fighting unit to pop in. I suppose a lot of them have fire duties to attend to. I had hoped that Emily might come down and give me a hand but – '

'Emily, much to everyone's surprise,' interjected Roger, 'has volunteered for firefighting duties.'

'Well I hope she'll be useful. She certainly hasn't contributed much to our community in recent years,' said Mrs Parker, building up a momentum of indignation as she cleared plates away. 'You know poor John Carmody had to nurse his sick wife all by himself for years. Years, literally years, without any help from Emily.'

'As I recall it,' said Roger Burton, reluctantly letting himself be dragged into the conversation, 'the son, Jack, wasn't much help either.'

'I suppose he wasn't, but one expects a daughter to attend to certain duties. And by the end, poor Maeve had problems that only a daughter should have been allowed to attend to. No woman wants her husband to do the sort of things that John Carmody had to do for his wife all by himself up there ...'

'Mrs Parker,' he said, using her formal title to try to jolt her back into polite conversation, 'Maeve had the choice of staying down here or going into a nursing home. I think at one stage, she also had the choice of moving into one of her son's rental flats in the city. She chose to stay here, she chose to stay with her husband and her husband chose to have her here.'

'But if Maeve had been in hospital, the rug would never have fallen off her lap ...'

'Accidents can happen anywhere. Haven't you ever sat too close to a heater and felt your trousers singe?' Roger Burton looked down at Mrs Parker's stockinged legs and added, 'I suppose you haven't. But it happens. Unfortunately Maeve wasn't able to stamp the fire out. Or run away from it. Didn't the coroner conclude that she was asleep when it happened?'

'It was probably a blessing in disguise in the end, wasn't it? I don't know how Jack Carmody would have coped with the last stages of Maeve's illness. He could barely carry her from her bed to her chair. He obviously felt he couldn't leave the house for long, couldn't go into Sydney for the day or anything.'

'You visited them every day, didn't you? You must have been of immense help and comfort,' said Roger Burton as he stopped his pacing by the window and looked outside inquiringly.

'Oh, I don't know, I suppose I did what I could, but – ' Mrs Parker paused as she recalled the last few times she had called on Maeve. 'I suppose it might have had a good effect because the last few times I saw Maeve, she seemed much perkier. Happy almost. She asked me to help her tidy up her paints. And she asked me to arrange some of her favourite paintings in front of her chair. I was going to lift them onto the easel for her but she said she just wanted to look at them ...'

Mrs Parker's voice trailed off. But the image of Maeve stayed with her. And with Roger Burton. It seemed to hang in the air between them, this memory of Maeve, surrounded by paintings in her studio. So final. So succinct. So suggestive, neither felt like exploring it further.

'Come on,' said Roger, 'I'll show you how to operate a knap-sack sprayer.'

Chapter nine

In the half-light of his one-room cabin, Bo concentrated on the nothingness in front of his face. His body was immobile. Almost imperceptibly, his ears twitched as he tuned into the sound coming from outside the cabin. Familiar. But strange. Slowly and with complete silence, Bo unwound his body, rose from his spindly chair and padded over to the door.

Bo's dog, Sheila, was already poised on the rock ledge that formed the outer courtyard of Bo's domain. Bo followed his dog's gaze. Something was stirring under the old ironbark tree. The rustling in the leaf litter was unmistakable. But Bo continued to stare into the shadows under the tree. Then he saw it. The shiny black tail of a red-bellied black snake now disappearing behind the trunk.

The sounds of snakes or lizards moving through dry bush litter were as familiar to Bo as the sounds of lorikeets landing in the ironbark early in the morning; as familiar as the slapping sound that the old wallaby made as it bounded down the hillside on its tail. Bo could hear a snake thirty metres away on a still day. If he listened long enough, he could gauge the size of the snake by the sound it made moving across brittle leaf litter. The biggest snakes around his cabin were pythons. Harmless pythons.

But not all the big snakes were harmless. To this day, Bo avoided the rocks near the top of the hill where he had once stepped over – nearly on – a brown snake. By the time Bo had seen the snake, it had whipped itself back into striking pose and was cursing Bo with a hideous hissing sound. Bo had leapt half a metre into the air, without a wind-up. The uncoiling snake had followed his legs as they left the ground and its fangs hit his trouser leg mid-air. Fortunately, the snake's aim was skewed by Bo's leap so the fangs banged against his leg rather than pierced it. As Bo landed a metre from the spot where he left the ground, the snake recoiled for another shot. But Bo had taken off by then. Hit the ground running. He'd never been back into that area. There is nothing worse than an angry brown snake. Except perhaps an angry brown snake with a memory.

The sight of the black snake wouldn't normally have concerned Bo. It wasn't aggressive and was only a danger in spring when it lay sunbaking on tracks. The only thing that upset Bo about seeing the snake was the fact he'd never seen a black snake at night. Black snakes, like humans, slept at night.

Bo continued to listen to the snake to gauge where it was going. And maybe why. He presumed that this was one of the snakes that shared a nest to the west of his hut. But this one was heading away from its home. Bo thought about it some more. It wasn't tearing off in panic, it was just shifting bases.

Standing sentinel on his rock ledge, Bo felt the night give him a hug. It was a hot hug, but the night seemed calmer than it had earlier when the north-westerly was blowing. The north-westerly wind had brought a lot of debris into the hillside. The soot hadn't seemed particularly thick but by early evening Bo noticed that the water in the bird bowl was scummed with ash. With the north-westerly easing, the air was less choked but the atmosphere seemed more charged.

Tonight the wind had an indecisive quality to it. It was not a quality that made Bo feel comfortable. He felt pressure in his bowels and thought he should move them now, while he still had the opportunity.

Bo loped off into the bush, with Sheila following at his left heel. Bo's walk was the first thing bushwalkers noticed when they spied him off the marked tracks collecting wood or carting rocks. His arms hung loosely just to the front of his body, as if they were used to carrying nothing but his balance. His torso was always held erect but his legs moved with a loping grace. The carriage may have looked arthritic but it was extraordinarily successful at moving him through the bush.

If one looked closely at Bo's walk, it was obvious that the right leg always led and the left followed. As a child he had tended to favour his right leg and, over the years, the right had gradually taken over. The right-foot motion tended to lead Bo in an arcing direction in the bush. A fact that Bo mentally compensated for when he was in strange territory.

Bo gave no indication that he was aware of his strange gait. He was neither selfconscious nor worried about it. Even when the art gallery woman had asked him if he had an injury, it didn't occur to him that she was talking about the way he walked. In fact, Bo gave the impression that he neither knew nor cared about how he looked. Certainly, he had the appearance of someone who never looked in a mirror – an uncorrected body. Free of primping, preening, posture corrections and masks. Never owning a mirror and rarely having the opportunity to catch himself inadvertently in other mirrors, Bo would often have markings on his face for days before they were accidentally wiped off. Tonight, Bo had just smudged his forehead with a bit of ash that he had scooped up from the water bowl. It would probably remain there for days.

The only photographs he had of himself were the family portraits on his shelf – one taken when he was five years old, another when he was eleven. If Bo ever pictured himself, he imagined he looked like a slightly taller, hairier and older version of the boy sitting on the front verandah of the Strathfield house. He looked nothing like that. He looked like nothing you would see on the streets of Strathfield. Or on any streets.

Within minutes Bo reached the toilet he had dug earlier that year in the lee of a giant rock. Bo squatted over the hole in the ground and stared at the *Reader's Digest* page he had carefully torn out of the 1962 May issue and tucked into his back pocket as he left the cabin. It didn't have any pictures on it. It was always disappointing when his toilet page didn't have pictures. He couldn't see words in anything but bright moonlight. And he rarely wasted torch batteries on the familiar trip to the toilet. But if there was a picture on the page, he could remember a lot of the stories from the time when his brother read the *Digests* to him nightly. The *Digests* were both precious and useful to Bo. Yesterday he'd tried to lug most of them down to the waterside to save them from the fires. But he'd only managed to drag a few dozen copies down when Carmody had started complaining about the weight of the parcels. The rest remained in boxes under his bed.

After he had used the page and had repositioned a flat rock over his hole, Bo padded back through the bush. The familiar track told him much about the state of the bush. The track was worn bare. Nothing green had shooted along its edges all summer. Puffs of dust trailed after him. And tonight the track was busy. The ants were still awake. Like the snake, they were busy. Purposeful.

When Bo reached his cabin he felt restless. His home didn't feel right tonight. It had been disturbed. All its most useful and familiar items had been moved down to the waterfront. What was left seemed more like a shell than his home. He decided he wouldn't be sleeping tonight. He grabbed the kerosine lamp and a gnarled branch that was in a corner of his cabin and slipped outside.

The outdoor fireplace was Bo's favourite spot. He had built the fireplace with rocks that had tumbled down the hillside onto the relatively flat area around his hut. The fireplace was big. It grew bigger all the time as Bo still collected rocks and placed them carefully into the dry-stone construction of the fireplace. The design of the fireplace owed more to the shape of the rocks than to any linear plan. In fact, John Carmody had once quipped that Bo was the only man alive whose stove was bigger than his

house. Tonight the fireplace was empty. Bo positioned his outdoor chair next to its hearth and propped his branch on the grill.
For a long time Bo sat staring at the branch, waiting for inspiration, waiting for the branch to show what was within. Sometimes
the art in the branch, the life to which it alluded, was apparent
from the moment he first saw it. He could see it in the twist of the
limb or the joint of a branch. His goanna was the most obvious.
He had only to gouge out a few splinters of bark around its tail to
immortalise the goanna in the branch of an ironbark. But mostly
Bo had to be patient. Like tonight. Bo emptied his mind and let
his eyes move over, around, above and inside the wood. He
might sit for hours like this, only moving when he got up to shift
the wood into a different position. Sometimes the wood didn't
have a story. Or it refused to reveal itself to Bo. These pieces he
either threw up the hillside or, if he was feeling stubborn, they
would be perched against a tree outside his hut. Eventually these
were lost to rot, ants or the tangle of underbrush.

Those that did finally reveal themselves were rewarded with a
whoop of joy. Then, in a frantic rush, Bo would carve away at the
wood, chipping, chinking, slicing, shaving and sawing. The
branches that reluctantly showed themselves were the most
exciting because what was revealed was subtle. It could be the
branch of another tree hidden within the wood, or a rocky outcrop. Once he excavated the watery image of a fish from a piece
of yellowbox that washed up on the shore. On a limb of an ironbark, he carved the wing of a bird caught in a moment of flight.
These sculptures were so finely etched that sometimes he could
barely see the image he created. They were his favourite pieces.

But those alluring pieces didn't sell. The art gallery owner from
across the bay always told him to concentrate on animals. Every
month or so when she made the trip across from the peninsula
and trudged up the hill with a couple of empty hessian sacks, she
said the same thing. Sometimes she shouted it at him, as if he
were deaf. Usually Bo didn't care that she shouted at him. He'd

just tuck his head into his shoulders a little so he couldn't hear her shouting so much. But this just seemed to encourage her. One day when he was sick of her shouting, he shouted back. Sheila got so excited by his shouting that she jumped up and began barking at the woman. The woman almost fell down the hill.

Mostly, by the time she had sorted through his work and shouted at him not to do so many 'obscure' pieces, he couldn't wait for her to leave. In the end she would tuck a few twenty-dollar notes into his hand, stomp down the hill with the pieces and swear not to come again.

She always came back. She'd been coming since Beryl Parker told her of his sculptures (somewhat derisively) seven years ago. And they still sold well. Bo didn't need the money, but he liked taking it from her. He liked to watch her peel the notes off the roll and pat them into his hand. He could see it hurting her, he could see her face pinching in on itself. The transaction cost her. Not him. He didn't even have to negotiate much. He just sat with Sheila by his side. Once when the woman lent towards Bo to press the money into his hand, Sheila began growling. Strangely, the woman took this as a sign that the money wasn't enough. She peeled another note off her pile, staring at the dog from the corner of her eye. It was the staring that Sheila didn't like. The dog continued growling. The woman peeled off another note. Then another. She kept peeling them off until greed got the better of cowardice.

Bo didn't know that the art gallery sold his pieces for between $350 and $550 each. And he probably wouldn't care, if he ever did find out. He may have cared if he discovered that she claimed the pieces were made by an Aboriginal person.

Time passed unheeded as Bo sat beside his empty fireplace and waited for the wood to declare itself. How much time, Bo would never know. He had moved out of clock-time many years ago. After a while, Bo noticed a shift in the wind. It had moved subtly to the south. The wind, even though it was gentle, was bringing dirtier air swirling into the lamplight. The dust danced around, diverting Bo's attention. When a gust of wind whipped down the hillside and slapped up the dust around the fireplace, Bo felt he could no longer ignore the presence that had arrived on the periphery of his vision.

He knew it would come. He went back into his cabin to get ready. As he prepared to go down the hill to meet up with the firefighters in his unit, he didn't know what he dreaded most – fighting the fire or having to mix with a crowd of people again.

When he left his cabin again, he looked to the south-west horizon and was not surprised to see the blood-red fury. Heaving on top of a not-too-distant ridge. Panting like an animal.

Chapter ten

Emily lay in the bunkbed in the spare room with a weariness that surprised her. She catalogued her body the way she'd been taught in yoga. 'Right thumb, right finger, palm of the hand, back of the hand, wrist, lower arm.' Every part of her body that was touching the bed felt weighted. Pinned down with weariness. She felt like Gulliver strung out over the landscape of her mattress.

But her mind was whirring. As she recapped the day, she marvelled at the speed with which her life had moved from cappucino belt to hillbilly territory. In all the hubbub she hadn't told her father that she'd lost her job yesterday. But she supposed he wouldn't have been too surprised. Jobs came and went without fanfare in her life. Her father would probably think … what? What did her father think of her life? That she was a career hobo, unable to stay with anything long enough to make a mark? Or that she was riding the bronco of the modern workforce, getting off and on the horse with the only assurance that she'd end up with a sore butt at the end of the day?

Her father, thought Emily, held his job in the engineer's firm long enough to qualify for long-service leave four times. He had been awarded three sets of placemats, two sets of company cufflinks and a gold watch. Now he did charity work. Giving back, he called it.

Emily heard the creaky spin of a door handle further up the hallway. It sounded furtive. As if someone didn't want the handle to make a noise. She listened for footsteps, for the unselfconscious footsteps of a sleepy-headed person seeking nightly ablutions. Nothing. A creak of a floorboard, maybe.

Oh my God, she thought suddenly, he is coming to me. The blond with the wizard smile is making his move. She had considered this possibility earlier that night, when her father had grudgingly suggested that Tony Thomas sleep the night in Jack's old room. Tony Thomas had hesitated momentarily and then, just before he nodded assent, he'd glanced at Emily as if seeking her approval. Or her complicity.

But she hadn't seriously thought Thomas would creep into her bedroom; that he would come for her from the shadows of the doorway; that he would appear at her bedside, staring down at her prone body with a panting presence; that he would tear the sheets off her, decisively but not violently; that the dark shadow of his body would loom over her, nestle into her folds, claim her in the darkness.

She'd rehearsed for this moment. Many times. Not that night but in the summers of her youth. One summer she seemed to spend every hot night preparing for an encounter with the lover at the door. The summer of her sixteenth year. She'd read scores of books – Sidney Sheldon, Jackie Collins, Jilly Cooper. *Fear of Flying* over and over again. She'd played card games. And she'd made telephone calls to girlfriends. But mostly she'd waited for that special man to spin the handle on her door and walk in to claim her.

Years later, when she discovered that men were not knocking her door down in the rush even if they knew where she lived, she realised that that summer marked the end of her enchantment with men – a premature end to the life of a romantic. Now, as she heard footsteps padding down the hallway, she hoped she was about to be proved wrong.

Posing sleep, Emily softened her facial features. She set her imaginary camera two metres from her bed and tried to see herself as the night-prowler might find her. She tilted her head back on the pillow and let her mouth open slightly. With one arm already thrown back over her head, she languorously pushed her breasts and buttocks out. The sensual S-bend. The pose of erotic abandon. She mentally checked herself with the camera. Yes, it was the classic nude pose of Marilyn Monroe. She let the image ooze through her body. Like an invitation to sex. The pose held the promise of sex, the fantasy of sex, the history of sex and the aftermath of sex. And then some more sex. As the dark shadow stopped outside her bedroom and slowly began to push the door open, Emily held the pose.

The shadow was above her now. Emily could hear the pant of a low breath. She tried to still her own breathing. The tension was exquisite. Where would he touch her first? Would his touch be soft and uncertain or firm and over-powering? What sort of approach was she hoping for? Would she be able to feign sleep for long? For the duration?

'Come on, Emily, it's time to get up and face the music.'

The sound of her father's voice shocked Emily into wakefulness. For a terrible moment she thought that her father was answering her telepathic messages. Her father's next words failed to explain his presence.

'Don't panic, Emily, just don't panic on me please.' She'd heard words like that before. That's what the rapist would say when he threw his gloved hands around the victim's mouth. Perhaps not quite as nicely. But the words were the same.

When John Carmody saw that his daughter was retreating stiffly into her bed covers, her eyes wide and uncomprehending, his worst fears about his daughter's presence in the Bay were realised. He tried once more to reach her.

'The fires are coming again and we need to get ready,' he said plainly and decisively.

When Emily heard this, the fog of erotica lifted. Quickly she placed herself in reality. She was in the spare bedroom. Her father at her side waiting impassively. She could hear Tony Thomas fumbling around in Jack's bedroom. She reminded herself of the fires on the hillside. As her dreamy state left her, she sighed with relief. Just the fires, she thought.

Scuttling out of bed, Emily had a barrage of questions for her father. But he was already walking away, no doubt concerned for modesty. Emily pulled on the musty old army trousers and dull white T-shirt that she had been wearing all day and tried to gauge what was happening in the household.

Thomas was talking on the phone when she entered the lounge room. By the tone of his voice, the telephone call was a work call although it didn't have the cadence of a news report. Her father was clanging with something in the kitchen. 'Emily,' he called from the kitchen, 'can you pop over to old Mr and Mrs Grey and escort them down to Mrs Parker's house?'

Emily walked down the hallway towards the back door. Her thoughts were still preoccupied with erotica. She hoped she hadn't called out Tony's name. She hoped her father hadn't noticed the Monroe pose. She was so bewitched, she had arrived at the open back door and was looking outside before she'd had a chance to prepare herself. Her mouth fell open and she felt the breath leave her lungs even before she got to the back step. Her father's calm demeanour had done nothing to prepare her for the sight to the south-west. The angry force was surging on the horizon. It seemed to see her. To sense her. Emily's skin tingled. With shock. Or fear. Or something between the two. Unthinkingly, she cringed and tried not to look at it. She grabbed the door handle and forced her eyes to look down at the back steps. The glow of the fire seemed to radiate off her skin. Emily lifted her face and peered at it from under her eyebrows, as if trying to avoid attracting attention. Emily felt it challenging her. It appeared to know her, to be beckoning to her.

Emily forced herself out the door and walked around the back of the house. She allowed herself only to see the track. Approaching the pale blue fibro walls of the Greys' house, Emily was relieved to see lights on inside. She didn't relish the idea of awakening two eighty-four-year-olds with the news that their love nest was about to be devoured by fire. But as she approached the ajar front door and peered inside, she could see they were already up and about.

'Yoohoo,' said Emily, pushing the door further open and edging into the lounge room, 'it's Emily Carmody here. Are you both awake? I've come to help you get down to Mrs Parker's.' She tip-toed through the lounge room, noting its clinical bareness. All the nick-nacks of the Greys' lives had been carted off to safer territory. Imagining the effort that the old couple must have put into collecting their nick-nacks, packing them and transporting them to safer ground, Emily suddenly appreciated how the threat of fire was having a great impact on many people's lives. She imagined the Greys sitting in this lounge room over the last few days, debating what needed to be carted off to safety, what might remain and whether anything would remain of their house by the end of the week.

Mrs Grey was first to greet Emily. She tottered into the lounge room, still buttoning her cardigan. Emily noticed the buttons weren't done up straight but she felt the circumstances didn't warrant an upbraiding. The old woman was nervously brimming with questions on the fire. It took only a few minutes for Emily to get testy. Why, why, why, she thought, do old people want to discuss everything in minutia? Her unease grew as she felt a gust of wind arrive in the house. The gust intruded like a stray dog, circling around the room, searching, sniffing, nudging up against them. Mrs Grey was still prattling when a second, more powerful gust whipped into the house and rattled the loose handles on the windows. Emily snapped, 'Is Mr Grey ready to go yet?'

Emily strode into a dimly lit room that she assumed was their bedroom and saw Mr Grey perched unsteadily on the edge of his bed, grappling with the laces of his boots. She whimpered when she saw Mr Grey's thickened, gnarled fingers attempting to thread metre-long laces through the eyes of his boots. His fingers had the dexterity of small balloons. Why, she thought closing her eyes, would an eighty-four-year-old choose to wear army boots to walk down the hill to the neighbour's house?

Standing over him, breathing tightly, Emily realised that the old codger was dressed in army fatigues. A terrible sympathy tore at her soul. What did he think he was going to do in this fire? Man the pumps? Drag the fire hoses across the burning ground? She murmured greetings to him and he responded by smiling briefly in her direction. A gust of wind rumbling through dry leaf litter outside the window tested her patience. She desperately wanted to get down on her knees, shove Mr Grey's arthritic hands aside and do his laces up for him. She resisted. Knowing that for some old people indignity is worse than death.

'Now, dear, I've left an old McLeod tool out the back for you. And there's plenty of water in the tank but don't use it until you have to. If we run out of water, we'll have to spend the next few weeks at my son's house. And I don't want that – '

'Mr Grey,' Emily interjected, 'I won't be staying here. I can't stay here and keep the fire off your house.'

Mr Grey stopped his attempts to lace his boots and stared up at her. 'Well, why are you here?'

'I'm going to help you get down the hill to Mrs Parker's.'

'We know the way to the Parkers', dear.'

'I know, I know, I just thought you might, you might – ' Emily searched for a phrase that offered dignity to the Greys' flight, 'need some help with something,' she said, looking around his bedroom for something heavy and awkward that might need carrying.

'Very nice. But we're all right, you can go now.'

'No, no I'll go down to Mrs Parker's with you. It's right near the hall and if we're evacuated we will all have to go to the community hall. I should go and check the hall while I'm down there so I may as well accompany you down the hill.'

Mr Grey did not say too much more. Emily felt he resented her presence now. She didn't care. She wasn't going without them.

She didn't want to have to charge up to the Greys' house later to try to rescue them. Nor did she fancy going over the scene with police, explaining where the old people had been standing when she last saw them alive.

After an eternity of ten minutes, the threesome took off down the hill. Huddled against the elements as they tottered down the pathway, Emily glanced to the sky and saw birds flying silently overhead. The sight disturbed her although she couldn't say why.

By the time they had made it to the edge of Mrs Parker's garden, they heard a siren boom. It came from the hall and ricocheted across the bay. Emily was delighted. A more joyous hoot she hadn't heard since the last day of last term at high school. Gently steering Mrs Grey to the left with the hand that was cradling her elbow, Emily said, 'We'll just do a quick left-hand turn here and head straight for the community hall, ladies and gentlemen. That sounds like the siren of evacuation to me. I think our boat is about to come in.'

Chapter eleven

'Who set the siren off?' asked John Carmody, striding into the hall where a dozen of his neighbours had already gathered.

'I got a call from the police, John. They said everyone should move down to the hall and be ready for the water police to arrange evacuation,' said Roger Burton.

'The police? Rang you?' said Carmody as he gently pulled Burton away from the hub of neighbours and lowered the volume of his voice.

'I suppose they rang me because I'm chairman of the Bay Association. I …' added Burton struggling for clarity, 'I'm with you. I don't know how or why they decided this but, umm, there you are.'

'The siren is meant for emergencies.' Carmody was addressing absent authorities rather than Roger Burton. 'It's supposed to signal unforeseen danger. Imminent danger. This is preposterous.' He paused. Gathered his thoughts and continued railing against the unseen authority. 'Those fires are at least two kilometres away. They may not even reach the area if the southerly blows itself out early. In the meantime, if a spot fire starts up, we can't do anything about it. We're supposed to huddle down here in the hall and wait to be lifted out?'

John Carmody was pacing the floor in front of Burton. His voice was not loud but the others in the hall had stopped talking and were watching him. 'There are still a lot of things to be done up there.' Carmody was addressing Roger Burton now. With conviction. 'We've got to lay out the fire hoses at the Solomons' and O'Conners'. We have to make final checks of all the houses.'

Carmody looked around the hall at the attentively silent residents. 'For God's sake,' he added, 'half the people in this hall should be up the hill with knapsacks ready to fight a spot fire. We should be planning how we're going to do a backburn.'

'They're evacuating everyone,' said Tony Thomas, walking up to Carmody with his mobile phone still in his hand.

Carmody turned on Thomas with hostility. He'd passed Thomas on his way down to the hall. Thomas was doing a live news report from the track and had cornered one of the neighbours for an interview. Carmody had skitted past the pair but had still heard Thomas's final statement to his microphone ' – terrorised little community fleeing the roar of another fire front'. As he strode down the track, Thomas's hyperbole ragged at Carmody. It was not so much the reporter's words that riled him. He was inured to media hype. It was the tone of his voice. It was the lascivious way Thomas said the words. Carmody realised that Tony Thomas was excited about the disastrous turn of events.

But already Carmody was forcing himself to calm down. He needed this media person. He may want to slash his ego with a few perfectly coined insults – he'd been practising some earlier that night – but he knew he might need the scumbag later.

'Listen, if you want to be of some use to us down here,' Carmody said as he faced the reporter in the hall, 'you can tell us what you know of the fire front that's heading this way.'

While Carmody was fingering the air in front of the reporter's chest, another resident, Harry Keogh, came into the hall. Briefly everyone turned to look at the new arrival. Keogh nodded silently to the sea of faces but he had the impression that people were not looking at him. They were looking at something else that arrived at the same time. The opening of the hall door had allowed angry gusts of soot to charge inside. The gusts whipped around the corners of the room, billowed up the walls and, as the door closed again, becalmed in the air above the residents. The soot wafted gently down around the people, settling in their hair, on their skin and, finally, on the floorboards.

'I know nothing more than you know,' retorted Thomas. 'There's a dirty great fire howling down the ridge and it's heading straight this way.'

'Can't you tell us what fire headquarters is saying about the front? Give us some information we can use?'

'I don't know what they're saying. I deliver the news, I don't own it,' said Thomas, tucking his mobile phone into a flap in his jacket.

'Well, your sort of news is useless to us,' said Mr Burton, chirping in from Carmody's left shoulder.

'It's not meant to be useful for you,' said Thomas, 'it's meant to be interesting for everyone.'

The mood of the room was heavy. Most of the residents were listening to the exchange from the front of the hall. Carmody, Burton and the reporter were in the middle. Emily edged up towards them. She felt obliged to smooth the tension. Already most of the residents thought of Thomas as a friend of hers. She too felt responsible for him. Although she wasn't sure whether this intimacy owed more to her nocturnal fantasy than it did to any real cameraderie.

'Listen everyone,' she said. 'I don't know if you realise how serious these fires are. Tony was telling me earlier that ash from these fires is falling in New Zealand. They are getting food parcels from Germany sent to fire headquarters. The President of the United States is said to be concerned!

'The whole world is worried about these fires,' she continued. 'Canada has offered to send us their computer software, which will predict exactly where the fires are, where they are heading and enable the army to fly over these areas and water-bomb the fires with a precision that – '

'Can you hear any planes overhead?' interjected Carmody. 'Can you hear any giant bomber planes dousing these fires tonight? What makes you think that a Canadian computer will be able to handle a Sydney bushfire better than us?'

'What makes you think *you* can fight a fire?' said Thomas, who had stepped back from Carmody and found a chair. As he said this he languidly propped his feet up on another chair. Even from that position he commanded the attention of the room. 'I can't see any yellow uniforms here tonight so obviously none of you are members of the bushfire volunteer brigade.'

'Roger Burton trained as a volunteer but that's not the point. Volunteer brigade members are not the only people who are capable of fighting fires,' said Carmody. 'Half the men here have had years of experience fighting fires. We all do our bit for maintenance procedures, we've been – '

'It doesn't matter how many times you've torched your backyards, if you're not an official firefighter then the authorities won't recognise you. You've got to be evacuated with the rest of them.' Thomas was examining his hands as he said this.

'We're as competent as anyone for fighting these fires – '

'Oh, you've got to be kidding,' said Thomas now facing Carmody, 'These fires are travelling in a six-kilometre-wide front, they have a few years of dry bush to consume along the way and a hot westerly to push them along. And you people are going to greet them with an overgrown hoe in your hands?' Thomas glanced dismissively at a McLeod tool.

Carmody had had enough. He turned, grabbed his helmet and strode to the door. Halfway to the door, he spun around and pumped his finger at the figure of Thomas. 'You, mate,' he said, 'don't even know what direction this wind is coming from! This is not a westerly. This is a southerly buster. And tonight that is not good news. Tonight, the buster is pushing this fire into the area at the rate of knots. And I'm not going to wait here for some Canadian computer, or some fictitious bomber plane to deal with it. And I'm certainly not going to wait here so some suburban cops can take me to an RSL club for the night while my place burns.'

Carmody's exiting boots echoed across the hall. Almost immediately, Roger Burton grabbed his helmet and strode after Carmody. The remaining group of residents stared at the backs of the two men and quietly considered what they feared would be one of the toughest decisions they would ever face.

The invitation lay heavily in the air. Emily swivelled her head from her father to Thomas, imploring Thomas with her eyes to do something. Surely, she thought, Thomas should be in charge here. He should exercise some authority and stop her father. He knew the procedure, he was in contact with headquarters. He should do something.

Thomas snapped a cigarette from his soft-pack, refusing to acknowledge the tension in the hall.

'Dad, you can't go out there again. We've been told we have to stay here,' she yelled as her father reached the door.

'Emily, I'm not asking anyone else to come with me. It's a decision everyone should make for themselves. I don't expect you to come,' said Carmody, adding with finality, 'I'll see you later.'

Emily's mouth was agape. Not only had she failed to stop her father but he had voiced something she did not want to think about. She shouldn't have to go out there into the fire, she told herself. Besides, she wasn't allowed to. Everyone was supposed to stay here. Arguments tumbled around in her mind. I'm a woman, they wouldn't expect a woman to go out there. And the law says we all should stay here. The authorities, the police, the media, they all say we should wait to be evacuated. Who am I to question them?

As Emily struggled with the jumble of thoughts, another neighbour followed the men outside. Then she recalled what she'd said to Mrs Parker on the track that afternoon: 'If the wall of flames from the west comes to town … I'll be in there with a bloody garden hose …' Her words resonated in her mind. Emily glanced towards the trestle table at the front of the hall. How could she offer to help with tea and scones after that statement? Would Mrs Parker remember it? And remind her of it? Emily looked at the McLeod tool that Tony Thomas had just sneered at. What the hell was she going to do in a fire?

Emily's dilemma wasn't made easier when a fourth man left the hall, propping open the door so he could carry a knapsack out with him. The wind entered the hall again. It carried a heavy load of debris. It shoved dust up the noses of the remaining residents. A few began coughing. Perhaps signalling their sensitivity to the force outside. Explaining their continued presence inside the hall to all those who heard the coughing. And convincing themselves of their need for shelter. As the door closed, silence descended on the hall.

The closing of the door seemed to close off options in Emily's mind. She let her mind fall into the void of weariness. Her gaze drifted across the hall. She saw a piece of ash dance indecisively in the air. Released from the wind, it was marooned in the quiet air like a boat without a rudder. Emily stared at the piece of ash to save herself from looking elsewhere. She wondered where the ash had come from. She switched on her imaginary camera and took it back to the birth of the ash. The camera saw the big piece of ash being torn off a tree in the heart of the fire. It focused on the ash as it was thrust up into the sky, carried up on the intense heat of the flames. Up past the branches of the trees, up above the tree line, beyond the reach of the flames into the cooling night sky. The ash had hung in the night air for a moment before it was picked up by the southerly wind. The wind pushed the ash to the north-east over the crowns of trees, over the small valley, over the roof of the Hegartys' house. The ash was cooling by then, losing its red glow. The camera saw the ash break in two and then continue travelling onward and downward, past the Curries' house, around the giant macadamia nut tree in Bo's backyard, over Carmody's roof where oranges were still damming water in the gutter, down the track and, suddenly, with a final gush, into the hall.

As the air cooled beneath it, the ash began to fall. It fell like a drunken sailor, weaving its way down along the warm eddies of the hall. It made a quick dive for the seat in front of her but just before it hit the back of the seat, it changed direction. It settled on Emily's hand.

Emily switched off the camera and looked down on her hand. The ash was still there. The wafer-thin piece of ash lay next to her left knuckle. She wondered whether it would blow itself off her hand. She hoped it would flitter away. It stayed on her hand and when Emily tried to brush it off, it smudged. Emily felt claimed. Marked.

The sound of television broke Emily's reverie. She could see the residents gathering around it. They began shushing each other as the introductory jingle to the news was played. Emily dashed up to the front of the hall and politely but insistently pushed her way to the front of the crowd.

The sight of a glitzy city hotel full of sharp suits and elegant women almost made Emily sigh with envy. Even the appearance of the toady Minister for Emergencies Services, Fred Hanes, surrounded by pretty-faced reporters made Emily homesick.

'Arriving at a cocktail party earlier this evening,' said the voiceover on the news report, 'the minister said that in future all those who lost their houses because of the fires would be given hotel accommodation.'

The scene switched to a close-up of the minister's face. 'The government,' said the minister, facing into the camera, 'is doing everything it can for the victims of the fire. If they have any grievances, I would expect to hear directly from them.'

The news footage switched to a shot of the reporter standing in front of the ritzy cocktail party. 'Earlier today, two victims of the Beattie Street fire revealed that they had been forced to spend two nights in a Masonic Hall where the toilet was located in a shed out the back and there were no facilities for washing – even for the simple task of washing their hands.' As the reporter said this, the vision switched from the glitz of the city hotel to the rear of an old hall. The camera panned around a stinking outhouse and rested on a hole in the wall, where no doubt there was once a handbasin.

'Did you all hear that?' shouted one of the residents. 'The government's going to put us all up at the Hilton for the night!'

A few other residents giggled. Another piped in, 'The minister said those who lost their homes would be in hotels, not those who get evacuated. We're going to have to be content here – ' Then another voice intoned, 'At least they had a toilet, have any of you remembered that this hall doesn't even have that?'

Emily, who had been trying to follow the news item without being distracted by the comments around her, shushed the group again. As their attention turned back to the news story, they could see the footage of Mary Peck running from her burning house with her bird cage in her hand. The footage was gripping. Even the fourth or fifth time. The position of the news camera in the centre of the road, the dirty grey smoke that formed the backdrop and the terror on Mary Peck's face as she ran down the centre of the road was incredibly similiar to the famous footage of the Vietnam War where a young naked girl was caught fleeing a napalm attack.

The image of Mary Peck running from her burning house was also tragic because, if you looked closely at the film, you could see that her bird was already dead. It was a lump on the bottom of the cage. The hall of residents hushed. This footage still brought a shocked silence whenever it was broadcast. And it was broadcast often. Tonight, though, in this smoky community hall, the footage also brought a frisson of fear. The residents focused less on the bird and more on the smoking inferno behind Mrs Peck. They craned to see whether her house had been devoured yet. They searched her face for signs of their own fear.

When the television news switched back to the scene of the minister at the cocktail party, the residents remained mute. It was Emily who broke the silence.

'Jack! That's Jack,' yelled Emily to the group as she caught sight of her brother milling around behind the minister. Even as she said this, the image of her brother had disappeared from the screen. The pretty face of the late night news presenter was filling the screen again.

'It was Jack,' Emily said to no one in particular. Another resident stretched forward and turned down the volume on the television. 'What was he doing there?' Emily muttered, more to herself than anyone else. Then, when the full irony of the situation had unfolded in her mind, she said indignantly, 'What the hell is Jack doing at a cocktail party, when we're all down here?' As she said this she looked around at the faces of the people surrounding her. As if to see who might have an answer. They looked embarrassed on her behalf. No one said anything.

Emily broke away from the group slowly. Still incredulous at the sight of Jack. The other residents parted silently to let her pass.

'You look like you need a smoke,' said Thomas, trying to break Emily's reverie as she wandered towards the back of the hall. He tossed a packet of cigarettes to her from his chair.

'Thanks,' said Emily. She caught the packet as it was lofted towards her.

Emily lit the cigarette and drew back with ballooning lungs. Her fifth cigarette in three years lacked none of the magic of the first. She inhaled again and, after a brief pause in her lungs, let the smoke leave her body through well-spaced lips. Still standing in the middle of the hall, she thought she should join someone – either sit with Thomas sharing a cigarette or mill around with the other residents. She looked at the small groups of people at the front of the hall. She knew most of them by sight, not necessarily by name. She knew most of their stories from her father and her unavoidable encounters with Mrs Parker, but they still seemed like strangers. She could see they weren't entirely comfortable with each other either – they talked to each other like close strangers. The way you talk to someone when you are forced into a relationship by proximity rather than choice.

As she watched the white smoke of her cigarette get acquainted with the more ethereal smoke of the bush, she noticed that old Mrs Grey was sobbing while her husband stared into the ether.

'Oh, Mrs Grey,' said Emily, quickly walking over to the old woman, 'the men are going to be all right. I'm sure they've just gone out to fix a few things up and they'll be back in no time.'

Mrs Grey stared into Emily's eyes, nodding. 'Do you think the fire will wipe out all the houses?' asked Mrs Grey, gathering a voice from the bottom of her throat.

'No, no I don't think the fire will wipe them all out,' lied Emily.

'Our house is further into the bush than anyone else's house, except for Bo's. They will be the first ones burned.'

Emily pictured the Greys' house. She'd always envied their house, its isolation, its sense of belonging to the bush. She didn't know what to say to Mrs Grey now. Platitudes seemed inappropriate.

'I wish I'd had time to take the Chinese rug out with us. It was my mother's. I remember playing on it as a child. It had such a thick, soft pile I would imagine it to be an emerald sea. It still has a grape juice stain that my brother made when he knocked my drink over in, in, 1916. Imagine that.' Mrs Grey did just that. Then added, 'Mr Grey thinks it still smells of the First World War!'

As she said this, she looked towards her husband. Mr Grey wasn't listening. Or didn't appear to be.

'But you got most of your precious things out, didn't you?' continued Emily.

Mrs Grey stared into the space in front of her. Emily could imagine her cataloguing the items that had been carefully placed in old cartons. Photos, documents, their wedding certificate, a few cheap and chipped statues, two old books, a pile of old silver trinkets, her royal wedding memorial tea cup, some doilies –

'Yes, Maeve,' said Mrs Grey, breaking from her reverie, 'I think I got the things that matter out of the house. After all, Mr Grey and I are both here, and that's all that really matters.

Emily smiled sadly at Mrs Grey. In the circumstances she thought it best to let Mrs Grey's mistaking her for her mother pass without comment. Her mother, thought Emily suddenly, would have handled this a lot better than she had just done. She would have known what to do in a disaster like this. She would have known her role.

'This must be awful for you, Mrs Grey,' said a solicitous voice from behind Emily. Hearing the sympathy in Thomas's gravelly voice, Emily turned to see him beside her. His brows were knotted with concern as he pointed his microphone at Mrs Grey.

'How long have you been living here in Flint Bay?' Thomas continued, staring forlornly into Mrs Grey's eyes.

'Oh, oh, I think it's forty-three years now,' said Mrs Grey, struggling for clarity.

'And your cabin up on the hill, you built that with your husband?'

'There was a two-room cottage on the land when we bought it in, um, in I've forgotten the exact year. My husband and I fixed up the old cottage and built the extra rooms on the back in, um, I think it must have been 1958.'

'It's a very pretty cottage,' said Thomas.

Mrs Grey wiped the tears off her face with impatient hands. During Thomas's questioning she had straightened in her chair and rearranged her dress. The propriety of an interview was important to Mrs Grey.

Emily watched this exchange with increasing incredulity. And anger. Thomas's solicitousness towards Mrs Grey was exposed in all its cynicism by the microphone that he held discreetly between himself and Mrs Grey. Emily kept expecting Mrs Grey to put a stop to the interview but the intensity of the conversation between them seemed to exclude her. And the rest of the room. And perhaps normal sensitivities.

'Where are you planning to live if the fires destroy your cottage?'

Even before Mrs Grey had a chance to digest this last question, her husband rose in a roar. 'Who gave you the right to interview my wife?' Mr Grey spluttered through teeth that were a little loose-fitting. 'We don't have to speak with you!'

Mr Grey wrapped his arms around his wife and gently hoisted her upright so they could walk to the other end of the hall. As he negotiated through rows of empty seats he turned again to Thomas. 'The fire is outside, sonny. The story is outside. Not in here with us,' said Mr Grey. Invigorated by anger, he added, 'Or are you too scared to get out there with the other men?'

The Greys turned their backs on Thomas and walked stiffly to join Mrs Parker and most of the other residents at the trestle table. Emily sat in embarrassed silence beside Thomas. Her silence, she thought, was as much a chastisement of Thomas as Mr Grey's outburst. Sitting mutely while he fiddled with his tape equipment, Emily half-expected Thomas to mumble an apology or an explanation. When, after a few more seconds, he had still said nothing, Emily glanced at him from the corner of her eye. He appeared to be blushing. Emily felt herself soften. Perhaps he didn't deserve the spit-laden vitriol of Mr Grey. Maybe they didn't understand what a journalist had to do to get the news. Was it fair to blame the system of news-gathering on the people who carried the microphones?

Emily breathed deeply and stretched her neck so she was staring at the ceiling. She envisioned herself from the perspective of the ceiling. She placed her imaginary camera on the light bulb that hung from the ceiling and pivoted the camera slowly around the room. It picked up two silent figures sitting in the middle of the hall and a knot of people buzzing around a table at the far end. Emily switched off the camera when she heard Tony Thomas muttering.

'Who are these people anyway?' he asked.

Emily looked at the other residents from the perspective of her chair. 'Well, Mrs Parker has been here for yonks. Her husband had lived in the Bay all his life and his father lived here too, although in a different house. Lots of these people have been here for generations ... Bo, that wildman you meet before, has lived here since the sixties. His family has had a weekender down here for decades, although I don't know what happened to the rest of the family.'

'That bloke is the weirdest thing I've ever seen. Positively simian,' interrupted Thomas.

Emily paused. She wasn't sure what simian meant. It didn't sound nice. 'Oh, I don't know about that,' she said. 'I think he's a bit of a savant.' Emily wasn't sure what savant meant either. She'd heard it used to describe Dustin Hoffman in a movie about a strangely gifted child. It was something to do with weird. But nicer. Certainly nicer than simian.

'Bunch of hillbillies, as you said,' said Thomas. Emily squirmed as Tony Thomas delivered her words back to her. It seemed okay for her to call the residents hillbillies. It didn't seem right for the reporter to make the same judgement.

'Dad has always joked that Flint Bay is a secretive place, that people come here to escape something. In the early days of Sydney settlement, scores of convicts escaped north and set up bark huts on the protected beaches of the area – lots of them didn't survive here for more than a few years. The ones who did survive were those who were able to farm the rocks for shell food or trap wallabies, and those who could fish without falling victim to the sharks that used to swarm here.'

'Sharks?' said Thomas.

'There used to be heaps of them. People would get taken by

sharks while standing in knee-deep water. And it happened all the time,' replied Emily. Seeing Thomas's attention straying she continued with her history.

'Later, the area became known as Smuggler's Cove when rum was the chief commodity of the community. Most of the rum for the settlement came in through the heads opposite Flint Bay. Even when free settlers began taming the northern beaches of Sydney in the nineteenth century, no genteel person ever felt safe in these parts.' As Emily related the history, she realised she was using the words her father had used. 'The whole northern area of Sydney was renowned for smugglers, escaped criminals, the socially retarded, boaties and fishermen. They all lived as neighbours but none of them would have asked too many questions of anyone else.'

Emily looked at the huddle of people around the trestle table, as if she suddenly saw them as descendants of the vagabonds and escapees who once lived here. She had always assumed that people became reclusive simply because they were living in a bush area – that the environment redesigned the person. Looking at the residents tonight, she wondered whether they were a bit that way before they came to the area. Perhaps they had simply found the right postcode for their personalities.

Tony Thomas was still fiddling with his tape equipment when he noticed Emily had stopped talking. He looked up at her. She looked strung-out. He couldn't decide whether he liked her looks or not. Sometimes, especially when she smoked, she looked husky, like a relaxed Judy Davis. But at other times she looked too sharp, a bit mean-faced. He took his eyes back down to his tapes and added, 'You know a lot about the area. Do you live here too?'

'No, no,' replied Emily giggling with embarrassment. She had noticed Thomas appraising her in a suggestive way. She'd felt a flush rise through her body under his gaze. He looked dangerous when he wasn't smiling. A bit cold-blooded. But exciting too.

'I don't live here,' she continued, 'my dad just tells me lots of stories about the place. I hardly ever listen to them but obviously I've retained some of them.'

'You seem to know the history off by heart,' continued Thomas. Emily paused to think about this. She too was surprised at how much she had retained. Perhaps she was more at home here in Flint Bay than she admitted. She wondered whether an environment could claim a person against her will. Whether a group of people could claim a new member against her will. And if Thomas thought of her as one of them, whether it had already happened. She changed the subject. 'I could do with another cigarette, if you're not rationing them already,' Emily said to him.

Thomas pushed the cigarette packet across the chair towards Emily and, as he stood up, said, 'He's wrong, you know. That old man, Mr Grey. The story is here with the people. Not with the fire. Fires don't talk, weep, yell or hurt. Especially not on radio. The story of the bushfires is a story about people.'

Emily watched Thomas wander off down the hall. He found his tape recorder and began setting things up for another report. He checked the read-out on the face of his mobile phone. She looked at her watch – almost eleven p.m. He never stops, she thought. Briefly, she wondered what was driving him. Tried to envisage how he might see their drama. She wondered what he was looking for down here in Flint Bay. An experience? Or an award?

Chapter twelve

Jack left the cocktail party full of uncertainty. What had Tom Cole meant when he said the front was moving into the western foreshores? Did he mean it was getting close? That it had arrived already? Or it might move in by tomorrow? Was he kidding him? Jack wished he'd had the sense to ask Cole about it rather than making the smart comment about sending down the helicopter.

He found his car, beeped its doors open and let himself settle into its leather embrace. He revved the engine and let the climate-control conquer the smoke that had sidled into the car with him. He had never seriously thought that fire would threaten his father's house. Even in the smoke-bound city of the last few days, Jack still thought of the fires as he thought of car accidents. They happened to someone else.

He remained unconvinced driving home up the highway. The sweet-smelling car wound its way effortlessly along the ribbon of tarmac, surrounded by psuedo-Tudor houses that wished they were in England. This, he thought, looking out at the lower reaches of the North Shore, belonged to a different world to that of fires. How could fire come this close to the city? How could the verdant belt of garden suburbs be threatened with a scourge that belonged to outback territory or colonial Sydney? It shouldn't happen in a post-industrial city where every second house had inground sprinklers.

Jack punched the radio button on. And almost missed. He was still piqued – at his father, at Jane, at the smarmy bureaucrat, at his wife. And whoever else came into his mind. He was also pissed.

The radio crackled into life: '... is coming under increasing pressure to solve the victims' accommodation crisis as the state of emergency nears the end of its fifth day. When the minister entered a cocktail party earlier this evening, he seemed tetchy with reporters about the issue.

'"The government is doing everything it can for the victims of the fire,"' intoned the voice of the minister, '"if they have any grievances I would expect to hear directly from them and not from you blokes."

'The minister is obviously under great pressure in this emergency. The opposition has already suggested that he should form a bipartisan committee to handle it and the federal government is known to be concerned about the handling of the situation.

'Of course, all eyes are still on the nine major fires burning out of control, one of which is nearing another housing settlement as we speak – '

Jack adjusted the tuning on the radio to rid it of crackle. Briefly he lost the station altogether. He cursed and slowed the car down. He tuned back into the radio in time to hear a mention of the words 'Flint Bay'.

'The fire storms have been heading this direction all day. The six-kilometre-wide front, fanned by the hot north-westerly, has been devouring the national park. Firefighters have been unable to do anything except watch its progress,' hissed the report. 'By this evening, when I arrived in this sleepy little bay, the writing was on the wall. This fire was going to sweep through the community of Flint Bay. As I speak, scores of residents are running down the hill, abandoning their homes and belongings, clutching pets and loved ones, frightened for their lives.

'I suppose in the scheme of things this is just another terrorised little community fleeing the roar of another fire front, but to the residents, this is their home, their life. Earlier I spoke to Beryl Parker ...'

As Jack heard the familiar echo of Mrs Parker's voice, he had
visions of a war zone. The towering flames howling above the
roofs of the houses of Flint Bay, crackling and exploding.
Residents stumbling down the hill, the old Greys half-dragged out
of their home by army reserve soldiers. His sister screaming as she
fled a wall of fire. His father retreating to a flotilla of boats that
was waiting in the bay with engines revving.

Jack Carmody tightened his grip on the steering wheel and,
with the bravado of wine, ignorance and fear, swung the car over
the double lines and pointed the nose of the Jaguar towards the
northern peninsula.

After a few minutes, Jack allowed himself to think about what
he was doing. Going down there, he thought. To do what? Jack's
mind slipped into blank again. Flames, booze, tiredness and
deflated lust were taking their toll on his intellect tonight.

Banging his father's number into his mobile phone, Jack listened as the phone's loud speaker buzzed. Burr, burr. Burr, burr.
The phone rang through the silence of his father's house. Jack
imagined the house abandoned. The ringing of the phone confirmed its loneliness. He wondered whether the house was
already on fire. Briefly he wondered if it might be dangerous to
ring a house that was on fire. It might electrocute his phone.

'Stupid, stupid,' he snarled at himself as he banged the hang up
button on the phone. The silence seemed incriminatory. Given up
already, the silence intoned.

Jack tried to think of someone else to ring. He mentally trawled
through his list of contacts. People in legal firms, on the Bench,
local and state politics, a few in media, medical specialties and
bureaucracy sprang to mind. None seemed appropriate. He
couldn't try Tom Cole again. There must be someone else. Jack
had always prided himself on his contact book – it had a nice
spread across the circles of influence. If a client needed a boost in
almost any department, Jack had a contact for it. He'd once been
able to help rescue a paraplegic client from a horror of a nursing

home by getting his friend in the Department of Health to arrange for an inspection of the nursing home. He'd been able to get Sarah into a law course at university through an old friend in the vice-chancellor's office. Jack had once quipped to one of his partners that everyone he could ever possibly need in life was listed somewhere in his contact book, except a plumber. The partner had replied that no one knows a friendly plumber because no one wants to be friends with someone who charges ninety dollars an hour to sort through your sewage. 'Not unless he's a lawyer,' quipped Jack.

Now he would have to add firefighter to plumber.

As Jack neared the northern waters of Sydney he noticed the air outside the car darkening. Howls of wind were throwing dirty black palls across the road. Almost like fog, he thought. But fog wasn't as dirty, mean or menacing as this stuff. Driving along the deserted main road with smoke-fogged street lights dimly showing him the way, Jack felt he was driving into hell. No one else was around, none of the houses were lit. Maybe no one was at home. Maybe everyone up here had been evacuated. The fires may have jumped the bay. Maybe no one had told him he was driving into …

Jack slowed his speed. He tensed so he would be able to see or hear whatever was coming his way. He'd had this feeling before. This feeling of not knowing what everyone else knew. It had been a stinking hot afternoon in the late sixties. He'd driven his old FJ Holden down to the surf and ran like a madman across the searing hot sand, stripping off his clothes as he neared the water. Still running, he'd leapt over the small surf, dived under and started swimming for the horizon. When he'd felt his body cool, he'd stopped swimming and turned onto his back to float. Out past the breakers, the water was calm. And empty. It took Jack a while to realise he was alone. A minute or so. Suddenly he'd spun himself upright and looked around him for company. There was nobody in this surf, which stretched a kilometre across one of the most popular beaches in Sydney.

When he squinted towards the beach he could see lifeguards waving to him. It wasn't a cheerio wave. Jack felt his lunch push against his sphincter. The beach, he realised, was closed. It wasn't closed because of rough surf. The surf was gentle. It wasn't closed because of blue-bottles, he thought, looking gingerly around him.

Even as he started swimming for shore, Jack knew why the beach was closed. There had been a shark alarm. Everyone had left the water. No one was entering the water, except madmen who charge down the beach without looking at signs.

He expected to feel a sickening crunch on his thighs any minute. He swam with his head clear of the water. He could see lifeguards readying a boat. He wondered who would reach what first. He hoped to God he wouldn't see the shark coming. If a shark is going to get me, he thought, I don't want to see it coming. Jack swam. Madly. Wildly. As he reached shallower waters where he could just stand, he wondered whether he could run faster than he could swim. He felt capable of running on top of water. He tried to run in chest-high water. It felt like running in mud. He could see a small crowd of people staring at him from the water's edge, unwilling to venture further. He could see himself in this scene. Caught between the lifeguards on the shore and a circling shark, running in slow motion.

The road wound around the northern beaches, taking Jack into its darkening heart. Jack longed to see another car. The dimly lit light poles waved him onward, past dark houses, past overgrown canopies of suburban bush patches and finally down to the picnic grounds that looked out over Flint Bay. Jack turned the car into the carpark that faced the western horizon and recoiled from the scene across the bay.

It was glorious. It was, he thought, rolling the word around his mucus-thickened mouth, glorious. Across the inky bay, the hills of the national park were being devoured by a wild party of flames. They seemed as high as the hills themselves. The sky was throbbing with an orange glow. The dark hills were etched into relief and the bay reflected a deeper crimson.

Jack blinked back tears at the majesty of the world alight. He felt himself enveloped in the force of the fire. The flames flickered in the pupils of his eyes, the glow turned his white shirt a hazy pink. He was being kissed and embraced by the force. Not realising that he had been holding his breath, he took a gulp of air and swallowed a hard glob in his throat. Opening the car window, he felt the burnt tinge of cool air hit his cheek. Strange, he thought, that any wind coming from the direction of that inferno would be cool. The wind was carrying the din of crackling bush, the whooshing sound of fire that moves through the bush like the wind. Wind on fire.

The aroma of burnt bush was deeply evocative. It carried memories of camping weekends, of loitering around barbecues built on twigs, of his father burning off carefully raked piles of leaves on still Saturday afternoons. Jack tried to make sense of the scene, to bring the dimensions of reality to the scene. He knew the hill closest to him was big – a hundred, a hundred and fifty metres high. And the flames that were consuming the crown of that hill were almost as high as the hill again. It didn't make sense. Nor did his feeling of awe. This, he thought, should be the worst sight in the world. It *is* the worst sight in the world. How can I marvel at it? How can it be so beautiful?

Struggling out of the car so he could stand at the open door, Jack leaned on the roof of his car and rubbed his open hands over his face. Even when he left his hands cradling his face, he could still see the glow of the fires in the blackness of his eyelids.

In the fires of his mind, he tried not to see his father and sister. He tried not to place his father's house on the map of that fire. It wasn't near the homes, he told himself. It hadn't swept into the Bay. He agreed with himself. The fire wasn't at his father's doorstep. Yet.

Jack banged his palms onto the roof of the car. 'Okay,' he said, 'I'm here. I'm coming over. I don't know what the hell I'll do when I arrive on that hellish hillside but I'll come and share your fire.' As Jack said this to himself, he opened his eyes, tore his jacket off and threw it into the car. He slammed the car door shut and strode over the small park towards the waterfront.

His mind engaged again, Jack looked around. He was surprised there was no one else here. He looked along the line of cars; one or two of them had sight-seers inside. But nothing else. No fire-fighting crews. No police. No army volunteers. He thought the place should be teeming with activity. Again he felt as if someone had failed to tell him something.

He was running now. Along the beach. Looking for ... a boat, he told himself. I need a boat. No, no, he thought again still running, a ferry. I should be able to catch a ferry. He looked up at the wharf. It was empty. He slowed to a jog, trying to think more clearly. A water taxi, he thought. He sped up again as he remembered a water taxi sign on the boatshed next to the wharf.

By the time Jack arrived at the boatshed he was puffing. He knocked on the huge, timber rolling doors. Pathetic, he thought. *He* could barely hear the knocks. He paused to get his breath before yelling out.

'Yoohoo!' Jack cursed himself again. The call sounded like the slightly embarrassed call of a neighbour asking for a cup of sugar.

'*Yo!*' he yelled more firmly, 'Anyone at home! Yo! I need a taxi.' Jack waited. He expected a reply. A light to turn on. A door to open. Nothing. After another thirty seconds, he called again.

'All the taxis went out earlier,' said a voice behind Jack. He spun around to find a young man standing with his arm resting over the shoulder of his girlfriend.

'I need to get over the bay,' said Jack quickly. 'Do you have a boat?' The man shook his head.

'Do you know anyone down here who does? Or someone who knows one of the neighbours who might have access to a boat?'

The man shrugged his shoulders. Jack heaved a breath in disgust and began to move off. The girlfriend said to his back, 'There's a rowboat down on the beach. It's got oars too.'

Jack waved without looking back and began running along the beach. He too had seen a small rowboat when he'd first jumped down onto the sand.

As Jack closed on the boat, he saw it was tiny. Held two adults, maximum. He slowed as he neared it. Its oars were tucked neatly under it, the tips just protruding. Jack stood over the boat and looked towards Flint Bay again to re-examine the distance across the bay. He half laughed as a big breath left his body. I'm going to face *that*, in *this*? he said to himself, looking at the red glory across the bay. It seemed to ridicule him. To mock him. To call to him. Teasingly. He was mesmerised by the sight again. It was so awe-inspiring, he just wanted to sit down on the sand and watch its dance, absorb its energy and feel its light, dusty rain on his skin.

He tore his eyes away from the sight across the bay. It's the last place in the world anyone would want to be, he said to himself, so why am I rushing to get there? He stared at the rowboat again. Indecision and fear had turned him to stone. 'Just do it,' he told himself as he grabbed hold of the boat's sides. 'Just fucking do it.'

Jack dragged it down to the shore. His shoes made a sucking sound as they sank into the wet sand. The boat was surprisingly light. The oars probably weighed as much as the boat. At the water's edge, Jack balanced the oars in the boat as he prepared to leap nimbly into the boat. He leapt and was ricocheted towards the other side of the boat. He wobbled inside the boat for a few seconds. As he did this, he could see that the couple he had met earlier were watching him from the park. The man was still standing with his arm around the girl. Jack readied the oars and began rowing. He asked himself how long it had been. About twenty years. The last time he had rowed anything was when he was a schoolboy. The small boat veered erratically as Jack rowed in the shallow water. He swore repeatedly as his rowing skills failed to make a reappearance. On one stroke, he hit a moored yacht. He swore at the yacht. He was sweating so hard, his suit pants were wet and clinging. He kept looking behind himself to see where he was heading. And to see what he was about to hit. He couldn't believe he could put this much effort into rowing and still not be clear of the moorings. How long will it take to cross the whole of the bay? What are the chances of making it at all? Jack glanced around. The bay widened to his left. It widened into the Pacific Ocean. Jack stroked again, a little harder. The wind was coming from the south. Jack was rowing into it. Would it push him off course? Into the Pacific Ocean? Jack put more effort into it. He heaved back on an oar so vigorously, he lost balance and the oar whacked his kneecap. Jack roared in pain. He let go off the oars and nursed his knee. The throbbing echoed through his body. He squeezed his eyes together. A tear escaped each eye. He told himself not to cry. But the very thought made him teary. He let the boat drift.

When he felt the throbbing subside, Jack opened his eyes. He flushed with shame as he imagined the couple looking at him from the shore. He closed his eyes again. He didn't want to witness his shame. He let the boat drift back to shore.

Jack felt the boat nudge the bottom a few times before the rocking and jerking of its beaching was too much. He got out and pulled it back up the beach. He didn't look around. He didn't want to see if anyone was still there. He walked stiffly back to the car and settled into the driving seat. It was only then that he allowed himself to look around again. The couple had gone. The carpark was quiet. The fire looked triumphant.

Jack watched the fires through the windscreen. He wound up the window. As the distant din of fire retreated, he could hear pop lyrics on the car radio. When he turned on the air-conditioner, the air cleared of smoke and the aroma of leather returned. Jack slumped back in the car seat. He was, he thought, sore, wet, hung over, exhausted and … he thought of something else. And still over here. He stared out the windscreen towards the western horizon. The boats off the beach were turned into the wind and they, too, were watching the spectacle on the horizon. Absurdly, he felt like he was at a drive-in movie.

Chapter thirteen

As soon as he left the hall, John Carmody felt calmer. Striding up the hill with a knapsack banging against his back, his mind was full of priorities. Together with Roger Burton and the two others who had followed him, he had carved the neighbourhood into divisions. Four men to check twenty-five houses. Not a lot, but enough. Ignoring the whipping southerly that was amplifying the ripping and cracking sounds of the approaching fire, he mentally catalogued the things he would have to do as he checked his neighbours' houses.

He was mildly, but pleasantly, surprised. In the last few days, he had never been certain that he would be able to transcend the drama ... but as he strode up the hill he was invigorated with purpose. The anguish of waiting was over.

Carmody thought of surgeons who were able to dig into the bodies of accident victims without acknowledging their tormented faces. He thought of lawyers who could rise in court and demolish the reputation, the career, the spirit of the person sitting on the other side of the courtroom and never once think of the person as a fellow human being. It was the luxury of purpose, thought Carmody. Those who had a role to play in a drama could rise above it. Escape it even.

By the time he had reached his house, Carmody had observed the exact state of the area that he was to oversee – the seven houses that had been placed under his care stretched over an area of three hundred-odd metres. He knew which of the houses were most vulnerable; which would have to be protected first. He knew which of the householders he could trust to have prepared their houses for the fires and who would have done a sloppy job.

Heading west to those houses that would be first threatened, Carmody kept scanning his immediate surroundings for signs of ash. The stuff that was falling now was big, flat ash. Some pieces felt hot as they landed on his skin. He tried not to think of the mountain of flame that was heading in his direction. He knew roughly where the front of the fire was. He didn't need to imagine the awesome strength of nature on the rampage. The elements at their chaotic best. Nature as the demented drunkard, lurching across the landscape, smashing everything in its path, leering at man's efforts to stop it, pissing in the face of authority.

The fire, thought Carmody focusing again, was in the small dip in the hillside that lay just to the south-west of the face of his hillside. It would have just moved through one of the biggest kitchen middens in the area. He smiled when he thought of the giant pile of shells, bones and rock fragments. None of that will be destroyed, he thought. Nor will the rock carvings. No wonder middens and rock carvings were the only surviving witnesses to Aboriginal life pre-settlement. Fires wiped everything else out. Eventually and inevitably, everything in the Australian bush was wiped out by fire.

As he strode up the hill, covering the few hundred metres of bush that separated houses from waterfront, Carmody thought of those who had fought fires before him. He sympathised with the early settlers arriving from the damp, misty streets of England into an endless stretch of landscape that erupted into fire every summer. He recalled reading in an ancient copy of the *Sydney Gazette* an account of the fire of 1805. That fire had almost wiped out the northern half of the colony – from Lane Cove and everything to the west and north. And what was the response from the governor? An order banning the smoking of pipes or carrying of firebrands near haystacks. As if that would make a difference. In the misty homelands of early settlers, fires may have only posed a problem near haystacks but in their new country, fire could race across the continent. How strange it must have been for the pasty-faced English. No wonder they feared Aboriginal people with the gourds of fire they carried with them like a giant packet of matches. A report in a later copy of the *Gazette* knew where to lay the blame for fires. 'Accidents are frequently to be attributed to the uninterested heedlessness of the natives, in transporting fire sticks from place to place and leaving unquenched their fires,' the *Gazette* had said. The report continued that white settlers must take responsibility for fires 'as there is no possibility of preventing dangers arising from the common habits of a barbarous race.' Such ponderous reports missed something. Aboriginal people weren't threatened by fire. The people who were devastated by fire were those with something to lose – those who owned crops, houses, barns, livestock. Aboriginal people trod lightly on the landscape. They had nothing to lose. Nothing that wouldn't replenish itself. Fire was a white person's problem.

Carmody started his rounds at the Greys' house. He climbed the hill behind the house and saw that their downpipes were plugged and water still lay in the gutters. All their windows were closed. The small space under their cottage had been blocked off with sheets of corrugated iron to prevent ashes from flying under-neath the house. Carmody knew the Greys had experienced bush-fire before. It showed. But, he thought, spying the garden hose laid out over the lawn, it had been some time since their last fire. The hose looked pathetically optimistic against the howling dance on the horizon. It might be able to cope with a spot fire but, if it came up against this front, it would melt even before the flames reached the boundary of the property. Carmody briefly envisioned the face of a man standing in front of a fire holding a hose that had just melted. He was relieved most of the neighbours were in the community hall.

Moving onto the next house, Carmody made a tally of his neighbours. Most, indeed, were in the hall. Mr Burton, Bruce

Leonard and Solomon had followed him out of the hall. Bo …
Carmody hadn't seen Bo since earlier that evening. He stopped in
his tracks, trying to envisage where Bo might be. The cabin? The
water's edge, waiting around his rowboat, up in the hills near his
caves? Bo, he decided, could be anywhere. But wherever he was,
he was probably all right. If anyone knew the moods of the bush,
it was Bo. He read his environment like others read street signs.
Carmody began moving again, thinking of Bo. It was Bo who had
warned Carmody of the vulnerable state of the bush last winter. Not
in scientific descriptions. Bo had mumbled something like 'ground's
getting thick, John' when he passed Carmody along the track. It
was not an off-hand comment. Bo never made off-hand comments.
He never said anything unless it was important. So Carmody had
dwelt on the comment, remembered it as he was walking through
the top track the next day. By the end of that week, Carmody had
checked his old fire hoses, the petrol pump, and had even cleared
a few dead bushes from the side of his verandah.

Approaching the next house along the hillside, Carmody felt
the ground beneath his feet soften. He took another step. His foot
made a splash. The ground was soaked. Not just soaked, it was
running with water. He followed the source of water, his mind
unable to come to grips with any logical reason for the hill to be
bubbling with water. Reaching the rear of the house, Carmody
heard the source. Water was pouring from the tap at the base of
the water tanks. Someone had turned on the tap. And left it on.

In a community that lived on the water levels in their tanks, this
was unthinkable. In Flint Bay, people had been bankrupted and
still been able to live here, they'd been jailed, divorced, infirmed,
crippled and mentally broken down and still been able to live
here. Septic systems had broken down and people had stayed.
Fridges had been bare and they'd gone fishing. But no one could
stay without water.

With a fire approaching, water was the first and last line
of defence. Water was dammed in gutters, sprayed over dry

weatherboards, soaked into roof tiles. In the absence of a carefully carved fire break, water was imperative for a safe backburn.
Without a few hoses to control a backburn, even a controlled fire
could turn back on the firefighters.

Carmody rushed, as fast as his gammy knee would allow, up to
the tank and turned the tap off. He knocked his knuckles on the
rings of the tank to discover how much water had been lost.
Water remained in only the last three rungs of the tank. The
Mathews' house was almost indefensible. As Carmody groaned
with incomprehension and sadness, he heard the gushing of
water from further to the east. Running, loping along to the next
house, he headed straight for the back where he knew the water
tanks were. He'd helped paint these tanks just a year earlier – a
dull grey/green colour that was designed as an apology to the
natural bush environment.

By the time he'd got around the back of the house, he'd
guessed what he would find. Another tap, fully open, letting
mega-litres of water rush out over the lip of the bucket that was
placed there to catch drips. A stream of water was already eroding
the ground under the house, pushing small stones, children's toys
and old boating equipment out from under the house and further
down the hillside.

Carmody twisted the tap off and tapped the rungs again. About
eleven rungs left. He did some quick calculations. With the scarce
rainfall of the last year, most of the tanks down here were only
half full or less. This tank may have started the day with only fifteen to twenty rungs of water. It was down to eleven. The
Mathews to the west had only three rungs. Whoever had done
this was moving along towards the east and wasn't too far in
front.

Already rushing off in the direction of the Purves's house,
Carmody could see the figure of a person hunched at the rear of
the house. Carmody almost shouted, 'Stop.' The cry was in his
throat when he realised he would have to do more than shout.

Something in the figure's movements suggested that a vocal rebuke would not have much impact. Carmody began closing ground between himself and the figure. The sounds of his approach were swamped by the gushing of water and the howl of the wind through the casuarina stand. He felt like a silent avenger, swooping on a scene of carnality. Then Carmody realised something else. He wanted to manhandle this person. He wanted to tackle the figure with a full body blow, wrestle the scum to the ground, grind his face into the fresh ooze, slam his knee into the puny back and …

With each pained step Carmody took to this, this – it was a man, he could see now – he felt anger clogging his throat, his jaws lock. He felt a fury rising from his guts. A fury that, even in the blood-lust of anger-yet-to-be-spent, frightened him. What if I start kicking the man and never stop? Just kick him and kick him and – and what if it feels good? What if it feels so good to lay a boot in that I won't stop?

Pounding over to the man, Carmody felt himself split in two. One part of him was striding across a rocky garden with his eyes locked onto its prey, blood rushing in his ears, heart pounding, chest expanding with gasps of anticipation and arms held stiffly in a pose that could only be used for pummelling. Another part of himself was slightly above this figure, hovering around tree level. It was watching the scene with no ability to intervene. It was able to rationally predict what the figure storming over to the house might do to the man who was still oblivious to the presence of another. It didn't like the projected outcome.

By the time Carmody had closed the distance, he was almost running. His step was light with power. His body dense with anger. He didn't recall the first contact. He simply became aware that he was rolling in the mud with the man. In slow motion. Watching the look of utter surprise cross Bruce Leonard's face as he yelled, 'Whhaaatt.' Carmody didn't remember much after that – except glimpses of Leonard's face disappearing into the mud, rising again, mouth agape, sucking mud. From somewhere just behind him, Carmody heard the snarling of an animal. It sounded like a pissed-off bear. He suspected but was too preoccupied to realise the sound was coming from deep within himself.

Carmody paused. As the blood subsided in his head, he heard the voice of reason break through. 'Cut it out. Cut that out, now.' The voice seemed to come from a distance. Carmody closed his eyes, poised over the prone figure. When he opened them again, he was startled. Roger Burton was coming up the hill towards them still yelling, 'What the hell is going on!' Carmody wasn't sure what was going on. He looked down at Bruce Leonard pawing the mud with his hands, his head tucked down into his shoulders and a pathetic voice making pleading sounds. Carmody's knap-sack lay next to Bruce Leonard. The bottom corner had traces of fresh blood and hair.

'He was letting all the water out,' said Carmody blankly. He loosened his grip on Bruce Leonard's shirt and pushed himself into an upright position.

'I was flooding the hill,' said Bruce, pausing to spit something from his mouth. 'If it's soaking wet, the fire won't have a chance.'

As Bruce turned his head, hesitantly, to face his neighbours, both Carmody and Burton stepped back. Bruce was a mess. Blood, mud, old ash, skewed hair, rumpled and torn clothes, an eye that was beginning to bloat. A messy package of a human being.

'That,' said Roger Burton to Bruce, 'is the dumbest thing I have ever heard.'

Bruce pushed himself off the ground with great effort. 'I sup-pose you two think you can fight this bastard fire with a garden hose?' He spat into the ground. Part of a tooth hit the earth. 'If flooding the hillside is the only thing I can do to fight this bastard, then that's what I'll do. I'm not going to sit in a hall with a bunch of women while the Bay burns.'

Bruce Leonard's head fell forward into his hands. Roger Burton stared at him silently. He didn't dare look at Carmody, who was facing the ground behind them.

Carmody was appalled at himself, at the monster that had reared from inside him. Most shameful was the fact that the monster was familiar. He'd lost his temper before. Twice. Both times with awful consequences. He thought the demon was buried forever. Buried beneath old age and remorse. He was frightened at its return.

By the time Carmody and Roger Burton had half carried, half dragged Bruce Leonard down the hill to the community hall, he looked a worse mess. Mrs Grey almost fainted when the three of them literally fell into the hall. Beryl Parker took one look at the scene and began fossicking in her bags for the first-aid kit. Everyone else stood staring at the scene, waiting for an explanation. Everyone except Tony Thomas.

'What happened to him?' asked Thomas.

'He had an altercation with a snot-nosed possum,' said Burton. Menacingly to discourage discussion.

'Don't give us that. What happened?' repeated Thomas.

'It's over with now, let's just get back to fighting these fires,' said Burton.

Tony Thomas looked incredulously at Roger Burton and, reading guilt into his silence, turned to Carmody. 'What did you do to him?'

Carmody fought for self-control. Before he could respond, Bruce Leonard lifted his bloodied, muddy face and leered into Thomas's face. 'Piss off, will ya?'

'I'll find out,' said Thomas to no one in particular. 'You can't expect to bash a man to within an inch of incoherence and get away with it. There are still laws that apply, even in cases of emergencies.'

Thomas felt the press of bodies as residents circled him.

'Why isn't a young man like you helping fight the fire rather than harassing old women? asked one of them.

'You're not doing *us* any favours,' joined in Mrs Parker. 'You're just taking our stories and using them for your listeners' entertainment. This is not a public service you're doing, you're just satisfying the public prurience – '

'Why don't you do a decent report on us for once,' injected another, 'come on, do a decent report while we watch.'

Thomas could see this getting ugly. He felt he was caught inside a stoning circle and he had nothing to shield himself with. Except righteousness. Quickly he tried to switch to mediation mode, think of a calming statement; something that would diffuse the anger. Nothing. He could think of nothing. Someone thrust the mobile phone into his hand. Someone else was saying, 'Go on, let's have a decent report.'

Thomas stared dumbly around him. From behind the front row of people, Carmody pushed through. Only he and Bruce Leonard had failed to be swept up in the emotion. He watched the anger. Happy at first. Then vindicated. Then concerned. Then when they shoved the mobile phone into the reporter's hand, he'd seen what should be done.

'Lay off,' said Carmody. 'There's no way we can make this creep do a news report that he doesn't want to do. Are we all forgetting that the fire is roaring into our valley? That we have only an hour or so to prepare; that we should be up the hill checking for spot fires?'

The mob didn't move. Carmody looked at the reporter. Then he saw the mobile phone in his hand. 'We don't need him to distract us,' Carmody continued, 'but we could use his mobile phone.'

As Carmody focused on the phone, Thomas squeezed it closer to his chest. Carmody's intervention had returned a bit of gumption to Thomas. He needed the phone. It was the link with his news room. It was his link with rescue services, with water taxis. It was his link to the real world. Without it, Thomas thought, I am stuck with this bunch of hillbillies, forced to wait for help like them. Caught in hell's waiting room.

Carmody's claim on the mobile phone had been a spontaneous one, but as he stared at the device he began to realise what a powerful tool it could be. They could take it up the hill with them and co-ordinate a backburn. They could use the phone for calling fire headquarters.

Carmody stretched out his arm towards Thomas, ready to receive the phone. And doing so, he got an inkling of what the withdrawal of the phone might do to Thomas. Sensing the shift of power, Carmody smiled at Thomas. The quiet smile of a winner. Carmody and his small band of fire-fighters exited the hall.

When they saw Thomas push the phone into Carmody's hand, the rest of the residents also recognised the importance of the hand-over. As they saw this, their anger dissipated. Thomas without his communication lines was no longer a threat to them. He seemed to shrink as he turned away from the group.

Emily refrained from looking in his direction. Losers, she thought, deserved the space of silence. Instead she leant back in her chair and took herself off in her imaginary camera. It roved around the ceiling, taking in the scene below. Tony Thomas was perched on the edge of a chair, intently cleaning his tape recorder. Emily was a few rows of chairs in front of him, turned away from him, staring into the rafters. Most of the others had drifted off to the television set, now switched on. The remaining residents were arranged in stiff rows in front of it, their attention to the screen total. Emily's imaginary camera zoomed in on the television. The screen was full of flames. It was a familiar picture. Not just because the sight of flames was now becoming such a common occurrence. It was the contour of the land being devoured by flame that was familiar. Emily jerked up in her seat as she focused on the screen herself. It was another news item, another fire. But not just another fire. Emily quietly lifted herself out of her chair and walked towards the television, still not taking her eyes from the screen.

'Is that – ' Emily murmured before she stopped herself asking the question. The television camera was now panning back from the fire. Across Flint Bay. She groaned as she realised this television footage was being taken from one of the suburbs across the other side of the bay. They were filming Flint Bay's fire. Emily had reached the other residents in front of the TV now. No one said anything. They could barely hear the commentary of the fire because someone had turned the volume down earlier. No one wanted to turn it up. They stood watching the film of the fire that was arriving behind them.

The howling outside was getting hotter, denser. And louder. If they turned around now and peered out the southern window, they would see what's on TV, she thought. But no one stirred. Then Emily turned from the group, scooped up a helmet from a chair and strode towards the door of the hall. When she felt the eyes of the group following her out, she half turned and said, 'I'm off to help fight the fire.'

Chapter fourteen

Emily regretted her decision as soon as she'd closed the hall door behind her. The wind raced down the hill and slapped her around the face, as if it had been waiting for her like a thug in an alley. It no longer had the coolness of a southerly. These winds had just passed through fires. They were warmed up, dirtied and confused.

The air before the fire front seemed to belong to its own weather system. It swirled around, changing directions, whipping to and fro. Crazy winds. Emily felt the wind ripping at her skin, scorching her eyeballs and slapping her senseless. And she felt her resolve fade. She turned back to the door. She couldn't do that either. She couldn't go in there and face the waiting again. She'd waited. She'd sweated it out. She'd served tea with Mrs Parker. She'd huddled with the old women and bewildered men. And yet, and yet, she thought, turning to face the hill again, she didn't want to face the thug up the hill, either.

'You're an arsehole, Thomas,' Emily spat back at the hall door. She breathed deeply. She didn't know why she had said that. He was hardly to blame for the creature up the hill. But he'd let her down. She'd thought that he would be her lightning rod to reality. She'd clung to him in the hope of remaining in his reality, the real world. That reality had slipped away. Emily slapped at the door-jamb of the doorway and began stomping up the hill.

Forcing her legs to move, she wondered whether she might be going to her death. If she was, she felt she didn't have any choice in the matter. But she wasn't going far, she realised, if she didn't have a torch. Emily kicked the ground as she looked along the dark trail. To go inside, even to retrieve her torch, was unthinkable. She might never come out again. Pausing, panting with emotion, Emily looked up the hill and saw torchlight moving in the bush near her father's house. Well, someone's up there and I know the path well enough. Without another thought, Emily willed herself up the hill.

Soon, sooner than she'd anticipated, Emily neared the wavering torchlight and in the dim light could just see the outlines of her father's body.

'Dad, Dad,' she roared. Or what she hoped was a roar. It was more the echo of a roar. But it worked. She could see her father turn in her direction and then flick the torchlight on her face. 'I'm here,' she said.

Carmody's torchlight caught Emily's face like a still photograph. The moment the torchlight hit her features, they were frozen in a pose that resembled the classic wartime moment – a distressed woman, battered and dirty and bereft.

'Emily,' Carmody said in a tone that was half question, half relief. 'Emily,' he said again. He felt happy, relieved, confused and finally tender. Waves of love swept over him. In the freeze-frame of the torchlight he could see his little girl's pain. And her courage. And her fear. As she climbed the last few metres to her father, Emily wanted to throw herself around his ankles. She even looked at his boots and half imagined herself clinging to them, wrapping herself around his ankles. Instead, she said with a sobriety she didn't feel, 'I've come to help.'

Carmody chanced one hug of his girl. A deep warm hug that he hoped would say all that he couldn't. Gently pushing her away from him, he said, 'Nice to see you. Come on, we've got lots to do. Grab the fire hose for me, while I try to get the pump going.' Carmody kept talking as he passed the heavy fire hose to Emily. 'Bo has just joined us, so we've got a decent crew together. We only need half a dozen to handle a backburn, as long as the wind isn't too nasty. But it's dropping already. Southerly busters generally only last about twenty minutes, and this buster has been raging for a good half-hour already. Can you feel it dropping?'

Emily nodded. She couldn't hear everything her father was saying. The wind was whipping it away before the words reached her. 'I thought the fire was creating the winds,' she said, fright constricting her voicebox.

'It's a bit of both.' Carmody sounded enthused with purpose. 'But the southerly that was behind this front is certainly easing.' Emily nodded. She didn't believe her father but she could see his enthusiasm, she could follow his gestures and she could sense his power. Emily looked down at the thick hose that was weeping small droplets of water. It wasn't turned on at the moment but it had obviously been turned on. Standing in the middle of a clearing holding the hose, she felt stupid. Like a gardener in hell. As her eyes adjusted to the murky blackness, she could make out other figures to the east of the house. One, she knew, must be Bo because of his strange gait. The others she couldn't recognise through the smoke. Soon she felt another presence behind her. In the quietening of her mind she could hear it better now. Roaring and crackling. She could see its glow reflecting in the windows of the house she was facing. Even as she stared away from it, she could see that the glow was lightening the ground around her.

When Emily finally turned to the west and saw how close the fire was, she almost dropped the hose and ran. One part of the fire front had fingered out in front to the main line and was only one or two hundred metres up the hill. The flames were as close as they were tall. She didn't run but stood transfixed by the flames. As she looked into the fire, she could see its dimensions – first the smoke, then the flames, then the blackened quietness behind the flames. She could see the destructive power in the blackened trees that formed the third dimension of the fire. Staring insensately into this monster that had been stalking her for days through the media and then here on the hillside, she realised what she was looking at. She was looking at her own cowardice. She could see all the cowardly things she'd even done approaching her. All the things she should have done but was too afraid to do, all things she should have been but didn't become because it was too hard.

'Dad, the fire is on our hillside already. Dad, it's here. Should we be here too?'

'Well, we were here first.' Carmody yelled. 'Come on, Emily, we've got the backburn started. The others have gone further along to the west to control it there, we have to keep an eye on it here.'

When Emily turned towards the bush that lay just behind the string of houses, she was amazed to see flames had just started licking up the hill from behind them.

'What have they done?' she said, her voice rising in pitch.

'Emily, keep a hold of yourself, this is the backburn. Roger has started it on the western edge and we'll move it along to the back of the houses and let it burn up the hill to meet up with the front.' As he said this, Carmody busied himself checking the operation of a drop torch. A shaft of flame dropped from the container onto the grass. He quickly extinquished it with his boot. 'It's a simple strategy. We start a little fire here so it will burn the fuel in front of the main fire and hopefully stop the huge bloody thing moving into our area.'

'That's the most stupid thing I – ' Emily's response was cut off by the sound of a huge tree hitting the ground. Hearing its branches cracking down through the branches of other trees did nothing to prepare her for the thwack as the trunk hit the ground or the rumble in the earth she felt through her boots.

Emily leapt. Even before her feet hit the ground, her eyes were darting around looking for a refuge. Carmody let go of the drop torch and grabbed her by the shoulder. He tried to stare into her eyes but when he couldn't reach her, he slapped her lightly around the face.

'Okay, okay, okay, okay,' said Emily. 'I'm fine, I'm fine.' She stepped back from him with an indignant look on her face. 'It's okay to be scared of this, you know. Most sane people would jump if a giant forest came crashing down in front of them.' Emily was huffing, more with hurt pride than fear. 'The sound of the bush going to hell is not something I'm familiar with. It may be an old story to you but I can't be blasé about it.'

'You're right,' said Carmody, 'but listen, you don't have any experience of handling this sort of situation. Why don't you go back to the hall? Mrs Parker will need some help – there are some scared people in there and that scumbag might make – '

'Look, Dad, I'm here. I've made the decision. Let's get on with it.'

'Put this on your back then,' said Carmody, putting his knapsack onto her back. 'I'll handle the hose after I've lit my section of the backburn. Just stay close to the house and keep an eye out for any spot fires. Remember you have to look *down* the hill for fires. You have to make sure no spot fires start in the bush in front of the houses.'

'You don't have to talk to me as if I'm a moron,' said Emily.

'Okay, just keep your eye out.'

Once he'd set Emily up, much like a tin soldier in a backyard battleground, Carmody returned to the line of earth that they had scraped clean of vegetation over the previous few days. It wasn't an immaculate job. Not many of the oldies could muster much enthusiasm in the heat of the last week. But it would hold. With some ceremony, Carmody lit his drop torch again and let its flame hit a small pile of leaves and twigs. He repeated this every few metres along the stretch of ground that demarked the area to be burnt from the houses.

Carmody loved watching the match-stick flames. This was the sort of fire he was familiar with – flickering hesitantly, nudging up to a new pile of leaves, crawling along the landscape, never far from a quick extinction. He was expert at coaxing fire. A long history of burning raked leaves in suburban gutters; of burning rubbish in incinerators; of camping fires; of burning overgrown tracks, grass verges and sausages had earned him the reputation as The Arsonist. The tag stuck for a few years, especially after he was rapped on the knuckles by the pollution authority for burning rubbish. But the nickname had lapsed from use in the last few years.

Carmody looked along the line of flame. He returned the drop torch to the back step of the house and picked up the fire hose to stop the flames edging back down the hill. The backburn line was not uniformly cleared of vegetation so occasionally fingers of fire crept down the hill. These Carmody quickly doused. The flames were growing quickly. Within a few metres of their origin, they had expanded in size, spread, noise and power. They were like boisterous children, keen to leave the safety of the parents' feet.

The slope of the ground meant most of the flames marched straight up the hill away from houses. Still, Carmody kept a strict watch on his patrol area. One could never predict the progress of a backburn. He'd only participated in a few controlled burns, but he'd seen enough to know they were like playing poker with the bush. You did everything you could to predict its path – you knew wind direction, wind strength, the humidity of the air, even the humidity of the foliage. You would know the lie of the terrain, the type of vegetation and the amount of fuel on the ground. But when fire hit the bush, it was a free force. It moved in directions you underestimated; it may not move through the area you wanted burnt, it might move too fast. It could be disastrous if it moved too slow.

Tonight, he and Roger Burton had decided to be conservative. They lit the backburn well in advance of the fire front – parts of it would burn for half an hour before it met the front, other parts would meet its rival within ten minutes. They didn't want to risk a slow take-up to a backburn, considering the size and speed of the flames heading their way. There is nothing more pathetic than trying to stop an inferno with a few smouldering leaves.

They almost didn't try a backburn that night because of the strength of the southerly winds. The winds that were bringing the six-kilometre front to their backyards could also push a small backburn onto the houses. But in the last fifteen minutes the winds had abated slightly and in the end they decided the steepness of the hill would outweigh the force of the southerly. Fire races up hills. The steeper the incline the faster the fire, and hillsides that were as steep as the one that fell into Flint Bay worked like bonfires.

As the infant fires left him, Carmody felt relief. For the first time in almost a week, he felt hopeful. Soon, he thought, it might all be over. As if seeing his relief, a dust-laden, smoky whirl of wind howled down the hill and stung him in the face. Carmody buried his head in his chest and felt the searing on his neck and his hand as two live embers hit him. Okay, he said to himself, it's not over yet. Too early for relief. And then, to the fire he whispered, 'But you'll get yours, just wait, you'll get yours.'

When the dust and smoke cleared, he looked along the line of neighbours who were nudging the fire up the hill. It was a loose-toothed line. The demarked area wound its way behind houses, out-houses, old dunnies and barbecue areas. Why they needed to protect a stone barbecue area from the fire, no one had explained. But no one said it was stupid. Some bits of ground are worth protecting. Ritual places. Places like barbecues.

While remaining vigilant along the backburn line, Carmody couldn't resist following the small flames up the hill. The licks of heat were converging on the wildfire with a lot more courage than size. He could understand why so many people would be baffled at the concept of this small line of fire defeating the big monster. It seemed insane.

The backburn was converging on the top of the hill – it almost looked as if it were being sucked into the big fire. As it went higher into the hill, Carmody lost sight of the distance between the backburn and the wildfire. The thought occurred to him that the backburn might die, it might not have enough fuel to reach the top of the hill; the southerly might rob it of vigour. He willed his small flames onwards. He could hear occasional yells of instruction and comment from the other firefighters. He wished he were near enough to talk with them. Carmody's eyes strained as the backburn neared the top of the hill and the oncoming wild-fire. He held his breath. Once, then again. Then he heard it. A massive explosion. It sounded like an oil tank going up or a boat exploding. When Carmody heard the explosion of superheated air, he knew the backburn had done its job.

Carmody breathed deeply but didn't relax. He turned along the line of burnt-out vegetation and told himself to check for spots. Suddenly he heard a telephone ring. It sounded ridiculous. Carmody laughed as he looked towards the nearest house. It wasn't coming from there. Then he remembered the mobile phone in his back pocket, the one he had used earlier to warn headquarters that they were going to attempt a backburn. He'd also used it to talk with Roger Burton who was working from a house at the far end of the line.

'Hello?' Carmody said.

'Tony? Is that you?' Carmody suddenly remembered whose phone he had and how he had come into possession of it.

'Ah no. Tony's gone for a quick leak. He asked me to mind the phone.'

'Tell him to ring the office when he gets back.'

'Sure. Bye.' Carmody found a red button and hung up. Carmody grimaced to himself as he forgave himself for the lie. And he continued mopping up along the line. Within ten minutes, the phone rang again.

'Yes?' said Carmody.

''Who's that?'

'John Candle,' lied Carmody.

'It's the news editor of Radio 2YX here. Is Tony back?'

'No.' Carmody couldn't think fast enough to invent another lie.

'Well can you tell me where he is? And why you've got his phone?'

'I'm not sure,' said Carmody in answer to both.

'You're not sure!' Carmody could hear the incriminations in the news editor's voice. He wondered whether he might be charged with theft.

'He went off to check out the fire. He should be back soon – '

'You said he'd gone off for a pee. What game are you playing at? Why did Tony leave his phone with someone else?' The news editor was thinking aloud. Carmody let him draw his own conclusions. They would probably be less incriminating than any excuse Carmody could offer. 'He'd better not be in trouble,' continued the news editor. 'If our man is in trouble we want to know. We'll send the bloody national guard down there to haul him out.'

Some lives, thought Carmody, are obviously worth more than others.

'Listen, we're all a bit preoccupied with a fire down here at the moment,' said Carmody, suddenly jack of the bloke on the other end of the line. The news editor interjected again and said something about lawyers and police. Suddenly the obvious occurred to Carmody. He hung up. From now on, thought Carmody, I'll only be using this thing to make calls. Not receive them.

Pushing the phone into his back pocket, Carmody saw the others approach him along the backburn line.

'We licked that bastard, didn't we!' yelled Roger Burton as he closed the distance between them. The firefighters exchanged back-slapping banter for a few minutes before Roger Burton said, 'What do you think our chances are of popping down the hall for a quick cuppa?'

Carmody looked up the hill. It was a smouldering battlefield. Smoke rose from the skeletons of bushes, fallen tree trunks, the trunks of trees still standing and from mounds on the ground. Embers flashed red across the hillside and several trunks were still burning. The threat to their rear had disappeared but it was still very possible that a live ember would find its way from the back of the houses and land in the stretch of bush at the front.

Carmody turned back to Roger. 'You'll only be gone twenty minutes or so, won't you?' Burton nodded. 'Well if you blokes are only going for a quick cuppa, Emily and I can handle it,' replied Carmody. Roger Burton raised an eyebrow on hearing Emily's name. 'She came up to help.' Carmody added, 'She's around the front of the houses.' Reading reluctance in Burton's silence, 'She'll be fine. She has a knapsack. And, given the chance, she has a good brain too.'

Burton and the other three men disappeared down the hillside. Halfway down, Roger Burton turned back to Carmody and yelled, 'Bo has already gone further up the hill. I couldn't talk him into a cuppa.' Carmody nodded. He watched them disappear and quickly scanned the hillside below to see if he could see Emily. He couldn't, but wasn't surprised. If he had been able to see her, then she would have been in the wrong position.

Carmody began walking along the line of fire break, looking up at the blackened, smouldering hillside and down to the unburnt bush that lay between the houses and the water. He passed three houses. Still intact, he said to himself proudly. All of them saved. And not just houses. Lives, they'd saved lives. And more than that, they'd saved people's weekends, people's holidays, their history and their future. When he thought of the people of the Bay, he never thought just of neighbours in their houses. He thought of the soul of the place; of the histories of the people who had passed through the Bay; of their memories, which were still carried in the land. He thought of the belongingness of the people to their area. All that, he thought, has been saved from the fire.

He heard rather than saw the snake. A frantic rustling across the burnt ground. He poised to get his bearings when the snake shot out in front of him. With a hot belly and its instincts skewed by the fires, the snake was doing everything it shouldn't have been doing. Charging at a man with its fangs bared. This snake, thought Carmody, mid-air in a jump he hadn't realised he was making, was not going to run away in fright. Almost before he hit the ground, half a metre away from the snake's hissing head, Carmody spun backwards and rolled down the hill. And kept going.

Carmody was almost relieved at the velocity of his fall and how far it was taking him away from the snake. He tumbled over boulders and old logs that had been removed from the clearing line. He crashed through a few small bushes and then he felt himself falling through the air. And he heard a crack as he landed. Then, slipping a few more metres down the hill, he crashed over a small stone wall. As his body settled into the ground, Carmody lost consciousness.

Chapter fifteen

Emily felt like a dork. Patrolling the front lawns of the neighbours' houses with a knapsack sprayer strapped to her back and an old woollen rug hanging limply from her hand. Stupid. Especially as she was facing away from the fire. But she remembered her father's words: 'You've got to keep an eye on the bush corridor in front of the houses because that is where spot fires could occur. Just remember you've got a blanket to smother small fires and a knapsack to tackle something bigger. If necessary you can even use the blanket while you're spraying,' he'd said before disappearing up behind the houses to check along the line of backburn.

Emily was unconvinced. She kept looking behind her to see what the real firefighters were doing. She could hear the shouts of instruction crossing the hillside between firefighters; the shouts were sometimes inaudible for the roaring of the fire front and smashing of trees and limbs hitting the ground. Sometimes she could see her father pass along the line where the backburn had started. The backburn was already fifty metres up the hill, lighting bushes and even small trees.

She'd tried not to look to the west. To the fire that glowered at her. That was almost upon her now. Emily recalled what the politician had said a few days earlier. 'If your backyard meets the bush, prepare for the worst.' She wondered whether the politician had wanted to say 'prepare to meet thy doom'.

To distract herself from the approach of the wildfire, she looked into the night sky. In between the swirling capes of smoke, she could see the ash falling from the sky. The ashes glowed against the bruised night sky. She watched their progress towards the ground. At first she thought of them as fairies, dancing on the wind, two-stepping down to earth. Some burnt out before they hit earth, some twinkled brightly on the ground before fading. When she thought of them more practically, she realised that these ashes were falling more heavily to earth. They were bigger, heavier and brighter than those she'd seen earlier. One fell onto her arm and burned her. She slapped at it but it left a red afterglow on her skin. After that she appreciated how spot fires could start.

Her gaze returned to the hill. To the progress of the backburn. It was nearing the top now and closing in on the fire to the southwest. As it closed the distance the backburn grew more ferocious. As if puffing itself up for the encounter. Emily was entranced by the imminent showdown at the top of the hill. She could not be convinced that the smaller fire would defeat the monstrous one. Like a football supporter, she willed her side on. 'Go, baby, go,' she chanted under her breath with her fist up around her mouth. She was prepared for the meeting of the fires but she wasn't prepared for the explosion set off when the two fires met and the superheated air in between was briefly crushed. She dropped her blanket and fell to the ground. If she hadn't witnessed the fires meeting, she would have imagined that someone had ignited a bomb. Or a can of petrol. Emily kept her head close to the cool grass. She didn't want to look but curiosity got the better of her. The explosion, she saw, had completely extinguished the flames for just a moment before oxygen returned to the scene and the flames leapt back into life. The fact that she knew the blast had been created in the fire made her feel a little easier. But not much.

It worked. Within minutes of the fires colliding, she could see the tally the backburn had taken on the wildfire. Deprived of fuel, the wildfire was wounded, limping around the top of the hill looking for support, for a bush to burn, a bit of undergrowth to

chew on. It was directionless. It couldn't go back and there was
nothing to draw it forward. That hellishly hot fire front was now
reduced to a series of fractured fires, trying to eke out its
remaining life in the crowns of trees, or in fallen logs or a few
patches of unburnt brush.

As the monster on the hill above limped into oblivion, Emily
felt easier, more centred. And increasingly superfluous. She
looked around for firefighters. Someone to talk to. She wanted to
know if it was all over. Was she relieved of duty? She wanted to
talk to someone about the backburn, celebrate it. Still crouched
on the cool stretch of grass, Emily found a more comfortable position and began fiddling with the nozzle of her knapsack instead.
She'd spun the nozzle through every setting before it dawned on
her that she might still need the knapsack. Spot fires, her father
had said. Was that still possible?

She got up and walked across the front lawns of the neighbouring houses, if only because it seemed a more useful thing to
do. As she paced she thought of the people still waiting in the
hall. She visualised Tony Thomas. He didn't seem as good-looking
in recall. His chin was weaker than she'd first noticed. His lips
thinner, his presence vapid. He still had a dazzle of a smile but his
eyes never smiled. She thought of her wet dream a few hours pre-
viously. The virtual sex scene. She felt disappointed in herself for
even thinking of throwing herself at such a creep. Still, she supposed the virtual encounter was more enjoyable than any real
encounter would have been.

'Got to get my jollies somehow,' she said aloud to herself. The
word 'jollies' reminded her of Mrs Parker, the doddering old bag
who had nevertheless marshalled food resources like a trooper.
And emotional resources. Emily's stream of consciousness swung
onto an image of her mother. Memories of her mother always
appeared when she thought of stoics.

Emily recalled her mother's strange relationship with Mrs
Parker – supportive but estranged. In fact, they had so little in

common, Emily wondered whether they shared anything else apart from gender and a postcode. Mother was not as fussed with appearances as Mrs Parker; nor was she particular about standards of housework or getting the dinner on the table by six p.m. or attending every P and F meeting; or the occasional swear word.

Emily tried to spin her mind back to earlier that evening. To recall what her father had said about Mum. He seemed to want to say something about her when he was sorting through her letters. Emily was still ambling along the boundaries of the properties, keeping a desultory eye on the bush. She wasn't at all surprised when she found herself approaching the foundations of the cabin that her mother had called her studio.

As her illness worsened, her mother had spent more time in the studio. She didn't seem to complete many drawings but she claimed she was busy. The last time Emily saw her mother, she'd wandered into the studio and caught her staring out the window. She must have been staring for a long time because it took a few seconds for her to realise someone had walked into the room. In those few seconds, Emily saw what had become of her. She had a glimpse of the mother as child, as the needy member of the family, not fully competent. Her mother had become less of what she was before, less of a mother, and as Emily caught her face in profile, she could see that this was just the beginning. Her mother was on a rapid journey to dependency. She would never be mother again.

When her mother noticed her presence that day and turned to smile at her, Emily also saw the sadness in her. The warm but wan smile was like an apology – as if she was sorry for what she had become and what she would become for her daughter. Later, after she had left her mother's studio, Emily told her father that her mother needed more care, perhaps daily visits from a nurse; she suggested that if her mother were back in Sydney they could all visit her every day. Emily decided then she wanted to spend as much time with her as possible. She could sense a deadline.

'She's not going anywhere,' her father had said. 'She wants to be here. I'm more than competent to handle whatever comes.'

'But Dad, I'm not saying you're doing a bad job. I'm just saying – ' what had she told her father? 'I'm just saying that I want to help. Be here for her.'

Emily kicked at the remains of the sandstone foundations. She had had no impact on her father. She could remember his lips tightening and his averted eyes. Even when he suggested that she bring more paints for her mother the following weekend, it seemed like a push-off. She'd purchased the paints in Sydney the next day but she'd never had a chance to deliver them.

Emily squirted the sandstone foundation with her sprayer. Then she noticed that the area wasn't burnt. Although the cabin was some ten metres up into the bush, someone had drawn the back-burn line around the foundation stones. Only her father could have gone to such trouble to save a pile of stones.

It was strange really. After her mother had died, her father had dismantled the studio within a day. Most of it was undamaged by the fire that had killed her mother. It was, in fact, smoke that had killed her. The toxic fumes of cheap furniture alight, the poison of burning plastic. The studio was blackened and partly charred but it could have been saved. It could at least have stood in the backyard for a few days – until after the funeral – until after the mourning period. But by the time Emily arrived the next day, it lay in pieces across the backyard, seemingly torn from the foundations.

Emily recalled how she had felt when she arrived at Flint Bay. She'd barely finished walking up the track to the main house when she saw that her mother's shelter had been hurled across the yard. Emily had been too shocked to say anything about it at the time. And she'd never raised it since.

Suddenly realising how much time she'd spent mooching around the foundations, Emily looked around her. She had heard the voices of men a while ago when she was patrolling the front section. Now she couldn't see anyone up the hill, nor could she

see her father along the crooked line of backburn at the rear of
the houses. She scooted around the front of the house to resume
her patrol. Scanning the hill below her, she saw a plume of smoke
rising from the ground twenty metres in front of the Leonards'
house. She ran towards the smoke, water sploshing around in the
knapsack and nozzle in her hand. She tried to tell herself it was
just a cloud of smoke settling on the ground. Even as she got to
the edge of the lawn to look down at the smouldering bush she
could see the small flames.

'Dad, Dad,' she yelled across her shoulders as she watched the
small circle of flame spreading outwards. 'Dad,' she yelled,
turning to look up the hillside to where the backburn line started.
'Shit.' She charged up the hill, over the lawns of the neighbours,
along her father's front lawn and around the back of the house.
Panting like a dog, her back bruised and sore from the knapsack,
Emily scanned the backburn line looking for her father, for firefighters, for anyone.

'Where the hell are you, Dad? Come on, come on, there's a
new fire around the front.' Emily's cries disappeared up the hill
and were swept away on the abating southerly. There was no one
there. Just the black ground in front of her, still smouldering, still
glowing under logs. There were a few flames licking the corpses
of logs, like bush carrion.

No one up the hillside. No one patrolling the backburn and
obviously no one in front of the houses where the small fire had
started. Emily did not have to do too many calculations to discover that she didn't have time to charge down to the hall for
help. She was alone with the fire.

'Fuck you!' Emily yelled into the ground. 'Fuck you,' she yelled
again, this time lifting her head so the words could escape up the
hillside. She was yelling at no one in particular. At the ether, possibly. At the fire. But it felt good so she yelled again. And again.
Then the curse became a chant, 'Fuck you, fuck you, fuck you.'
The chant grew more rhythmic as Emily turned and stormed

down the hill. Chanting and stomping across the lawn, she turned around the house into the front lawn and saw that the ring-worm of a fire she had seen just a minute earlier now had pretentions. It was consuming a small bush. It was as big as a picnic rug. And spreading fast.

Thinking of the picnic rug, Emily raced further down the hill to grab the old rug that she'd discarded earlier. When she reached the edge of the lawns, she leapt into the bush and pounded her way through the ten metres of vegetation that separated her from the fire. Not bothering to push bushes aside with her hands, she walked through them, stomping and stumbling over knotted branches. All the while she was staring at the fire, glaring at the fire. She had no idea what she was going to do. She was driven by anger, frustration, by the southerly that was blowing gently at her back. And by the lack of any other option.

As she stormed up to the ring of fire, Emily let go of her chant and began to roar. She bashed at the fire with the old rug, whipping it with a violence that flattened some of the flames but forced others out onto unburnt ground. Still roaring, still cursing and sometimes growling, Emily threw the rug over the burning ground beneath her feet. She felt behind her back for the nozzle of the knapsack. Adjusting the nozzle to a fish-tail spray (she was relieved that she had fiddled with the nozzle earlier) she directed the spray onto the bush that was burning just metres in front of her. The bush sizzled in anger.

'Gotcha, ya bastards,' she yelled at the flames. She flailed the fires close to her heels with the rug and doused those on the other side of the circle with sprays of water. Within a minute her feet began to heat up, her eyes were searing with ash and debris. The radiant heat that was hitting her face was being cooled with mists of water from the fish-tail spray. Her voice was almost raw but still she roared at the fire, cursed it, spat at it, snarled.

As she saw her work having an effect, Emily's mood lightened. She began whooping as she tackled the last perimeter of flames.

Then she was kicking at the flames, spitting at them, pointing the nozzle right into the heart of small flames and yelling, 'Suck on that, sucker!'

Within minutes, the fire was just a circle of black. Emily, with a trigger-happy hand, aimed the nozzle at anything that even looked like crackling. She stalked the circle, silently goading flames to reappear. 'Come on. Have another go,' she whispered. 'Let's see what you're made of.' Her feet warmed on the burnt ground, her eyes were inflamed with debris and passion. Just one flame dared to spring back to life. It wrapped itself around the branch of a dead-looking bush.

'Scccwitt.' the sound of the spray knocking the flame down sounded sweet. Emily patted her knapsack. She inspected the bush to ensure the flame had got the message. And then she resumed a patrol around the small circle. Soon she felt alone. And she knew the fire had died.

Emily stood silently inside the circle of blackness. Her hands, throbbing with heat, hung limply. The blanket draped from her hands to the ground. Smoke rose from the circle like gauzy curtains, filling her nostrils and brushing against her hair. It was not comfortable standing on the scorched ground but Emily was reluctant to leave the vanquished territory.

She felt remarkably pleased with herself. She looked around her burnt territory, smiling to herself. She was not just pleased, she had never felt more alive. And calm, the sort of serenity she had never experienced before and never thought possible. Not under a million crystals. Not after a half-day isolation tank session. Never.

She felt calm not just within herself but calm within her surroundings. Looking out beyond her circle to the gum trees, the casuarinas, the pathway, the sides of cottages, the water just visible between the thick waterfront vegetation and the sky bruised with smoke, she had become a seamless part of the environment. She didn't want to move for fear of destroying the moment. She never wanted to lose this feeling of belonging to the flow. She had a place here, here in the environment, here in this moment of time and she didn't want to lose it. Still standing quietly, her body was starting to ache and she liked that too.

Emily had no idea how long she was there. Finally she felt a chill of cooling sweat. When she looked up into the sky, the reflected glow of fire had disappeared. There was no sound of fire, no sound of men. Only the sound of a yacht's clinking tackle reminded her where she was, and that she was still alive.

When she stretched her arms to the heavens, she felt every muscle lodge their complaint. Her back felt so bruised, she wondered if she might have damaged the discs. Her arms were a spent force. They hung loosely by her side and resisted all attempts to engage them in any work. Her feet were throbbing and her throat felt so ripped, she dared not say a word or breathe too suddenly. She felt great. Emily picked up her blanket and walked up to her father's house. To celebrate with a cup of tea.

Chapter sixteen

Boisterous with friendly taunts and deprecating references to events just shared, Roger Burton and three firefighters pushed into the hall. Mrs Parker was passing the door when they burst in.

'Oh my God, look at you all. What on earth have you been doing?' said Mrs Parker, clasping her army jacket closer to her chest.

The men stopped in a messy knot of bodies and, as if just realising they possessed bodies, began inspecting themselves. The lower parts of their clothes were black and shedding soot onto the floor. Their hands were scratched, rubbed raw and slightly swollen. Their faces were smudged with different hues of grey and slashes of black. Their eyeballs were so red they looked as if they were desperate to get out of their sockets. Hair that had been under helmets or slouch hats was matted with sweat, ash and suppression.

As they stood in front of her, the smell of burnt wood, sweat and the awful sweetness of spent fear settled into the room. Mrs Parker twitched her nose, took another look at Roger Burton and began to giggle. 'You look like a mob of boys who've just discovered a dump down the road,' she said, adding in a more practical vein, 'I don't think I've got enough face washers for all of you.'

'Beryl, we don't need a face wash, we need a cup of tea,' said Roger.

'You're not going to touch my good china with those filthy hands of yours.'

'Do you mean to tell me that you hauled your good china down here for emergency catering?'

Mrs Parker winced slightly. She wondered what basic rule of safety she had just breached. Perhaps china would smash in heat and injure someone. Maybe it helped spread germs and hepatitis or, God forbid, AIDS. She glared towards the reporter's bag further down the hall.

Roger Burton read her alarm. 'It's just that carting china down here was beyond the call of duty, Beryl, that's all.' He gave her a reassuring tug on the arm. As he neared the trestle table, nodding at a few of the other residents on his way, Roger Burton detected a strange mood in the hall. People seemed a little silent, withdrawn. Natural enough, given that it was after midnight and they'd been marooned for hours not knowing whether their houses were still standing. But there was something else, he thought, quaffing a couple of cups of water before pouring himself a tea from the hot urn on the table. These people seemed embarrassed.

Roger Burton turned to face the room, sipping on the tea. He supposed they all knew the backburn had been successful. That they had been keeping a watch on the fire's progress from the hall. A few insipid smiles from residents seemed to confirm victory. Then he noticed that the reporter's equipment was still perched on a chair but the reporter wasn't in the hall.

Pulling Mrs Parker aside, Roger asked her where Tony Thomas had gone.

Beryl looked embarrassed. 'There was a bit of an incident,' she said, hoping that Mr Burton would leave the matter there. She turned her back to him and busied herself with cups and saucers on the trestle table. Roger Burton waited, sipping on his tea.

'Beryl, what happened?'

Mrs Parker huffed and took him by the elbow to the corner of the hall. She looked around for two chairs. Then decided to remain standing. Roger Burton was looking impatient.

'The reporter, what's his name, Tony, saw a police launch pull up at the wharf about an hour or so ago. He dashed outside and along to the wharf. We were all looking from the windows but we didn't follow. The reporter seemed happy to meet the police. He may have known them. He was chatting and back-slapping them. Then he seemed to be explaining a lot of things to them, pointing to the hillside, to the fire. The fire must have been halfway along the hillside when this was happening. We could see the police looking at the fire from inside the launch.' Mrs Parker breathed deeply and continued.

'The reporter came back to the hall to tell us that the police were ready to begin evacuations. Six of us could go with the police launch and the rest could wait on the end of the wharf until the water taxi arrived – ten minutes or so. The reporter started packing up his equipment.' Mrs Parker paused. Roger Burton was getting testy.

'Okay, Beryl, so why aren't you all on the launch now? What went wrong? What did you do when the reporter told you to evacuate?'

Mrs Parker shrugged her shoulders. 'Nothing', she said as if she found it hard to believe. 'Well, we didn't do nothing, we just – well Bruce Leonard began fiddling with the broken water sprayer. He just turned his back on the reporter and got busy with the sprayer.' Mrs Parker thought about this. It seemed inadequate to describe what had gone on. Roger Burton, however, was beginning to comprehend.

'Then,' continued Mrs Parker, 'someone else began reading a book. A few people began pouring themselves some more cups of tea. When I saw they needed more tea – ' Mrs Parker paused again, obviously still struggling for comprehension ' – I began wiping some of the freshly washed cups for their tea.'

'What did the reporter do?'

'He said – well I suppose he got angry. He started saying, "Come on, you all have to get out of here. Don't you know you're being evacuated and if you hang around too long the police will forcibly drag you out of here?"'

Roger Burton urged Mrs Parker on with a nod of his head.

'The reporter stormed up to Bruce Leonard and told him to tell everyone to get their stuff and get out. Bruce stood up – his face was such a mess, puffy, pulpy, one eye was bulging – and he just looked at the reporter and then sat down to fix the sprayer again. The reporter stormed off to the wharf again.'

'So the reporter has gone back to the peninsula with the police?'

Mrs Parker shook her head. 'He went back to the launch and was throwing his arms around and pointing at the hall and then a policeman got out of the launch. But a radio call must have come in because the policeman stopped, turned back to the boat, listened for a while and then hopped back into the launch. They left.'

Roger Burton clanked his cup into its saucer. Momentarily, he was stuck for words. 'But I thought everyone was dead keen on getting evacuated,' he said, partly to Mrs Parker, partly to himself. Mrs Parker took a breath as if to say something. Then she stopped herself. She looked perplexed. She shrugged her shoulders.

This time Roger Burton breathed deeply. 'And the reporter?' asked Burton again.

'He came back and said the police had been called off to the other side of the bay where there were some campers caught on the water's edge. He said they would be back.' Mrs Parker reflected on what the reporter had told them. Belatedly, she got stroppy about it. 'The reporter sounded such a bully! As if he were a policeman himself. Or privy to the plans of the police. He talked to us as if we were a mob of unruly schoolchildren.' Mrs Parker was gathering steam. Everyone in the hall could hear her now. 'As if we'd be frightened of a few policemen! We would just tell the police "thank you very much but we are all fine here, we don't need to be evacuated – "'

'Beryl,' said Roger Burton interrupting, 'what happened to the reporter?' He said this slowly and firmly. Mrs Parker glanced around at the others scattered around the room. None of them was near enough to hear Mr Burton's question but everyone knew what was unfolding. And none were stepping forth to assist with the telling.

'The reporter stayed. He sat down and began recording another news item. As soon as he started, people in the hall quietened so they could hear him. Soon the whole hall was quiet, listening to him speak into his tapes.'

Mrs Parker breathed deeply and began in a faster voice, as if speeding through the telling would lessen its impact.

'He said something like we've all gone crazy,' continued Mrs Parker, 'although he didn't use those words. He said something like the tension is so great here that people are having trouble hanging onto reality and then he said something about John Carmody and the scuffle between him and Bruce. He said we'd all defied authority and faced heavy penalties when the disaster was over and then ...' Mrs Parker paused to describe a happening that was beyond her experience, beyond even her imagination.

'The reporter stopped talking into his microphone then. A few people had got up from their chairs and moved over to him. They were all standing around his chair, staring at him as he taped his report.

'It was like there was an angry circle of bears around him. Then someone who was standing in front of me – we were all standing around the reporter by that stage – someone said, "Go on, Tony, tell them what you've been doing in the fire."

'Then someone else, it may have been Mr Grey, said, "Yes, Mr Reporter, tell them how you have been tormenting elderly women, reducing them to tears while you hide in the hall with the women and old men."'

Mrs Parker paused. Roger Burton leaned towards her. He urged her on. 'Come on, Beryl, what happened then?'

'The reporter, who'd been quiet for a while, started his tape machine again. He spoke into the microphone and stared at everyone while he spoke. He said something like, "At this moment I am surrounded by a mob of angry people who, in their desperation, are trying to take their anger out on anyone or anything. At the moment I am that "anyone". And then he stopped talking. But he left the tape running.

'That made everyone really mad. I'm not sure why they would be so mad that he left the tape on but it – it seemed aggressive. One of the neighbours, Brian I think it was, leant forward and pressed the stop button on the tape. Someone else came forward and took the microphone from the reporter's hand. Then someone took all the equipment from him. He started saying things like, "I'm just doing a job, I'm not meant to be a hero, I'm not meant to get involved."' Mrs Parker stopped again, as if she could hear the reporter's yells.

'It was too late for all that. And everyone was getting so het up and then old Mrs Grey started crying and before I knew it, Christoph – ' Mrs Parker stopped mid-name. She looked into Roger Burton's eyes, trying to tell him with her eyes. Roger Burton returned her gaze. He looked serious and comprehending. 'After a few minutes the reporter made it outside. He didn't go far. Just down to the rock near the water. I suppose he's waiting for the water police to return. Do you think - ' Mrs Parker paused. Roger Burton was backing away from her towards the window. When he reached the window, he looked outside. About twenty metres along the waterfront he could see the hunched form of a man squatting on a large flat rock.

Roger Burton returned to Beryl Parker's side. He breathed out deeply and stared into the ceiling. He noticed thin brown streamers woven around the rafters. He was about to ask Mrs Parker about it when he realised the festive streamers were, in fact, tape. From a tape recorder. He imagined the rest.

'And then, Beryl, I suppose you all kicked up your heels and had a party.'

Mrs Parker glanced up to the ceiling and grimaced. 'We got a bit carried away.' She shrugged her shoulders. 'It seemed a good idea at the time.'

Roger Burton saw several faces in the hall looking in his direction, obviously waiting to gauge his response. This, he thought, is something I don't particularly want to adjudicate. He wrapped his palms around the tea cup. It was cool and empty. Beryl Parker saw his gesture and suggested another cup of tea. With a thirst still unslaked by numerous sprays from the knapsack, three cups of water in the hall and a cup of tea, Roger nodded and followed Beryl. Their return to the refreshments table seemed to signal an easing of tension in the room. A few residents broke away from their coterie and joined Roger and Mrs Parker at the trestle. In the relative quiet, he noticed the television had been turned off.

'Did our fire feature on the TV?' Roger said to the small group of people who had gathered behind him as he poured water from the urn.

'Yep,' replied old Christopher Downs, whom Roger had hardly noticed earlier in the day. 'We could see the fire up the hill better on the TV than we could out the window.'

'So you saw the backburn?'

'I think we saw the start of it. They were filming from the other side of the bay so the detail wasn't too clear.' Christopher Downs paused. 'We turned it off when they said the houses of Flint Bay had been destroyed.'

Roger Burton looked incredulous. Christopher Downs continued. 'We knew they'd made a mistake because when the reporter said Flint Bay was destroyed, the camera was focusing further around the foreshores to Steel Bay. So they were probably referring to Steel Bay. It looked pretty bad there. The fire made it down to the foreshore – '

'But they said Flint Bay. They told everyone our houses had been wiped out,' interjected another resident.

'Christopher rowed out into the bay in a dinghy to check what was really happening. He could see all our houses still intact. And he could see the start of the backburn – ' said another.

'I was pretty bloody angry when I got back,' continued Christopher.

'It was just after Christopher came back that the police launch arrived and the reporter went out to meet them …' said Mrs Parker, trailing her sentence for someone else to pick up.

The others were silent. Roger Burton felt strange surrounded by these people. He had known most of them for years, mostly on a neighbourly basis. They seemed strangers to him tonight but they seemed like family to each other; the way they finished off each other's sentences, the way they told the story as one. He glanced around them. They stood in a tight circle around him. He felt the pressure of their stares. He tried to block them out to retrace what they had told him. Something they had said had briefly raised alarm bells. He trawled through the story – the bashing of the reporter, Christopher going out in a dinghy, the TV news … he saw it then.

'You said the fire looked bad at Steel Bay?' he asked of no one in particular.

Christopher Downs answered. 'It swept over the hill and right down to the water. Nothing would have survived its path. It hit the water and began spreading out along the waterfront …' As he said this Christopher too saw the threat. So too did most of the others.

'Has anyone bothered to check back along to the east to see if it's heading around the bay towards us?' asked Burton. The heads shook. 'If that fire – ' he paused, thinking aloud. 'It's still got a slight southerly breeze behind it. Unless one of the brigades has stopped it from the water, it will be heading along the waterfront and around the headland into Flint Bay.' Burton was already placing his tea on the table and checking his watch. He'd been in the hall for almost an hour. He swore to himself and began striding out of the hall. His firefighters, who were lounging on chairs at the back of the hall, spotted him leaving and hastened after him.

Even when he stepped outside the hall, Roger could see that the
night air had muddied again. He scampered up the first incline of
the hill to see to the eastern edge of the strip of bushland that separated houses from water. As he scanned along the corridor of
bushland, he could see that there were no spot fires, but he didn't
expect to see them. Not with Carmody and Emily up the hill. As he
continued stepping up the steep incline of the hill, his view of the
eastern corridor improved. He could sense the fire before he saw
it. When he saw the plumes of smoke rising from the tip of the
headland, he was more angry than surprised.

Running back to the hall to retrieve the knapsacks and tools
they had left just outside the door, Roger Burton was making a
few quick decisions. The fire was heading for them from the
south-east. Even though it was heading into the southerly and
therefore couldn't travel too fast, it was heading along the water
and their houses would be uphill from it. And fire, he knew,
travels four times faster when it is travelling up a steep hill.

There was only a relatively small amount of bush between the
waterfront and most houses, a few hundred metres. So any fire
moving through that area wouldn't normally build up much heat.
But the ground in front of the houses had been allowed to collect
debris for six or seven years.

When Burton got back to the hall, he realised they'd have to fill
their knapsacks again. He had planned to do it even before he
came down from the hill but he'd thought the worst was over. He
felt like kicking himself. He kicked the knapsack instead.

'Roger, it looks as though the fire has already moved in front of
the Lumleys' house. It won't be long before other houses on the
far eastern perimeter are in its sights,' said Trevor Purves, who
had scouted further along the hillside.

'How close?' said Roger, filling his knapsack under the tap
attached to the outside wall of the hall.

'It's twenty, thirty metres from the Lumley house,' replied
Purves. Burton was systematically filling knapsacks. And thinking

of strategies. Hoping to God that he was thinking clearly. Knowing that he had to think fast.

'Then we won't be able to fight from the threatened houses,' he said. 'If it's that close already it will be too late and too dangerous by the time we get up to the houses. We don't even know whether there's a fire hose fitted to those houses.'

Roger Burton paused. 'I think we'll have to fight this one from the waterfront and move in on the flanks. We should have two guys down here along the waterfront, taking the sting out of its progress along the hillside and the others should start attacking it front-on. We'll be limited in the amount of water we can get onto the fire. We should be able to set up a fire hose and pump water from the bay. But apart from that we've only got knapsacks. It's too dicey to go up the hill.'

'Does that mean,' interjected Tony Dwyer, 'that we're going to sacrifice those houses that are closest to the fire at the moment?'

Roger Burton didn't answer. He didn't think he had to answer. These blokes weren't stupid.

'And what about Carmody?' said Trevor Purves.

'And his daughter? And Bo?' said another.

The crew were hauling knapsacks onto their backs while the last two were being filled. The questions hung in the air. Burton, willing the water to fill the knapsacks faster, remained mute. The others weren't sure whether Roger Burton had heard their questions. He had. He'd been churning the same questions around his mind for the last few minutes. Ever since he realised that Carmody's house was one of those threatened by fire. Surely, he thought quickly, Carmody and his daughter couldn't have missed this fire. What were they doing up there on watch? Burton tossed the question around his mind for a few more seconds. Then he concluded that it was a question he couldn't hope to deal with at the moment.

'No doubt, we'll meet up with them along the way,' he said.

Chapter seventeen

Emily flopped on the lounge. It felt strange to be in her father's house again. It seemed like a long time since she was last here. She listened to the kettle gathering steam on the stove and breathed deeply. She could smell the residue of tobacco smoke from the cigarettes she'd shared with Tony Thomas earlier that night. It mingled with the bush smoke that had infused her clothes and hair while she was beating the spot fire into submission.

She inspected her hands. They were black and grey with ash. 'I must look like something you'd find in an ashtray,' she said to herself, lifting her hands disdainfully away from her body. 'But,' she added, 'I could do with another cigarette.'

Breathing in languorously, Emily relived the joy of that afternoon when she'd drawn back on her first cigarette in years. She considered searching the kitchen rubbish bin for stubs. She tried to recall how deeply the stubs would be buried in the bin. They'd be on top of the carrots, cheese packaging and diet cola cans. Beneath the container of almost-empty avocado dip and half-finished tomatoes.

'Get a life,' she said to her lungs. 'I am never going to be that desperate for a cigarette again!' To distract herself from the pining in her lungs, Emily scanned the room. Except for the furniture and bookshelves, it was full of empty spaces. All the memorabilia, chintzy china, tourist souvenirs, old mugs and photos had been hastily removed from their positions. Their absence had left a patchwork of blank spaces on the walls and on tops of shelves. She tried to refill the bald patches. It wasn't difficult. The framed tapestry of a cat belonged above the mantle, the picture of

Grandfather would have hung beside it, the needlepoint rural scene hung near the door, the giant wooden salad tossers hung down the architrave of the door.

Emily looked back to where the needlepoint rural scene once hung. She remembered sitting with her mother while she worked on it. For one long evening Emily had sat at her mother's feet with a roll of maroon tapestry wool, cutting new lengths for her when she needed it. How long ago? She must have been a teenager. It was the most boring job but – Emily sought the right feeling – it was soothing. Mother liked to talk as she did needlepoint. They talked of everything. And nothing. Stories, events and jokes. Her mother's evening chatter seemed to wash over her. Emily looked to the bald patch again better to envisage the rural scene. She could see it now – she'd cut not just the wool for the maroon roof of the homestead but some of the blue wool for the sky and the gold wool for the wheat. All woven with stories of their lives.

Emily took her eyes off the bald patch and continued searching the room with her eyes. 'Such eclectic taste, Dad,' Emily murmured in the chiding tone an interior decorator might use. But even as she said it, she realised that it was not her father's taste. The room was still her mother's room – every item of decoration had been chosen by her mother.

Emily pushed herself upright and scanned the room for something that had been bought during the last eight years. Nothing. She stood up and slowly turned around the room, briefly putting her imaginary camera to her eye. There must be something new. Books, yes, okay, there were some new books. But nothing else. The house had stopped renewing itself when her mother died. Emily let her arms, which had been framing her camera view, fall to her side and saw her father's house as if for the first time.

One of Emily's favourite mindgames was to guess a person's favourite era by looking at their house. Most elderly people picked the forties to settle into sameness. In the forties homes, furniture was big, stuffed and criss-crossed with wear patterns.

The carpets showed the tracks between bathroom, bedroom and lounge room and sometimes there was a milling spot near the TV, where the radiogram once stood. People whose heyday belonged to the fifties betrayed their sentimentality with Aboriginal ashtrays, kidney-shaped side tables and faded pastel paints in linoleum kitchens; the sixties crowd were less status-driven, preferring to flop on orange vinyl lounges crouched low on a moderne rug of mission brown and russet.

After she had decided in which era the house decor had frozen, Emily would try to guess why the people in the house had given up on decorating. Did a house simply reach a state where it was finished? Done? Perfect? Or did the inhabitants of the house lose interest in embellishing their living spaces? Some, she suspected, had run out of money. Sometimes, especially in old people's houses, time stood still when the spouse died. Those houses would become living memorials, the body imprints in armchairs testifying to the deceased. She was spooked by those houses. Now she was a bit spooked by her father's house.

Emily wandered down the hall, curious to see whether anything in her father's house had changed. Opening the door to her father's bedroom, she could see the ghosts of her mother's home-decorating in every bald patch on the wall, in every dust-free ringmark on the furniture. Then she noticed the box on her father's bed.

'Shit, look what he forgot,' Emily whispered as she walked to the box of letters that her father had been dipping into when she arrived in his room – when she shrieked her way into his room.

She sat down on the bed, near the box. But not too near. The box seemed to have a presence. As she peered over its rim at the neat piles of postcards, letters and documents, she could almost feel the secrets wrapped in old ribbons. Emily continued to sit. Establishing her claim to territory. When there had been no objections to her presence, she moved closer to the box. Then she saw a letter written in her own hand. Using this as an excuse, she

picked up the pile of letters and retrieved the one that was written
in her hand.

Judging by the lined paper, she'd written it at school. Judging
by the handwriting, she was aged about fourteen years. As she
started reading it, she recalled the exact time and circumstances:
science lab, late morning, sitting next to Heather Larson.

Dear Mum,

I'm sorry I lost my temper at you this morning. I don't know why I do that.
I hate myself when I leave home without kissing you or at least saying
goodbye. I hate it when I see you go quiet and sad. I promise I'll never kick
Jack where it hurts again.

P.S. But can you tell him not to hide dead goldfish in my bed again? After
all, I'm not the only one who's supposed to remember to feed them.

Emily fell back on the bed laughing. She wrapped the letter close to
her chest as she remembered the procession of goldfish that had
moved in and – very soon after – out of the goldfish bowl. She'd
buy two and within weeks they'd die. So she'd buy some more and
soon those too would be flushed down the toilet. She was, Emily
now thought, the world's first serial pet killer. She didn't know why
she persisted in buying new fish. Or why she hadn't checked what
she was doing wrong with the old fish. She could only recollect
that having a pet was very important to her at that stage.

Emily sorted through the pile to find more of her letters. She
found one that had amateur scrollwork scribbled around its
perimeter, suggesting a formal document. Judging by her handwriting, she was only ten or twelve when she wrote it.

Dear Dad,

Can you hereby witness an agreement between your daughter, I, Emily
Carmody, and your son, Jack Carmody, regarding a arrangement about

bedrooms. For one year I will have the big bedroom at the back of the house and, exactly a year after I move my stuff into it, it will be the turn of Jack. This agreement cannot be underdone by any arguement. If we move house, I will get the best room.

Signed, Jack and Emily

Emily giggled at the scrawl of a signature that the young Emily had obviously practised with abandon – the loopy scrawl of an eleven-year-old sophisticate.

'And why didn't I become the lawyer of the family?' she asked of no one.

Carefully, guiltily, Emily picked up a letter that had been poorly refolded. She unfolded it so she could refold it properly and place it back in the box. It was, she saw through eyes that were trying not to look, the letter her father had been reading yesterday.

She didn't intend to read it, she told herself. It had fallen open and she'd just seen the start of the letter as she was refolding it, she told herself as if rehearsing an excuse. She recognised the writing as her mother's but it had a different quality to it – it was neater than her normal writing and the letters were smaller and tighter. As she started to read it, the letter unfolded beneath her hands.

Dear John,

It is almost midnight. I fear I won't sleep tonight. Strangely I don't feel tired. The treatment was brief and went without fuss. The nurses are mostly very patient and helpful although I do feel a bit of an impostor. When I look around the ward at the other beds, well most of the women here are young and have such busy lives. I feel, words escape me. Perhaps if they would be honest to me instead of saying all those things like 'we'll have you right in no time', and 'when you're on your feet again'. I feel so embarrassed when they say that, as if I'm dragging the chain. Sometimes I get angry and want to tell them that the next time I'll be on my feet again is when I'm on my way up to the pearly gates.

A woman on the other side of the ward died yesterday. They try not to let the other patients know when someone dies. I knew before the nurses did. The woman's bed had been still for at least an hour when a nurse started her rounds. As soon as the nurse came to the woman's bed, she signalled for the other nurse and closed the curtain. After a flurry of activity, the nurses and doctors left the ward. Soon after, an orderly wheeled the body out on a trolley. Under a sheet, of course. I don't know why but I expected things to be quiet in the ward after they moved her out. Perhaps even tearful. But, at least, quiet. It wasn't. The nurses were so busy changing sheets, wiping away traces of the woman. They sprayed her plastic mattress and rushed new linen onto the bed. When they whipped out the woman's name from the name plate at the top of the bed, well that was it. She was gone. Obliterated. It happened so fast. Everyone seemed in such a great rush to forget the woman was ever there. Just hours later, another woman was moved into the bed. I couldn't look at the new patient. It's strange, John, but I haven't been able to look in the nurses' eyes either. Why? I don't know. Maybe I don't want them to see that I'm scared. Maybe. But then again, maybe I don't want to see what is behind their eyes. I'm afraid I'll see their impatience.

But such talk doesn't do anyone any good. John, I would like to think that this will not last interminably. I would hate to think that I could end up in a nursing home with nothing but the morning tea trolley to look forward to. John I don't want to come back here again.

I am getting tired now. Perhaps I will be able to sleep tonight. There should still be four or five frozen stews in the freezer. If it has been very dry this week, can you water the pot plants?

I look forward to seeing you on Friday. I long to see you on Friday.

Love, Maeve

Emily flopped back on the bed. The words of her mother had resonated with pain and fear – despite the polite tone, because of the polite tone. She could envisage her mother lying in a hospital ward, staring up at the high ceiling, waiting for time to pass, trying to tread lightly on the nurses' timetable.

'I didn't know you were lonely, Mum,' she whispered. 'And I didn't know you were scared.' She clasped the letter to her chest, warming the thin paper with her body heat. 'Why didn't I know how you were feeling, Mum? Why? Was it because I didn't want to know? Or because you didn't want me to know?'

Emily recalled the early stage of her mother's disease and the days she had spent in hospital. Mother didn't want to go to hospital. She had insisted to everyone that it was a big fuss over not much at all. She'd hated hospital but at least she wasn't in pain at that stage. Pain came later, much later. Something in Emily's memory didn't ring true. Emily racked her mind to recall the small details of her mother's stay in hospital. It was summer. Hot and humid. Late summer. Emily suddenly saw the discrepancy. Her mother had been in a private room. She was not in a ward as her letter implied. Emily snapped the letter back up from the bed to check the date on it – July 12. Just a month before the fire killed her. Emily hadn't even known that her mother had been in hospital a second time. She had no idea then, or even later, that her mother had been hospitalised just before her death.

John?' a voice echoed from down the hall.

Emily leapt onto the floor and stashed the letter into the box. She thought about hiding the box but quickly decided that would be incriminating. And useless. Who could be calling? she thought, striding down the hall. And why is he looking for Dad? Nearing the end of the hallway, she noticed the air was smoky again. She remembered putting the kettle on. Must have boiled itself to a mist, she thought.

Turning the corner of the hallway into the small vestibule, Emily crashed into Bo. Both leapt away from each other. Almost rebounded off each other. Bo quickly settled himself. Emily kept retreating. Bo was a sight from a Spielberg make-up room. He was covered in soot, his eyes startled white and his mouth red, moist and almost sexual in contrast.

Emily was still backing away from him, stuttering that her father wasn't there, that he was with the other firefighters, when Bo's smells caught up with her. They came in layers. Burnt wood, she could overwhelmingly recognise, stale breath, yes, a doggy smell, and finally, overwhelmingly, a musky smell that pushed its way up through the burnt wood overtones. The smells insinuated themselves at the back of her head. They were more unsettling than unpleasant.

'I thought it must be John here,' he said.

'No, not here.' Emily tried to recall what had happened to her father. He was supposed to be watching the backburn. But that had finished. When she couldn't find him to fight the spot fire, she'd presumed he must have gone down to the hall or moved along the other end of the Bay. How the hell was she to know?

While she was trying mentally to relocate her father, Emily noticed Bo's extraordinary beard. It was patchy in growth. Some parts were thick and wiry, other parts were almost bald. Like he'd started shaving himself and then changed his mind. Talk about a bad hair day.

'The others went back to the hall,' said Bo. 'Don't know about John.' Pause. Obviously still thinking. 'You'd better come with me.'

Emily got the impression Bo had issued this invitation with utmost reluctance, like a boy whose mother has insisted he ask the nice girl to dance. Emily intended to let him off the hook.

'Bo, I'm fine. I'm fine here in the house. The backburn's done. It's all settling down and umm – ' pausing. Looking for a way out of the conversation. 'It's all over, Bo.' Emily fumbled for words under Bo's insistent presence. He wasn't meeting her eyes – he had his head turned down and his eyes were darting around different spots of the floor. Emily felt she would have more success arguing with the dog.

'Bo, don't look so worried,' she said, slapping her hands together in mock merriment, 'I'll tell Dad that you called in, when he gets back with the others.'

'You better come up the hill with me,' said Bo.

Bo was finding this encounter stressful. His dog empathised with light whimpers. He was almost tempted to turn on his heels and leave the woman. But she was John's daughter.

'Fire has cut you off from the hall.'

Bo stopped talking when he saw the shock on the woman's face. She hasn't seen the fire yet, he thought. Slowly, almost gently, he pointed behind her, through the kitchen window, which looked north-east.

Emily turned around, reluctantly, almost suspiciously. Through the big kitchen windows she could see that smoke was billowing up towards the house from the small stretch of bush that separated the houses from the waterfront. She walked a few steps into the kitchen to see out the kitchen window better. The smoke seemed to be coming from the east, from the area where she had pounded a spot fire into submission just a little while ago.

'I put it out,' said Emily turning to Bo, 'I put the spot fire out. It was definitely out when I left it – '

'It came from around the headland,' said Bo. He hated hysterics. He didn't like women much either. Maybe because of the hysterics. 'The fire has come around from the other bays. Moved along the waterfront.' Bo mumbled. He shrugged his shoulders, as if he were partly to blame for the fire, taking on some of the responsibility for it. 'Sudden. Was sudden,' he added, trying to explain. Failing.

'Okay, okay. Let's get down to the hall,' said Emily, striding back towards him.

'Can't do that,' said Bo, 'we should – ' Bo tipped his head towards the back of the hill. As if the gesture would finish his sentence. It didn't suffice. 'Up the hill. We should go up the hill.' He was shouting at her now. As if she were deaf.

Emily looked at Bo as if he had just crawled out of his dog's anus. Spurred by the horror of spending any amount of time with the half man/half animal, she dashed out of the kitchen and onto the verandah to map her escape down the hill.

There were only a few hundred metres of bushland between most houses and the waterfront. Just a splinter of bushland, but it was enough to allow the fire that had come around the headland a funnel into the bush suburbia.

'We can run west, behind the houses. Then when we get far enough in front of the fire, we can dash down towards the water,' Emily called from the verandah.

'Burnt ground will be safer. We should go up the hill.'

The tone in Bo's voice suggested such intransigence that Emily began to worry. Bo's nature was something that Emily had speculated about but never seriously contemplated. The speculation had been scary enough.

'Caught between a wildfire and a werewolf,' she muttered to herself as she walked in from the verandah.

'I have to visit the bathroom,' she said to Bo, disappearing into the hallway. She wanted to give herself time to think of an alternative to spending the night with Bo on a burnt-out hillside. But even as she left Bo and his body odour behind her in the hallway, she was beginning to realise she didn't have much of an option. Emily's gut began to ache.

When Emily disappeared, Bo tried to figure out where John Carmody would be. He had been sure he'd find him here, in the house. He tried to remember the last time he had seen him. Maybe at the end of the backburn line? Yes, walking along the eastern edge of the backburn. Looking happy. But had he gone down the hill when the other firefighters had gone down for tea?

Without the woman to distract him, Bo mentally recapped the events from when he had left the group of firefighters. Perhaps along the way he would remember where John Carmody had gone.

'I'll go now,' Bo had said to Roger Burton when the decision was made to head down to the hall for a quick cup of tea.

'This ground is still pretty hot,' Roger Burton said, nodding his head to the blackened land that lay between him and the hut.

'Few things I want to do,' Bo said. He handed the knapsack water sprayer to Burton.

'Don't you feel like a cup of tea?' Roger persisted. Bo shook his head.

Bo loped off, his dog at his heels and the stares of the others on his back. Roger called out after him, 'Beware of the widow-makers!' Bo nodded in acknowledgement. After a few more seconds he felt alone. The men must have turned around and started down the hill. For a minute longer, Bo headed in the direction of his hut.

When he thought the other firefighters were in the hall or at least out of sight, Bo turned and began heading back east. He wasn't in a hurry to make it back to his place, he knew it had been saved. He had some exploring to do. His hunting ground had been transformed. The territory he knew as a dense tangle of scrub, tight-knit casuarina stands, tall redgums and ironbarks had disappeared and been replaced by seared earth.

Fire exposes everything, thought Bo. The hillside was barren now. A bare-butt hillside of rocky outcrops. Purged of green, the rocks held the only remaining claim to the land. Even the trees that were still standing looked uncertain of their future. Bereft of leaves and most of their branches, the trees looked more like giant twigs that had been upended and pushed into the soft, ash of the ground. Ghosts of the forest.

The fire had also exposed the true shape of the hillside. The little gullies, the steepest inclines, the relatively flat rock ledges could all be appreciated anew when they were stripped of the clothing of foliage. Bo knew the shape of these areas through the soles of his feet. He had walked over them so many times. Now, for the first time, he could see the shape of the land.

While the ground smouldered and all other residents sipped tea in the hall, Bo had roamed the burnt-out hillside, scavenging for 'treasure'. His eyes scanned for bits of wood that were showing their spirit. He picked up gnarled and scorched branches, bits of exposed roots and skeletons of saplings. He turned them over with his boots and cradled their warm corpses as he searched them for signs of a story.

The hillside was a strange place that night. Still smoking in some spots, still warm under the boots in other areas. The only part of the hill that wasn't black was the thin track that wound around the back of the houses. Bare earth couldn't burn. The abating southerly air skipped around the hillside, creating small eddies when it met warm air from smoking logs. Occasionally a tree would crash to the ground – without warning, apparently without reason. Bo wasn't worried about the widow-makers. He knew which trees were most likely to fall and he kept his distance from them.

As he rambled across the hillside, Bo also kept an eye out for more practical, man-made treasures – old and forgotten tools, jerry cans, bits of old machinery and even the foundations of homes long forgotten. Aboriginal carvings might be exposed, middens and old garden beds of the convict settlers. These, he knew, were of great interest to John. The spirit of those who lived here before him was important to John. Not so much to Bo. Of all the practical elements exposed by the fire, Bo would pay most attention to those things that had been lost along the bushwalking trails. With penknives, coins, drinking containers, tin plates, spoons, sometimes watches and compasses dropped along the trails, Bo could replenish supplies in his house. But he didn't collect any of these treasures tonight. He remembered their position for retrieval in the coming days. The idea of spending the next few weeks rediscovering his hillside and its exposed treasures filled Bo with excitement.

During the time he had spent re-exploring the hillside, Bo had been distracted three times. First when an old wallaby had hopped into view further up the hill. It was a mess. Its coat was half burnt off and it hopped awkwardly. The wallaby turned towards Bo. Although it was a fair distance up the hill, Bo could see the stark terror in its eyes. It was, Bo realised, a corpse already. Its nerve endings just hadn't got the message. The second disturbance was when he noticed a plume of smoke coming from in front of one of Carmody's neighbours. Bo couldn't see the source because the fire was on the other side of the houses, but even as he noticed it, he could see that it was being extinguished. The yelling and hollering that came from the area suggested it was being beaten to death.

A little later, when he was turning over an old log, Bo was disturbed for a third time. He heard his dog whimper. It was not a hurt whimper or a sad whimper. It was a fear whimper. Bo looked down the hill and saw smoke coming from the east – from the eastern waterfront, in front of the houses. Bo was curious but unafraid. He knew burnt-out land was one of the safest spots to watch an oncoming fire. But then he had noticed lights in John's place. And he remembered that John had not been with the other men when they left for the hall. The dog's whimpering made him feel uneasy. He scrambled down the hill to check that John was all right. And instead, he had found Carmody's daughter.

'I need to find my cap,' said Emily, walking down the hallway to appear at Bo's side. Too close. For both of them. They both took a step back. Emily began fossicking in the mess of fishing tackle, torches, raincoats and brooms that lay behind the back door. She didn't know why she wanted a cap. To shield her, she supposed. If not from the fire. Then from the sight of it. It might provide a fringe to face the fire.

She grabbed a Lumley Insurance cap that had fallen from the rusty hooks onto the floor and, as she turned away from the mess, she picked up the rug that her father had handed her earlier that evening. It was dirty, singed and still smelt of fire. Bo stared at the woman. As if seeing her for the first time.

'Blanket,' said Emily, proffering the rug for Bo's inspection, 'for fighting fires.' She let the rug drape to the floor and lifted the cap off her head. 'Cap,' she said, 'for keeping my head in an emergency.' Bo didn't respond to Emily's joke.

'Come on, let's go and face our future,' said Emily without enthusiasm.

Chapter eighteen

'Brring, brring. Brring, brring.' The ring of the telephone seemed to come from a great distance, as if it were a church bell ringing from many hills away. Gradually the ringing got closer. And louder. Carmody opened his eyes. And saw blackness. He thought he might be dead. But he doubted they had telephones in heaven.

Focusing on the ringing, Carmody became aware of his surroundings. Face down in a pile of compost, nestled near a cool sandstone wall. He turned his face to see down the hill. A house. He was fifteen to twenty metres from the rear of a house. He focused again on the phone. It must be relatives ringing the owners of the house to check they are all right. Only worried relatives let phones ring for so long.

Carmody let his face slump forward again. No, he suddenly thought, the ringing wasn't coming from inside the house. And it wasn't the ring of a normal phone. An image of the mobile phone flashed in his mind. Then he felt it lying against his backside, still in his back pocket. Even as he realised this, the ringing stopped.

Alone in the darkness of the compost pile, with the fog of his brain and a growing awareness of acute pain radiating from his leg, Carmody attempted to roll onto his side and free his hand so it could retrieve the phone. He almost fainted with pain. The pain began shooting up and down his body like lightning strikes. He clamped his teeth together and set his jaw. He told himself to be brave. The ringing continued.

On his second effort, the pain was, if anything, worse. But Carmody managed to shift his arm out from under his body and began to move it slowly down his body to his back pocket. By the time his hand had reached his bottom and pulled the phone ever so slowly out from the pocket, the ringing had stopped. With even greater effort, Carmody's hand carried the phone along his torso, up his neck and finally rested it beside his face.

Carmody lay there expecting the phone to start ringing again. Minutes passed. As he stared at a half-rotten banana peel that lay between his face and the phone, Carmody felt relieved that these neighbours didn't compost meat or soggy cereals. This compost mound was sweet-smelling, warm and soft as an old horsehair mattress.

Still the phone was silent. As the pain subsided, Carmody decided that he should ring for help himself. He began thinking of whom he should ring. Even as he thought of who might be able to rescue him the phone started ringing. He opened his eyes and saw the green face of the phone flashing the word 'call'. Pressing the green button quickly, Carmody was suddenly lost for words.

He croaked. Then, for want of a better word, said, 'Yes?'

'Tony, is that you? Tony, where the hell have you been? Where the buggery are you?'

'Not Tony.' Carmody's pained voice silenced the person on the end of the phone. Carmody suddenly recalled whose phone he had taken. Or stolen. Then he began appreciating why these callers were so persistent.

'Who is it? And where are you?'

'It's John Carmody, and – I'm – I'm not sure where I am.' This was taking more energy than he could ever have believed. Carmody felt a buzzing set up in his head. He felt faint. He willed himself to keep talking.

'I'm hurt. I need help.'

'Okay, okay. I'm the night news editor of Radio 2YX. I can contact the police for you but you have to tell me where you are. Are you still down at Flint Bay? Is Tony there with you? Is Tony all right? Did you find him earlier? Sorry – I'm going too fast. One at a time …'

The phone line went dead then. Carmody stared into its green face. He felt his hopes sinking and his enchantment with the device deflating.

The phone rang again. Carmody was quick on the uptake. He didn't want to upset the temperamental device. 'Hello?'

'Have you got a battery light on the phone?' said the voice.

'I don't know. I can't see properly.'

'Well if you can't see a light, your battery is okay. It's probably just the reception cutting out. Tell me where you are.'

'Behind one of the houses,' Carmody replied. 'Tony is …' as Carmody tried to find the words for community hall he felt his mind being dragged into a huge void. His words echoed around an infinite chamber. His head fell into the banana peel.

'You there? You still there?' the little voice beamed out of the mobile. 'Just take a deep breath and get your energy back before you attempt to speak again. I'll wait here. Take it easy, take it easy.' As Carmody lost consciousness, the phone settled back into piles of tea leaves and old lettuce and the voice disappeared into the ether.

Chapter nineteen

'Who's hot for a fire story?' Jay Willocks yelled across the news room. There were only three people left in the room – a young cadet who appeared to be talking fervently into the phone to her boyfriend, an old hack who was tapping away on a keyboard writing late night news summaries for an English paper, and Mike Cottee. The news editor's eyes landed on Cottee's head. And they didn't budge until Cottee reluctantly looked up.

Cottee took his time walking up to the news editor's desk. As he neared he said, 'So have we lost ten thousand homes to the fires yet? Is that what this story is about – I get to interview the ten thousandth home to be burnt?'

The news editor thought about making a quip but reconsidered. He needed to stroke Cottee into this story. 'Yeah,' he said, 'that was a cynical ploy by the minister wasn't it? Announcing the apocalypse on national television. Do you think he is truly stupid or was there some strategy behind it?'

'I don't know and I don't care,' said Cottee, pulling a chair in front of the news editor's desk and propping his feet on it. He looked at Willocks still standing with the receiver of a phone in his hand. Every so often Willocks put his ear to the receiver as if to listen to something. 'Shouldn't you hang that thing up?' said Cottee.

'No, this is where the story is. We've got a story happening on the end of the line,' said Willocks. 'Remember how we lost contact with Tony Thomas?' Willocks paused for Cottee to answer.

'Yeah, when Tony went for a bog in the bush,' replied Cottee.

'Well, yes. But remember when we rang again, some bloke

picked up the phone. He said that Tony had gone to check out the fires and hadn't returned,' continued Willocks.

'That may have been what Tony told the bloke with the phone,' said Cottee, uncrossing and recrossing his feet on the news editor's desk. 'We figured Tony was doing a "Barry Wells". Maria was taking bets on how long he would hide out in the bush before he would fight his way back through the fires to be miraculously saved by his sheer determination and courage! I gave him twelve minutes,' said Cottee.

'I hope you're not in charge of the news desk when I'm in Bosnia,' said Willocks, pushing Cottee's feet off his table. 'Didn't it occur to any of you that he might be seriously lost? That he might be hurt? Or in danger? Reporters have been seriously hurt in these fires already and you – '

'Oh come on, Jay. The only reporters who have been hurt are those who figured that a few burnt toes were worth the enormous exposure they would get for their pain, the follow-up interviews in the women's magazines, the pay-rise the stations would give them so they wouldn't sue for workers' comp and the fact that they would become almost – '

'Mike, are you shitty because I asked you to come back from that cocktail party down town?' Willocks waited for an answer. Cottee shrugged. 'You don't seriously think I'll let one of my last remaining senior reporters get drunk at a cocktail party while we're in the middle of the biggest catastrophe – ' Willocks waved his hands down the news room. 'Look who I've got left to cover the fires!'

'Get our action-man reporter back from Noumea,' interjected Cottee. Willocks stopped gesturing and looked at Cottee for a few seconds.

'Murray is dying to get out of Noumea. He is supposed to be on his honeymoon and he says he hasn't lifted his head out of the newspapers, radio and TV to look at his new wife much less ...' Willocks let the sentence trail. 'He can't get a plane out of

Noumea until Monday so I told him not to bother, it'll be all over
by then. Unless we're lucky – '

'Murray would love to get his arse burnt in these fires. I can
imagine the hospital scene now.' Cottee was obviously taking the
mickey.

'Okay, okay. The Barry Wells accident may have been a stunt.
Scott Gormley may be a handsome face in search of an accident
but let's face the reality we've got here. We haven't heard from
Tony for two hours. I've tried to contact him twice and all I got is
this bloke who doesn't know where Tony is. As soon as I begin
questioning this bloke in depth, he switches off the phone. Now,
after a long silence, the phone is back on and this same bloke is
dying on the other end of it.'

'Dying? Really dying?' Mike Cottee was suddenly interested.

Jay Willocks held aloft the receiver that he had been holding in
his hand throughout the conversation. Then he pointed his finger
at its earpiece. 'He has passed out. You can hear breathing when
you listen carefully. He's badly hurt. He could hardly speak to me.
Says he's trapped behind a house down there. I don't think he's
got long to live.'

Mike Cottee took the receiver and listened intently. After a few
seconds, he thought he too could hear breathing. He began imagining the report he could do with this receiver in his hand. He
wished he was a television reporter. He could imagine the camera
panning up towards him from the back of the room, panning in
on a solemn-faced reporter who is holding a phone in his hand.
'Listen,' he would say offering the handpiece to the camera, 'to
the sound of death in the fires. Listen to the sound of another
victim of the fires, another …'

'I'll do the story,' he said to his news editor, putting his hand
out to take the phone. 'I've got a great intro for it already.'

With Cottee already cradling the receiver to his chest, Willocks
moved his papers off his desk and ambled across to a spare table.
'It's your baby but I'll ring the police and pass on the details about

this bloke. Seems he's trapped. Probably under a tree or something or part of the house has fallen on him. His name, by the way, is Carmody,' he continued.

'Do you think something sinister has happened? Like he may have been in a fight with Thomas and maybe hurt Thomas, maybe something worse, and now he's lying injured, maybe with Thomas dead next to him – '

'Mike,' Willocks interrupted, 'stick to the facts as we know them ... if you need to speculate, be restrained. Remember, understatement is sometimes scarier than hyperbole.'

Mike Cottee put his ear to the phone again and listened. He could hear waves. He couldn't tell if they were waves of breathing, of distant surf, waves of static or of wind. He was being lulled by the waves when the thought suddenly struck him.

'Jay, how long has the mobile been turned on?' he called across the space between the desks.

Willocks whispered a curse to himself. 'You're right, he could lose power. Let me think ... Thomas has probably had the phone off the charger for a couple of hours – four, maybe six hours. We should have twenty clear hours but he was using it quite a bit ...' He did the calculations at the same time as Cottee. For every minute spent on the phone, ten minutes of charge was lost. 'Mike, you'd better hang up. It will save power. It's probably a better idea anyway. If you hang up and then keep calling back, the ringing of the phone might bring him out of unconsciousness. If you keep the line open, the power could go at any time.'

'But I was going to do the next news report with the phone,' Cottee was gesticulating at the handpiece, 'and hold the phone to the microphone and, you know, let them hear the sound of, sounds of ...'

'Sounds of what, Mike? Dying? The sounds of someone dying?' Willocks, shaking his head, 'If I'd known you were so keen to do a blood-curdling award-winner I would have sent you into the fires on Monday. Next time, Mike, next time, you get to go.'

'Can I still use the phone angle in the story?' said Cottee.

'When you're ready to do the report, I'll get on the end of another phone and do some breathing for you. In the meantime, keep trying the number and see if you can get the bloke to wake up again.' Pausing. 'Oh and Mike, what sort of death rattle do you want – light, barely there breathing or a raspy, smoky breath?'

'Thanks, Jay,' said Cottee, knowing his news editor would be able to pick exactly the right tone of breathing to cause the most alarm. Then he banged the number for Tony Thomas's mobile. He imagined the mobile rining at the other end, a ringing that was echoing around the fire-ringed community of Flint Bay. The call of the phone that was failing to stir a dying man, he thought. The ringing of a phone that would be subsumed by fire at any moment, he thought.

'Hey, Jay,' Cottee yelled across the desks, 'is it dangerous to be on the other end of a phone that is being burnt?'

'Not if you're on the right end of the phone, Mike,' Willocks replied.

Chapter twenty

Emily was having trouble keeping pace with Bo. How could someone move so rapidly, so nimbly, and never move his upper body? she thought. Especially such a wiry old man. Old? Emily couldn't decide how old Bo was – possibly forty-five but just as likely sixty-five. It almost seemed as if Bo aged to a different clock to everyone else. Certainly the wildman could not be time-cast by a dated hairstyle or his wardrobe, or even by his wrinkles. In Bo's world, age was measured by scars, bumps, nicks, limps, lost digits and other infirmities. Emily had no idea what year Bo had landed on the earth but he was moving over boulders, through thickets, and around sandy banks like a young man.

During their escape up the hill, Bo never turned to look at her, to inquire after her welfare or ensure she was still following. But his dog did. Every few metres, the mongrel would turn and look at her as if annoyed that she was following. Once or twice the dog lifted her upper lip to begin a growl but Bo yelled at Sheila even before the dog had released the growl.

After an exhausting few minutes, Emily grew annoyed at Bo's stupid plan, at his indifference to her welfare and at his dog's petulance. The next time the dog turned to check her progress, Emily growled back at it. It wasn't a loud growl. It wasn't a particularly threatening growl. Emily's growl wasn't much more than a baring of her teeth. But no one had growled at Sheila before. Sheila didn't enjoy the experience.

The dog charged at Emily like a keg on wheels. Emily looked up in horror. The dog bounding down the hill towards her had such speed, momentum, height and such a pissed-off look on her face that Emily froze to the spot. With split-second decision-making, she concluded that she couldn't run; there wasn't a climbing tree within sight and she certainly couldn't fight. As a yelp of fear burst from her diaphragm, she turned to face down the hill. Bracing her body to withstand the imminent blow of the dog, she wrapped her arms around her head.

Emily's yelp alerted Bo to his dog's attack but by the time Bo had turned around, seen what was happening and yelled 'No' to his dog, Sheila was within three metres of Emily. The yell from Bo aborted Shelia's planned leap onto the woman. But it couldn't stop the dog's momentum.

Emily felt the dog crash against her legs. She was bowled over. Literally. The dog took her legs from under her and kept heading down the hill. Emily flipped and landed on her back. She was so winded she didn't notice that she was sliding down the hill, scraping her legs on sharp rocks and fallen branches.

She hadn't got her breath back, even when Bo appeared above her. Her mouth was gaping at the sky like a netted fish. Gulping for breath, Emily willed herself to faint. When she saw Bo's face appear above her, she was torn between wanting him to give her breath and wanting to die. She thought she might prefer to die than to have Bo do mouth-to-mouth resuscitation.

With one arm, Bo flipped Emily into a sitting position. That action was enough to get her lungs working again. As Emily panted with relief, she felt a wave of emotion tingle through her body. Relief and shock shivered through the nerve ends of her body, washed over her mind like a thick balm. Then, without premeditation, Emily burst out crying. Her face contorted with a series of thick, mucusy sobs.

'Why me!' she yelled down the hill with her arms flailing out to encompass the fire front; to encompass the mongrel dog that was now looking sheepish below her and the wildman behind her.

'Why, why, why – ' Emily's curse was subsumed by sobs. Thick, ratcheting sobs.

Bo stared in horror at the woman who was lashing the ground
with her hands and wailing like a banshee. He might have been
fascinated at such a sight, if it weren't his responsibility. But he
couldn't walk away from this strange creature. Bo gave her a few
more seconds to see if dignity would return. But the sobbing was
swelling. She looked as though she might lie on the ground and
refuse to move. He bent down to her and lifted her by the elbow.
She had no resistance left. He half escorted, half dragged her the
last hundred metres or so to his place. The dog followed a few
paces behind, obviously mortified that someone else had usurped
her place at Bo's side.

Emily's sobs were subsiding by the time they arrived outside
Bo's house. Emily didn't know it was Bo's house. She thought it
was a shed. As it lay on a rocky outcrop surrounded by a swathe
of burnt-out bushland and the remains of a grassy paddock in
front, she felt the shed was probably a good place to shelter from
the fire. It was only when Bo ushered her inside and sat her on
his bunk that Emily realised she was in his home. Sitting on his
bed. In the middle of the bush. Isolated from the world. With a
feral dog outside the door. And a wildman beside her.

Emily filed these facts in her mind as Bo busied himself in a
corner of the room. An inventory of horror began to build. Even
with the aftermath of sobs reverberating through her body, she
was acutely aware of the room's smell. It filled her nostrils, the
back of her head and the upper part of her palate. It was … it was
mainly the smell of maleness. The sort of smell she encountered
walking into her father's place after a long absence, or the sort of
smell that is in an all-boys' house. It was the smell of body odour,
of pheromones; the faint odour of urine and unwashed bed sheets
and sweaty clothes. Overlaying these odours was the smell of old
tea and damp tobacco. Lastly there was the clear, almost astrin-
gent smell of kerosine.

I'm a goner, she thought, closing her eyes and bringing her fists
to rest on her cheeks. Any second, this creature will turn on me,

shred the clothes off my body with his sharp nails, push me back
on this rotting mattress and have his animal way with me. And
then douse me with kero and burn me alive.

'This will hurt a little,' Bo said, from a position that was very
close to her face.

'Please, please. No, no, please,' Emily whispered urgently as
she opened her eyes to confront the horror.

Bo tipped a bottle of hydrogen peroxide onto an old hanky. 'It
should be cleaned.'

Emily stared in silence while Bo focused on her leg. In the dim
light of the cabin, Emily noticed that her old army trousers were
torn. Shifting forward to look at her leg, she could see a frightful
gash on her calf. Then she felt the sting of the peroxide as Bo
dabbed the gash with his hanky. Too late, she wondered if she
could get AIDS from a dirty hanky.

'Whoooaahhh,' Emily moaned. Bo looked into the face of the
woman for the first time. He had serious reservations about her.
Now that her face was screwed up in demented pain, he felt nervous about her. She reminded him of a hatchling – scrawny, bird-
faced and hairless. He wondered why she had hair on her head
but not on her legs. How could someone have legs that were as
white and bald as the palms of his hands? When he looked at the
legs, he wanted to run his hands over them to see if they were
hose. But he could see the blood flowing from the skin so he
knew the baldness was not artificial. Bo recalled a boy in his
boarding school who had lost every hair on his body – the hair on
his head, his eyelashes, eyebrows, the hairs on his arms and legs.
That boy was deeply disturbed - 'traumatised' the priests said.
Perhaps Emily is disturbed, thought Bo. No wonder Sheila didn't
like this woman.

Emily had thrown herself back on the bed but as soon as the
stinging eased she pushed herself upright. Didn't want to give him
any more ideas. Bo had retreated to a dark corner of his hut. Still
sucking air through clenched teeth, Emily felt she had to make

conversation. If she got him talking, he would remember that they were both human beings, both social creatures, that they both belonged to the world where rape and murder were not allowed. Conversation, she thought, was her last link to the real world. The world where men use razors, dogs wear collars, houses come with fences and survival means making it to payday.

'So Bo,' she said with false bonhomie, 'what do you do?'

Wrong, wrong, wrong, she thought as Bo turned slowly from his corner, chewing the question over in his mind.

Bo was indeed chewing on the question. Do? he thought. What do I do? He thought of the things he did. He walked a lot. He cooked a little. He read his magazines. Do? Do? What do I do? He thought of other connotations. Did she mean what they were going to 'do' about the fire now? He looked around his room for inspiration. Then he saw a branch. He pointed at it. 'That,' he said.

Emily looked at the branch propped on his table. 'Oh really!' she said, having no idea whatsoever what Bo was referring to. But she wanted to keep him distracted. So she lifted herself off the bunkbed and wandered over to the branch to pick it up.

'A goanna,' said Bo.

'Ummm,' said Emily. She wondered what level of IQ she was dealing with. A man who thinks a branch is called a goanna has got to have an IQ around the speed limit.

Emily pretended to view the branch. But her eyes were scanning the room. She spotted the kerosine lamp and felt that at least her fear of being doused with kerosine was unfounded. She searched for weapons. For hidden guns and sharp knives. Every so often as her eyes darted around the room, never veering to Bo who stood at her back, she glanced at the branch again. A goanna, she thought. She almost groaned the word.

Then she saw it. In the golden glow of the kerosine lamp, she could barely discern it. But as she held it up to the light, she saw a perfectly formed lizard skittling along the branch.

'There!' she exclaimed. 'There it is! Oh my God, it *is* a goanna.'

Bo looked askew at the woman, misgivings growing by the minute.

'This is great,' she said, looking up at Bo. 'Have you done any others? You must have, this is so good. Where are the others?'

Bo gestured to a few spots around his hut where finished pieces awaited the return of the gallery owner across the bay. Emily took one of the pieces down from a shelf. With a frisson of excitement, she studied the branch. It was like find-the-picture puzzles. She stared at it for a good half-minute, turning it carefully, examining it from afar, then closely. Shrugging her shoulders with embarrassed disappointment, she handed it back to Bo. Then she saw it. Taking the branch back, she held it in her outstretched hands and said, 'It's a tree, isn't it! It's the branches of a weeping tree. And there's a pond underneath!'

Bo grimaced and blushed. He felt tingles of excitement listening to the woman's triumphant gushings. No one had been so enthusiastic about something of his before. Or not for a very long time. It was a strange feeling. A strange, dangerous, heart-thumping sensation. Bo was more nervous than ever. And he liked the feeling.

Emily was now picking up the rest of the pieces that Bo had indicated just a few minutes earlier. 'I'm going to find all your secret treasures in these branches.'

Bo smiled in acknowledgement. Or he tried to smile. It had been so long that it didn't quite work. His mouth twitched. Unfamiliar territory. The smile slipped into a grimace.

Emily didn't see Bo's attempt at a smile. She was transfixed. For minutes she sat on the bunk, picking up each of the pieces in turn to discover its art. She was calmer now, more solemn. She could see that these branches did not reveal themselves too soon. It took patience and perhaps an open mind to see what Bo had created.

Time passed silently. Emily was immersed in her search for art. Bo was standing by his one window, looking down the hill. He felt like a stranger in his own home with this strange creature, who had filled his room with shrieks of delight, yelps of pain and a perfume that was soft, warm and powdery – like the aroma of his mother. He was keen to keep moving but felt immobilised by her presence.

Finally Emily found the secrets of all the branches, except for one. She felt defeated. And disappointed with herself for her inability to see beyond the branch.

'This one defeats me,' she said to Bo, handing back his branch.

'Me too,' said Bo.

'What do you mean?' asked Emily.

'Nothing there. Couldn't find it,' said Bo.

'You mean you haven't sculpted this one?' Emily asked. When she saw Bo agree, Emily threw her fist to the ceiling and yelled, 'Yes!'

As Emily's whoop fell to earth, the room was silent again. Sitting on the bunk, smiling to herself, Emily drew a mental picture of herself in the room. Slowly she became aware of Bo standing in the corner, alternately looking out the window towards the fire and looking in her direction. She saw again her compromised position on the bunk and gazed around the room in search of a conversation. She spied a family portrait propped against the window.

'Is this your family?' she asked, pointing to the portrait.

Bo looked towards the picture as if seeing it for the first time in a very long time.

'Mum, Dad, bruvver and me,' he said.

Emily pushed herself off the bunk and went to the window. Picking up the framed portrait carefully, she could see that it was a classic, pre-war family portrait. Everyone was posing on the front steps of the family house. Father at the rear was a head higher than everyone else and his hand rested proprietorially on his wife's shoulder. Mother looked intelligent but withdrawn. Her hands hung loose at her sides, as if they were itching to get working again. The older boy was almost a teenager and his jaw jutted forward in a macho pose. The younger boy had ears that waved at the world.

'You?' Emily asked placing her finger on the boy with the jumbo ears. Bo nodded.

'What happened?' Emily blurted the question out without thinking. She immediately felt embarrassed. 'I mean do you still own the house?'

'Sold it. Don't need that,' Bo replied as he began to pace.

'You sold the house here at the Bay that was once next door to this hut too,' Emily said, more statement than question.

Bo shrugged. Emily stared at the house in the portrait. It would never have occurred to her that this wildman had come from a privileged background. If she'd been asked to envisage Bo's child-hood, she would have imagined a poor bush house with a weird child and alcoholic parents. She could have pictured him inside a wolf's den more easily than she could picture him on the rolling turf of a majestic home.

'You should take the photos to a safe place,' Emily said, staring into the charms of a past generation and, in particular, the self-assured look on the face of young Bo. Or Anthony as he was called in the handwritten list of names at the bottom of the photo.

Bo looked at them again. He hadn't even thought about moving them down to the water. But now that he looked at them he supposed they were the sort of things that most people would want to save. To him they were always just there. In the back-ground of his cabin. Like memories themselves, quaint but of no relevance. Just background noise. Certainly they weren't useful, like the old magazines.

'I should help the others with the fire,' Bo said suddenly, step-ping over Emily's outstretched leg to open the door.

'What will I do?' she asked, breaking her reverie with Bo's pre-war family home.

Bo was already outside the hut with his dog circling eagerly around his heels.

Chapter twenty-one

Jack twitched into wakefulness. His bum was numb. His mind was a jumble of sleep, grog, sinusitus and regrets. As he scanned the scene outside his Jaguar, he realised the world had moved along. He'd lost touch with time but he wasn't sure whether he had fallen asleep or switched off.

He leant forward and caressed his kneecap. He could almost feel it swelling under his palm. He patted around the knee in gentle exploration. It felt thicker, fatter than he remembered. Bound to require surgery. Hesitantly he stretched his leg out in front of him. It's amazing I can still move it, thought Jack. Another victim of the fire. Jack shook his head in empathy.

Looking towards Flint Bay, he could see nothing through the heavy smoke. He thought of his father and the other residents. 'Sorry, blokes. I'm useless to you now,' he said to them as his hand continued to knead his knee. What would they be doing at this moment? Hiding? Evacuating? Fighting the fires? He tried to imagine residents strung out along the hill with hoses, picks and whatever … The image was slow in forming. His memories of the Bay were as insubstantial as his visits. He knew the track up to the house, the route to the corner beach and he knew Mrs Parker. But, as he tried to reconstruct his father's house in his mind, Jack realised he had only ever seen the place through the unfocused eye of a guest. Always taking in the panorama, never the details. He knew the view from the verandah but he couldn't remember how high the verandah stood off the ground. Or how close the bush was to the verandah. He knew there was a sweep of lawn but he couldn't recall whether it was wide enough to provide a good fire break. He knew there was a water tank at the back of the house. But he couldn't remember if there was just one tank or two, or even three.

He tried to place his father and Emily on the hillside. He could see Emily clearly. She was in the bush, dressed in fatigues, shouting something, frantic, angry, yelling at others to do something. Like a fly braining itself against a window. He saw his father. Quiet, purposeful, doing something diligently. Smoke was shrouding him. His father was thinking … Jack tried to think of what might be on his father's mind. He came up with a blank. He was saying … What would he be saying? The image of his father receded. He was an ethereal presence on a smoky hillside.

'I don't know the bastard at all!' Jack suddenly said to himself. Again he tried to place his father on the hillside with the other residents. With Emily and her frantic yells, with Mrs Parker and her pokiness … his father was … his father was not there for him. His father's face was turned from him, looking into the bush. His body stiff and unfamiliar. His eyes, if he could just see into his father's eyes. Jack forced the image of his father to turn to him. He could see the eyes now. Expressionless. His father's eyes told him nothing. They seemed to upbraid him with detached recognition.

Jack broke his daydreamy stare. He shook his head and blew air softly out of his mouth. 'I know Mrs Parker better than I know my old man,' he whispered to himself.

He looked across the bay. It occurred to him for the first time since the fires had swept through Sydney that he might have seen his father for the last time. It occurred to him that his father might be facing his death at this very minute, that he might be dead already. 'Have I never seriously contemplated that possibility? In all this drama, I never once seriously considered that Dad might …' In his silence, he answered his own question. The thought that his father may have already died flooded the back of Jack's eyes. He felt his sinuses clog with mucus. If he survives, Jack thought as he pressure-cleared his sinuses, I'll get to know him again. I'll spend time with him. Reach out. In his mind, Jack built scenes of meaningful evenings spent with his father on the deck of his Killara home. He felt invigorated with purpose. I'll have real talks with him. We'll go out to dinner together. We'll go to the rubgy club. Maybe regularly. Every Thursday night. Jack imagined garrulous, blokey evenings spent with his father in the rugby club, sharing ribald jokes and football scores. He felt liberated by his resolutions. Forgiveness too. As if intentions were half the solution.

Wiping his sweaty palms down the front of his shirt, Jack looked across the bay as the smoke cleared. And he looked more intently. Something had changed. The fires. The fires had changed. The big front that had swept in from the west looked as if it had been blown to smithereens. All that was left of it was a hillside dotted with smoke trails, occasional flares and slow-burning tree trunks.

But a new fire had sprung up on the headland to the south-east of Flint Bay. It had snaked its way around the southern foreshores and was about to turn the corner into Flint Bay. Jack shifted in his car seat to get a better view. He pressed the squirt and wipe func-tion of his windscreen wipers to remove the grit that was filming his vision. Whether it was the cleaner windscreen or a sharper mind, Jack suddenly appreciated the danger of the new fire. This fire would sweep around the headland and cut off the houses from the water.

'Shit, shit, shit, shit, shit', Jack said, now fully alert and thor-oughly confused. At that moment the *Best of the Beachboys* faded and the pips of a news bulletin echoed around the cabin of the Jaguar. Jack turned the volume up.

'Sydney, in the early hours of Saturday morning. A city still ringed by fires. A city sitting under a heavy pall of smoke. A city counting the toll: the lost houses, the lost pets, the lost bushland and perhaps the loss of yet another life. This is Mike Cottee with a special round-up of the Sydney fires.'

As the news tune wound down, the radio faded to silence. Jack turned up the volume again. He could only hear the sound of distant waves coming through the radio.

'Do not touch the volume dial,' boomed the voice of the reporter. 'That faint sound you just heard is the sound of a man in deep trouble. That is the sound of a man trapped in the fires to the north of the city. He can't speak. He is barely alive. No one knows where he is, but thanks to the modern technology of a mobile phone, we can hear his struggle for life and, with any luck, we might be able to get him out of there.

'Just a few hours ago, in the small community of Flint Bay, one of our reporters, Tony Thomas, tracked off into the bush to check out the fire situation. He hasn't been seen or heard of since. Instead, from our news room in the city, we have been monitoring the fate of a resident of Flint Bay as he lies by the mobile phone that belongs to our reporter, Tony Thomas.

'We have marshalled the resources of police and fire crews to Flint Bay to help with the rescue. There is not much else we can do to help the victim, but he does have one lifeline. It's this phone (pause to listen to the faint breathing sounds). It's not much. But we in the newsroom have been endeavouring to maintain the spirits of the wretched man on the other end of this line. As you can hear (pause to listen to more breathing) it's a faint hope.

'Perhaps as a city, we could all put our prayers and our hopes behind this man, who is just hanging onto life. Perhaps we could all pause for a minute and give this man, this man whom we only know as Carmody, our best wishes and our prayers.'

Jack had feared the worst when he heard the reporter mention Flint Bay. When he heard his father's name, he felt his spine chill. His eyes misted and his heart felt as though it was floating in the middle of his chest. He feared he might float away at any minute. He heard the sound of light breathing. His father's breathing? Or his? He didn't know. No, no it must be his own breathing. He could feel himself getting lighter in the head, the buzzing of an imminent faint. He forced himself to fix his eyes on the hillside of Flint Bay. Just across the bay, yet so far away. He began to think that he was watching a movie again. It seemed so unreal, so beyond his reality, so out-there.

Jack banged the dashboard to dislodge his thoughts. He made a move to get out of the car. I'll bloody swim across the bay, he thought. I'll drive, float, sail, swim or fucking fly over the bay, he thought. Then he saw his mobile phone.

'Of course,' Jack said to himself as he phoned the number that the radio station repeated ad nauseum through the day to take requests for favourite hits. His call entered a computer queue.

'What request would you like?' said a voice on the end of the line. Thank God, thought Jack, it's a woman, not a computer.

'I need to speak to the newsroom ... I know this is not the phone number but if you can't put me through just tell me the number ... it's a bloody emergency, woman. I'm not trying to get a cheerio on air, it's an emergency.'

The sharpness of Jack's voice frightened the hit requests operator into giving him the newsroom number. Even as he punched the number into his mobile, Jack had no idea what he was going to say.

''Lo, newsroom,' barked a voice at the other end of the line.

'Ummm, umm, listen,' said Jack, utterly unable to put words in the right sequence, 'my name is Jack Carmody. I heard ... on the radio ... just then ... that ummmm ...'

'It's Mike Cottee here, Mr Carmody. Are you related to the Carmody we have on the end of the line?'

'Father,' still struggling with logic. 'That's my father.'

The voice on the other end of the line was silent. Jack had no hope of continuing the conversation so he waited.

'Jack, did you say your name is?'

'Ummm. Jack. Jack Carmody ... my – '

'Oh Jack, yes of course. This is truly awful. It must be terribly hard for you to ... do you mind if we tape this, Jack? It might come in handy later, if we need to … umm, you know … refer to it when the search for your father gets under way …'

'Sure, sure,' said Jack annoyed that the reporter was side-tracking him, 'I'd like to know where he is … what I can do … we have to be able to … do, you know, where he is?' growing exasperated with tremors that were robbing his throat of moisture and his brain of logic.

'Hold on a minute, Jack Carmody, let me explain,' said Cottee, afraid that he had a panicky fish on the end of the line. 'Your father is somewhere in Flint Bay. We have been endeavouring to pinpoint his location but he keeps lapsing into unconsciousness. It must be terribly difficult for you.'

The official tone of the reporter was rankling Jack. 'Yes, yes, it is hard. But I just want to know …'

'Are you down there in Flint Bay, at the moment?'

'No,' said Jack. 'I tried to get across there but I'm stuck on the peninsula. I'm looking across the bay to the hillside now. It doesn't look too good …'

'What can you see?'

'The main fire has dwindled. But there's another front coming around into the Bay from the south-east headland. They probably can't see it from inside Flint Bay so if you could contact the authorities and get a message down there about the new front, see if that – '

'Yes, okay, we'll be telling authorities immediately about that new development. Tell me, how do you think he would be coping right now, trapped in a fire storm, wounded, weak and – '

'Oh, hang on! I'm not going to answer those sort of questions. If he is hurt, I want him out of there.' Pausing. Then angrier. 'I don't want to do a post-mortem now.'

'Of course not, Mr Carmody. I'm sure we can all understand your fear and torment – ' the use of the word 'we' rang bells in Jack's mind. We? We can understand your torment. Suddenly Jack saw who the reporter meant by 'we'.

'Are you taping this?' Jack interjected. 'Will you be broadcasting this?'

'We asked your permission, Mr Carmody,' said Cottee, using the royal 'we'.

'Not for airing it! You said something about a tape. What's this about an interview?' Jack yelled.

'With all respect, Mr Carmody, you can't withdraw permission after the interview.'

Jack was silent. His anger had returned some clarity to his thinking. He'd been fooled into an interview. A pathetic sounding interview, at that. He should not say anything else without thinking it over.

'Mr Carmody?' Cottee's voice inquired.

'I'm still here.' Jack was silent again. He began thinking like a lawyer. He'd dealt his best card – an interview. But he could still play on the possibility of another, more thoughtful interview. He could dangle an exclusive arrangement before the reporter. He could play on the reporter's sense of decency. But that was a wild card.

'For the moment, Mr Cottee, I would prefer it if you didn't broadcast our conversation,' said Jack, pausing to enable the reporter to turn off the tape recorder. Big hope. 'As you can understand,' he continued, 'I'm very keen to speak to my father. If you could tell me the number of the mobile phone that he has in his possession I might be able to discover where he is. We might be able to direct emergency workers to him.'

This time Cottee was silent. The professional tone of the son put him on edge. He also wanted to continue the interview, get some family history, a bit of scene setting. And tie him up exclusively. At least for twenty-four hours.

'I'd like some sort of response to my request,' said Jack to the silence.

Cottee guessed the subtext of that comment. It meant, 'You are on the record and if you don't tell me how to contact my father, I

will have you before every court in the country when he dies.'
The import of this conversation finally hit Cotttee.

'Of course I'll give you your father's number. We no longer
have him on the line. We hung up to conserve power in his
mobile phone. But I'm happy to give you the phone number, I
just ask that you don't speak for too long. We are not sure how
much power the battery has left. Also,' Cottee paused here for a
swallow, 'if you could ring the station back when you've finished
talking so we can know what's going on, assist with authorities
and,' Cottee's voice was tailing off a little, 'we might speak at
more length.'

'You want another interview,' said Carmody.

'Well, we're happy to assist you in saving your father. I would
hope that you might repay the courtesy and grant an interview.'

'Another interview, you mean,' said Jack.

'Another interview,' concurred Cottee. Jack shook his head in
disbelief. Here was a reporter playing on *his* sense of decency.
But he had already decided to do another interview. He hoped
that a new interview might prompt the reporter to can the earlier
drivel. Although he suspected that his tears, fears and hyperbole
were exactly what the station wanted to air.

'I'd be happy to do another interview,' said Jack. 'Perhaps you
can hold off broadcasting our first conversation until I've spoken
to my father and got back to you. I'm sure I'll have much more
insight to offer, after I have contacted my father. Don't you think?'

'I'm sure too,' said Cottee. An answer that promised absolutely
nothing.

Chapter twenty-two

Bo scampered down the hill with his dog in position at his right heel. The dog's vigorous wagging said she was happy to be alone with Bo again. Bo had mixed thoughts upon leaving Emily. Mostly he was relieved. No woman had ever been inside his place before. Even the woman from the art gallery would never go inside. He would meet her outside the hut and negotiate in the chairs beside the outdoor fireplace. Suited her. Suited him.

Now a woman had been inside his place. She had burst into his room, flopped onto his bed and displaced him to an uncomfortable corner. She claimed his home with her scent. When she had quietened and the awful smell of fear had left her pores, her sweet smell had reached around the room and touched everything. Including him. Including Sheila. Sheila hadn't liked the smell. Bo could see her nose twitching in irritation. Bo liked it. It was talcy. It was the smell that had hugged him when he used to throw himself into the bosom of his mother. The smell of tears and comforting and strokes across his forehead. It had been a long, long time since he had nestled into the soft folds of his mother's body. Emily's smell, lapping around his room, brought back all those memories.

It had unnerved him too. He hadn't smelt softness in so long, he didn't know how to respond. When he found himself staring at the white baldness of her legs, he was worried that he might do something ungentlemanly. Not anything indecent. But he wanted to touch. He desperately wanted to touch her leg. Just once.

He was relieved too. To be out in the bush again with the warm, black ground beneath his boots and his dog panting behind his ankles. Talking to people exhausted him. And his talk with Emily had been longer and more … more challenging than any conversation he had held in a long time. Sometimes, he felt himself shrinking when people spoke to him too much. As if their talking was stealing a little bit of his soul. That's why he kept to his own tracks along the Bay. Tracking across the hill on a higher, barely visible track than the one that others used down near the water. That's why he rarely met the morning ferry to buy provisions. He bought food in bulk and infrequently. He caught the ferry over to the peninsula early in the morning. Those mornings were the only times that he was separated from his dog. Sheila was a possessive dog. She hated it when Bo would insist that she stay by the door of the hut while he went down the hill with a big hessian bag to catch the ferry. The dog would remain disconsolate, whimpering to herself while Bo travelled on the ferry. Sheila would remain beside the hut while Bo did his shopping in the corner store that lay three kilometres across the water from Flint Bay. Then as soon as Bo had paid the shopkeeper and was turning to walk out of the shop, Sheila's ears would prick up. As Bo took the first steps towards home, Sheila would begin bounding down the hill towards the wharf. Sheila was always on the wharf when Bo alighted. Always.

As Bo got closer to the fire front, he could see firefighters trying to tackle the fire from the waterfront. From his vantage above the line of houses, still in the burnt-out area, Bo could see that they were having limited success. A fire hose, drawing water from the bay, was dampening the fire's progress along the hillside. Other firefighters with knapsacks were having less success. No one was trying to fight the fire from uphill. Already one house was on fire. Strangely it was the second house along from the eastern end of the hillside. The first house in the line of fire had been spared. Not through any special efforts or precautions. Simply because fire was capricious. Another three houses were threatened. The next ten minutes would tell which of those houses might end up in flames.

Bo felt Sheila breathing heavily on his sock while he mentally tracked the best route down through the houses to the waterfront. A loud whooshing thump set Bo off down the hill again. Probably a can of petrol, thought Bo. Boat fuel or mower fuel, stored in a house. A column of smoke and fire from underneath one of the threatened houses confirmed Bo's speculation. Another house is a goner, he thought.

'Bo! Bo! Over here,' yelled Roger Burton, spying the dark figure of Bo scampering down towards the front track. 'Good to see you. Can you give us a hand here?' Burton continued as Bo closed the distance between them.

Roger Burton was fifty metres in front of the fire. Although he carried a knapsack on his back, he wasn't doing much firefighting himself – his role seemed one of directing the men working the flanks of the fires. Fighting this sort of fire with a knapsack was a bit like trying moral suasion on a fire. As if reading scepticism on Bo's face, Burton continued, 'I need to set up another fire hose further along the track, if we're going to stop this fire before the next lot of houses. Can you take this knapsack from me and keep closing in on the fire as it moves along the water?'

Roger Burton wasn't waiting for an answer. He already had the knapsack off his back. Bo nodded as he accepted the knapsack and looked along the line of men who were further back along the flank of the fire. There was one man with a hose, three or four with knapsacks. There was a lot of smoke, not much drizzle.

'Carmody down there?' said Bo, the knapsack still propped against his legs.

'No, no. We think he went back to his house. We saw lights on there. I presume he headed further uphill or tracked back westward when he saw this coming around the headland,' said Burton. He took advantage of the moment to squirt water drops into his eyes.

'Wasn't him in the house. Was his girl,' said Bo.

'How do you know?' said Burton, trying to focus on Bo through his watering eyes.

'I saw her. Took her out. Up the hill. To my place.'

Roger Burton was blinking wildly at Bo now, trying to clear his eyes. He stared into Bo's dark and wizened face, which was framed by a wild tizz of hair, beard and eyebrows. Still blinking, Roger saw that Bo's over-sized hands were absently working the nozzle on the knapsack. He saw Bo as a woman might see him. As a frightened woman might see him. Alone on a fire-swept hillside. Dragged to a lonely hut. At that moment, a veil of smoke swirled around the wildman, giving him an ethereal image. Worse, Bo didn't budge, cough, squint his eyes or try to fan the smoke away. He looked comfortable in the smoke. Unperturbed, immutable.

'You took her to your hut?' said Burton, fishing for more information.

Bo shuffled his boot on the ground and refused to meet Burton's gaze. The knapsack tottered over and hit the ground. He knew he shouldn't have stared at the woman's bare leg. He tried to remember whether he had touched the leg after all. Maybe he had. Maybe Mr Burton knew he had. Women were always trouble. Always trouble.

'She's all right,' said Bo, trying to answer all the questions bobbing around in the other man's head.

Roger Burton banged his forehead with his hand. All right? All right! he thought to himself. Burton stalked around in a circle while Bo kicked earth distractedly. What the hell does that mean? thought Roger. Does it mean she's mucked up but she's still alive? All right! Does it mean she has been brutally raped but she's okay because she's up there in the hut comatosed with trauma? What does 'all right' mean to a man who is so anti-social that he sends his dog chasing after the art gallery owner who is kind enough to pay him a few dollars for bits of bark?

'What the hell does all right mean?' Roger Burton shouted. Surprising himself, Bo and the dog. Sheila bared her teeth, growled and began to move out from behind Bo's ankle. Bo kept banging the ground with his boot. He was inclined to leave the rest of this exchange to Sheila.

Roger Burton's mind was still flashing with images. A white girl, a dark, unknowable man, a hot hillside, flames, burning flesh, silent screams of a gagged woman, a dog as witness and accomplice. The growl of the dog, padding towards him, brought him back to the reality in front of him.

'Okay, okay,' said Burton, addressing the dog more than Bo. 'She's okay, is she?' Waiting. Peering under Bo's matt of hair, trying to contact his downcast face.

Bo nodded. Sheila stood her ground, still growling. Burton's hands were lifted in the classic calming pose. For himself as much as for the dog.

'I've got to take your word for it. I can't stay here and try to squeeze a sensible conversation out of you. I've got to get that hose. Just concentrate on the front of the flank, Bo. Don't go up the hill. Don't go up to your hut until I get back. Okay?'

Bo nodded. He didn't find the courage to talk again until Mr Burton was heading off. 'Where is Carmody?' Bo yelled after Mr Burton. Burton just threw his hands up in the air and kept going.

The radiant heat of the fire warmed Bo's forehead as he searched the ground in front of him for a memory of Carmody. Bo had been on the western perimeter when Carmody had been patrolling the eastern end of the backburn. Bo looked up towards the houses, through shrouds of smoke. Carmody had been behind one of these houses the last time Bo had seen him. Virtually straight up the hill from where he stood now. Bo had a bad feeling. Carmody wasn't the sort to disappear during an emergency. He wouldn't find a bolthole and sit it out.

Leaving the knapsack, Bo began scuttling up the hill. He cut a circle around the approaching fire to reach the loose-toothed line

of houses. He was on alien ground. There was no track leading
straight up the hill so he pushed, brushed and leapt his way over
bushes, bracken, old wire and the odd bit of junk that hadn't
made it down the hill for the council clean-ups. He felt alien, too,
around these houses. These houses that were built for views and
warm nights on timber verandahs. These houses had never
looked more ill-at-ease in their environment than they did tonight.
Bo could almost feel their discomfort as he skirted around the
back of one of them. He'd always thought the houses were follies.
They were built as if disdainful of the bush – above and beyond
the ground. They were loaded down with air-conditioners,
heaters, flyscreens and water heaters – to keep the bush at bay. At
night they were lit, inside and out, so the dark could never
penetrate. Bo couldn't understand why people wanted to live in
the bush if they did everything possible to detach themselves from
the feel of living in the bush – its quietness, its darkness and
its moods.

Bo was only three houses along from the eastern end of the
bay but he couldn't travel further east. The fire had arrived there
and was dancing inside two of the houses already. He had to trust
that Carmody wasn't in there. He turned towards the west and
scuttled along the back of the houses. Bo kept close to the walls
to avoid the smoke. It was much thicker up the hill than it was
below. At times, the smoke turned a bilious green. This was
smoke from the burning houses. It was noxious with man-made
materials. Sheila began to whimper. Bo was normally receptive to
Sheila's calls. Her whimpers had alerted him to fierce storms while
he was out in the bush just as her barks had scared off innumer-
able snakes that were lazing on tracks. Bo was so attuned to his
dog, he could tell the level of danger by her sounds. This sort of
whimper usually indicated a threat that the dog could do nothing
about – a storm, or fire.

Tonight, the dog obviously didn't think it was such a great
idea to be heading off into a fire. Bo barked at Sheila to stop

whimpering. Over time, Bo's communication with his dog had lapsed into pidgin English. 'Cut it out' gradually became a gutteral-sounding 'krroouut'; 'come on' became 'carrrnn'. Sheila understood these commands perfectly and responded happily to them. But the sounds of Bo disciplining his dog were a source of fear for many other residents of Flint Bay.

Bo almost yelled at Sheila again, when, seconds after she finished whimpering, she started barking. The tone of bark forced him to stop and look around. The dog was facing towards the back of a small stone wall. A pile of debris was lumped under the wall. As he neared it, Bo could see the green fluorescent face of an instrument. Never having seen a mobile phone, Bo presumed the instrument was a toy and, keen to move along, slapped his thigh at Sheila to keep moving. But Sheila wouldn't budge. Bo was forced to move back and take her by the scruff of her neck. Then he saw the prone figure of John Carmody.

He looked dead. His body had the limp, careless pose of the dead. Bo stood still, trying to figure what had killed John Carmody, trying to decide whether the threat was still here. No, he thought, there's no danger lurking. Just – just death? Now Bo began to move forward, reluctantly. He didn't want to rush to the body. He didn't want to know too soon that his friend was dead. 'John, John,' he called. Or rather whispered. It seemed rude to yell. He kept walking towards the body. He could see Carmody's face now. His eyes were closed, his features were relaxed. Too relaxed? Bo was above the figure now and lowering his own body to the ground. Still hoping, still calling quietly.

'John, John,' said Bo. He crouched beside Carmody and moved his face close. He stopped breathing for a few seconds, better to hear for a breath from Carmody. Nothing. But then a raspy breath. And another. Bo began breathing again. Sheila whimpered quietly.

'John, John.' Carmody heard the call from a long way off. It sounded as if his name were being carried on the breeze. He could imagine the wind whispering his name as it rustled through the casuarina trees beneath his house. When he heard his name again, he wondered whether he was dead. Maybe angels were coming down to take him up. Or the banshee was calling.

A powerful smell suddenly raked at the back of his nose. The smell dragged him back from the tops of the casuarina trees. It pulled him back to the rear of this house and the pile of compost. As Carmody met his consciousness again, he opened his eyes.

Carmody saw the wild and dark face of death peering into his eyes. The banshee has come, he thought, closing his eyes and screwing up his face in preparation for the kiss of death.

'It's me!' said Bo. He read the unrecognition on Carmody's face. 'Me. Bo,' he said, trying to chase the consciousness that he could see was slipping away from Carmody again.

Carmody still held his breath. He forced himself to recall the face that had loomed into his vision. Hair everywhere. A gaping mouth that seemed too red. Organ red. An odd smell coming from the mouth. Eyes that were – eyes that were worried? Carmody took a breath and opened his eyes again.

'Bo,' said Carmody. A smile tweaked at his cheeks.

As Bo started mumbling an apology, Carmody interrupted, 'Mate, do me a favour.' Pausing for an unsatisfactory breath. 'Get your dog off my leg.'

Chapter twenty-three

Emily watched Bo disappear down the hill. He looked like a rap dancer with an arthritic back. As she stared down and across the hillside to the eastern fire, she had to agree with Bo that she would be safe up here in the hut surrounded by burnt-out bush. Even though the fire had claimed one house near the headland, it hadn't made any inroads behind that house. Emily craned to see her father's place through the stand of casuarinas that separated it from the neighbour's house. She couldn't see it. But she guessed where it stood in relation to the fire. Too close, she thought.

After a few minutes of willing the fire away from her father's house, Emily stood back from the window and looked for something to distract her. Music, she thought, I haven't heard music in … seemed like years. She searched the shelf for a CD player. Then kicked herself. 'As if a wildman would have a CD player!' she chortled. She began looking for an old cassette player. Or a radio. Or a TV. Or … Emily stopped scanning the shelves when the thought hit her that this man may not even be connected to electricity. She searched the walls for power points. There was nothing. She saw the kerosine lantern burning lowly in the corner and realised that the lamp was not for romantic effect.

'Shit. This man is living in the last century.' Her gaze shifted around the room, warily. 'Noooo, couldn't be,' she added, more to fill the void in the room than to convince herself. Emily remained silently upright. She was almost expecting someone to contradict her.

'He must be connected to gas. He might still use gas lighting.' She searched the floor for gas outlets. But only for a few seconds.

'Of course he bloody isn't. No one down here is connected to gas,' pushing herself up off the sun-bleached wooden floor.

For no particular reason, Emily thought of the documentary she had once seen on haunted houses. One of haunted places featured was a guesthouse in the Blue Mountains. The new owners had moved in and been using the phone for a couple of months when, one day, they had trouble with the phone. They rang the telephone company. When the electrician came, he told them that the guesthouse wasn't even connected to the telephone system. There weren't any phone lines coming into the house. When he followed the cord of the phone they had been using for months, it wasn't connected to anything.

'Oh shut up!' Emily said to herself. The last thing she wanted to dwell on in this prehistoric hut was a ghost story. Emily moved over to the bunk and sat down gingerly, so as not to disturb too much...dust. She looked around the room again.

'Well, how does he bloody live then?' Emily set out to answer to her own question.

She picked up her imaginary camera, adjusted the focus and began slowly shifting the camera around the room. The focus settled on the middle of the room and she began her voice, 'Here, in the middle of the room we have a pot-bellied stove. So we know that this creature needs warmth in winter. Which means? Yes, he is warm-blooded. Okay, let's move on.' Emily rose off the bed and spun the camera around to her left.

'Here we have a wardrobe. Well, that's a bit generous. We have a space for hanging clothes. A very small space for hanging clothes. And in it we have...' she continued fossicking through the hanging space, 'one old suite, circa 1960s and a greyish shirt, which is just hanging onto the threads in its collar and...a raincoat.

'Hummmpf,' Emily let the clothes slip back into the wardrobe and paused. 'There must be some more clothes,' she said to herself, then to the camera, 'I think we might find them in this wee cupboard here.'

Emily opened a small cupboard on the floor with a flourish it didn't deserve. 'Aha! Here we have it. We have a pair of trousers. So we know he owns two pairs of trousers. We have here a woollen jumper, which has been darned,' she pulled the jumper out of the cupboard and turned it around in her hands. 'Yes it has been darned at least half a dozen times. With different coloured wool. And we have two T-shirts, a couple of socks and a little treasure basket.'

Emily pulled a small basket from the cupboards and began riffling through it. 'Here we have the emergency kit. Spare shoelaces. Needles, thread. And here are those bundles of wool that have helped salvage Bo's jumper. And a pile of string and a pair of scissors. Amazingly sharp.'

Turning the scissors around in her hands, Emily's camera focused on the fine serrations along the blades of the scissors. They had been hand-sharpened. She tried to imagine how someone would sharpen a small pair of scissors. She had never sharpened anything in her life. If her knives or scissors got blunt, she would buy another pair from Woolworths. God, sharpening something like this pair of scissors could take ages.

There was a neatness to the basket of necessities that struck Emily as being pre-planned. It wasn't just neat in itself, it was neat to a plan. Like a travelling salesman's suitcase. It had a practised neatness. Even the clothes in the cupboard had a studied simplicity about them. Emily zoomed the camera in and out trying to see the pattern to the packing, the meaning behind the simple collection.

Then she saw it. It was exactly what swagmen had packed in their swags. How did she know this? Emily mentally dropped her imaginary camera as she racked her brain. Oh yes, Henry Lawson. His stories were full of the details of the lives of bushmen. She remembered the Lawson stories she'd studied at school. She couldn't recall the title, but one of his stories had lovingly described all the necessities of life that were rolled into a swag –

spare trousers, needles, patches, a blanket (preferably blue because it didn't show the dirt), a pen and, hanging off the swag, a bag of provisions, a billy and a small frying pan.

In that same story, Lawson told of one old swaggie who had died on the track. He'd been found with arms hugging the earth and his swag smothering him. His swag was full of things that he didn't need but couldn't resist – one leg of a pair of trousers, a pile of rags, papers, a jam tin, medicine bottles, rusty nails, pots without handles. Emily's English teacher had said that greed had killed the swaggie. But that teacher was a bit of a commie.

Emily placed the basket back in the cupboard and closed it. The handle of the door was a piece of wood that swivelled. The wood was worn shiny and smooth. It would have looked chick in one of those rustic kitchens that the designer magazines are always cooing about. But this handle wasn't made to impress.

Emily checked the other handles in the room. All the cupboard handles were timber pivots. The door didn't have a handle. It had a large, bent nail that you swivelled to open or close. Another nail was outside. 'Phew, Bo, the insurance company wouldn't be impressed with that set-up.' Checking the single window, Emily saw that it was hinged from the top and was opened simply by pushing it out. A stick propped the window open. On closer inspection, Emily could see that the window could be battened down against storms. There was a nail hole through the frame of the window and an old, rusty nail laying on the ledge that could be dropped through the hole and into the window frame. 'Maybe that old swaggie wasn't so crazy for keeping rusty nails, after all,' Emily said the memory of her teacher.

Slowly, almost hesitantly, Emily put her camera to her eye. She was no longer sure what she was looking for but she felt she should complete the picture. The camera moved to the kitchen. 'Just two steps to the left is the kitchen,' Emily said in voiceover. The camera found a tiny bench that served as a kitchen. Emily fell silent.

In a space that wasn't much bigger than a chopping board stood a bag of flour, a bag of sugar, a packet of tea-bags, a jar of Bonox, a wrinkled pouch of Drum tobacco, a box of matches, a jar of Vegemite, a mug, a plate, a knife, a fork and two spoons.

'Oh look,' Emily said as the mellifluous tone of her voiceover began faltering, 'the man has two spoons.'

Emily started crying then. She thought she was going to laugh. But she cried instead. 'This is pathetic, Bo. Nobody lives like this any more,' she said, trying to stifle sobs that she kept expecting would turn into laughter. Emily turned around the room, gesticulating to the evidence of Bo's life, 'Haven't you heard of the dole, Bo? The pension, food coupons? This is pathetic.' She waved her hands around the hut.

'Look, he has two spoons,' she said in an attempt to be facetious, 'he has two spoons. How extravagant! Who does he think he is? Is he a bloody chef? What the hell does he want with two spoons?' Emily slapped her head as another wave of tears hit the back of her sinuses. She felt herself getting angry but she had not idea who she was angry with.

She grabbed the spoon and held it up as if to display it before a camera. 'This is the spoon that broke the camel's back. You let that be a lesson to you. Don't let rampant materialism lead you into getting two spoons or you'll end up flat on the track, buried beneath the sag of your possessions.'

Emily kicked the cupboard door and stepped back to Bo's bed, where she let herself fall face-first into the bed clothes. The scratchy blanket was strangely comforting. She could smell the remnants of socks, of body odour, of unwashed hair and the cloying maleness within the fibre of the blanket. She rubbed her face into the scratchiness of cheap, old wool. She could feel the layers of old dust – dust that had blown off the hillside years ago; dust that had walked in on Bo's boots and settled on the floor of the hut. Dust that was getting muddy with her tears.

After a while – Emily had not idea how long – she stopped

crying. Sitting stiffly on Bo's bunk, she tried to compose herself. She wiped her cheeks, patted her face and let the quiet of the hut take her. When she looked at the kitchen again, she said, 'Sorry, Bo.' She paused to swallow a mucus plug and then added, 'I'll put the camera away.' She quietened now. 'No more cameras, Bo. I promise, no more cameras.'

When the quite returned and her pulse settled, Emily's eyes found the pouch of Drum tobacco. 'Sure,' she said to the absent Bo, 'I'd love a fag.'

She stepped over to the kitchen bench (she could almost reach it from the bed) and took the pouch. Settling on the bed again, she carefully rolled a cigarette. She rolled a thin cigarette, the sort of thin cigarette she thought Bo would normally roll. As she lit the smoke, she drew back deeply. The tobacco was stale and crinkly dry but it didn't have the acrid staleness that ready-made cigarettes get after a few days. It tasted great to Emily. She drew back again and felt the pores of her lungs quickening with appreciation.

'God, I love smoking.' Emily looked around for an ashtray and noticed one on the pot-belly heater in front of her. She leant over and tapped her cigarette into the ashtray. As she did this she realised that this was probably where Bo sat when he was smoking. What the hell does he do here? she thought, imagining Bo sitting here on the bunk in a dimly lit room, smoking. Just smoking. Not listening to music. Not talking to people. Not reading, not in this light. Not watching television. Emily looked around the room as if searching for something hidden. As if there should be something more in Bo's life.

'Maybe not,' she replied to herself. 'Maybe this is all there is?' Emily dragged on the thin cigarette and took in all the room offered. She thought of monks retiring to caves in mountains; she thought of bushrangers and outlaws, escaped convicts and, in modern times, the crazy drunks who slept under freeways.

She spied the family photograph that she had left propped against the window just half an hour before. The happy boy with flappy ears stared back at her. How could a man who had such a nice upbringing, end up here? she thought.

As Emily recreated Bo's privileged upbringing in her mind, she recalled something her father had said about Bo inheriting the family home, or homes. And how her had sold them and lived off the proceeds. The thought occurred to her that Bo might be rich.

'Fuck me,' she whispered, 'this is the home of a rich man?'

After a while Emily began an exploration of Bo's daily life. She conducted the search through his life with more diffidence this time. There was no riffling through cupboards or gawks of distaste.

Eventually Emily pieced together the elements that she thought comprised Bo's day. She found the packet of Lux tucked under the foundations of the hut, next to the water tank. She found a big, flat, clean rock that she thought he might use to squeeze water out of freshly washed clothes. She found the old string of clothesline that was woven through the low branches of a macadamia nut tree. She found mango, avocado, lemon and orange trees dotted around the expanse of bush grass. His diet, she thought, was better than most. She should see his rubbish bin in the giant, burnt-out steel drum that stood near the lemon tree and the pile of salvage that littered the rubbish area – old fishing nets, an old Weber barbecue trolley with its grill ripped out. Later she recognised the Weber grill on the big fireplace – 'So much for high-tech barbecues' she told herself. She found an axe and some small cutting and chipping utensils. She found the medicine box that Bo had pulled out from the back of a cupboard to treat her leg earlier that night. When she was replacing the medicine box – a shoebox really – she found an old fork that was jammed at the back of the cupboard. She pulled the fork out, wiped it on the back of her pants and spat on it to polish it up. When it was clean she carefully placed it on the kitchen bench, next to the other fork. Bo will be pleased with this find, she thought.

Emily stepped over to the window and peered down the hill. Even from this distance – a hundred metres or so – she could feel the heat of the flames. So too she could see the red and orange of the flames reflecting in the dirty windowpane. She watched the progress of the fire. Three houses consumed, maybe two others threatened. Although she couldn't see them, she could see the effects the firefighters were having on the fire. There must have been half a dozen of them. Below the fire. From the behaviour of the fire – its quenching, its smoke, its patchwork progress – she could almost determine what the firefighters were doing. Three houses, half a dozen firefighters and one fire. Emily's forehead rested against the windowpane. And I'm caught up here, keeping a tally of the event. Like a race caller. A viewer, always reduced to the role of a viewer. Separated from life by a pane of glass – a window or an imaginary camera or a television screen. But there was always a pane of glass between herself and life. She lifted her forehead off the window and raised her arms in a circular motion around the pane of glass. Her fingertips left tracks on the grimy glass. She stepped back to look at the effect of her stokes. For some reason she expected the strokes to have a curvaceous look, a languorous tone to them. Instead they looked tense. Manic even. The red glow from the fire found the tracks in the glass. It looked like the fire was colouring in her strokes. The sharp red tracks of frantic strokes reminded her of a mental patient pawing at the window of a barred institution. No, she thought, I know what it reminds me of. She tried not to remember but the image was there already. It was a story that she had first heard as a girl. It had stayed with her. She had even researched the story once. And found it was true. It was the story of how they used to bury people who were in coma, thinking they were dead. It happened in previous centuries. When they couldn't determine whether someone was truly dead. Or maybe they just couldn't wait that long. They'd bury the people alive and, sometimes, the shock of suffocation woke the people from the coma. And they would find themselves in a coffin, in the dark, under a lot of soil, slowly suffocating. Then they would try to claw their way out, they'd tear at the lid of the coffin, breaking fingernails, splinters and sometimes fingerbones. Buried alive. She couldn't remember how they discovered this. Whether some relative had insisted they dig up the body; whether someone at a burial service had heard cries. No, she thought, they discovered this when they were occasionally forced to relocate graveyards. They'd dig up the coffins, open the lids and discover … what? The body with long, bony hands still frozen in mid-air, rigor mortis of a frantic scratching?

Emily reversed away from Bo's smeared windowpane as if it were contaminated. 'This is how Mum died,' she whispered to herself. 'In a room just like this. A single-room studio. With smoke filling her nostrils and – ' Emily was slowly spinning in the middle of Bo's hut. The walls seemed closer now. As if all four walls had taken one step in, moved one step closer to each other. Or maybe two steps. Everything seemed close – the walls, the air.

Emily was panting slightly. Her face screwed up. Caught between a sneer and a scream. She spun slowly around the room. A coffin of a cabin. Emily was whimpering now. She looked over to the windowpane again. A pall of heavy, dense smoke drifted up the hill, past the window. The smoke … it was the smoke that killed her mother, she thought. She looked at her finger tracks on the windowpane. Drawn in desperation. Buried alive. Suffocating under –

'Fuck me! I'm outta here.' Emily lunged at Bo's door. She half fell over something on the floor. She kicked at it, then saw that it was the rug she had carried up from her father's house. She picked it up and ripped the door open. It opened lopsidedly. She had ripped it clean off its top hinge. She didn't stop to inspect it. She was off. Down the hill.

Chapter twenty-four

'Can you move, John?' asked Bo.

'I can't. If I could just drag myself ... I can't.' The two were silent for a while. Then Carmody continued, 'There seems to be more smoke.'

'A new front come around the headland,' Bo replied.

'That's trouble,' said Carmody. 'Close?'

'Ummm,' said Bo. They lapsed into silence again. The sounds of fire consuming timber were carried up the hill on smoky breezes.

'Can you drag me down the hill, Bo?' said Carmody, closing his eyes so he wouldn't unduly influence Bo's decision.

Through the timber foundations of the polehouse behind which they were sheltering, Bo could see the edges of the fire. It was already in front of this house, although further down the hill. Bo wasn't too good at physics but he knew that his sixty kilos of wiry muscle couldn't hope to drag an eighty-five-kilo man a few hundred metres along a hillside and then down the hill in front of a fire. Too much could go wrong.

'No,' Bo replied.

Carmody wasn't surprised at the lack of sentimentality in Bo's voice. Facts were facts to Bo. He never mourned the impossible. He never argued with the muse.

'Well, you'd better go, before the fire gets here,' said Carmody. 'Tell Burton where I am ... Don't let Emily come looking for me.'

'I'll stay,' said Bo, already looking around for some extra protection from the fire. It was heading up the hill with a mission.

'Don't be silly, Bo. Get back down the hill,' said Carmody, without either sentimentality or artifice.

'I'll stay.'

Carmody didn't argue any more. He let himself relax back onto the pile of compost while Bo busied himself with something under the foundations of the house. Carmody could feel himself getting warmer. He wondered whether he had a fever. Or whether the fire was getting nearer. I'm probably composting, he joked to himself.

After a few minutes, Carmody felt cooler. He opened his eyes and saw blackness. He guessed he must have lost consciousness again. Searching the blackness, Carmody could see a slit of light. He had been covered with something. As his eyes adjusted he looked above him and could see the outlines of an old door. He realised that Bo had propped it up against the stone wall. It had formed something of a cave. Further down his body, a white barrier had been propped up against the wall. Another door and something else further down, an old surfboard or something. Carmody was in a cool cave and, judging by the occasional waft of untainted body odour, Bo was in the cave too.

'Bo?' said Carmody quietly.

'Ummmm,' Bo's voice came from above Carmody's head and closer to the wall. Bo was obviously crammed into the cave. Carmody imagined him hunched up against the wall. A soft panting sound suggested that his dog was tucked in beside him. Carmody breathed deeply. Feeling inordinately relieved that Bo had stayed.

Carmody was silent for a while. He never felt the need to speak with Bo. He could wait with patience when Bo was around. He could feel himself giving into the rhythm of waiting now. The nothingness of waiting. When, just a little while later, Carmody felt the heat building on his unshielded boots, he spoke again.

'Is it getting close?'

'Hhuummmm,' replied Bo. Carmody waited for expansion. His toes told him the fire was very close. The roar of flames was louder. The fire was consuming the house. Greedily. Bo was silent. Sometimes Bo's simplicity was infuriating. Carmody felt his serenity slipping away. The heat throbbing in his feet and the roar in his ears were telling him what Bo wouldn't. Couldn't. Carmody wanted details, word-pictures. What he really wanted was to be talked through this.

As he opened his mouth to quiz Bo further, a plume of putrid smoke hit his lungs. It was the toxic smoke of burning polymers, of burning paintwork, of melting foam and smoking laminate. Dirty, putrid, green and evil, Carmody tried to cough it out of his lungs and a pain in his leg shot through his body like an electrical current looking for an outlet.

When the smoke passed, it left a lingering image with Carmody. It was the image of green/purple smoke rising from above Maeve's studio. On that day, eight years ago, when he watched his …

Carmody tried to break his stream of thought. He scratched his face with the hand that was propped just under his cheek. The disturbance to the compost pile brought an aroma of banana. Carmody reached in front of him, grabbed the banana peel and rubbed it under his nostrils.

But the image of Maeve stayed. He could hear her distant coughing.

Bo breathed lightly and pushed himself prone against the ground. The fumes were worrying him, too. They were nasty and very low. They were leaving only a narrow strip of clean air above the ground. With the planks propped over them, the smoke should rise up the sides and be carried up the hill on its own heat. There was obviously a downdraught forcing some of the smoke into their cave. But they couldn't move now. They were pinned. Their hope lay in being able to find clean air against the ground.

Bo realised he had a better chance of getting clean air than Carmody, who was on top of the compost pile – stuck up there, groaning, shifting about in a quiet panic, murmuring and whispering.

'Maeve, Maeve.' Bo heard rumbling whispers. It took him a while to realise what the sound was. His friend was hurting.

'It didn't take long,' Bo said obscurely. 'It was all over for her.' He added, without much more illumination.

Both men were silent and very still. Carmody chewed the words over in his mind, trying to attach sense to them, trying to find a meaning other than the one he feared was intended. Finally, after a silence of minutes, Carmody insisted, 'How do you know, Bo? How do you know?'

Bo searched for the words that he had never expressed to Carmody. He took himself to the track where he had watched the studio burn all those years ago. It was the track between the old paperbarks. Bo couldn't remember where he had been heading when he saw the smoke coming from the studio. But he remembered the dirtiness of the smoke. He remembered stopping on the hillside. And he recalled how he had almost run down to the studio when he saw Carmody. But something had told him not to.

'She didn't cry,' said Bo.

Carmody thought about these words. He couldn't recall Maeve crying. He only remembered her rasping coughs. He could remember every one. If he chose to reel the memory through his mind, he could probably recall every single detail of her death – from the colour of the sky, to the music he had heard wafting out of his back door while he stood on the back lawn watching – it was a country and western song, 'Take me home, country road'. But in his memory, there was no other witness to the death.

'Were you up on the track?' Carmody said in a deadpan voice.

'Passing by,' said Bo.

Carmody tried to imagine Bo on the track that day. He couldn't. There had been no one around.

'If she was animal, she would have died long before – '

'She wasn't a bloody animal,' Carmody interjected. Paused. 'She was my wife.' He lifted his head above the indignity of vegetable peelings as he spoke of Maeve. 'She was my sick wife,' he continued quietly. 'She needed help and couldn't find it. She needed me and, in the end, I wasn't enough.'

A picture of Maeve's face loomed large in Carmody's mind now. It was a face of serenity. It was the image of her face when he had visited her studio just a few months before her death. He'd poked his head into the studio to see if she wanted her muffin and coffee yet. She'd looked so peaceful staring out of the window that it had taken him a few seconds to notice her rug. The corner of her rug had slipped off her knee and onto the metal frame of the electric heater. The rug was singed and the room was filling with the smell of scorched wool. But the rug was not alight. He had whipped it off the heater and taken it outside to stomp on it and toss dry earth over it. By the time he returned with the dirty, burnt rug in his hand, Maeve was smirking. Or trying to suppress a smirk.

'It's not funny,' he'd said as he folded the rug in on itself.

Maeve smiled at him again. Quietly, almost as an afterthought to herself, Maeve had said, 'It would save a lot of time and fuss.' He looked at her then. Looked into her face. They locked eyes for a long time. Finally he had looked down at his hands, which were twisting the rug around themselves in a ball. He wanted to ask her what she meant. But he was afraid of the answer. When he looked at her again and saw her face, he could see the answer.

Bo heard Carmody swallowing loudly. It disturbed him greatly to hear his friend choked with emotion. He thought of what he might do for him. He struggled to find words.

'Her spirit. It was gone.'

Carmody wanted to continue berating Bo but his throat was too clogged. He thought of what Bo had said. Did the wildman really say that? Or was he hearing his own voice? The words resonated so meaningfully that Carmody wondered whether he had thought the same thing before. Or whether Maeve had said something to that effect. Certainly the thought wasn't new. Maeve had gone before the smoke had choked the life from her.

Carmody lay his head into the pile of compost again. And felt tears drip across his cheek into the peelings. His sinuses were clogging with eight years of unspent emotion. He felt almost detached from himself. His mourning arrived in heavy swells.

The night and the smoke closed in around the man-made cave. In the house, fire was reducing toys, chairs, blinds, carpets and beds to shrivelled corpses. Most of the smoke joined the night sky. But sometimes a swirling, mad wind would push the bruised smoke out the back of the house and around the small pile of rotting vegetables and living flesh that lay against the stone wall. Time moved in strange patterns. Measured only by the regularity of the men's breathing.

Chapter twenty-five

When Carmody heard the ringing, he was in a deep dream. Water surrounded him. The water was wild, warm and viscous. Like muddy surf. He was extending his hand to a body that kept appearing just beyond his reach and just beyond his sight. He was stretching with every fibre of his muscles – for some reason he couldn't swim – but the body was always bobbing out of his reach. Then he heard the siren of the rescuers. Maybe the rescue team will arrive in time to save her, he thought. He tuned into the ringing sound, he willed the sirens to come closer, faster. As the ringing got louder, the dream began to fade.

'John, phone. Phone,' said Bo, tapping on his shoulder.

Carmody lifted his head. He could hear a muffled ringing. It sounded as if someone were sitting on the handset. Then he remembered the phone in his back pocket. 'Bo, I have a phone in my pocket.' As he said this, Carmody remembered that it was no longer in his pocket. He had taken it out to answer it and had left it near his face. 'No, not in my pocket. Somewhere here. The mobile. It was here next to my face,' Carmody said, quickly raking his hand through a pile of rotting vegetables and grass clippings. 'It was right here before you moved the stuff on top of us.'

Bo cocked his ear to the sound of the ringing. He recalled the green face of the instrument he'd seen when he first stumbled across Carmody. But he couldn't recall seeing it after that. He followed the ringing back to its source. Over to the other side of the compost pile. The ringing stopped. Sheila was quicker on the uptake. The dog scrambled over the compost, nudging Carmody's crook leg as she went. She crammed her nose into the crevice between the compost pile and the bottom of the door. The phone had slipped down the pile when Bo had propped the door over them.

'I forgot about the phone,' said Carmody. 'How could I forget it?'

'What? What?' said Bo. The fire was roaring now. Like a train coming through a tunnel.

'Doesn't matter, doesn't matter,' said Carmody. Talking to himself, more than Bo.

Sheila reversed out from the crevice with a mobile phone in her jaw. A saliva-covered, dirt-encrusted phone. She ignored Carmody's outstretched hand and dumped it in front of Bo.

At that moment, it began ringing again. Carmody nodded to Bo. 'Press the green button.' Bo stared into the face and pressed the button. He didn't speak into the piece. He couldn't remember what to say.

'Hello, hello. Are you there, Dad?' Carmody could hear the voice even though the phone was against Bo's ear. Or hovering near the ear. Bo didn't look as if he trusted the device.

'Hello? Dad?' Carmody could recognise the voice of his son.

Bo passed the phone to Carmody. Very slowly and carefully. Carmody could just see the expression of horrified awe on Bo's face. He smirked at Bo's discomfort. Then he began chuckling. 'It won't bite, Bo,' he said, his chuckles gathering momentum, feeding on themselves.

Carmody stretched his arm to take the phone from Bo. But he was in no condition to respond. He held the phone out over the compost heap while his head nodded rhythmically with laughter – a quiet laughter that occasionally lapsed into a whimpering chuckle. Carmody was surprised by his outburst.

'Dad? Dad?' the plaintiveness of his son's call tickled his sense of absurdity. And kept him laughing. He thought of all the bizarre ironies of his situation. How on earth did Jack get his number down here? Where was Jack calling from? What did Jack want to chat about? Carmody felt his nose dribble as he snorted a few more chuckles. Does Jack want to sugggest that I now move into that apartment at Bondi? Nice timing, Jack, my big toes are melting, my lungs are full of mucky smoke and you're going to tell me to ...

'Dad! Dad!' His son was sounding worried again. Carmody told himself to shut it off. Jack sounded as if he were in a chiding mood. Not another lecture, thought Carmody. No, no, Jack is probably just checking to see if his insurance policy is up-to-date. This last thought was a little too close to the truth to be funny. Carmody took a big breath and lifted the phone to the side of his face. Suddenly he didn't want to talk to his son. He knew it would be problematic.

'Jack Carmody, I presume,' John said into the mouthpiece.

'Dad, what's going on down there? Are you all right? You sound as if you're bloody pissed. They told me you were hurt,' said Jack. He paused to catch his breath. He knew he should be alarmed about his father. Instead he felt himself getting angry. How could the old man sit there giggling when his son was ringing to arrange his rescue? Ho, bloody, ho.

Jack *was* angry now. 'We've obviously got the wrong message. Judging by your gay mood, things are pretty honky dory where you are.'

John Carmody raised his eyebrow at the phone, already regretting that he had taken the phone from Bo. Perhaps he should hand it back. Bo would probably communicate better with his son than he would.

'I'm all right, Jack. What can I do for you?'

'Oh, don't be ridiculous,' shouted Jack. 'I'm trying to help you.' Pause. 'Jesus, you're supercilious sometimes.' Frustrated pause. 'What's that noise? Is that the fire?' Jack paused again. Then continued, 'God that sounds close. Dad, is that the fire?'

'It's certainly not a barbecue, Jack. Those flames have got more than fire-starters behind them – there's the odd couch, a bedroom or two, bit of lino – '

'Dad, what can I do, how can I help?'

'A bucket of water would be useful,' said Carmody.

'Okay, I'm not down there with a bucket of water, am I? I suppose you've got a right to be angry about it but … let's just stick with what we can do. What can I do from here?'

'Where are you?' asked Carmody, finally curious about what his son had been doing.

'I'm across the bay. In my car.'

'The Jag,' said Carmody, still kicking.

'Yes, the Jaguar,' said Jack, quieter now. Pausing. 'We should keep the recriminations for after the event, Dad. At the moment, I want to ensure that you are safe. I want to see if I can do everything possible to get you out of there.'

Carmody rested his head on the compost pile. As he did this, he looked across at Bo. His wild friend looked sad. Or disappointed. Carmody winced and breathed deeply.

'I'm sorry, Jack. It must be getting to me. Listen, I'm behind one of the houses. It might be the O'Conners' house. I've mangled my leg so there's no way I can move. The house is on fire at the moment – '

'You're in a burning house,' Jack interjected.

'Behind, behind the house. We're dug in.'

'We?' asked Jack.

'Bo and I. And Sheila. The dog. And a pile of rotting vegetables. And one phone.' Carmody paused. He thought of all the things he had just mentioned and he said, 'You know, Jack, I'm not sure which one of those things is most valuable to me at the moment. I'd hate to think it's this yuppie headpiece.'

Carmody suddenly sucked air in through his teeth as a flare of heat passed over his ankles. The sudden intake of breath made a raspy, hissing sound. Without even moving his head to look in the direction of the fire, Carmody could see the air outside the tent lightening. He presumed something in the kitchen must have caught fire. He hoped the O'Conners had taken their tins of petrol down to the waterfront.

He tried to bury his feet in compost to escape the radiant heat, but the compost pile was too thin and scrappy on its edges to provide much cover. He could hear his son yelling again. 'What was that? Are you all right? What was that sound?'

'Yeah, yeah, Jack. I'm all right,' said Carmody, suddenly thinking of Bo. 'You all right, Bo?' A grunt answered his question.

The fire was building to a crescendo. At least, Carmody hoped it was. He imagined it moving through the house like a drunk returning home. Crashing through the rooms, lurching around the furniture, searching for more. Its blustering anger roared into the night sky, screaming of a hunger that could never be sated, a temper that could never be quietened.

'Dad, we should be able to get a rescue team down to you. What number is the O'Conners' house?'

'They don't have numbers, Jack,' said Carmody, unable to hide his disappointed tone.

'Okay, describe it.'

'It's the white house with the blue roof and it's five houses along from the headland,' Carmody said. He felt spent now. It all seemed too hard. And too late. 'Jack, listen,' he said, 'this is all too late.'

'Don't talk like that,' said Jack, his words cracking on the fading line.

'I don't mean it's too late for ... I'm not being dramatic. But the fire will have passed in any case.'

The line went dead then. Carmody turned and looked at the phone. He could see the words 'no service'. Just as he pressed the red button to hang up, the phone rang again.

'Hello, hello, you there?'

'Yeah, Jack. I'm back,' said Carmody.

'Well, we haven't got long. Either your phone is running out of power or the fires are interfering with reception. We can't muck around. And I'm supposed to ring the radio station back and let them have a go.'

'What?' said Carmody.

'Don't worry about it, we don't have time to talk about it. Just tell me what you need – a fire boat, a truck to come down from the top of the hill, a helicopter?'

'Well, I'd hate to keep you from an exclusive interview with a radio station so I'd better put my order in fast,' said Carmody, hating the taste in his mouth but continuing regardless. 'Now a helicopter would normally be my first preference but landing may be a mite difficult – '

The line went dead again. Quiet settled into the cave. Even the fire seemed to have lost enthusiasm. Carmody's sarcasm hung heavily. As if to look for support, or a change in the conversational climate, Carmody sought Bo. He couldn't see him properly. Bo's head was poised over the ground, as if he was entranced with something on the ground – or wanting to escape into the ground. He waited for Bo to acknowledge him.

The wait was causing Carmody discomfort. It almost seemed as if Bo was saying something with his unreceptive body. A snub. Or a disappointment. Well, what the hell did Bo know about families! He'd never had to deal with a son with whom he shared nothing except a genetic code. It never ceased to amaze Carmody how different his son was from him. Jack liked all the things that he loathed – the social life, the city power circles, big cars, big homes, rugby union and modern dance. And he was useless at all the things that mattered. He couldn't change the washer in a tap! He said no one changed washers in taps these days. They just got new taps. He couldn't tell the difference between a wallaby and a kangaroo. One Easter, Jack had seen Flint Bay's ancient wallaby hopping along the path and yelled, 'Oh, look at the baby kangaroo!'

Once he may have thought Jack cute for such a comment. Later, when Jack was a teenager, he even found much of Jack's behaviour curiously ingenuous. But increasingly his son annoyed him. And disappointed him.

Carmody turned away from Bo. The light was dimming. The fire was probably on its way out. He imagined the blackened frame of the house outside the cave. He hoped the house had been well-built. Or the whole bloody lot might crash down around them. Now that would be hell – to be pinned under a poker-hot timber frame. Imagine not knowing that the houses down here don't have numbers! Did that boy ever open his eyes when he was down here and *see* what was here? Carmody thought of the times that Jack and his family, Emily and he had spent down here over Easters, Christmases and occasional long weekends. He could barely picture Jack down here. He could see Jack fussing around in the kitchen but he couldn't see his face. He wondered if Jack ever looked him in the eye. Or if he never sought Jack's eye.

Carmody was impatient now. He waited for the phone line to come good again. He looked across at Bo. 'Stupid technology, eh?' He said to Bo, wooing him into a conversation.

Bo nodded. Still not looking up from the ground. Despite the sounds of timbers splitting, of flames and furniture crackling, the cave seemed heavy with silence.

'He's worried about you.' Carmody looked up at Bo. He opened his mouth and gathered a breath to answer Bo. But then he wasn't sure whether Bo had said it. He waited for Bo to look his way, to acknowledge what he had just said. But the man never shifted his eyes from the ground.

Carmody stared at the banana peel that seemed to follow him around the compost pile. He flicked it away with his middle finger. The pause lengthened. Bo was infuriating company, at times. An insubstantial presence that you could never rely on. The phantom human – you try to treat him like a normal human being, and he turns feral. Then when you get used to treating him like a bush animal, he says something. Meaningful.

'Well, why should I start relying on him now?' Carmody said to the incriminating silence. 'I've never been able to rely on him before. Where was he when these fires started? Where was he when I needed help to build the studio? Where was he when – '

The rest of the sentence lay in the air. Even Bo looked uncomfortable. He shifted in his position. The dog shifted in sympathy. Or perhaps in the hope that they might be leaving this cave. Carmody was caught in the past. In one moment in particular. The day Jack came to the Bay and saw how difficult it was for Maeve to move around. It was when Maeve had called for assistance from the bathroom that Jack piped up with his idea of putting her into one of his rental flats with a medical alert alarm around her neck. 'You can't handle this any more,' Jack had said to Carmody after he had helped his wife out of the bathroom. Then Jack had explained how the medical alert alarm worked. He said that an old person could be left alone in flats for days, even weeks, if they had an alarm around their neck. If they got into any trouble, they'd just press the button on the alarm. 'We're lucky,' Jack had added, 'we can throw money at this problem.'

'Your mother is not a problem,' Carmody had replied. To no effect. Jack had then told him that the whole family could visit Maeve if she were nearer to the city, she wouldn't be living far from home, she would always be just a beeper away from help.

'Her home is here with me,' Carmody had told his son. He had left then. Got a raincoat off the back door hook and gone for a long walk, leaving Jack in the kitchen with his wife and boy out on the verandah and Maeve ensconced in her studio, out of hearing. He hoped.

When the phone started ringing again, Carmody groaned and let his head slump into the compost.

'I get it?' offered Bo when he saw Carmody's reaction.

'No, Bo. I'll get it. He's my son.' Carmody lifted the phone to his ear, pressing the green button with his thumb. 'Bayside funeral services, how may I help you?'

'I wish I could laugh, Dad,' said Jack in a voice that was cool and tidy. 'I've been onto the police. They've got a water police boat just south of the Bay. They said they'd get the boat to get up there. I described the house. Is there anything else you can tell me that will help them find you?'

Carmody was silent. He felt himself clogging up. He didn't know if he was angry, frustrated, tired, pissed off, relieved, sad or disappointed. Maybe he was a bit of all that. And some more. He opened his mouth to speak. He felt the plug of emotion in his throat. As if responding to a silent command, Sheila the dog suddenly bounded out of the make-shift cave. Carmody looked at Bo but he could see that Bo had not given any commands. He seemed just as perplexed by his dog's behaviour. Carmody hoped the dog had not sensed a snake slithering around outside.

The toll of the night was pressing heavily on Carmody now. His leg was swollen to three times its normal size. He could feel it stretching the trouser leg taut. It felt red and it throbbed with the beginnings of an infection. He was hoarse – with smoke, with shouting, with tiredness, with spent and unspent emotion. His eyes were red and gritty. His teeth were hurting because he had clamped them so tightly when the pain shook his body. But most of all he was tired of the whole thing. He seemed to have been living with fires for ages. As if they'd moved into his territory and decided to stay. He'd waited for them for an eternity. And now it seemed he had fought them for an eternity. And yet they still kept surprising him. Haunting him. Chasing him.

Carmody shut down his thoughts for a minute. He called his energies back to the present. Back to the son who was waiting on the end of the line. Nothing's changed, Carmody thought suddenly. My boy and I are still only ever talking to each other on the phone.

'Jack,' he said finally. Quietly. 'It's nice of you but I think it's too late.'

'Why, what's happened? Dad you sound hurt. What's happened?'

Jack's crackling words echoed around the cave. As Carmody paused to clear his throat, Bo lifted his head. Carmody could feel Bo's stare on the side of his head. He didn't dare look at Bo.

'Jack, I'm fine, I'm fine,' he said sounding quieter all the time, 'all I meant was I didn't want to put anyone to any special effort. But …' Carmody could still feel Bo boring into his head. Okay, okay, he thought. Let me go. Bug off, Bo. I'll bloody biff you, if you don't mind your own business … 'What I mean is, look it's great what you've been trying to do. I really appreciate you trying – '

'I'm not trying! I've done it. Whether you like it or not!' said Jack.

'I know, I know, I didn't mean to sound …' Carmody exhaled heavily. 'You're probably right. It would be nice to get some help up here. God knows what could happen next. That bloody snake could come charging down the track again and – '

'What snake?'

'Don't worry about it. Listen, there is one thing you can tell the police. Tell them to go straight into the community hall, next to the wharf. Someone there should be able to direct them to the O'Conners'.'

'Got it! Anything else?' said Jack.

'Ummm,' Carmody searched his mind. He could hear the finality in Jack's voice. But he didn't want the conversation to end yet. He had a lot to tell Jack. He thought he should try to tell Jack some of it. At least, he thought, he should give it a try. 'Ummmm, trying to think …' continued Carmody, looking around the cave, noting that Bo was no longer staring in his direction, that the light from the house fire was dimming, that the dog had not returned, that the banana peel was no longer in sight.

'Yes, Jack, there is something else,' he said finally, rubbing his face with a grimy hand. Carmody felt Bo's stare on the back of his head again. 'Tell the police to come to the back of the house. And Jack? Tell them if they find a pair of boots on the compost pile, they're too late.'

Chapter twenty-six

Emily bounded through the burnt landscape, searching for a safe passage through the houses down to the water. As she drew directly behind one of the houses that had caught alight, she could see the orifices of the house were spewing a rotten, black smoke. She could appreciate why nothing could survive if it were caught inside a house that was spewing smoke like that. She'd always imagined smoke as the stuff that wafted off barbecues – light, ethereal, promising food. Now she could see that smoke from a house fire was nothing like that. She recalled how she had leant into a barbecue once to see what it was like for her mother to die of smoke inhalation. 'You're an idiot, Emily,' she cursed herself under her breath.

She started to walk away from the burning house when she heard a growl. Emily froze. The growl was familiar. But she couldn't pinpoint where it had come from. Another growl. This time Sheila moved towards her as she growled.

'You!' said Emily. And then she was lost for words. What was Bo's dog doing behind a burning house, growling at her? The dog stopped growling and cocked one of its ears. It, too, seemed confused to be facing the growling woman again.

'Where's Bo?' said Emily. The question escaped her before she had time to think about it. Stupid, stupid, she thought, asking a dog a question. She shook her head and was about to start walking away from the dog – slowly – when the dog's gesture made her stop again. When she had asked the dog where Bo was, Sheila had turned her head towards the house. As if answering her. Or looking for Bo herself.

Emily slowly moved towards Sheila. 'Here?' she asked the dog. Then she lifted her head and called, 'Bo?' It was a half-hearted call. 'Bo!' she called more firmly. The dog was silent but its head was still half-cocked in the direction of the house. The sound of flames finding new fuel inside the house carried up the hill. Then –

'Oye!' Immediately Sheila tracked back towards the house, leapt down a small stone wall and disappeared.

'Hello?' Emily yelled fearfully as she edged towards the house, bending down to avoid the smoke and trying to see where the dog had disappeared to. As she neared, she could see a door propped against a stone wall – no, two doors were propped against the wall and something else too and a pair of boots were sticking out –

Emily yelped in fright. The boots that were sticking out from under the fallen door were motionless. And skewed at a strange angle. Dead, she thought. Bo is dead.

The appearance of Bo, reversing out from the cave-like structure silenced her. Emily threw her head down in her hands and murmured, 'Thank God, thank God.' She continued murmuring into her hands, 'Oh Christ, thank God he's not dead! Oh God, he's alive.' When the logic of the situation caught up with her, she stopped murmuring and cranked her head out of her hands. Bo was walking towards her. The boots were still sticking out of the cave. She froze. She didn't want to ask the question. She didn't want to think about it. She stood stock still and watched Bo approach.

'He's okay,' said Bo, reading her panic. 'Bad leg but okay.'

'Dad? It's Dad?'

Bo nodded. Emily crouched low, scrambled around Bo and disappeared under the propped door. She could see her father was already smiling as she focused on his face.

'Good find, Emily,' said Carmody.

Emily busied herself tending to her father. She pulled a small foil pack of prescription painkillers that she kept with her all the time. 'Chronic headaches,' she'd told her doctor. She never had headaches but she'd grown to like heavy painkillers after she'd been prescribed them for an abscess on a tooth. They gave her a gentle drowsiness that killed pain, insomnia and even sadness.

After Emily had given her father two tablets and draped his exposed feet with the rug she had dragged down the hillside, she leant back inside the cave. Bo and his dog were just outside. The fire was less intense now. Bo only pushed his head inside the cave when a plume of smoke was occasionally sucked down to the ground.

They sat in silence for a while. There was both too much to say and nothing that could be said. Each of them trawled through their thoughts, looking for a place to start but overwhelmed by the enormity of what had happened, by the density of their emotions. Bo felt he should say something to the girl about what had happened in the hut. Or what didn't happen in the hut but might have happened. Or, recalling Roger Burton's fury at him, what might have happened in the hut according to others' minds. And he gave up.

Emily too had so much to say to Bo – about his hut, what it had told her, what she had finally seen in it, how she could see the beauty in his life, how she had found an extra fork. And she gave up.

She thought of her father and all the things she had to say to him. About what she had discovered in his house; how she had glimpsed his sorrow in his house; how she was beginning to understand how he had lived since her mother's death and, yes, about her mother too; about her death. And she gave up.

It was Carmody who broke the silence. His thinking was becoming clearer as the painkillers numbed his hurt. He almost felt comfortable, hugging the warm pile of compost while the drugs washed over him. His mind was drowsy but, at the same time, sparkling clear. As if his thoughts had been freed from tension.

'You brought your mother's rug to protect me,' he said to Emily, tilting his head back on the compost so his words would travel easily to his daughter, who was still leaning back against the wall.

'What?' Emily leaned forward.

'The rug you put over my feet just then, it was Maeve's rug. I gave it to you yesterday to help you fight spot fires.'

'I'm sorry I wrecked it. It's covered in soot. It's all singed – '

'It was singed before,' Carmody interrupted.

Emily thought of the rug – blackened, gnawed by flames, smelling of a thousand cigarettes. She was about to dismiss it from her mind when something in her father's tone made her re-examine what he had said. 'It was singed before,' he'd said, not in a dismissive tone but in a manner that suggested more.

She cocked her head, better to see his eyes. He was staring at her. Intently. She knotted her eyebrows in question.

'She burnt it herself,' replied Carmody. 'It was an accident. She was sitting in the chair with the rug on her lap. The rug slipped off her lap and onto the heater. By the time I came into the studio, its edge was singed but it hadn't caught alight – '

'But that's how she died,' interjected Emily. 'That's how the coroner said she died – a rug slipped onto her bar heater.' Emily was trying to catch up with her own thoughts. 'You mean the same thing had happened to her before? The same sort of accident?'

Carmody didn't reply. The answer was obvious and there was no easy explanation. He felt the pain of Emily's unfolding shock. And his own pain too; a rubbing against old wounds. His head dropped. Why does Maeve's memory bring so much chafing, he thought? Don't wounds ever heal so decisively, so toughly that nothing can knock the scab off any more? Isn't it –

'But why – ' Emily started to say something but stopped. Carmody could see her searching the space in front of her for words. Or understanding. 'Why didn't you do something? Why didn't you – ' Emily was literally grabbing the words with her groping, gesticulating hands – 'move the heater away from her? Or take the rug? Or warn her?' Her voice was squeaking with stress. 'Or keep watch over her?' Emily paused. With confusion or anger, Carmody couldn't be sure. Judging by the tension around her lips, she was getting angry. 'You'd been given a warning, for God's sake!' Emily lifted her hands to her shoulders and threw them down to the ground. 'It was a warning from God and you ignored it?'

Emily was sucking on her knuckles. Carmody wasn't sure whether she'd hit them on the ground or she was trying to stem tears.

'A warning of what, Emily?' he asked. 'That she was going to die? That Maeve didn't have long to live? Don't you see, she was dying anyway.'

'Anyway?' said Emily her voice still pitched tight. The word rankled. It implied another action. A contrary action. An excuse. 'You say "anyway"? What do you mean "anyway"?' Her hands were poised arthritically before her face.

This is too hard, thought Carmody, turning away from the claws which were wanting to squeeze an answer from the air, threatening to throttle the truth from him. How do you put into words that which has always been unspoken? How do I explain the sense of conviction, of doing what seems deeply, intuitively right? No, no, not right. But something that must be done. Carmody's face sought the comfort of the compost pile. As his nose nuzzled the vegetable and grass clippings, he smelt the sweetness of slow decay. And he longed to join in the process. To join the pile of life matter returning to the ground. Ashes to ashes.

He heard a stifled sob from Emily. What to tell her? Does he tell her of Maeve's wishes? Carmody could see Maeve's eyes before him. The knowing, compassionate look she gave him when he was chiding her about the singed rug. The silence they shared when they both realised what had happened; him looking down into the rug that he was rubbing distractedly between his fingers, Maeve searching his face. It was a silence more informative than any conversation he'd ever had.

Carmody turned his head to face towards the door that shielded him from the fire. There wasn't much heat left in the fire now. It seemed to have lost its fight. And its soul. It sounded more like a sulking force, kicking around the few pebbles left in its path, still blowing off plumes of heavy smoke. He couldn't see Emily from this position, nor Bo, nor his dog. Suddenly he felt a gust of violence.

Willing herself not to cry, Emily could see her father grappling with her question. As his silence extended, her fears compounded. The silence reeked of guilt. But even as she waited for an answer, she couldn't face up to the reality of the word herself. 'Anyway', 'anyway', the word stunk of every weak excuse she'd ever used.

The cave felt close. Emily's breathing came with difficulty. Stifled sobs, tension, the soup of smells from the putrid smoke, the compost, Bo and his dog. And something else. The rotten carpet smell of fear. Her system was closing in on itself. Her breathing was like a rasp.

Before she'd even thought about it, Emily threw her legs and arms at the door propped against the wall. It seemed to explode off the wall, flipping up and sliding down the hill. The other door slipped sideways. Immediately she could feel the radiant heat of the dying house fire.

'Was it like that, Dad?' Emily asked. 'Is that how it happened?'

She looked towards her father then. His face was turned to the ground. Images of his face flashed before her like a fast-rewind. Funny faces, sad faces, closed-off faces, hurt faces. She could see the younger faces of her father. They were happy faces. Carefree faces. And the face of her father that night when he saw her running up the hill to him. A loving face. But did he have another one?

Then she got an image of Bruce Leonard's face. Leonard's face earlier that evening when he had stumbled into the hall with blood and pulp seeming to hang from it, hands covered in blood, blood spatters all over his clothes as if he had shaken himself like a dog. She tried to remember what her father's face had looked like when he walked into the hall behind Bruce.

'No.' The answer came from somewhere else. Not her father. Emily tried to focus on reality.

'Wasn't like that,' the voice said.

Bo, thought Emily. It was Bo who had spoken. She listened but didn't turn to look at Bo.

'You saw?' she asked quietly. 'You were there? You saw it all happen?'

Bo glanced briefly towards Emily and, almost imperceptibly, shrugged his shoulders.

Relief flushed through Emily's body. Her father was not a killer. He didn't do it. She let her face drop into her hands with relief. She tried to imagine Bo and her father on the lawn outside her mother's studio that day. Standing outside the burning studio. Watching? Bidding farewell while fire – She couldn't recreate the scene. Nothing seemed right. Nobody could watch that. Nobody could – Emily searched for logic. If it 'wasn't like that', what was it like? If he wasn't a killer, what was he?

'But why didn't you do something when you saw what was happening?' she said.

A timber support crashed somewhere inside the house. The three looked at it. The fire was dying. The back of the house had been reduced to skeletal frames so they could see inside. Chairs still faced each other in conversation mode but reduced to their metal frames – only their intentions remained. In the kitchen the sink was supported by its drainpipe, the bench and drawers surrounding it had been burnt to ashes. The fridge and stove stood stoically. A patch of daisy wallpaper was still visible above the stove. A bookshelf in the lounge was still burning but everything else was smouldering – quietly, haphazardly and without soul.

'Just answer me, please,' Emily continued as she stared into the innards of the house. 'Wasn't there anything the two of you could have done? Strong, you're both strong, you could have carried her out, she might have been, you must tell me what you were doing and, Mum, what Mum was doing because – '

'She was drugged,' Carmody turned his head to face his daughter and spoke clearly and quietly. He didn't like the pitch of Emily's voice. It was distant. Unconnected.

'The coroner's report said that she had taken a lot of painkillers. She'd obviously stored them for quite a while. She was drugged. Maybe even comatose – ' Carmody continued.

'But what did you do for her? Did you try to save her?'

'For what, Emily! Save her for what? For bedpans? For the hospice? Save her for mouldy stemmed carnations left in the plastic jug by her hospital bed?' Carmody stared towards Emily. He felt a lump swell in his throat. He ratcheted it down his throat. 'Sometimes,' he continued, 'the most courageous thing you can do is nothing.'

Silence took over then. It hugged them and carried them off into the clearing night air. After a while, the coolness of the night air settled on them. It told them that the fire had been quenched. They probably realised this but none made a move to go. Even the sounds of firefighters moving in the burnt-out area on the other side of the house was barely registering on their silence.

'Over here! I can see … yeah, I can see them behind the house here … yeah, two, no, no, three or four of them.' The cry was coming from a policeman. An excited young policeman who had skirted around the back of the burnt-out house to discover Bo, Carmody and Emily and a dog slumped around the back.

Emily watched him pick his way carefully over pieces of the wall that had fallen onto the side path. She felt almost removed from the scene. She didn't feel like yelling a response to the policeman, or whooping, or crying, or doing any of those things one imagined one might do if one was about to be rescued. She was content to watch him pick his way through the rubble, swearing as a bush swiped a charcoal mark across his trousers. When the officer found a clear spot in the rubble, he swung his spotlight onto the trio and yelled, 'You all right there?'

Caught in the white light of a super-powerful beam, Emily slitted her eyes and said to her father, 'They've come for you, Dad. The police. They've come for you.'

Chapter twenty-seven

'Your Excellency, Madam, ladies and gentlemen and students. It gives me great pleasure to present these bravery awards. Given the traumatic events of the last year, we have a large contingent of people who are going to be awarded. I suppose every one of them would prefer if circumstances hadn't brought them here today. But emergencies in life – though hard to live through and hard to recover from – are an opportunity for the hero inside to come to the fore.

'I know, from the government's perspective, this past year has been a great trial. We have had to endure a particularly snide Opposition. I lost one of my ministerial colleagues, Gai Hill, due to a campaign of villification for what was, in fact, a sensible handling of the historical grants scheme. For a while on Saturday night, March 14, I thought we might face the final test of courage. But, thanks to a few loyal voters, we came through the other side of that testing election.

'And I think we came through that trial because of the courage that *we*, the government, showed during those tragic fires of last summer. I think the people of this state were sending us a 'thank-you' note for the tremendous effort during that emergency.

'Some of you here today may remember something that I said just after I'd dashed back from a brief family holiday to take charge of the emergency. I told the people of this state that we were likely to lose thousands of houses. I told them that the fires were so widespread, so ferocious, that we were taxed beyond our limits. It was a tough thing for a minister to say but, in hindsight, I think that statement fuelled the fighting capacity of all our people. I think it became something to bring us all together. During those long days I spent at bushfire headquarters, I saw the valiant efforts of all involved. It was those gallant efforts that prevented a far greater catastrophe from happening.

'As a result of that effort, we only lost a hundred and thirty houses. We *should* have lost thousands. The fact we lost only a hundred and thirty shows what a great effort we can muster when we have *real* leadership.

'I'd like to take this opportunity to announce some new measures for dealing with fires. In the future, emergency bushfire fighting procedures will be handled by the defence forces. A special unit within the army will be set up and equipped with the latest technology for fighting fires. With an initial grant of ninety million dollars from state and federal governments, this unit will be equipped with two aerial water-bombers and a high-tech fire detection system with digital communications networks and displays, which will offer real-time control of all resources.

'This initiative is not meant to negate all the hard work and bravery shown by volunteer firefighters. It is simply meant as a recognition of the difficulty of their work and the risks they have faced. How can we ask these brave Australians to risk their lives again? I don't think we can. In today's society, we need to tackle this age-old scourge of the Australian bush with the best technology we can lay our hands on, not with the raw courage of its people. We've gone beyond the days when we rely on a McLeod tool and a long garden hose to fight fires.

'In addition, the government is introducing new codes for building in bush settings. Again, these codes are not meant to drive people out of the bush – although the bushies may have to learn how to handle a lawn-mower.' The minister paused to smirk at his quip. 'Basically these codes revolve around the idea that in a bushland setting, houses will have to have guttering and roofs that meet the new standards; every window will need to be shuttered; foundations will have to be completely covered and there should be a twenty-metre buffer of clear land between the house and any native bush – whether that is lawn, water or some nice pavers. As I said, get mowing, blokes.' The minister shared another grin with his audience.

'I won't keep you any longer. His Excellency is waiting to present the awards. I might just suggest that those award-winners who *do* want to say a few words, keep it brief. We have a lot of awards to present and some nice tea and cakes to tuck into afterwards. Thank you all again.'

Fred Hanes stepped back from the podium. Humbly he bowed his head in acknowledgement of the applause. Since the fires, he'd given virtually the same speech a dozen times. He had arranged for it to be reprinted in seven department gazettes and newsletters. The same sentiments had cropped up in a dozen-odd media interviews he had given since summer. It worked every time. People loved it. He didn't mind giving the speech either. He felt he owed it to the people.

As the applause chattered across the lawns of Government House, Jack Carmody riffled though his prepared notes. Sarah, sitting next to him in the third row, whispered through her teeth, 'Jack, the minister just said to keep it brief. What are you doing with all those notes?'

'Lay off, Sarah. These are just a few prompts in case I forget to thank people,' said Jack, still staring intently at his notes. 'There's a lot of people to thank,' he added distractedly. 'There's a lot of people whose role has not been properly recognised through this whole business.'

'Have you got the bit about us living in Killara right? West Killara, Jack, west Killara,' said Sarah, also not looking at her husband.

Jack stopped reading and gave a sigh. Sarah had been carping on about this Killara business since he had known that he would have to accept his father's bravery award on behalf of his father.

'Why can't he accept it himself?' Sarah had asked two months ago in the kitchen of their Killara home. Their west Killara home.

'He'll be in hospital. He's been waiting to have this reconstructive surgery ever since the fire. He says there is no way he is going to postpone the surgery. His precise words to me were: "There's no way I'm going to put off fixing my leg just so some politician can get all puffed up over offering an award."'

'Well, what about Emily then? She should accept it. Wasn't she down there for the fires?'

'Well yeah, but she's – ' Jack let the thought lapse.

'She's what? A woman!'

Sarah, thought Jack, never let a ball-kicking opportunity pass her by. 'Noooo,' he replied, 'she's not used to public speaking.' He had then rustled up a quick bowl of cereal. Mornings at home were getting briefer all the time. Sarah had continued to stare out the kitchen window, searching for solutions.

'What about his friends? Doesn't he know a lot of people down at that Bay who might – '

'Sarah, what's the big deal about me accepting an award for my father? Don't you think I can make the speech?'

'Don't be silly, you won't have to make a speech,' said Sarah, looking more worried than before.

'I won't have to but I'm going to. My father deserves a bit of a tribute and I'm going to give it to him. And there are a few other people who might deserve mention – '

'You're not the minister, Jack. At these sorts of presentation ceremonies you're supposed to walk up, put your hand out, bow to the Excellency and clear off,' Sarah had said. And then she turned around, picked up his newly poured bowl of cereal and tipped the contents carefully into the bin. 'Why do you pour so much cereal into the bowl if you never finish it?' she'd chided.

'Sarah, I had just poured the cereal. I just turned around to find a spoon and …' Jack let it go as he noticed his wife's fraught expression. 'What is really bugging you about this awards ceremony?'

'I don't want people to think we come from Flint Bay,' Sarah said finally.

'Why would they?' asked Jack.

'Because you're getting up on a stage to accept an award for your father who fought the fires in the wilds of Flint Bay.'

'What's wrong with Flint Bay?' Jack had asked. He stopped stirring his coffee then. He had never thought there could be anything wrong with living in Flint Bay. It was a nice enough place for a bush holiday house. Sarah only visited begrudgingly but he always assumed she was uncomfortable with her in-laws rather than the house itself or the area. He couldn't imagine that people might think it an undesirable place, but something in Sarah's tone of voice told him he may have missed something here.

'Well?' Jack had prompted Sarah as she fossicked around the pantry.

'Nothing's wrong with Flint Bay if you like bull ants, outside toilets, hermits, spiders, snakes and fishing for your dinner,' Sarah said finally. 'I don't like any of those things. *We* don't like any of those things. That's why *we* don't like it there. But if people see you talking about your "family home" there they might think we *do* live there,' Sarah said this with such gusto, she was obviously relieved to get it off her chest.

Jack paused. He tried to appreciate Sarah's point. He didn't always agree with her. But she was usually right about these things. Jack thought about how others might react to the idea that he lived in Flint Bay. It might be nice to be thought of as a tough bushman, as a heroic firefighter. He imagined the applause as he accepted an award for firefighting. He pictured himself on the podium wearing moleskins and an Akubra. And maybe a five o'clock shadow. He saw the admiring faces in the audience. Then he saw the faces of his partners in the law firm sitting in the audience. They weren't smiling. Or clapping. He saw his wife's point.

Since that day, Jack had rehearsed the speech often. Even as he flicked through the speech today, with the rows of heroes already filing up to the stage, he couldn't resist teasing Sarah. When she asked him about the Killara note, he hit his hand on his forehead and said, 'I knew there was something I forgot!'

Sarah wasn't in the mood for teasing, 'You forget to say that, Jack, and I'll – ' she stopped herself. Her mouth closed in on itself. Jack stared at her, waiting for her to finish her threat.

'It doesn't matter now, anyway. It's too late,' said Sarah.

Jack was startled and looked to see where the line of heroes had reached. He presumed she meant he had missed his turn. The seats two rows in front of him had just emptied. He hadn't missed anything. He turned to query Sarah but dropped it when he saw the fine lines around her mouth pursed in anger.

Watching the heroes file up to the stage, Jack noticed that none of them gave speeches. A couple said a quick thank you to their parents or their wives or their mates, but not much was said beyond the "thanks, Mum" genre. Still, he thought, most of these people were simple bush folk. They couldn't string a few words together even if, like Jack, they had people to impress.

At the end of his row, heroes began shuffling out. Jack grew nervous. Perhaps he shouldn't say anything. Perhaps it wasn't his place to talk about the fires. When he stood to join the shuffling queue, his wife threw a no-nonsense look in his direction. That settled it.

'Ladies and gentlemen, if I could just say a few words on behalf of my father, who unfortunately is in hospital today,' Jack said, leaning over in front of His Excellency to access the microphone.

'I won't take a minute. As I said to my friend Tom Cole when I was lobbying for more resources for my father's patch of bush, "Just give me a fire truck and I'll be outta here."' Jack laughed at his own joke. He scanned the audience for signs of supportive laughter. Most of the audience was occupied slapping other people on the back. Sarah was looking at him. Intently. And a few journos were chewing on pencils while they looked for something to write about. Still, his first payback had been made. Just two more to go.

'Unfortunately I don't live in the bush. The only flames that threaten Killara come from a Weber barbecue on a Saturday afternoon.' Jack smirked at his joke. He was now fully in command of the microphone, having nudged the Governor to one side. 'But my father does live in Flint Bay and was there for those dreadful fires, along with the rest of the Flint Bay community.

'I only wish I could have been there. But like most of Sydney I was just an onlooker. I did my bit – organising a rescue team down to my father's side – but for the most of it I was forced to sit and watch. My father was indeed very brave for co-ordinating the firefighting effort down in the Bay and, indeed, for managing to stay alive while pinned down with a broken leg in a burning house. If the truth be told, my father didn't want me to send a rescue team for him. He didn't want to endanger their lives.

'Anyway, most of you would have heard my father's plight on Radio 2YX so I won't bore you with details.' The crowd below him was not bored by the speech. No one was listening. But this didn't deter Jack. 'But this is something I hope none of us ever have to live through again. None of us should have a close encounter with fire.' (Jack particularly liked that phrase. It gave an eerie feel to the speech.) 'And this government has the courage to admit that people and bush can't live closely together. People need protection from the bush and this government is going to give that protection!' (Third score settled.)

Jack raised his small medal into the air in a gesture reminiscent of the football grand finals. Not many people noticed. As he was escorted from the stage by His Excellency's secretary, Jack caught sight of Tom Cole, standing beside his minister. He looked chuffed. He noticed two of the reporters scribbling in their notes. He presumed they too were impressed. He saw his wife as he nudged past her to his seat. He couldn't read her expression.

An hour later, Jack was still trying to work out Sarah's mood. They were sitting in the bar on the fortieth floor of a building overlooking the Harbour. Jack had insisted they go somewhere to

celebrate. Sarah tried to tell him they didn't have anything to celebrate, that Jack hadn't done anything to celebrate about. For
Dad, replied Jack, we're celebrating on Dad's behalf.

Now they sat twiddling plastic sticks in their cocktails. Jack
plucked a cherry off the rim of his glass and began sucking on it.
Sarah looked at him with a pained expression. Jack knew she was
pissed off then. He tracked back through his speech to see if he'd
made any faux pas. He couldn't find any. On the contrary, he
enjoyed his little asides. Especially that joke about the only fire
threatening Killara coming from a Weber barbecue. He looked at
Sarah again. She seemed far away.

'Did you like my joke about the Weber – '

'Jack, we're separating.' Sarah said it so fast that Jack briefly
thought she must be making some comment about a barbecue.
He repeated what she said in his mind again. He heard the flat
tone of her voice again.

'*We're* separating?' he asked. He wasn't at all clear what she
meant. At least he wasn't willing to take it on board without a lot
of explanation.

'We-are-separating,' Sarah replied slowly. 'That means we are
no longer going to be married. And we will probably get a
divorce.'

'I said we lived in Killara …' Jack gazed uncomprehendingly
into her face.

'Oh, come on, Jack. It's got nothing to do with your stupid
speech.' Sarah lifted her glass and downed the rest of her drink.

'Where did this come from, Sarah?' Jack still held the cherry
between his fingers.

'I've been thinking about it for a long time, Jack. There's
nothing left between us. We should lead separate lives. I'm not
asking you to move out of the house. I assume you won't insist I
move out. I've drawn up a plan for how we can divide the house
in two. Then it won't upset Joel too much. He should be able to
move between the two areas. Roughly I'll take the front of the

house and you can take the back section. The only thing we have to share is the kitchen and if we agree to use that only at certain times then we can avoid seeing each other at all times except – '

'Whoa, whoa, slow down, Sarah.' Jack placed the cherry in the ashtray while he tried to gather his thoughts. Sarah turned around and signalled to a waiter for another round of drinks. Jack was still incredulous. 'You're dividing up the cutlery already and I'm thinking we're here for a celebration drink. Can we go back a few paces?'

'Oh Jack, let's not make a drama of this.' Sarah breathed heavily and stared out the window to avoid Jack's stare. 'It shouldn't be a surprise to you. We haven't had a marriage in a long time, we've shared a charade. This will just … just complete the charade.'

Jack was gobsmacked. All he could think of was that marriages didn't end like this. They ended with fights, rages, tears, biffs, recriminations, violence and only after lots of threatened walk-outs. Marriages don't end with a chat about the division of cutlery.

'I thought we had a good marriage.' Jack said this quietly. He felt he should probably be ashamed of this comment. Sarah's incredulous stare confirmed this.

'You thought we had a good marriage? Get serious. What does a good marriage mean to you – cereal on the table every morning? A bit of sex every so often? The odd civil word to each other?' Sarah was silent for a moment. 'Did you seriously expect me to wait around in that emotional vacuum you call "a good marriage" forever?'

'You could have said something before this,' said Jack.

'Nothing would have made any difference. You're not up to it, Jack. Sorry, "up to it" is too much of a value statement. You're never going to be able to satisfy what I want – '

'What's that? A bigger house in Killara? A Palm Beach week-ender? January ski trips to Aspen? A housekeeper who comes more than once a week so she can press the Arab sheets you insist we buy?'

'Egyptian sheets. They're Egyptian sheets, Jack. And yes I want all that and more. I want to strive for whatever is possible. I want to have a real relationship. I want to love passionately … I want one more chance at life. I don't want to start "settling" for things. Once you start "settling" for things, your whole life becomes a boring compromise. Now that I've got my law degree I want to have a go at a career, and go at it full bore. I want to run, jump, push until I'm exhausted, tilt at the impossible, find someone with whom I can share a giggle, someone who'll have a shouting match with me, someone who will take me to the places I want to go.'

'And you'll do all this from the front half of the house?'

'That won't be for long. Just until we've found our feet.'

'Just until you've found your feet.' Jack felt numb now. Sarah's soaring spirits as she'd talked of her future had left him feeling hollow. Every plan of hers was a slap in his face. He felt numbness invade his body. And he didn't fight it. Less room for hurt. He knew he should welcome numbness into his heart. For an extended stay.

The waiter appeared behind them and placed the drinks on their table. Jack chug-a-lugged the remains of his first drink. I'll be doing a lot of that now, he thought. Sarah sipped at her new drink. Jack could tell by her stiff body language he was on borrowed time already.

'How long,' he said quietly, 'how long has it been a charade, our marriage?'

Sarah shrugged. 'I don't know. Gee, Jack, was it ever anything else? Can you ever remember it meaning much?' She paused, then added, 'That's not entirely true. It had promise. At one stage, early on, our marriage had the promise of going somewhere. I honestly don't know why it didn't.'

Jack nodded. He was beginning to look at the relationship in a detached way. Maybe that was the way he should discuss it with Sarah. Detached, cool, calm. Get some sense back into things. Some resolution –

'Maybe you always needed more intimacy than I did. Maybe all women do. Has it occurred to you that our rift may be more about the current battle between the sexes than any personal failing of ours?'

'It doesn't matter what caused the rift, it's there. God, Jack, I tried to live without intimacy for the sake of comfort. I turned off emotionally. I expected nothing of you, or of Joel or of myself. But I was dying. I was growing sour, hard, brittle and increasingly resentful. I'm not that sort of person deep down inside. I want to give myself another chance at intimacy.'

Jack nodded, trying to agree, trying to find some opening for negotiation. 'Why can't we have another go at intimacy?' he asked looking into her eyes, as if to establish there was some communication between them beyond words. 'We should have had this discussion ages ago, we should have got counselling.' Jack was becoming more animated. 'For God's sake, I need intimacy too. Sometimes I long for – '

'I honestly don't think you've got it in you,' Sarah interjected.

'How on earth could you make that judgement of me?'

'Look at your family, Jack. Look at your father. Is there any empathy, openness, vulnerability, sense of sharing in him? With a father like that, why would you expect to be able to achieve intimacy?'

Jack sipped at his drink while he thought this over. His drink was almost empty. He didn't want to finish it. He knew it could be their last drink together. 'Dad wasn't always like that. He only got that way after Mum died.' Jack placed his drink delicately on the table. 'He turned off. He had to, it was his way of coping with grief. I tried to reach him but he wouldn't let anyone help.' Jack's voice slowed. He was surprising himself. He hadn't thought this way about his father before. He had always assumed that his father's coolness towards him was dislike. Perhaps it was something else. Certainly he'd made efforts to bridge the gap. He recalled the phone call between himself and his father on the night of the January fires. How many times had he pleaded with Dad to let him help, let him get help? And what had he received in return? A few wry comments.

Sarah was searching for money in her wallet to pay the bill, which had arrived with the last drinks. Jack could see the wrap-up. He could see events moving along without him. He didn't feel that things had been settled at all. Something more should be said, he thought. Something formal, maybe. Something of an explanation, maybe. Or clarification. Only one thought came to mind.

'Who gets the Weber?' he asked. Sarah didn't reply. He didn't expect her to.

Chapter twenty-eight

'Do you want another cup of tea?' Mrs Parker called from the kitchen. Roger Burton mumbled a reply. She couldn't hear a word of it. Her hearing had been getting weaker for years but she was loath to visit a specialist about the problem. Her uncle had used an ear trumpet. She knew they didn't prescribe trumpets these days but she didn't want to test this theory.

'Sorry, you'll have to speak up, the radio is turned on,' she said, raising her voice so Roger could hear her in the lounge room.

'Yes, thanks', he yelled back.

Mrs Parker looked very pleased with herself. Not too many people said yes to a second cup of tea with her. Especially not Mr Burton, who moved in and out of her home like a visiting medical officer on rounds. With more duty than interest.

Roger Burton mooched into the kitchen with cup and saucer in his hand. 'I thought I might stay and listen to the midday news program to see if there's any mention of that awards ceremony that John Carmody was meant to be at.'

Mrs Parker took the cup and saucer from his hand. He seemed relieved. For some reason, Roger Burton never felt comfortable handling Beryl Parker's china. As if it were too precious for his meaty maw. 'No trouble at all, Roger. I'll brew up a fresh pot. Do you think we'll be able to hear John's name on the radio broadcast?'

'No, Beryl, they don't broadcast lists of names like they used to. Air time is too precious for that,' said Roger, sitting down to the radio set at the kitchen table.

'Well it seems to me the radio stations don't do us any favours any more. I mean what were they chattering about when we needed to know the progress of the fires? Their silly reporters getting themselves into trouble! And all the weeping fire victims! It's all very well but we could have done with a bit more information. They're all just flibbertigibbets!'

Roger Burton grimaced at her choice of language. But knew better than to ask. Judging by the flourish with which Mrs Parker had used the work 'flibbertigibbets', it was her word for the day. He turned up the volume on the radio and peered into its face to identify the station they were listening to. 'It doesn't seem to have prompted you to change stations,' he said.

'I only listen to the gardening program,' Mrs Parker said, standing sentinel next to the kettle.

Roger and Mrs Parker were silent as they listened to the midday news. There was only a brief mention of the bravery awards ceremony in the main news items but the station was promoting a special feature on the aftermath of the fires on the twelve-fifteen feature spot.

From her kitchen window overlooking the back garden, Mrs Parker could still discern the backburn line that had saved her cottage last summer. On the side of the line nearest the house, there was native grass and a few scraggly bushes. She'd always intended to start gardening in her backyard but it took all her efforts to keep the front garden looking decent and the backyard seemed to belong more to the bush than to her house. On the bush side of the backburn line stood the weirdest-looking vegetation she'd ever seen. Black ghosts of trees were sprouting brilliant green shoots from every direction – they grew under old branches, spotted along the main trunk and tufted on top like a botched hair-transplant. Mrs Parker didn't have much confidence in the gum trees recovering their shape. They all looked malformed to her. She wondered whether she should raise the possibility of cutting them down and planting some new trees. Perhaps at the next Flint Bay Association meeting. But the television shows and newspapers had been so ecstatic about the regrowth in the forest, she presumed there must be something important about keeping old trees – something she'd missed. Something she couldn't see from her kitchen window.

The ground looked pretty, though. Lots of green strappy grasses and ferns had sprouted from the black soil. In some places the ash was white. She didn't know why some ground was covered in black ash and some was white. She thought of asking John Carmody when she saw him on the track a few months ago. But she was sure the answer was something simple. Something she'd missed.

'It's hard to believe it was a black mess just nine months ago,' Mrs Parker said to Roger as she turned away from the window to tend the boiling kettle. Roger Burton wasn't listening. His ear was cocked to the radio, which was introducing the special on the fires with the resounding noise of fire – that dreadful whooshing and roaring of a train that's always coming towards you. But never arrives.

'Yes, that's the sound most of the state never wants to hear again. That is the sound of fire in Sydney last summer. Most of us now recognise the sound of fire but, for some of us, that has become the soundtrack of their nightmare. Welcome to our special report on the aftermath of the fires. I'm Mike Cottee.'

In the pause that followed the introduction, the volume was raised on the fire sounds. Against the whooshing sound, a woman's cries could be heard, 'Whaaaaa, whiiiwhhaaa, ahhhha.' Her cries piercing. And familiar. Most people now recognised the wailing of Mary Peck. They'd heard it dozens of times during the state emergency and they hadn't been spared since. Mary Peck's desperate escape from her house, with her budgie dead weight in the bottom of the cage, had been included on a television station's promotion. Most Sydneysiders now heard it once or twice a day. Schoolchildren responded to the sight of Mrs Peck dashing down the road with her dead budgie by singing a bastardised jingle, 'Dead, dead, deady! Your chicken is ready.' Not everyone had grown so immune. Roger Burton's back tickled. It was an unpleasant sensation.

'Not another round of wails!' said Mrs Parker, turning to Roger with her fists on her hips.

'Settle down, Beryl. Let's listen for a minute and see if John Carmody gets a guernsey.' Mrs Parker perched on the edge of an armchair opposite Burton. She always perched when she had visitors.

'The minister today announced that future bushfire emergencies would be handled by the army,' the reporter's voice boomed from the radio. 'The minister was speaking at a bravery award ceremony for some of the heroes of the January fires. "A special unit within the army will be set up and equipped with the latest technology for fighting fires ..."' the minister's voice seemed to drone.

With a growing sense of ennui, Roger Burton listened to the minister detail how the military would take over emergency fire operations. 'They just don't get it, do they?' Roger Burton was addressing Mrs Parker but he was looking at the ceiling. 'These politicians saw tens of thousands of firefighters tackling the most monstrous fires in fifty years and yet they turn around and say we can't handle it. They won't trust the average person to have the common sense, the courage and the will to protect themselves and their houses. For God's sake, Australians have been fighting fires in their backyards since we first jumped off the tall ships and all of a sudden we can't do it any more? We're helpless victims? We need a man in uniform to do it for us?' Burton let his thoughts drift off. Mrs Parker twisted a hanky in her hand and didn't answer him. She could see Mr Burton wasn't really addressing her.

The radio report filled their silence: '... reminded at a ceremony today of some of the heroes of Sydney's terrible fortnight. There were bushies, firefighters, suburban mums and dads and even a few kids lined up to accept awards for bravery. I spoke to some of them about their experiences in the fires and how they have, or haven't, settled back into life since the summer scorchers – '

As the radio reporter talked with some of those at the ceremony, Roger Burton's attention vacillated between the stories
being recounted on the radio and his experience at Flint Bay.

When he heard the radio heroes tell how they fought their
fires, Roger Burton relived the tactics that he and the other firefighters had used during the emergency. He still kicked himself
for leaving just John Carmody and his daughter on watch after the
backburn. Sure, there were no live embers falling when they went
down to the hall. Logs and trees up the hill were smouldering –
would smoulder for days after – but the wind had dropped so ...

He had been around that route many times since then.
Debating the reasons for the decision. With himself and others
down at the Bay. It didn't get him far. Just kept him awake at
night.

Tuning in to the interviews again, he heard someone talking
about the native animals she had saved. Roger Burton did a quick
tally of the animals that had been saved in his area. And those
that had been lost. The old wallaby that used to eat the young
citrus trees in his backyard hadn't been seen since. A goner. There
was a baby goanna living further along the track but no sign of a
mother. Another goner. There hadn't been too many snakes
spotted at the end of last summer. Beryl Parker had even crowed
about St Patrick taking them all away from the Bay. But this
spring, a young brown had been spotted on the pathway so St
Patrick obviously hadn't been thorough enough. He knew that Bo
had found several skeletons of wallabies, snakes and the odd feral
cat. No one had seen a snot-nosed possum since the fire. But
then, no one had seen the much-vaunted snot-nosed possum
before the fire either.

Roger Burton's stream of consciousness pooled around Bo for a
minute. Of all the people of the Bay, Bo seemed least perturbed
by the whole thing. If anything, he seemed a little happier with
the denuded bush. He had gathered a pile of promising-looking
branches at the back of his hut. And he was busy chipping and

shaving several of them. A few weeks after the fire the woman from the art gallery had visited Bo and told him that burnt art was 'hot'. She wanted as much burnt artwork as Bo could produce. Roger Burton didn't tell Bo, but he had heard that the art gallery woman was selling Bo's work as an Aboriginal's celebration of fire.

As the radio interviews droned on, Roger listened to the tears of survivors. He had never cried. Then or now. He had never felt like crying – there wasn't time during the emergency and there wasn't much point after it had passed. Briefly, he had felt pained when he saw the faces of old Mrs and Mr Grey as they confronted their shell of a home. But even as he escorted them around the house, holding Mrs Grey firmly under her elbow, his mind was too full of rebuilding plans to be diverted by sadness.

It was only when he heard others crying that Roger Burton was forced to wonder whether his career in bureaucracy had made him too cool and detached or whether the emotional tide had changed during his lifetime. He usually concluded the latter. It's bloody high tide for tears these days, he would tell himself.

'… and of course our own reporter Tony Thomas did not escape.' The mention of Tony Thomas's name broke Roger Burton's reverie. And that of Mrs Parker.

'Why, that rat!' said Mrs Parker.

'Shuushh,' said Roger Burton, turning up the volume as a rebuke to Beryl.

'Tony, you've been up against the wall of flame. You were almost overcome with smoke. Can you tell us what it feels like to be in the middle of an inferno?'

'Sure, Mike. It's something that lives with you forever but, of course, I was only one of scores of media people who covered the fires,' said Thomas.

'Yes, Tony, but only a few of you managed to get caught in the fires. Listeners to our late night program will vividly recall those terrible few hours when you went missing down at Steel Bay. That very night that we dialled your mobile phone number and discovered an injured man was on the other end of the line. Tell us about that, Tony.'

'It was Flint Bay, Mike, not Steel Bay but no matter. Yes, well that drama occurred right at the end of the emergency. I went down to Flint Bay as the fires moved across the national park. It was a strange little place – '

'Strange indeed,' interjected Mrs Parker.

' – frightened community huddled in a small hall. I spoke to many of them that night. They were frustrated – very frustrated – and scared, but there was little any of them could do. They were forced to wait most of the night for an evacuation.'

Roger Burton listened transfixed. He couldn't believe that a history that was not his history – that was not even the history of the residents of Flint Bay – was being recorded as the history of his community. He felt strangely violated. As if this stranger was riffling through their stories and claiming them as his own; stealing their history with his technology.

He tuned into the interview again. Listening for details. He heard Tony Thomas talk of Mr and Mrs Grey. He heard him recount the tension in the hall. Most of these details were superficially correct. But the package was different. The package wasn't the truth. Not his truth.

'... and how did you manage to get lost in the fires for all those hours and survive, Tony?'

This, thought Burton, is the big lie. This, he thought, is where the reporter who was exiled to a rock for most of the night is publicly transformed into a hero penetrating into the heart of the fires to report truth, justice and the 2YX way. Tony Thomas's pause was confirmation of that.

'It wasn't that long, Mike. Really it was more of a misunderstanding – '

'You did get lost in the fires, didn't you, Tony?' said the host, miffed that one of his own colleagues might squib on him.

Tony Thomas exhaled. He'd never got used to this lie. He

wasn't even sure how it had started. His exit from Flint Bay that night was still a jumble of scenes in his memory. He remembered the water police boat pulling up at the wharf of Flint Bay for a second time. He'd scampered over the rocks and sprinted along the wharf and met the police as they jumped off the boat. They asked him for directions to the O'Conners' house. He didn't know then but they had arrived to look for the injured John Carmody. He presumed they'd come back for him and the other residents. When he told them that he was a radio journalist, the captain had turned to him and said, 'Well, we've found you, now we just have to find your phone.' Tony had jumped on the police boat then. He wasn't going to let it go anywhere without him on board. The policeman behind the helm didn't question him. One look at his smashed in face convinced the officer that the reporter had every right to hitch a ride out of there.

He had travelled back on the police launch with John Carmody strapped to a stretcher and his daughter beside him. Thomas hadn't said a word to them. They didn't say anything to him. It was as if they had never met. It was a policeman who'd handed Thomas his grubby mobile phone. By the time the police launch arrived back at the peninsula, a junior reporter from the radio station was waiting for him. Tony tried to recall details of the scene.

'How did you find your way out of the fires?' asked the junior reporter as Tony had stepped off the police launch.

'I don't know,' Tony replied. Not interested.

'It must have been hell to be stuck out there for so long?'

'Certainly bloody was,' Tony had replied thinking of the eternity he had spent with the hillbillies.

'You've obviously been injured by the fires,' continued the cub reporter.

'Give us a break, mate, my nose is killing me. I've got to get some help. Sorry, I'll speak to you again as soon as I get something for my nose.'

And that was it. By the next bulletin, the cub reporter had told everyone how Tony had been dragged out of the fire by water police; that he had broken his nose in the fires; and that it was a miracle that he survived. The next morning, Tony had thought about explaining the mistake. But when he thought it through, he didn't know how he could explain what had happened to him in hillbilly hall. Or how he had 'lost' his mobile phone. How, Tony thought, do you publicly announce that you are not a hero?

In the past nine months, Tony Thomas had let the lie live. But he still didn't feel comfortable about it.

'I know it's hard for you to go through it again,' prompted Mike Cottee, 'but …'

'No trouble, Mike. Yes, I did go out into the fires. I wanted to check the position of the main fire front and see whether any houses were endangered – '

'And you left your phone with Mr Carmody? In retrospect that was a very lucky thing for Mr Carmody but not so lucky for yourself, Tony.'

'Yes, I must admit that I now sleep with my trusty mobile tucked under my pillow. But that night Mr Carmody needed the phone for a while to co-ordinate the firefighting – '

'So residents *were* involved in fighting the fires that night? I thought they were evacuated,' said Mike Cottee, who was growing testier with his colleague's lack of zest for this interview.

'Yes, a few residents were fighting the fires. And they did quite a good job of backburning. Although there were obviously limits to what they could do because it was their backburn that set off the spot fire. And, of course, it was that spot fire that wiped out houses on the western edge of the Bay.'

That statement hit Roger Burton like a blow to the stomach. All the recriminations he'd levelled at himself through sleepless nights. All the arguments he'd had with neighbours. All the useless platitudes that people like Mrs Parker had delivered to him. They had all been negated by one sentence on air. An incorrect sentence. Fire headquarters had told them that the fire had come around the headland from the other bays. It wasn't a spot fire set off by the backburn. But that fact amounted to nothing now. Roger Burton slumped forward a little, his forehead found a hand to rest in. He willed himself to forget it. He told himself it didn't matter.

'He not only lies about where he was during the fire but he can't get the lies right!' injected Mrs Parker. 'He said we lost houses in the west! Only someone who had no idea what happened that night would say we lost houses in the west.'

Roger Burton listened to Mrs Parker with disinterest. He no longer cared about details. The history was out there now. It belonged to everyone. There was no way it could be rewritten.

'Why don't we ring the station and tell them exactly where Tony Thomas was that night? Expose him!' Mrs Parker said, revelling in the opportunity for meddling. Bigtime meddling.

The radio was replaying the sound of fires again. Roger Burton presumed the special had concluded. He turned his attention to Beryl Parker, observing her mischievous eyes and the way her hands clasped together in a let's-get-down-to-business pose. She had leapt off the arm of the chair and was pacing excitedly. He thought he should have a hose to turn on her. Instead, he tried to deflate her kindly.

'I've been through this with you already, Beryl. We can't tell anyone that the reporter wasn't up the hill checking out the fires because that would make a liar of John Carmody. Remember what he said to the radio station when he had the mobile phone?' Beryl Parker looked confused. 'He told them that the reporter had gone to check the fires. And that he'd left the phone with him. What will the radio station think if we now tell them that Carmody was lying and that Carmody stole the phone from their reporter?'

Roger Burton paused to let this scenario sink into Beryl's mind. He wondered what sort of punishment was attached to stealing equipment. He wondered whether stealing a media group's equipment was as serious as stealing police equipment.

'I suppose,' said Mrs Parker thoughtfully, 'the radio station wouldn't be impressed with what we did to the reporter in the hall, either.'

'Actually, Beryl, I never found out exactly what went on in the hall but by the looks of the reporter's face in the newspaper the day after – '

'He told the newspaper he had been injured in the fires,' Mrs Parker piped in.

Roger Burton sniggered. He turned to Beryl, noting for the first time that she was dressed in her Sunday-best clothes, and he snorted, 'You know, Beryl, maybe the reporter does deserve the hero status, after all.'

'You mean for putting up with us?' said Mrs Parker.

'Well, it's another trial, isn't it? Perhaps Tony Thomas is the brave survivor of a night with the Flint Bay ferals.'

'So you don't think I should ring the station and tell them that it was the houses on the east of the Bay that got burnt?' she asked.

Roger Burton tuned into the radio again. A talkback segment was on. Tony Thomas was answering questions from listeners. Sounding pretty sure of himself too.

'I know the talkback number, I ring it all the time,' continued Mrs Parker, reading her friend's mind.

'Let's just send him a little cheerio,' said Roger Burton, slapping his thigh. Mrs Parker hustled over to the sidetable to retrieve the phone. She carried the phone to the kitchen table, whipping the long cord out behind her as she went. She had no idea what Roger Burton wanted to say to the reporter. But, judging by the smirk on his face, she suspected it was cheeky.

'Hello, is that Tony Thomas? ... Oh good, this is Roger Burton from Flint Bay, Tony ... Yeah, good to hear from you too. I just wanted to say a cheerio and also point out something that you said ... No, it won't take long ... No, I can say it quickly. Tony, the houses that burnt down were on the east of the Bay, not the west.'

Mrs Parker could hear the delayed transmission from the radio set, which had been turned down low for the interview. Crouching over the table to pin her ear to the radio set, she giggled as she heard the silence that followed.

'Is that right, Tony?' piped in Mike Cottee.

'Well,' said Tony laughing quietly. Nervously. 'If Mr Burton says it is, then I'll take his word for it. I'm no bush baby, the east side of a hill looks much like the west side to me.'

'But, Tony, didn't you say you went to the west side of the Bay to check out the fires?' said Mike Cottee, probing for something.

'Well, it's all west of the Pacific Ocean to me. But seriously when you're in the middle of an inferno, you're not sure how to get out of there, much less which is east and which is west.'

'Okay, Tony. I think the station needs to buy you a compass,' said Mike Cottee with his eye on the clock. Thirty-five seconds to twelve-thirty. 'Thanks for your call, Mr Burton. Is there anything else you'd like to tell Tony?'

'No, that's it. Just tell Tony we're all followers of his career down here in Flint Bay. We'll be keeping an eye on him.'

Mrs Parker giggled as Roger Burton returned the handpiece of the phone to its receiver.

'Should we have told him that we still have his tape machine in the hall?' Mrs Parker walked back over to Roger Burton. She whispered this as if the radio reporters might still be able to hear them. Or perhaps out of guilt.

Roger Burton had to think for a minute where the tape recorder had ended up after the residents had left the hall for their homes or, in a few cases, to bunk in the homes of neighbours. Then he remembered. After they had finished stacking the chairs, someone had pushed the tape recorder under them. Burton visualised the chairs. They were stacked beneath the trophy wall, where civic pride badges, articles of association certificates and letters from important people hung in frames.

'No,' said Roger Burton, 'I think his equipment belongs on our trophy wall.'

Chapter twenty-nine

Emily stared at the pair of ducks fighting in the bay. From her position on the verandah of her father's house she couldn't see whether they were fighting over a fish or having a domestic. When one duck yabbered back at the other, she giggled. It looked exactly like the sort of domestic arguments that are played out in kitchens every day.

'Don't let him badger you into submission,' she yelled out to the duck she presumed was the female, if only because it was losing to the bigger duck.

Her shout embarrassed her. It bounced off the roof of the verandah and seemed to echo across the bay. Even the ducks looked nonplussed for a brief second. Emily looked around the neighbourhood to see if anyone might have heard her. She never felt alone at the Bay now. No matter where she was – on the verandah, the track, the bush or on the beach – she sensed that someone was passing by, or listening. Or looking from afar. When she had scanned the area and decided that it was unlikely anyone had heard her shout, she suddenly noticed what she was doing with her hands.

While leaning against the timber railing of the deck she had been picking at a spot of dry rot in the railing. Judging by the raw appearance of the splintering timber, she'd been picking at it for some time. Today. And possibly the day before. Emily patted the cavity in the railing as if to salve it. When she lifted her palm again, she could see the outlines of the tree from which the timber had come. There was a knot just below the surface. Emily blew at the dust and shavings in the cavity. In the calm spring afternoon, the shavings seemed to take a long time to reach the ground but they disappeared quickly in the lizard-skin markings of the earth. Looking back into the cavity and then across to the hillside across the bay, she shrugged. Timber came from the forest floor, eventually it would return there. It all does, eventually. Whether through shavings, demolition or … Emily looked back at the cavity she'd worried into exposure. It's only the timing we have a say in, she thought.

Patting the wound in the railing, Emily half-turned to see if her father had noticed her vandalism. He had been fossicking around the cabinets in the living room, looking for something he said he wanted to show her. Already he was on his way out to the verandah. Judging by the smirk on his face, he'd found it.

Emily noticed him having trouble negotiating the verandah door with a newspaper in one hand and his walking stick in the other.

'Hang on, hang on,' she chided as she walked across the verandah to the door, 'wait for me to open it. The doctor said you'd be a bit of a cripple for a few weeks after the operation so take it easy, will you?' Emily opened the door and attempted to take her father's elbow. Without lifting his eyes from the newspaper, Carmody briskly moved his elbow out of Emily's clasp and continued along the verandah.

'Jack's big day!' Carmody announced. 'All you wanted to read about Jack's day with the local heroes!' He flourished the newspaper under Emily's eyes. Emily took the paper, annoyed at his cryptic drama.

'If you sit down, I'll read it,' she said. As Carmody rolled his eyes and plonked precariously into the old lounge that graced the verandah, Emily began to read.

The story on the awards ceremony was headlined, 'Local Heroes'. Most of the front page of the peninsula newspaper was occupied by a photograph of the people who had received bravery awards. About seven in the photograph had their faces circled so readers would know which of the heroes were locals. She read the story. Much of the copy was concerned with where the heroes lived. As if their postcode was of more interest than their story. The 'local heroes' came from a ten-kilometre radius of the peninsula – a generous definition of the word 'local'. Emily wondered how you would feel if you were a hero who lived a suburb away from the imaginary radius that qualified as local. Like a second-rate hero, she supposed.

'Can you see him?' Carmody said impatiently.

'Hold your horses, I'm reading the story.' Even as Emily said this she began scanning the photograph for Jack's face. She didn't even think to look at one of the circled faces so she was surprised when she finally spotted Jack's face peering out from a circle. He looked very satisfied with himself. He certainly didn't look as if he were there by proxy. Looking at the small type below the photograph, Emily searched for his name. There! 'Jack Carmody of Flint Bay.'

Emily burst out laughing and let the paper fall to the floor. She turned to see her father smirking.

'Jack Carmody of Flint Bay,' she repeated to her father's face. 'Jack would die if he saw that. You know how Sarah feels about this place. She thinks it's hillbilly town. And now,' she gestured to the paper on the floor, 'all her pals with weekenders on the peninsula will think ... and Jack's colleagues!'

Emily turned to her father again. 'Has he seen this yet?' Carmody shook his head. 'Do you think we should call him?' asked Emily. 'Let him know? Warn him?' Carmody's expression was noncommittal. 'Go on,' continued Emily, 'call him.' Carmody went to lift himself off the lounge.

'Don't worry,' said Emily, already walking to the verandah door, 'I'll get the cordless phone and bring it out.' Emily disappeared for a few seconds. Carmody looked across at the hillside opposite and felt the chill of late afternoon pat his skin. His face had lost its smirk.

'Do you remember his phone number?' asked Emily, re-appearing with the cordless. Carmody shook his head brusquely.

'Well, what button is it on the most frequent numbers?' Carmody shook his head again. Emily, waiting for his reply, looked up at her father. She noticed the sadness that had settled on his face. She started to ring directory assistance. She looked at him again. He was looking at the distant hillside, obviously not wanting to engage in the conversation.

Emily pressed the hang-up pad and said more breezily that she felt, 'Ah forget it, if you call him I'll have to speak to him and I don't feel like a fight this afternoon.'

She headed back to the kitchen and mooched around the fridge and the pantry, and froze when she heard the call come from the back door.

'Yoohoo, anyone home?'

She looked for an escape route. She cursed when she realised there was no way she could escape without being seen from the back door. It was too late anyway because she could hear Mrs Parker edging along the hallway while cooing her 'yoohoos'.

'Ah Emily! Good to see you,' said Mrs Parker. Emily planted a smile on her face and glanced out to the verandah. She could see her father sink into the lounge a little as he recognised the archly enunciated voice of Mrs Parker. Emily began walking through the lounge room and out to the verandah knowing that Mrs Parker would follow.

The older woman trailed Emily, making a curious squishing sound as she crossed the lounge. Emily turned back to check the source of the sound and saw the knee-high wellingtons. Mrs Parker had begun wearing the boots after the fire, when she noticed that the blackened ground of the Bay was turning her stockings grey. Nine months later, she was still wearing knee-high boots with her paisley-print dresses.

'They'd *l-o-v-e* those boots on Oxford Street,' Emily whispered lasciviously to Mrs Parker.

The elderly woman had no idea what Emily was referring to but Emily's tone told her she didn't want to know. As Carmody saluted Mrs Parker's arrival with a raised hand, Emily sat down firmly next to her father. As if to remind him that they had to share the duty of Mrs Parker.

'I must say, John, your house is looking a bit tired next to the neighbours' houses. Such bright, shiny, new houses! We'll all have to start keeping up with the O'Conners, the Watts and the Greys and Lawsons.' Mrs Parker gesticulated to the houses on both sides of Carmody's house, as she followed Emily to the middle of the verandah.

'It's remarkable how the fire picked off a house here, two houses there, and left some houses in between untouched.' Mrs Parker's comment didn't warrant a reply. They'd heard that comment scores of times over the last nine months. Carmody, always polite, raised his eyebrows in agreement.

'Oh, I see you've got the local paper too!' said Mrs Parker to the two silent faces on the lounge. Carmody went to stand up, as if to offer Mrs Parker a seat, but Mrs Parker gestured him down again with her hands. She didn't stop to interrupt her monologue. 'Isn't it a nice photo of Jack! I'm sure he's very proud of himself. As I suppose you both are – '

'There's nothing to be proud of,' interrupted Emily. 'Jack was just standing in for Dad. If you remember rightly, Jack wasn't even down here for the fires.' Emily chided herself for her tone. She knew Mrs Parker didn't deserve her rudeness but she was unable to stop herself.

Mrs Parker smiled thinly at Emily. For a few moments no one said anything. Emily sank deeper into the lounge, biting the inside of her mouth. Mrs Parker looked busily at the view and Carmody concentrated on tapping his foot. A chill south-westerly zephyr nudged around the corners of the verandah, gently flapping the top page of the discarded newspaper.

'I saw that nice woman from the art gallery on the peninsula the other day,' said Mrs Parker pointedly. She waited for a response but Carmody just looked bemused and Emily cautious. 'She said she had a visit from a young lady from Flint Bay.' Mrs Parker paused again. Carmody glanced at Emily. Emily concentrated on the floorboards of the verandah.

'She said a young woman stormed into her shop demanding to know why the shop was advertising native artwork.' Emily groaned at Mrs Parker's half-baked version of her encounter with the art gallery woman.

'That "nice woman from the art gallery"' said Emily repeating Mrs Parker's words, 'was advertising Bo's work as the traditional artwork of an Aboriginal person and she was selling the pieces at twenty times the amount she gives to Bo. The first is illegal and the second is immoral.' Emily folded her hands over her chest and mashed her lips together. She could feel both of them looking at her. She wished she wasn't blushing. Wishing it away made the blush worse.

She blushed every time she heard Bo's name mentioned. Sometimes she'd feel herself flush at the thought of him. Strangely, in the eight or nine months since the fires, she'd never encountered Bo here at the Bay. And she'd been down here often enough. A dozen times. Along the track. To the beach. Bushwalking. Once or twice she thought she saw him further back into the bush. More a feeling than a sighting. But their paths never crossed. She didn't know what she'd say if they did meet. The first time she came back to the Bay after the fires, she'd prepared something to say, just in case she ran into him. Something about a fork. But they'd never met and she'd since forgotten what she would have said to him. In fact, she was growing hazy about what really happened on the night of the fires. That she felt embarrassed whenever she tried to remember, worried her. It was almost as if she and Bo had shared an intimacy. Not sex. Not sex. She was reasonably confident they hadn't had sex, but she had to reel back mentally through the events of the night to convince herself of this. These rewinds inevitably slowed at the moment Bo ministered to her wounded shin. She could still see the crazy frizz of Bo's head as he knelt in front of her. And the exquisite tenderness with which he had dabbed the dripping hanky onto her wound. Like an artist putting the finishing touches to a canvas. And then, as the hydrogen peroxide soaked into her blood vessels, sending her into a paroxysm, she recalled Bo's mortified expression. Staring at her with big … yes, big brown eyes, then staring down at the wound as if he were considering sucking the peroxide from her system to stop the pain. She could see him swallow with difficulty while she spun around on his bed, grabbing the thin pillow and biting into it. Hugging the pillow into submission, moaning into its warm staleness. And then the silence that followed. Bo frozen into a kneeling position while her pain subsided in waves. Panting relief into the pillow.

No. No. They hadn't had sex. She told herself many times. But beneath the sound of denial was a sense they'd shared something more intimate than sex.

Carmody and Mrs Parker had stopped talking to each other and were looking at Emily. She looked at them with a start. Had she just spoken aloud? Said something … about Bo? She searched the air for the last words that had been spoken on the verandah.

'Emily?' asked her father. Obviously for the second time, 'Did you threaten to blackmail the woman?'

Emily groaned. She had no idea what Mrs Parker had just told her father but it sounded as if it was full of hyperbole.

'I just told the woman that unless she pays Bo a proper amount for his branches – I think I mentioned a sum of three or four hundred dollars – then I would tell the Department of Fair Trade that she was passing off artwork as Aboriginal.' Emily paused. Then added, 'The woman seemed more than happy with the deal.'

As she said this, Emily turned to her father. He was making a vain attempt to disguise his chuckling. She turned to Mrs Parker, who was making a good attempt to look vindicated.

'Four hundred dollars!' exclaimed Mrs Parker, obviously keen to prolong the drama. 'These things are only chipped away bits of bark. I've never seen anything in them and to ask four hundred dollars for them! It's positively prestidigitation!'

Emily mashed her lips together to prevent herself from making a quip at Mrs Parker's expense. And failed. 'Certainly, Mrs Parker, such a figure is no nugatory sum,' said Emily. Carmody, who had been trying to stifle his chuckles, could no longer contain himself.

Quickly Carmody stopped laughing and mumbled an apology. Mrs Parker continued. 'Well, I would have thought a young girl like you would have better things to do in life than persecute small businesswomen,' said Mrs Parker, trying to salvage some pride.

'Emms does,' said Carmody with a smirk still playing around his mouth. 'Next week she's off to start shooting a documentary.' Mrs Parker arched her eyebrows. Allowing Carmody to continue. 'She'll be tracking across the outback with all our bush artists.'

'Six, Dad, just six,' said Emily wanting to wrap this conversation.

'Oh, you mean those Aboriginal artists who do dot drawing?' said Mrs Parker. More of a dismissal than a query. She dusted down her floral dress as if she was clearing herself of contamination.

'Those bark paintings sell for a lot of money these days,' said Carmody. 'New York galleries are all over the best Aboriginal artists. Some of the pieces go for tens of thousands of dollars.'

'Really?' said Mrs Parker. Emily wondered if that was the first time that Mrs Parker had sounded impressed when talking about Aboriginal people.

'I think she likes you,' Carmody said after Mrs Parker had taken her leave and the silence of the evening had been allowed to settle on the verandah.

'Come off it,' retorted Emily, 'I'd rather rot in hell than become Mrs Parker's friend. I'd rather die than – no,' she added quickly after spying the local paper still flapping on the verandah floor,

'I'd rather live in Killara than become her friend.' Emily said this last comment with an expression of comic horror. Carmody winced in agreement.

'Poor Jack,' said Emily. To herself or him, Carmody couldn't tell. But he let the comment pass.

'You know Bo won't use the money from the art gallery woman,' Carmody said after a while. 'He'll just stuff it into his burial money jar.' Emily, sitting next to him on the lounge, just shrugged.

'Bo is so worried there won't be enough money to bury him next to his brother, he socks away every cent he gets,' continued Carmody. 'He must have thousands of dollars in that jar – '

'I didn't see any jar,' interrupted Emily.

Carmody thought about this for a while. Bo had showed him the jar of money a few years ago when he had asked Carmody to take care of his burial. The jar was hidden behind a loose piece of fibro wall. Carmody wouldn't have expected Emily to know where Bo's jar was but then, he never found out what did happen on the night of the fire when Emily was forced into the hut. He'd heard a few pointed comments among the residents. And, frankly, he wondered himself. But he left it to Emily to say what she wanted to say about the night. He waited again. Vaguely hoping she might expand on the subject. A pair of magpies cawed at the silence.

Now that spring had arrived, the sun loitered longer above the western horizon. Emily stared at the hillside on the opposite side of the bay. Still denuded, its rockfaces were glowing under the rays of the setting sun. At that moment, when the sun was beaming directly into the hillside, the rocky facades seemed to throb with reflected glory. Over the minutes of the sunset, the hill's energy ebbed and its gold escarpment browned. The hill lost its brilliance like a slowly fading smile.

Emily tried to imagine the eveningtide of the Aboriginal people who once lived on the hillside. She pictured the women settling young children into caves for the night. The crying, the cooing. The tidying up for the day, cleaning the cave floors of grit, stoking the fire with a carefully placed branch, bunking down for the night as they stared into the setting sun.

'Do you ever imagine the lives of the Aboriginal people who once lived here?' Emily was surprised at the sound of her voice. It reminded her how long the silence had stretched.

'I can hear them,' Carmody replied. Flatly. Almost to himself. Emily wanted to turn and look at her father to see if he was smirking or serious. But she didn't need to look to know. She stared into the fading brilliance of the hillside as she pondered his words. The shadow of night was moving rapidly up the hillside now. Creeping up to claim its territory, casting the bush in a different mood. A brooding presence. In the tide of darkness, she could imagine the convicts who had once escaped to the caves along the hillside. She thought of them toiling to terrace the steep hillside so they might grow vegetables. And she thought of the outlaws who had escaped authority by rowing across from the peninsula. She tried to imagine them getting comfortable for the night in draughty huts they had built on the site of older abandoned huts. What optimism to build their huts on the remains of others. Why would they have thought their attempts at life on the hillside would be more successful than others? Emily tried to hear the imprint of their memory through the sounds of waves lapping and the calls of evening birds.

'I suppose you can hear the whoops of escaped convicts, sometimes,' said Emily quietly.

'I don't think they did too much whooping,' he replied. Emily blanched. Not sure whether her father was taking the mickey.

The night had claimed the hillside now. Zipped it up for another day. The landscape slipped into primeval time. A time when all activity ceases and only the elements remain. Earth, wind, rain and fire. Was there ever a time when there was no fire? Not on that hillside, there wasn't.

Emily shivered. The landscape seemed morose in the darkness, as if it had slipped into a black mood. She'd seen its moods before. She'd seen it in a rage – tearing, roaring, unpredictable and vicious. A gaping mouth with a view into hell. She could never trust its benign facade after that. Love it, yes. Fear it, yes. But trust it, never.

The two of them sat in the audience of the sunset until the first mosquito of the night landed on Emily's thigh.

'Got you!' Emily muttered as she squashed the mosquito into her flesh.

'What?' said Carmody.

'I said "got you"' Emily said as she looked around her exposed legs for more hovering mosquitos. As she searched, she caught sight of her father's confused expression. ' – To the mosquito,' she added, 'I said "got you" to the mozzie.'

'Oh,' said Carmody, obviously disappointed.

Emily tried to think what her father might have expected her to say. She'd lost track of their last conversation. Perhaps the organisation of dinner was on his mind. No, she thought, he always seems surprised to see dinner arrive on the table. Emily winced when the thought occurred to her that this might have been one of those special silences. One of those awkward pauses that had haunted their conversations since the fire. The silence that begged a question.

Emily swallowed a lump of emotion and breathed deeply as if she was about to begin talking. And she stopped herself. If she said anything now, the subject would be raised; laid out on the slab for dissection; ready for scalpels to pierce old wounds. Emily exhaled slowly and quietly.

She'd wanted to know everything in the days immediately after the fire when emotions were coursing through her body, ready to burst forth at any trigger; when she wanted to tell everyone everything that had happened.

But the days passed. Most of them spent alone in her flat.

When she did see friends and they asked about the fire, she found she couldn't talk about it. Not with them. But she wanted to return to the Bay to talk about it with her father, she wanted to see the legacy of the fire in daylight, talk to the neighbours, find out their stories of the day. But mostly talk to her father.

The right time to talk with her father never arrived. And later when life resumed a routine pace, she began to think more coolly about what she wanted to know from her father.

What could she ask him? 'How did you know, for sure, that Mum wanted to die?' Or should she ask him, 'How is the business of dying planned? With a nod? A debate? A detailed plan? Or is it a contract that doesn't need words?'

The questions would spin through her mind like the questions in a quiz show. 'What was it like standing outside the studio listening to your wife die?' ... just ten seconds to answer and the prize is yours ... 'Did you hope for a fast ending or did you long for a last-minute reprieve?' ... and for three hundred and sixty-five thousand dollars the answer is?

Sometimes the questions would stab at her heart as if each word was a dagger. 'Tell-me-Dad, did-Mum-cry?'

These weren't questions she could ask. They hung in the landscape of her mind like strange mutated animals – no home to go to, no future to speak of. But they kept appearing.

In her darker moods she'd rehearse questions to ask him about her involvement in the death. 'Hey, Dad, did you block me out of her death because you were mad at me or because you wanted to spare me?' Or, 'If I had done what you wanted me to do, would you have made me an accessory?' These questions left her with sleepless nights.

Sometimes in more positive moods she'd frame questions that might quell their pain. 'Dad, did you feel a gust of freedom when her spirit left her body?' And, 'Did she whisper "thank you" through the wind in the casuarinas?'

None of the questions had answers. Nor would they ever have

answers. Even if, one day, she asked them of her father, she knew the questions would remain unanswered. She didn't know whether living with the questions was worse than living with inadequate answers. So she lived with the awkward silences.

Emily sneaked a look at her father from the corner of her eye. Tears tingled at the back of her eyes again. She guessed what he wanted from her. She knew the nature of the request that lay in the silence. But what her father wanted was nothing she could give.

She closed her eyes. Emily's eyes clenched hard as she recalled a thought that had occurred to her at about three a.m. on a winter's night when she had woken from a nightmare – I have seen his shadow and love him more for it, and fear him more.

Emily rubbed her face and expelled a breath heavily. As she opened her eyes, she found herself staring across into the hillside. The hill had disappeared now, the dark, brooding bulk indiscernible from the night sky. Its presence seemed stronger for its visual absence.

Carmody looked over to her when he heard her exhausted breath. Did he still have that expectant look on his face? Emily thought as she tried to see the expression on his face without looking his way.

I could raise the subject now. This is the moment to raise it. With the evening stretching before them and a brooding hillside as witness. If ever her mother's death could be carefully laid out for dissection, this was the time to do it. Emily breathed deeply again and looked across to her father's face. She smiled.

'How about dinner?' she asked.

'I thought you'd never ask,' said Carmody.